VALLEY OF DEATH

Indy slowed into a hairpin turn. A huge tree trunk blocked the road and he hit the brakes. Through broken branches he saw eyes peering at him and Gale. She rose in her seat, looking directly at the eyes. Then she slid down slowly.

Indy turned to look again at the tree blocking the road. Before his eyes it began to fade, until suddenly it wasn't there anymore. He shifted into gear; this time he didn't need Gale to tell him to go ahead.

They rounded another turn. He felt as if they drove suddenly through a *field,* a force field of some kind. Whatever it was, it made his entire body tingle, raised the hair on his arms and the back of his neck. Even his teeth seemed to respond to a vibration he couldn't place. Then it was *gone* and he *knew* they were on the other side of what Gale described as "the circle."

Finally he was in St. Brendan Glen.

All about him was horror and death.

The Indiana Jones series
Ask your bookseller for the books you have missed

INDIANA JONES™

AND THE

WHITE WITCH

MARTIN CAIDIN

BANTAM BOOKS

NEW YORK • TORONTO • LONDON • SYDNEY • AUCKLAND

This book is for
TREADWELL OF MOORDOWN

INDIANA JONES AND THE WHITE WITCH

A Bantam Book / April 1994

All rights reserved.
TM *and copyright © 1994 by Lucasfilm, Ltd.*
Cover art by Drew Struzan.
No part of this book may be reproduced or transmitted in any form or by any means,
electronic or mechanical, including photocopying, recording, or by any information
storage and retrieval system, without permission in writing from the publisher.
For information address: Bantam Books.

ISBN 0-553-56194-4

Published simultaneously in the United States and Canada

PRINTED IN THE UNITED STATES OF AMERICA

OPM   0 9 8 7 6 5 4 3 2

1

Three thousand feet above the rugged gullies and thick woodlands of the New Forest of southern England, wind blowing her bright red hair in a swirling billow, Gale Parker yanked back the throttle of the little training plane. The soft ticking of the engine at idle and wind sighing through wings and wires enabled conversation between the front and aft cockpits.

Indiana Jones, startled by the unexpected quiet instead of the engine roar that had become so comforting at this height, glared at the redhead as she turned to look back at him. Before she could speak, he pounded his fist against the cockpit padding.

"Turn it back on!" he shouted. He watched the nose drop below the horizon as they slid off into a downward glide. He didn't like it. He wanted to hear that engine, feel its vibrations, smell the exhaust. That was comforting; this was ridiculous.

Gale laughed at him. "Not to worry, Indy!" she called back. "I have to talk with you."

"Talk to me on the ground!" he yelled. His eyes widened as the high trees began to expand in size as the airplane kept drifting downward.

"This is only your first lesson!" she called back. A wing dipped down. Indy gripped the sides of the cockpit with white knuckles as Gale righted their little craft with a smooth motion. "Are you sure you want the aerobatics?" she asked, the wind thinning her voice.

"Yes, *yes!*" he shouted. "I don't want to waste time like this! For God's sake, start up the engine!"

"It's running, it's running," she scolded him. "It's idling. One of the things you have to learn. Indy, I'd rather we went into this easily."

"The words!" he demanded, shouting louder. "Stop talking like a woman and start flying like a pilot!"

She smiled, teeth white in the afternoon sun. "Whatever pleases you, ducks!" she called merrily. She turned around, then back again. "Remember, Indy! Keep your hands on the controls and follow through with me. Got it?"

He gripped the stick and planted both feet on the rudder pedals. "Got it!"

"Go with me, but don't fight me on the controls!"

"I won't, blast it!" he shouted angrily. "Just *fly!*"

He felt the throttle knob move forward under his left hand. Immediately the engine roared fully to life and the nose came back to level.

Her voice drifted back to him. "All right, luv! Here we go! Like you say, no holds barred!"

The nose dropped sharply. They seemed to be diving straight for the trees. The wind howled about him. Was she crazy? What was she doing *now*?

The stick in his right hand pulled back sharply toward him with a force so great he felt a brief pain in his wrist.

Abruptly the trees before him fell away and blue sky and white clouds were everywhere. He felt as if an elephant had suddenly sat on his chest and head and arms. His feet were leaden as Gale hauled back into a tight inside loop, the airplane rushing upward, continuing over. Through the upward climb, the centrifugal force, what these lunatic pilots called g-forces, mashed him down in his seat, hung his lower lip low, and sagged sudden bags under his eyes.

The pressure was gone; now he was hanging upside down. He was falling out of the airplane! No, he wasn't! His seat belt and shoulder harness supported his weight or he *would* have tumbled out of the cockpit. His stomach sent him a warning complaint, the engine roar abruptly ceased, the stick moved forward, then hard back again, and the wind's shriek increased rapidly as they hurtled downward in a wide soaring plunge.

He swallowed the lump in his throat, trying to focus on the controls. He gritted his teeth, determined to be the best student the lithe redhead had ever flown with. They pulled out into level flight, Gale advanced the throttle, the engine thunder comforted him, and without warning he felt the left rudder pedal slamming down. The right pedal came back and shoved his leg back and his right knee up, and in the same movement the stick slammed back against his body.

Gale whipped the trainer into a wild snaproll, hurling the aircraft forward through a gyrating, twisting maneuver that made mush out of the horizon. Indy could see only a blur of sky, clouds, and trees. He had no idea where he was and what he was doing as Gale followed up with another snaproll, then eased level.

Again she pulled the power back to idle and twisted in

her seat to look at him. "How you doing, ducks?" she called.

He swallowed a bitter taste in his mouth, felt his heart trying to jump from his chest. He tasted blood where he'd bitten his own tongue, but still he managed to offer her a smile. Gale recognized the signs; Indy's grin was more that of a death's-head than of someone having a good time.

He thought he heard her call out something like "hammerhead" before the advancing throttle drowned out her words. "Hammerhead?" What did a shark have to do with this? "Uhhhh." He realized the sound was dribbling from his own mouth as she hauled back again on the stick; they were going straight up now, and—

"We're too slow!" he was shouting uselessly beneath the storm of sound from engine and wind. The airplane went straight up, almost hanging on its propeller. As the speed fell away he felt it vibrate and tremble, and he *knew* they were going to fall out of control. The whole frame shuddered, and abruptly that left rudder slammed down again, the stick banged to the side, and the airplane went into a perfect rolling half cartwheel through its hammerhead maneuver.

Gale went straight up and straight down. She flew knife-edged maneuvers so that the wings were vertical to the ground. She rolled and jackknifed, whirled, hauled up into a steep climb, chopped the power, and slammed down on left rudder.

The world went mad as they whipped into a tight tailspin. He couldn't believe the scene before him. Over the red hair whipping in the wind and the blur of the propeller, the world rotated madly as they went straight down. But that was impossible! He forced himself to *think* through the cotton he felt being stuffed into his head. He knew his stomach was about to revolt, but through it all he realized he was seeing an optical illusion. It wasn't the world whipping about; it was *them*.

Gale kicked right rudder, shoved the stick forward, and the rotation stopped with a jolt that banged Indy's head on the side of the cockpit. Again they were level. Gale turned to see a greenish pallor across Indy's face. She knew the signs. "Oh, no!" she called aloud to herself. Immediately she crossed the controls—barely in time as Indy hung his head and shoulders over the edge of his cockpit and offered up everything he'd eaten the last day to the world far below.

He felt ghastly. He fumbled for a handkerchief. He felt as if he were drooling. His stomach was still upside down and he knew his eyes were crossing. But since he'd thrown up, he felt better, and—

The dry heaves hit next, and again he was hanging over the cockpit, hating the moaning sounds that rumbled up through his throat. He had nothing left to offer the wind, but his body muscles still spasmed. Finally he just hung along the cockpit edge in an imitation of a wet rag, looking straight down at the thick woods below. They were still over the New Forest, and through the yellow haze before his eyes he recognized the buildings and hamlet of St. Brendan Glen.

His senses took over swiftly. Something was terribly wrong beneath them. In that moment his unease fled, his stomach behaved, his mind went back to work.

Flashes of light pierced the high tree canopy, then bursts of red flame slivered upward. He stared down in disbelief. Those were concussion waves rippling along the treetops! That was Caitlin St. Brendan's home down there!

Her village . . . and it was being torn with explosions and spreading flames.

Indy banged his fist against the side of the airplane. Gale turned, grinning. Her smile vanished as she saw the distressed look on his face. As loudly as he could, he shouted to her, "Kill the power!" She rolled level, yanked the throttle back.

He pointed to the ground. "Caitlin!" he shouted. "Gale, look down there! Those are *explosions*!"

Thick smoke was already flowing across the trees. "Oh, no," Gale murmured. "We've got to get there right away!" she called back. "Hang on, Indy! We'll be on the ground in ten minutes!"

For the first time he didn't mind the wild curving power dive as she went at full speed for the grass airfield on Salisbury Plain. He couldn't miss the sound of desperation in Gale's voice. Down below, in the heavily wooded St. Brendan Glen, were Gale's closest, lifelong friends. Especially Caitlin, more than a friend, closer than a sister. A soul mate. Something horrible was happening beneath those trees. Indy was much too familiar with the flash detonation of powerful explosives and the outward-spreading ring of concussion waves not to realize that the remote hamlet was being ravaged by unknown assailants for some inexplicable reason.

Indy slipped lower in his seat, away from the wind that now shrieked past the little airplane in its reckless dive for a landing. A deep sigh went through his body. He had waited for months to break away from the demands of not one, but two universities. Albeit grudgingly, he had been given a sabbatical from Princeton as well as London University, and only days into his long-delayed freedom, he knew that whatever was going on below them in the New Forest was about to destroy any quiet in his life.

He had the feeling he was going to miss the tedium of the classroom.

On the ground, feet planted solidly within ivy-bedecked walls, Indy lived a life far removed from that of an explorer and adventuring archaeologist whose well-being, to say nothing of his survival, depended so often on his knowledge of local customs and language, his quick wit, and the physical prowess of a man as skilled at mountain climbing as he was at skiing across desolate arctic wastes.

His other, adventurous life was aided in no small degree by his skill with the powerful bullwhip and Webley .44-caliber revolver he was forced to use when his closest companion was imminent death.

But to the academic world he was Professor Henry Jones, learned teacher of medieval literature at Princeton University, a tall man of bookish habits in coarse tweeds, who peered owlishly through wire-rim glasses at his students. Those students, and the Princeton faculty, never knew when Professor Jones would appear on schedule to minister to the young minds awaiting him. Princeton had a special relationship with Sir William Pencroft, the crusty, wheelchair-bound chairman of the Department of Archaeology of London University. That relationship enabled Pencroft to call upon Princeton for Professor Jones's services for field research in hostile lands.

Jones's extraordinary skills in ancient languages were renowned throughout the world of archaeological studies. He delved into the past with an almost casual air, as much at home among ancient ruins as he was in the classroom. His research and investigations had taken him across Eu-

rope, through the United States, down to the diamond
mines of South Africa, and to Asian cultures still not
known to ethnographers. In every respect Professor Jones,
known in the field as Indiana Jones, a name he far preferred to his scholastic title, was a time-travel detective.
Ancient languages, artifacts, long-forgotten cities came
alive for him, and it was these skills that Sir William judged
invaluable.

But Indy could not be all things. Through the years he
had tried time and again to learn to fly an airplane. This
ability would shrink distances for him, open new vistas,
and gain him many hours otherwise lost in tedious surface
transport. In a recent adventure during which he had pur-
sued a criminal group bent on gaining international economic, industrial, and military strength, he had traveled in
a rugged, ugly three-engined beast of an airplane not only
in Europe and the United States, but also across the Atlantic Ocean. His time in the Ford Trimotor, which he helped
navigate and had even taken the controls of for brief peri-
ods, only hardened his determination to become a pilot in
his own right.

As a result of this desire, he now found himself several
thousand feet above the rugged gullies and thickly covered
landscape of the New Forest of southern England, flying
from a grass airstrip on the Salisbury Plain. Never had he
thought his instructor would be a woman! But he had
enormous confidence in the fiery redhead. She had been
aloft since she was a young teenager and had flown gliders;
since then she had progressed to everything from small
seaplanes to heavy airliners.

Gale Parker had become in many ways his partner in
their recent adventure—misadventure, he corrected himself—across continents and oceans. This in itself was a

drastic departure for Indy, who preferred to operate on his own, without having to care for and protect other people. However, the more time he spent with this woman, keen-minded and swift in her reactions, the greater was his respect for her.

They had met in the New Forest, by accident, when each was stalking the same wild boar. Indy used a powerful bow and arrow, she a crossbow of her own design and making. A slight rustle in the bush brought her about faster than he believed possible; then a bolt hurtled away and the animal fell with a steel shaft through its brain.

She fascinated him. He studied her features carefully and then he caught her by surprise. "Your name—"

"Gale Parker."

"That isn't your name," he said coolly.

"Oh?" An eyebrow went up; she tilted her head to study this stranger for whom she had an instant liking. There was something special about this man, a self-confidence evident in every move he made. And his eyes! They seemed, even in the brief time since they nearly collided in the thick glen, to miss nothing. They were piercing, knowing.

"Then tell me, stranger—"

"Jones. Indiana Jones."

"A strange name, indeed."

"But not as strange as yours." He laughed.

"Why," she asked slowly, "do you deny me my name?"

"Because it is English, and you have blood in you that is not from this land."

"You are perceptive."

He shrugged, waiting.

She amazed herself by telling him, "I am Mirna Abi Khalil. My father's name."

"Bedouin?"

"A ruler. A bloodline unbroken for hundreds of years."

He studied her carefully. "But your mother—"

"Sybil Saunders." She gestured in a wide sweep of her arm. "This is her home, and her own bloodline, too, has been unbroken for more than a thousand years here in the New Forest. She is of the early Wicca."

She watched his face, waiting for whatever expression might reveal his thoughts. She saw recognition and respect.

He nodded slowly. "The ancient religion," he said. "Then it must be your mother who had you change your name to Gale Parker."

"A witch's family has its problems in today's world."

"Agreed," he acknowledged. He looked about him. "And this, the New Forest, is your home?"

"I was raised here. Except for four years, which I spent in Germany with cousins. Hard schooling, flying gliders, learning different languages. I returned when I was eighteen. To here, my true home. That of my family."

"You don't live in the woods," he said, again studying her.

"Oh?" her smile was mocking. "Then pray tell me where *do* I live?"

"Where you are with friends, the comforts are all about you, the food is wonderful, and you commune with nature, and"—he paused, locking his gaze with hers—"what lies beyond everyday vision of nature."

"You do not tread lightly."

"No need to," he replied easily. "I understand. I have been here before. With the Romanies—"

"They care little for outsiders," she warned.

"I said I have been with them, joined their campfires, learned their names, shared their friendship."

"Remarkable for—" Her eyes widened and she stabbed a finger at Indy. "I know you!" She corrected herself quickly with a sudden shake of her head, her bright red hair swirling like a lovely mist about her face. "I mean, I know *of* you! You're the professor bloke from America—" Again she shook her head as if to force belief into her mind. "You were with the giants at Stonehenge."

"Yes."

"From what I hear, you did not interfere, with your presence, I mean, with the Dance of a Hundred Years."

"You are right. I did not interfere," he said, more stiffly than he liked. "And yes, I was finally accepted."

"Then it's a handshake between us that's called for!"

They clasped hands. "I'll give you some help with that boar."

"You would share the kill with me?"

"Of course," he said. "I'd be very pleased to."

"Then we eat here," she announced. "Look about you, Indiana Jones. Darkness settles about us, a fog that would make our way through these thick bushes and the gullies and ravines almost impossible. In the dark, the gorse bushes would tear our clothes to shreds. No. We will cut what we need from the animal, build a fire, eat as people ate here a thousand, even five thousand years ago." She smiled, creating a devastating warmth in the settling gloom. "I promise a hearty and delicious meal."

He bowed in deference to ancient courtesy, then eased the pack from his back. "I travel prepared," he said.

"Which means?"

He placed shakers of salt and pepper on a leather sheet.

"Red wine and a loaf of bread," he announced. "And if you like, some cheese."

"A feast!" she cried, clapping her hands. "Wonderful."

His hand dropped to his holster. Faster than her eyes could follow, the Webley was in his hands, hammer cocked back for instant firing.

"What would you shoot, my American friend?"

"I heard something moving in those bushes." He pointed. "If it's the mate to this boar, we could be hurt badly before we have time to react."

"Thank you," she said with deceptive calm. "There is no need. What you heard, the bushes rustling, no doubt were noises made by those who will share our kill."

"Who?"

Her laugh was the tinkling of silver bells. "Why, the people of the forest night, of course. We have always shared with them. Put away your weapon. They are friends. *And* what you heard was the carving of the boar. The finest meat will be left for us."

"The people of the forest night?" he repeated, his study of her expression piercing. "Would they also be known as the little people?"

"Perhaps."

"You're being something of a pixie yourself, Gale Parker."

"Would you start the fire, please? You ask so many questions!"

No food tasted better, the flavor of the boar heightened by the seasonings and wine he always carried on such treks. When they were done, she gathered ferns and moss. "We will sleep here tonight. Soon you will be unable to keep your eyes open, my new friend, and you will sleep deeply, indeed."

"What makes you so sure?" he asked, yawning. He *was* sleepy.

"The spell, of course."

He could barely keep his eyes open. "Spell?"

"You are accepted. We have nothing to fear. The little people will tend to our safety."

"That ridicu . . ."

Indy had awoken in a sea of drifting golden mist. He blinked, trying to remember where he was. Soft moss had been his pillow. He sat up slowly and saw the gold from the rising sun streaming through the trees. Gale sat against a rock, studying him. She smiled; all the good morning he could ever ask for.

They had worked their way through the New Forest to a picturesque little village, seemingly untouched by modern civilization. Everyone seemed to know Gale, nodding or waving to her. She led Indy to a bakery shop where they shared steaming biscuits and mugs of coffee.

In the days that followed, he became ever more impressed with this young woman. Behind the stalker of wild game in the forest lay a swift mind and an extraordinary spectrum of abilities. She was an expert geologist. She knew the name, history, and properties of every plant, bush, and tree they saw. She laughed at his surprise. "When you grow up in this forest, you learn all these things at an early age. It becomes second nature. You learn to live off the land, and if you are kind to the forest, it is kind to you."

"That include the little people?" he asked, half in jest.

She peered slyly at him. "It does."

"What do you call them?" he pressed.

"Oh, the world has its own names," she said airily. "Elves, faeries, gnomes, wee folk—"

"You haven't mentioned troglodytes."

"Ah, those are supposed to be the evil ones." She smiled. "The nasty denizens of the dark woods."

"You don't seem to believe in such evil folk?"

"I've never met any."

That had been answer enough—and all he could get from her on that matter. When she talked about her mountain climbing and geological expeditions, her flying, hunting—she'd even made more than sixty parachute jumps from airplanes!—he had realized how talented and rare a person was this Gale Parker.

Then he had been plunged into helping American and British military and civilian intelligence agencies on their wild pursuit of the international power group that had been amassing enormous wealth and military forces. A group that killed in cold blood, and shocked governments with their reported find deep within a South African diamond mine of a mysterious cube, reputedly thousands or even millions of years old, and marked with unknown cuneiform symbols. They offered the cube, which could possibly have unlocked secrets of an ancient alien civilization, with all the enormous ramifications of a technological leap into super-science, for no less than one billion dollars.

That was where Indy came in. Both the American and British governments sought his cooperation in attempts to decipher the mysterious, perhaps extraterrestrial, cuneiform markings. The deeper Indy went into the twisted snarls of international intrigue, power plays, and remorseless murder, the greater was his need for the speed, versa-

tility, and firepower of a rugged machine that could fly,
land, or take off from almost anywhere.

The investigation into allegedly ancient markings exploded into a constantly hazardous, life-threatening series
of confrontations in which Gale was Indy's almost constant
companion. When the flaming conclusion to the affair finally occurred, the two knew they were a formidable team,
had complete faith in one another—and Indy was more
frustrated than ever in still not being able to pilot an airplane.

He drove anything with wheels, navigated over seas and
oceans with great nautical skill, clambered up steep mountains—but he could not fly a plane. Every time the opportunity presented itself, *something*, including rather nasty
people who were out to end his life, would interfere.

Now his misadventures were behind him, he and Gale
were back in England, and he would use the young woman's skill as a pilot and flight instructor to win his own
wings. Off to the Salisbury Plain they went. Indy rented a
cottage. Gale was to teach him every possible hour, seven
days a week, a nonstop cram course—which was how Indy
always attacked new challenges.

Now, on his first lesson, after he had insisted that Gale fly
their little trainer through the gamut of aerobatics, he had
succeeded splendidly in turning green, throwing up, and
then . . .

Then the searing flashes, the leaping flames, and smoke
pouring above the treetops of St. Brendan Glen in the
New Forest.

Where Gale's mother and her closest friends lived.

Gale swung the trainer over the grass field, chopped the
power, and swung about in a wild approach into the wind.

She landed hard, bounced, gunned the engine, and tramped rudder to turn to the far end of the field where Indy had parked his sports roadster.

When she climbed from the cockpit, Indy was startled to see tears streaking Gale's cheeks. "They're dead," she choked out. "My family . . . friends . . . dead."

"How do you know?" he asked quietly.

She took a deep, shuddering breath, wiping tears from her face with the sleeve of her flight suit. She placed her right hand over her heart.

"When something like this . . . happens," she said falteringly, "we feel it here. Like a knife."

She grasped his arm. "Please, Indy. *Hurry.*"

2

Indy roared away from the Salisbury airport, tires spinning on gravel as he headed for the main road leading westward. Gale sat quietly to his left, her eyes almost vacant as she struggled against the emotional pain. Indy needed no urging to run his Bentley BG 400 to high speed. His car was a modified convertible with a powerful eight-cylinder in-line engine of 220 horsepower, and high torque that made it perfect for the winding narrow English roads. For perhaps twenty miles he drove along a paved highway; then Gale sat up straighter, pointing to a cutoff before them. "Take that turn to the right, Indy," she directed.

He eased off their speed, downshifting. The turn she indicated seemed more a country path than a road, tree branches hanging low over its surface. He started to question her, then reminded himself that she had lived in this country most of her life. He made the turn, ducking as branches whipped over their heads, and glanced in his rearview mirror.

Indy's eyes widened. The road directly behind them, the very road on which they were driving, skidding around

turns, dashing up and down the sharp rises and dips, was
gone! The dust clouds thrown up by the powerful car
swirled back, then vanished as if sliced off neatly by a huge
knife. He kept checking the rearview mirror. The amazing
effect continued.

"Gale, tell me about this road," he said to his passenger.

She looked up slowly, turned to see behind them,
shrugged, looked forward again. "Its not a road for everyone," she said at last.

"That makes a lot of sense." His sarcasm was obvious.

"I mean, only certain people can *see* the road. Normally,
I doubt if you could." She pursed her lips, thinking hard.
"But then again, being who and what you are, and everything you've done with the unusual, you *might* be able to
see it."

"I see it well enough to drive on it!"

"Yes, because I'm with you. Otherwise you'd never have
seen the turnoff."

"It's disappearing behind us as we drive. Like it rolls up
invisibly." He glanced at her. "You know that's impossible."

"Yes. But it's a magic road."

"A magic road," he echoed in a hollow voice. What
next? he wondered. A marching band of pixies blowing
bagpipes?

"I mean, it's used only by the people of the forest. It's
really a horse-and-cart trail."

They slammed and bounced around a rough turn. He
clenched his teeth to keep from biting his tongue. "I can
believe that," he grunted. "But what makes it magic?"

"Only certain people can see it. It's been like that for
hundreds of years. The old legends say it was used by sor-

Indy slammed on the brakes. He didn't conceal his sudden irritation. "You're playing word games," he said. "If there's a river and it's deep and you expect me to go plunging into the water, I expect more of an answer than you've given me."

She studied him carefully. He understood what was running through that carrot head. The lethal dangers they'd faced, the times each had saved the life of the other. The *trust* they had for—

She seemed to read his thoughts. "You trust me, Indy?"

"Don't ask silly questions. It's my life we're talking about."

"So go ahead," she egged him on. "Shoot the rapids!"

"A Bentley isn't a kayak," he said, almost snarling at her. But he jerked the gearshift down and back, floored the accelerator, and shot ahead. They started down a long slope, and through the trees he saw water ahead. The river and—

A blast of frigid air hit him with shocking effect. He felt as if he'd been thrust into a huge freezer. He glanced at Gale. Frost on her hair! *Frost?* Moments ago it was warm and comfortable, then suddenly . . .

He felt his ears, painful from the cold. His nose. Frost spread across the windshield. It was like the arctic!

There; the river. Straight ahead. No . . . not water. It couldn't be . . . but it was. In the few seconds he had had the river in sight as they rushed down the slope, the blue water had misted over and assumed the colorless sheen of *ice*.

The Bentley sped across ice, tires beginning to skid and slip. Just as he realized he was losing control they bounced up on the opposite bank, the tires dug in again, and he accelerated up and around a turn. By the time they completed the turn, his ears and nose were wet with melted frost and water was streaming down the windshield.

"The little people again?" he shouted above the roar of the engine and the howling wind.

"Yes!" she called back. "Just like the light that curves! They turned away the warmth of the sun!"

"That's impossible!" he shouted.

"I know!" she shouted back, laughing.

He couldn't argue with that infectious laughter, or the manner in which she accepted magic and sorcery as if they were as common as flowers and sunshine. Besides, he knew better than to mix his own battered perception with the task of whipsawing the Bentley through the horse trail. Too bad, he muttered to himself, they don't have the magic to turn this rutted mess into a decent highway.

Yet through it all he was grateful for the intrusion of fog and bent light and curving sunshine and the "little people" he couldn't see, but with whom Gale maintained a warm and friendly relationship. For these brief moments of wild driving and inexplicable magic, Gale seemed free of the terrible gloom and fear that somehow was being communicated to her.

He heard her laugh again, and then he knew there would be no more for a while. He could *feel* her misery. Several times he glanced at Gale and saw the lines of empathy appearing on her face. The closer they came to St. Brendan Glen, the more intense became Gale's mood. He was startled to see her flinch as though a wave of pain had shot through her body. Blood appeared at the side of her mouth; Gale had bitten down unknowingly against her own lip.

He forced his attention back to the road. "Gale, how much longer?"

"Twenty minutes, perhaps."

"You all right, girl?"

Her answer surprised him. *"No."*

He'd spend these moments better by trying to remember whatever he could of St. Brendan Glen. He'd been there before, but in the dead of night, and Gale had brought him there by the main highway that skirted around the dense forest and rugged terrain. But there was much he knew from his own studies and his years of travel through this part of England. He loved the southern part of this country, so stunning to the eye, so steeped in history, the ground almost hallowed with memories of races and cultures and religions long gone. This countryside had once been a bloody battleground for tens of thousands of men and horses, war machines, slashing swords and bludgeons. There was magic in the massive stone monuments of Stonehenge. Arthur and his knights had lived and loved here. Indy thought of Camelot. Of Utherpendragon and Merlin, of Excalibur and Caliburn. Of the Lady of the Lake . . . the marvelous intertwining of myth and fact, legend and reality that was known as the "mother of Britain."

It was not so simple a matter for an outsider to draw hard conclusions as to what was solid rock and what might be a phantom mountain. Whatever existed here had been sustained for more than a thousand years longer than Indy's own country even existed. Whatever it all was, it defied science, laughed at logic, tugged at the heartstrings, and sang of life and love and tradition.

Indy had always wanted acceptance within the inner circle here in the New Forest. Difficult enough for an Englishman; until now, impossible for a man considered barely one step above the savages English explorers had encountered during the colonial days of that strange far-away land called America.

Indy laughed to himself—at himself. He was like a colonist visiting a new and strange land.

His laughter faded in his mind. He wished fervently to banish the scent of death, the knife of pain he could almost feel emanating from Gale the closer they came to the Glen.

"S-slow down, Indy." Gale was forcing the words out. She was nearly doubled over. "It will be better," she gasped, "when we cross the line and enter the circle."

Indy slowed into a hairpin turn. A huge tree trunk blocked the road and Indy hit the brakes. Through broken branches he saw eyes peering at him and Gale. She rose in her seat, looking directly at the eyes. Then she slid down slowly.

Indy turned to look again at the tree blocking the road. Before his eyes it began to fade, until suddenly it wasn't there anymore. He shifted into gear; this time he didn't need Gale's words to tell him to go ahead.

They rounded another turn. He felt as if they drove suddenly through a *field,* a force field of some kind. Whatever it was, it made his entire body tingle, raised the hair on his arms and the back of his neck. Even his teeth seemed to respond to a vibration he couldn't place. Then it was gone and he *knew* they were on the other side of what Gale described as "the circle."

Finally he was in St. Brendan Glen.

All about him was death and horror.

3

St. Brendan Glen had remained a magical enclave for more than a thousand years. Its cottages were hewn of strong forest wood and buttressed with stones on all sides to withstand violent storms. The houses rose along hillsides, in ravines, on upward slopes, a fairyland of mystical structures, smoke drifting from chimneys, walks of wood and stone winding through flower beds of riotous color. In the near distance loomed a great hall, to Indy looking strangely like ancient Viking gathering places. The Glen people farmed their land, rode horses of magnificient stock, worked herds of goats and sheep and cattle. There were dogs aplenty, many pets, but huge Irish wolfhounds were trained as sentries and protectors of women and children. The Glen was a holdout from the past that had carefully blended in with the technology and science of the present, although the latter was so subdued it seemed barely to exist. The Glen made full use of electricity, but all the power lines were buried deeply so as not to offend the eye and clash with nature at its finest.

This was the St. Brendan family of Wicca in the New

Forest, remote and magical, part of earth and nature, where ancient legends were still believed and observed, where the land seemed of a time and nature separate from the England lying beyond the forest.

Then came the "invaders." Indy had seen their handiwork when he looked down from the training airplane. The spears of flame, the numbing shock waves; they could only be the largest of the blasts he knew were ripping through the forest community.

His worst fears were now before his eyes. This slice of earth, so much in harmony with nature and history, had been raided with all the butchery marking mass slaughters of the past. Bodies of men, women, and children were still sprawled, twisted like rag dolls in pools of dark red. Everywhere those who could fend for themselves were aiding the wounded. Thick smoke swirled about, billowing from houses still aflame, tongues of fire crackling amid the tree branches. People, bloodied and hurt, had formed bucket brigades, bringing water from the streams to prevent the fires from spreading.

Gale had asked that Indy remain by the car. Few people knew his face, and the air was thick with emotion. But Indy found it impossible simply to stand by as a spectator. He joined a line of people passing water buckets up a slope. The people to each side of him took an instant to study his face. No questions. He was aiding; he was no longer a stranger. When the fires were damped, he moved to the injured, helped with first aid, carried the most badly hurt on stretchers to the communal building atop the hill.

Hours passed. Time to try again to match the past with this devastating present. Indy had never before been in the Glen, yet he knew of St. Brendan, isolated within the gullied forest. There was no way to avoid this community so close to Stonehenge and its deeply mystical and religious ties to ancient times. Stonehenge, where stood the ring of giant stones that still baffled modern-day scientists, cast a spell of energy down through Salisbury Plain and all its holdings.

And the world-familiar ring of stones atop the hill of Stonehenge was but one central part of a far-flung pattern of ancient sites where the men and women of thousands of years past had charted the movement of planets and stars with an accuracy that defied modern-day science. The standing stones and mark stones were not restricted to the plain of Salisbury; they were found throughout the British Isles. They were so much more than huge stones weighing hundreds of tons; their structure, their shaping, their very arrangement formed an astonishing geometric pattern from which strange and powerful energies flowed across the countryside.

No two sites were alike. The stones, twenty and even forty feet high, sometimes stood on hard ground, rearing into the sky, monoliths around which the lives of the ancients revolved. Others were like great spears lanced deeply into the earth. Rudstone at Rudston and the Devil's Arrows at Boroughbridge in Yorkshire had been erected by some unknown, even unimaginable force. Today powerful machines and hundreds of men would be required even to move these structures, let alone drive them into resisting surface.

Indy had discovered the hard way that the stories about energies collected in these sacred sites were painfully true. The reality was all the more confounding because every attempt to "catch" such energies with scientific instruments, scanning for electrostatic, magnetic, or other known sources, were dismal failures. They indicated only stones of special and particular shape. Other instruments searched along the known spectrum, in the ultraviolet and the infrared. Nothing. So he was dealing with energies that might even be imaginary. But how could *imagination* exert a physical force? It might not be measurable with an *instrument*, but it could be powerful medicine when it swept into and against the human body.

Indy had tried everything he knew to learn about the energy folklore that had grown up around the consecrated circle of Stonehenge. It was a frustrating period of chasing shadows, or ghosts of what once was or once might have been—if it existed at all. He had pored over the thick volumes relating to Merlin, who had referred to Stonehenge as the *Chorea Gigantum*. Down through the ages, it was known also as the "Giant's Ring" and, with stronger reference to the energies locked in the great circle of stones, as the "Dance of the Giants." According to the ancient scribe who slowly and carefully penned the records, the great stones had to be positioned according to an ancient and long-lost formula.

There was more to this positioning, Indy concluded, than simply measuring the sweep of celestial bodies, a simple yet brilliant astronomical calendar accurate to the split second over a full year. That was the visible, obvious purpose.

But Merlin—ah, if he could only know for certain the existence and powers of this remarkable wizard! Merlin had demanded that the huge rocky masses of Stonehenge be positioned in such a way that they became an instrument tuned to invisible powers. That instrument played on those powers in a manner similar to a catgut bow drawn across the strings of a bass viol, producing a deep, groaning, yet melodious sound not attainable through any other instrument.

All energy follows patterns, Indy deduced, whether from a steam engine or a trumpet or a whatzit. Invisible energy wasn't magic; radio waves were as commonplace as wind and sunshine. Was the energy of the great stones, so carefully locked into position by order of Merlin, on the order of radio waves?

Indy concocted a homing antenna of his own design to discover a particular radio frequency, respond to that frequency, and then point unerringly to the source of the radio wave.

For power, he judged he could use the energy of his own body. After all, the human body *is* a biological-electrical machine. You could prove this easily enough if you grasp the end of the antenna connected to a radio. Immediately the reception grows stronger and the signal clearer. In this case the human body is an antenna.

He built a carrying frame about his chest and back, the antenna loop running to the extent of his outstretched arms and over his head. He felt self-conscious about wearing this strange device. *Looking like an idiot is almost too much to ask,* he lamented to himself. Suitably ensconced in his contraption, he climbed a ladder to a high flat rock, larger than a motorcar, at Stonehenge.

He still felt a bit silly until he began to turn, his body and his contraption acting as a huge loop antenna. Silliness evaporated when an electrical shock lashed through his body, right down to the soles of his feet. Mouth agape, he continued his turn and was astonished to see tiny electrical fires, tongues of blue flame, crackling about his mouth. Sucking in air created a tiny field of electrostatics, enough at this point (with Indy so perfectly matched to the ener-

gies of Stonehenge) to create the equivalent of rubbing
cat's fur briskly with a brush. He almost fell, clamped his
mouth shut, tasted the ozonelike burn of electricity, and
then froze.

Not because he wanted to. He was locked absolutely in
this position. Heat flashed up from his feet through his
body; he saw a white light surrounding him, followed by a
thunderclap and an invisible hand that seemed to smack
him broadside. He flew from the stone, arms and legs
flailing, to crash on the ground far below.

Good fortune was often Indy's lot, and so it was this
time. He fell sideways. His loop antenna yielded to his
weight and folded slowly beneath him in a wonderful de-
celeration that crushed the contraption but protected his
body. Except for bruises and scrapes on his face, burned
lips, and singed hair along his body, he was unharmed.

But he never again questioned that the ancients,
prompted no doubt by that infernal Merlin, had devised
the equivalent of a tremendous capacitor, a battery collection device that soaked up energies still unknown to modern science, and capable of unleashing that power in
devastating form.

But now Stonehenge seemed to be on the other side of
the planet. What Indy wore now was dried and caked
blood, soaked clothes, and mud. His hands were scraped
and his muscles sore from hours of "pitching in" to help
in any way he could. He had not seen Gale since they
arrived but wisely accepted the fact that she would appear
when time and circumstances were right.

The cries of pain from the wounded had subsided; gone
also was the crackle and snap of flames. The smoke had
thinned with the coming of night. New fires appeared, this

time from lamps and torches placed to light the area. They burned cleanly, with little smoke.

Then he smelled the gorse, a natural fragrance that rushed against the smell of blood and animals and humans whose lives had been abruptly ended. There was also the stench of gunpowder, a strange odor that always reminded him of being in a great train station or the subway. *Underground,* he corrected himself. *That's what they call it here.*

All diminished and then vanished before the fragrance of the gorse. He knew of this custom from the time he had spent with the Romanies, who burned the bush for fragrance in fireplaces or in open campfires. It had about it the strong smell of incense, and it rode the breezes of the night air as a pleasing perfume. A smile moved fleetingly across his lips. He recalled how the Romanies, those Gypsies of the New Forest, used the smoke of the gorse to catch their dinner. They looked for pheasants in the trees above them and set gorse bushes aflame. What was pleasant to the human was a devastating drug to the birds. One good whiff and they tumbled like overweight flightless chickens to the ground.

His own thoughts of eating proved distasteful at this moment. He moved to the trunk of a large tree, resting against the bark, and sat in a quiet half-awake, half-asleep state. Finally he fell asleep.

He awoke to Gale kneeling before him, holding forth a silver cup. "Drink, Indy," she said quietly.

He accepted the cup, the silver cool to his touch. The first taste told him he was drinking the alcoholic fruit of the juniper berry, almost unknown beyond the New Forest. It cleared the head and sharpened the senses. The delightful drink went down in a long, unbroken swallow. He was returning the cup to Gale and wiping his mouth with the back of his sleeve when his arm froze in midmotion.

Standing behind and to the right of Gale, her figure outlined against a distant fire so that much of her face was still shadowy, was the woman he knew at first sight could be none other than Caitlin St. Brendan. Daughter of Kerrie and Athena St. Brendan, descendants of the family line that had ruled in this great vale for more than a thousand years.

And Gale's lifelong friend, as close as any sister could be.

Indy rose slowly to his feet. Caitlin's presence had struck him with almost physical force. He knew he had never before met any woman like her—any person like her.

She stood feet apart, braced against the pain of the wounds that had torn her body. Her leather garments showed rips, tears, stains, and slashes from which her blood had flowed. Somehow he knew that most of the caked blood on her clothing was not hers.

The great sword she held before her, the wicked point just above the ground, spoke for itself. His eyes went from the woman to the sword. Indy knew he was seeing a weapon that belonged to legend. If he was right, he beheld the fabled sword of fire.

Caliburn.

The sword fashioned through direct order and instructions of Merlin for King Arthur. The fighting sword of the man who held court at the Round Table. The Sword of Sacred Fire.

Even now that seemed beyond question. Reflecting firelight, gleaming, the blade yet shone with an inner glow that came from the metal itself. Indy was struck dumb with the sight of the sword he himself had sought for years, if only to prove its existence. He had been through Glastonbury and Avalon, to the fields where the legends claimed Arthur had fought and won terrible battles. Indy had searched through abbeys and cathedrals, the halls of the great knights, the sacred assemblages of Stonehenge, and the many other portals to the past. Reports of the sword were so tantalizing they had led him on again and again when he was ready to abandon the fabled blade to the mists of legend.

His eyes moved slowly up from the weapon to the face of the woman holding it. Strangely, he had a fleeting impression of a Cherokee Indian. Firelight reflected from high cheekbones. She was a marvel of beauty and might. Neither her broad shoulders nor powerful grasp of the sword hilt reduced the grace and femininity that so impressed Indy. Jet-black hair, long and slender fingers of strength. And her neck muscles, again highlighted by the glow of nearby fires, told of athletic and muscular prowess.

Her eyes flashed. They seemed to miss nothing as she in turn studied Indy. Their long mutual inspection gave him the opportunity to recognize both power and pain in her face. Her leather tunic again captured his eye.

This woman should not be able to stand, let alone walk, he judged quickly. If he saw correctly, Caitlin had been wounded grievously in the battle that had taken place here. The slashes in her tunic had been made by blades that had penetrated to her body. He couldn't miss the round tears that seemed to mark where she had been hit by bullets.

How was it possible for her still to be standing? Then he thought again of the sword. There was more to the legends of Caliburn than the blade of fire, given its great power through special alloys and the sorcery of Merlin. For this moment he put aside objections of myth and legend. Here stood a woman who seemed to have been wounded so many times that she should have been dead.

But she was here, now, standing before him, and the legends of Caliburn became literal to him. *The scabbard!* That was it. *If* the legends were true, that is. But he'd already seen so much here that danced about the edges of reality.

He forced his thoughts aside, but he couldn't stop thinking about the scabbard. He started to speak, held back his words, rushing memory details as quickly as he could through his mind. According to legend, the scabbard could heal any wound it touched. Its healing powers, be they magic or psychic, would begin to work immediately. And— *Later,* he told himself.

Gale seemed to be in tune with the thoughts swirling in his head, even able to sense when he mentally put them aside. She lowered herself to the ground; Caitlin did the same. Obviously, the mysterious events were about to be explained.

"There are at least thirty dead here," Gale said abruptly. "Cut down, murdered, in cold blood."

"Another fifty hurt," Caitlin added. Her voice, despite her physical injuries and the shock of emotional trauma, was strong, yet subdued, as if her presence and her words were enough to emphasize whatever she might say.

"Who?" Indy asked simply.

"We are not sure," Caitlin said, then after a pause: "Yet. But we shall know who they are, and then we will find them."

Indy gestured toward the devastation about them. "They used high-power explosives. That much is obvious."

He settled to the ground beside Caitlin, who was sitting cross-legged, erect and proud.

"We saw from the airplane. The flames, and the shock waves of explosions," Indy went on. "Impossible to miss what was happening."

"They were—are," Gale said hesitantly, "mercenaries. They knew where this glen was, who was here. They planned well, they moved like . . ."

"Professionals?" Indy offered.

"Yes," Caitlin said. "Trained, practiced, ruthless."

"Go on, please," Indy prompted.

"What they did," Caitlin said, measuring her words, "was calculated, methodical, brutal. All to serve a purpose. They came here in motorcars. We don't know how many. They were upon us, in our midst, almost before we realized their presence."

"But—" Indy turned to Gale. "When we drove here, the roads that vanished, I mean—"

"That was afterward, Indy," Gale explained. "Before? No one has come here to harm another person for years more than I remember. *After* the attack, well"—she shrugged—"you have a saying for something like this."

Indy nodded. "We do. Locking the barn door *after* the horse has ran away. Doesn't help."

Indy looked to Caitlin. "They came in, without warning, and opened fire?"

"Yes. Explosive charges. Powerful enough to destroy buildings, kill people, set fires. The blasts . . . they demoralized our people before they knew what was happening. Then this group—"

"Forgive me for breaking in," Indy said quickly. "How many were there?"

"Perhaps twenty. After the explosions, they did not kill

and wound without reason. What they did was calculated. They killed to break the spirit of the people, who were already fighting back with arrows and spears. It is not a primitive defense. One of our arrows can penetrate the bodies of three men. But it was too late. They cut down our best fighters, then they killed several women and children. After that, they held children with knives at their throats. They laughed. If we did not do what they wanted, the children would die. At such a moment, demoralized and shocked as we were, there was no time to invoke the old ways."

Was he missing something? Indy looked to Gale. "They, *who* are they?"

"I wasn't here." Gale deferred to Caitlin.

"Their faces were evil, but they were strangers to me," Caitlin said. Recent memories seemed to set her eyes ablaze. Instinctively her grip tightened on the sword hilt. "As I said, they were professionals. They worked as a team. And they knew where to go for what they wanted."

Her last words made Indy sharply alert. Whoever, whatever this group was, they had come here, armed to the teeth, ready to kill and maim for something beyond mere killing.

Before he could ask more from Caitlin, she rose to her feet like a great cat. "I must go. I am needed." She looked up as if she could see through the night, across the hills and thick trees. "Besides, the others are close by now."

Indy showed his confusion.

"It has to be the authorities," Gale said quickly.

"We shall cloak ourselves," Caitlin added. "No one will be able to find their way here."

Indy climbed to his feet, gesturing. "Caitlin, that would be a mistake."

She looked at him, a questioning expression on her face. "You hardly know us, yet you make so strong a statement," she said slowly.

Indy knew he was treading on dangerous ground. This woman was seething inside with pain and hatred, wanting, needing to strike out. He felt he was much too close to that sword.

"I know," he told her. "Understand that I have no more liking for the authorities, the police, than you do, Caitlin. But there's no way you can keep quiet about what happened here today. The explosions, the fires. The friends of yours who were killed. And how many of the attackers did you and your people get?"

"Nine."

"You just can't make them vanish. Not without repercussions that won't die down." Indy glanced at Gale; she nodded for him to go on. "Besides, I have a few contacts of my own with the authorities. Right to the top, Caitlin. And they may know more about the people who attacked you than you imagine."

Her eyes fixed on him like those of a cobra. "You can learn their names?"

"I can't promise. Except that I promise to try my best," he said quietly.

"If anyone can," Gale broke in, "it is Indy."

Caitlin moved closer until she stood directly before Indy. He had never seen eyes like those. She was incredibly alive. An aura seemed to flow from her.

"Why would you do this?" she asked, her voice strangely distant.

Indy held her gaze, their eyes locked. That was one beaut of a question. She was right. Why *would* he do this?

"I don't *know* why," he told Caitlin. "Only that I will."

He was beginning to understand the urge to help her. She was everything he had found in his travels through the world. She was all the great women of history. The queens and the leaders, princesses and priestesses. Everywhere he had gone, through temples and pyramids, tombs and castles, fields of battle, the conquering of nations, all was here in this one incredible human being. To turn away now would be to turn away from everything he stood for. Even that didn't make much sense to him, but Indy knew, he absolutely *knew*, he was committed. Gale moved by his side, her two hands holding his arm. That, too, was a sign for Caitlin.

She made no speech, asked no more questions. "Thank you," she said, bowing slightly. She turned and moved into the night gloom between the fires.

"Do you know what has just happened?" Gale asked Indy.

"By God, I do *not*," he answered, more sharply than he intended. While Caitlin stood before him he felt mesmerized, engulfed in a flow of energy. Hieroglyphics and cuneiform and languages whispered from clay carvings and stone seemed to float about him.

"You have been made a part of us. Of all of us, here," Gale continued in answer. "Let me tell you something else, Indiana Jones. I've never seen anything like this. *Never*. It is as if . . ." She sought the words. "It's as if you two have known one another for hundreds of years. As if in some ancient time you were brother and sister, and now after a long absence you've been joined together again."

Indy turned to her. "When did *you* become a romanticist?"

Gale smiled, a secret she almost voiced. Instead she held her silence.

Indy looked about the Glen. "Before the authorities get here, Gale, you'd better tell me what happened. All of it. Everything," he emphasized.

"It's . . . terrible," Gale said, her voice faltering.

"You can fall apart later, Gale," he said, his voice deliberately harsh. "Right now I need information."

Gale nodded. She took a deep breath. "They tortured Athena. Caitlin's mother . . ."

4

In reflected firelight Indy saw tears moving slowly down Gale's face. That sight hit him with a force that was almost physical. On opposite sides of the world, he and this woman had flown and driven and sailed into and through danger. Never once had Gale Parker yielded an inch of strength, flinched from fire or steel. Yet those few words about Caitlin's mother acted like a knife in her heart.

Instinctively Indy rested his hand atop Gale's. "Hey, stop right there, carrot top," he said gently. "If this is too much for you, I'll—"

She wiped away the tears with the back of her hand and took a deep shuddering breath. "I'll be all right, Indy." She showed a bare trace of a smile, her sadness coming through. "You just never know when this bloody stuff hits you. Athena was . . . well, a second mother to me." She sat up straighter, strength flowing back into her body and mind. "I'll be fine, Indy."

He nodded, then thought of a question that had been nagging at him. He also knew if he guided Gale through her pain by seeking specific answers, she'd be better able to handle the shock of losing loved ones.

"You said they, these men, tortured Athena. Why? And how did they know who she was?"

Gale shook her head. "I can't answer all that. Only what happened."

"Then start at the beginning. From what I've heard and seen, this group came in by car. Drove here. They apparently knew exactly where to go. They also knew how important it was to hit this place with as much surprise as possible. That way no one could prepare any defense. Right so far?"

"Yes. Caitlin's already told you what happened. The first thing they did was to kill wantonly. To frighten everyone into submission."

"But they didn't succeed?"

"No. Some people were out of sight when the shooting started. They were coming in from the woods. When they heard the explosions and saw the fires, they ran as fast as they could. They had been hunting with longbows, spears, swords. Just as their ancestors hunted for food. Even as the . . . the—"

"Invaders—whatever. Go on."

"Even as they were shooting people the hunters fought back with their bows. They're powerful and deadly. They took down several of the attackers. But they couldn't do much against rifles, weapons like that. And the invaders split into two groups. Their leader, whoever he was, led a small group up to the great hall. Somehow, he knew that Caitlin and her parents would be there. By then Caitlin and some others were aware of what was happening. They let the men come into the great hall and then they struck back, from the sides, from high ledges inside the building."

Gale finished her own cup of wine that had been at her side before she went on. "Caitlin went charging directly at their leader. With her sword. They opened fire on her. From what I've learned, she cut down at least four."

Indy gestured to interrupt. "Wait a moment. You said they shot at Caitlin."

Gale nodded.

"And they hit her?"

"Yes."

"With rifles? Rifle bullets?"

"Yes. She was also in a battle with two men who had swords. She was wounded badly then."

"Gale, what you're saying is impossible. I've just spoken with Caitlin. She had enough holes in her clothing, where she was struck, to have fought with a dozen men. Yet she's walking around!"

"I know, but—"

"No, let that go for a moment. Apparently after this group got inside the great hall, the fighting stopped?"

"Yes. By now, the men in the open had grabbed several children, held knives to their throats. Warned Caitlin and everyone else that unless they gave in, stopped fighting, they would kill the children." Gale swallowed hard, struggling to continue.

"What then?"

"In the hall. They held Athena. Caitlin's mother. One man, Caitlin remembers someone called him by name. Scruggs, I think. I'm not sure. He was laughing. While two men held Athena he went up to her. He had a curved sword. He—"

Indy waited as Gale struggled to speak.

"He sliced off her ear."

Indy sat, frozen, listening.

"He threw the ear at Kerrie, Caitlin's father. Told him he would chop off her fingers one by one, and then go back to the other ear and then her nose. Kerrie broke free. He charged Scruggs. He had no chance. They grabbed him and sliced his Achilles tendon so he couldn't walk. They told him to give up what they came for or he would see his wife cut to pieces." Gale shuddered again. "Kerrie had no choice."

"Where was Caitlin during all this?"

"She had climbed atop the rafters, the big wooden beams, high in the hall. There was nothing she could do. Too many men, too many guns. Several men were carrying submachine guns. They would have opened fire on her. All she could do was to study the faces of the men, try to remember everything she could about them."

Indy sat quietly for several minutes. Gale seemed relieved to be able to lapse into silence, to regain her composure as she fought to relate the terrible events.

Finally Indy seemed jolted by a thought. "These people, the gunmen . . . *what were they after*? Why did they come here? What is so important that they'd brutalize and kill like madmen? This isn't some nickel-and-dime robbery. There's no way the government won't get into this affair. They'll bring in the heavyweights. Scotland Yard, they'll be in this up to their armpits."

He paused and looked directly at Gale. "What were they after? *And did they get it?*"

Gale stared at the ground.

"What was it? Jewels? Diamonds? *What!*"

"It's . . . it's for Caitlin to say," Gale murmured.

"You're not giving away family secrets!" Indy said, half

shouting. "You can't keep this *quiet*! When the police get here, they'll turn this place upside down and inside out *unless* they get full cooperation. Don't you understand, Gale? Some thirty people are *dead,* and—"

"Enough, *enough*," she shot back.

Indy rose to his feet. "You want to stay here or leave with me now?"

Her eyes widened, a hand raised in protest. "You're *leaving* us? After what you told Caitlin?"

"After what I told Caitlin, *yes*," he snapped. "This is like boxing with shadows. Everybody talks in half sentences. I said I'd help, in any way I could. But I can't help anyone by being led around blindfolded."

"I—"

"Go or stay—which is it?" he demanded. "I can't see any use in getting tangled up with the police. I'll sound like an idiot, and if that's what I'm going to be like, I'll do it all by myself. The last thing I need is help *like this*."

She didn't answer. Indy shook his head, disappointed, and started for his car. He didn't look back, but suddenly heard the sound of a woman running. He stopped. Gale was at his side, holding his arm. "Let's walk. Away from . . . from the smell of blood. It's easier to talk this way. And you're right. You'll have to find out. Even Caitlin will tell you."

He nodded. They walked along a path, deep in the woods, that rose to a nearby hill.

"They were after the map," she said in a rush.

"Gale, please. You can do better than that."

"Sorry. It's just that I've never spoken about this to anyone. For more than fifty years, Caitlin's family has been the keeper of a map. From what I understand, it marks the location of an enormous fortune in gold. Bullion, mainly. Also ancient gold statues and figurines. Supposedly they're from long-lost cultures or civilizations and they're priceless."

She turned to look at Indy. "That's not all. There are also coins. Coins from ancient Rome, from the Holy Land, and other places."

"You realize," he said slowly, "this could be worth hundreds of millions of dollars?"

"Yes, I know."

"These statues. Are they well-known? To museums, places like that?"

"They're known, but hardly anyone has seen them. I think they were part of a collection from somewhere here in England. And the coins, well, I've heard something about a special arrangement a long time ago between our government and the Vatican. I can't be certain of everything I've just told you, but basically that's it."

"And this map tells where it is?"

"Is, or was. I don't know."

"Where? The gold, or treasure, whatever it's called. Where is it supposed to be?"

"That's the crazy part, Indy."

"So tell me about what's crazy."

"It's not here. In England, I mean."

"Where, then?"

"I think it's somewhere in your country."

He froze. "In the States?"

"I *think* so. You'll have to get more information from Caitlin or her father."

"You're right. This *is* crazy. Why would a fortune in bullion, and statues, *and* coins have been sent to the United States? And when?"

"I've told you everything I know."

"I'm trying to figure how the Vatican got mixed up in all this."

"I can't tell you any more, Indy." Her voice was almost pleading. "I just don't know."

"Sorry. I didn't mean to hammer on you," he apologized. He was pushing too hard. She'd had enough in one day to break the spirit of a dozen strong women. "I'll wait to talk with Caitlin. Or her father."

"I can't promise they'll tell you any more."

"I wouldn't ask you to promise anything for someone else, Gale. But I'll bet my bottom dollar they'll lay it all out for me. That's the only way I can be of any help."

"Caitlin is going to need you."

"Didn't you say that the invaders were going to kill Athena if her husband didn't give up the map?"

"Yes."

"Five'll get you ten that they have another copy. I know they do."

"What makes you so sure?"

"These people are very sharp. They're survivors. More than a thousand years right here. Armies have marched through these woods, destroying castles and fortresses, churches, whole towns. But St. Brendan is still here."

"What's left of it," Gale said angrily, then turned her head sharply. "Indy, over there." She pointed.

Indy turned to see the lights of approaching cars. At least four or five. "The police. We'd better get back to the main hall."

Five police cars, each with four constables. *And* a division chief and a detective. They looked with disbelief at the carnage about them, at the gutted homes, still smoking. The sight of nine bodies, slain with arrows or crossbow bolts or hacked with swords, shocked them to stunned silence. When they were led to the great hall, where the bodies of thirty men, women, and children had been laid out in neat rows, covered with white cloth and silk, the policemen knew they were in over their heads. They moved slowly among more than fifty wounded, including children with glazed, uncomprehending eyes.

"It's a bloody war," the division chief said, unnecessarily. He turned to a constable. "Get a call in to London right away. We'll need twenty ambulances, from the looks of it. If they haven't got that many available, have them send up a lorry or two. The dead won't mind not riding in style."

They talked briefly with Kerrie St. Brendan. He gave them short and angry shrift, far more occupied with tending to his wife than answering questions from baffled "poppies with badges" scribbling useless notes on pads.

"Talk to my daughter," he snarled to the division chief. "You do my woman no good with all your prattling."

"Prattling, is it?" the frustrated, angry chief said to Caitlin. "He calls all this murderous killing prattling?"

"No. He does not. He faults only you," Caitlin said. She sat on a large stone before the entrance to the great hall, the police gathered about her, Indy and Gale to the side.

Caitlin had little to tell them. She detailed the sudden attack. "Who were they?" She shrugged. "Murderers."

"What did they want? Why would they attack you like this?"

Caitlin pointed to the nine bodies on the ground. "Ask them."

"I can't bloody well do that, miss. They're dead."

"You *are* alert," she said caustically. "I can't ask them, either."

"We'll do a full report tomorrow, miss."

"As you wish."

"We'll want to question everybody."

"You can't do that."

"Why not?"

"We have almost forty dead. The children are in shock, and," she said in a tone that brought the officer up short, "you will *not* bother the little ones. Their minds need time to heal."

"Well, you heard. We've got ambulances and some lorries on their way. We'll have to remove the dead ones. I'm sorry to do that at such a terrible time, but, well, you know, police procedure and all that."

"Take the trash." She gestured again to the slain attackers. "We bury our own dead. Here, in the deep woods."

"We *must* take them with us."

"You will not."

"I'm not going to give you any grief, miss. If not tonight, then tomorrow."

Caitlin stood up suddenly. To Gale, it was clear that a sudden thought had come to her friend. "All right. The trash leaves in the lorry. Or a garbage truck, it's all the same. Our people must be taken in ambulances. Treated with respect and dignity."

Relief showed on the officer's face at this sudden show of cooperation. "I respect your sorrow. I appreciate your help," he said as kindly as he could.

"Do what you must," Caitlin told him. "It does not matter. Nothing will avail you."

She walked off before the man could reply to her mysterious parting words.

                              o   o   o

The ambulances and a single lorry arrived. The police hauled the lifeless bodies of the attackers to the lorry and dumped them in like so many sacks of meal. They did not touch the people from the Glen; these bodies were carried reverently to the ambulances.

Indy stood with Gale in the shadows to the side of the activity. "I can't believe Caitlin did that," he said finally to Gale.

"You can't believe she did what?" came the reply.

"The way she gave in so suddenly. At first she refused to allow the bodies of her people to be taken away. Then, like throwing a switch, she changed her mind."

"She did no such thing, Indy."

"One of us is crazy, Gale."

She shook her head. "Neither of us. Trust me. Trust Caitlin. And be patient. You will understand soon enough."

"All right."

The vehicles started back for London in a loose convoy, red taillights flickering through foliage.

"We'd better be thinking about going back ourselves," Indy said. "Unless you want to stay here with Caitlin and her family."

Gale shook her head. "No. I want to be with you. You're going to have questions and I may be able to fill in some blanks for you. But, Indy, would you mind waiting awhile?"

"Something come up?"

"No, but it will. Perhaps in an hour or two. You'll see."

"You won't tell me what?"

"I'd rather not," she said. "I'm not trying to be mysterious, Indy. But it would be so much better if you could see what's going to happen instead of hearing about it."

He studied her for a moment. She was serious. He nodded. "Okay. I can use the time. Can you take me around to those people who were closest to the attackers? Those who heard them speak, saw how they acted?"

"All right. Let's start at the caves. That's where the injured are being taken. Where the Old Ones are mixing the herbs and potions to make them better."

"Doctors?"

"We have no doctors here, Indy. We never have. If you know the secrets of the forest, it will take care of you."

If he had never heard the word "witch" mentioned, even once here in St. Brendan Glen, just several minutes spent in the great caves beneath the rugged hills of the Glen erased all doubt that he was in one of the great strongholds of ancient Wicca, a religion and, in most ways, also the way of life of these people. Adults and children, many grievously wounded, lay on clean straw pallets pressed into strong bed frames.

To all sides, women both old and young tended caldrons bubbling and seething over fires, into which they dropped herbs and plants unknown to Indy, but clearly being boiled and prepared as medicine. He heard a child cry out in pain. Two women were by his side at once. One applied a green salve to an open wound, the other held a silvered cup filled with an opiate, crushed from berries and plants growing all about the Glen, to the youngster's lips. Within minutes, the sudden wails of pain subsided to whimpers, and then that pink glaze of pain that had been in the child's eyes was gone.

"You're a witch," Indy said to Gale as they followed the tunnels from one cavern to another. It wasn't a question or an accusation, just an acknowledgment of a fact. "I'm not unfamiliar with Wicca, or even the Celts or Druids, or their many offshoots, but this is the first time I have ever been deep inside such a religion. Belief, fanatacism; they intermix. But it's different here. It's, well, *natural*."

"I'm sure whatever I tell you, you already know from your research. Sometimes, Indy, I need to remind myself that you're a highly respected professor, known for your studies of ancient times. Not just here in England, but throughout the world."

"Don't be overwhelmed by what you hear," he said in mild protest.

"By what I *hear*?" She laughed. "Indy, I've *seen* you work, remember? I've seen you look at carvings and strange writings that utterly baffled men of great learning. You might as well be in a London club, pipe between your teeth, a drink in one hand, reading an ancient scroll as if it were a modern pulp magazine!"

"I wish I'd written that all down. Good grief, Miss Parker, that's the best description of me I've ever heard."

She grasped his arm with both her hands as they walked. "Go ahead, Indy. Ask away. I'll do my best."

"All this." He gestured with his free arm. "Has it always been this way?"

She shook her head. "Hardly anyone outside Wicca really understands what we are, how we came about. There are plenty of books that tell of—"

"Forget books. Tell me what you've learned from the time you and Caitlin were children here. That's *life*," Indy stressed. "Not some notes somebody wrote down for their thesis."

"You know that the religion dates back before the Christian era?"

"Yes."

"I believe it's an error to consider the earliest days of what we now call Wicca as a religion. It was essentially a pursuit of the occult."

"And occult's true domain is the unknown," he added. "Using your own words, based on the way you lived here, growing up, with Wicca as a part of your daily experience," Indy said as he sought a new source of information, "what *is* Wicca, this way of life"—he gestured to take in all of St. Brendan Glen and the New Forest beyond—"to you as an individual? This isn't idle curiosity, Gale. You may be able to tell me much more about the historical and archaeological facts of this area than I might get from all the official records put together."

Gale smiled at him. "I know precisely what you mean, Professor," she said in a friendly mocking tone. "When I read about us in the London newspapers, I'm never certain who they're writing about."

She pointed ahead and to the right, and they followed a line of torches along an upward incline. They emerged from underground along a short but twisting path, invisible to passersby, that brought them to a hill looking down on the Glen.

"There it is," she said quietly as they looked on flickering torches and fires. From this distance there was no sign of the horror so recently visited upon the Glen. Even the wind blew toward its center, so that the acrid smoke from destroyed buildings never reached them.

"Thousands of years ago, no one knows that precisely when," she began slowly, "leaders of villages and hamlets, banding together for food storage and protection against the elements and marauding bands, recognized that they knew very little of the world about them. What we call

Wicca today had its origins throughout Europe. In its strictest sense, it wasn't yet a religion."

Indy nodded. "As I understand it, Wicca was really the attempt to recognize the truth of life and then to practice it as a guideline. Go with wisdom instead of blindness."

"Very well put, Indy. It recognized that certain individuals had a skill, or instinct, for what *was* wisdom in making choices for all the people in their groups, and that their advice for the future just happened in the long run to be most beneficial for all. Wicca didn't rule; it *guided*. Those who wanted to follow, did so. The others were free to go their own way."

"So it wasn't organized, as such."

"Right. Unfortunately, there were selfish and greedy people back in those times, just as there are today." Gale sighed. "They were the ones who turned the ability to predict the future to their own ends. What was Wicca, a search for knowledge, became witchcraft, which debases what Wicca stands for. The people who used witchcraft were judged to be sneaks, ruthless, and when nothing else could explain away their growing power, it was said that they were in league with demons and devils."

"Which put them right up against the growing power of the church," Indy added.

"And Wicca, which had nothing to do with witchcraft, was tarred with the same brush," Gale said, her tone just a bit sharper. "Along came the game of casting out the witches, *all* of them, good and bad. No distinction was made between Wicca, which had evolved into a kind and useful religion, as much a way of life as a theological pursuit, and those who cloaked themselves in witches' arts, but were without morality or conscience." She shook her head. "Along came waves of oppression."

"In its worst form, the Spanish Inquisition," Indy said quietly.

"The Inquisition made tremendous profit from it. Gold, jewelry, homes, land, women kidnapped for brothels, slavery, and horrible tortures and killing. Depravity at its worst."

"In short, to hunt and condemn witches was to achieve power over others," Indy commented. "The old game of being top dog."

"So our forefathers, *my* ancestors—"

"Went underground," Indy finished for her. "Look, Gale, all this has been prologue. I want to get down to the personal level, *here,* in the Glen."

She nodded. "All right, so let me establish right off the old chip for you what Wicca is for us as our religion. We believe in a supreme being. Use whatever names you want. Ultimate Deity—whatever. I've never known any of us, including the Old Ones, to feel they were wise enough to comprehend what is supreme."

"Okay, I get the basic picture. You're also communing with nature, and—"

"That's not good enough, Indy. We don't commune *with* nature. *We're a part of nature and we live that role actively.*"

"Now we're getting down to it," Indy said with sudden satisfaction.

"How ever do you mean that?"

"I'll answer you with a question. How do you reconcile Wicca's acceptance of a supreme being with the, well, the magic I've already seen. The way roads seem to appear and disappear, little people I can't see cooking our dinner for us. Water that turns almost instantly to ice and becomes water again. Mists that form when everything *I* know about meteorology says they shouldn't. So I'll accept this as magic. How can you have both your religion *and* magic? They don't fit in the same picture."

Gale held her gaze on him. Finally she smiled and shook her head. "So brilliant, so talented, and yet so blind. Poor Indy! Bedeviled with the falsehoods of the modern world."

"What in blue blazes are you talking about?" he snapped.

"Indy, where does it say that a deep personal belief in something bigger than us, than all of us, must reject sorcery and magic?"

"Why, I . . ." He fell silent, perplexed.

"They fit as naturally as dark and light, as night and day. That's about as opposite as you can get, but they certainly go together wonderfully."

"Yes, I know all that. But what I've seen here violates the physical laws by which this whole planet operates!"

"It does *not*. Your problem is that you haven't yet learned to *see;* you haven't let your instincts free so you can *feel*. So long as you keep that stupid word 'impossible' in the forefront of your brain, you'll always be blind to the magic that's just as real as the invisible wonders of your world."

"Oh?"

"You sound like a partridge. But"—she laughed—"when you purse your lips like that, you look like a fish."

"Very funny."

"I'll say."

"What invisible wonders in my, our, world?"

"Remember when you climbed atop that main structure at Stonehenge? With that crazy antenna you wore around your body?"

He grimaced. "Knocked me into the middle of next week. Yes, I remember."

"What was the energy that threw you from the rock?"

He glowered at her. "I, uh—"

"You don't know."

"No, I don't. Do you?"

"Only that it's earth energy, and the rock is a focal point. Just like a magnetic stone will swing around a compass needle. You don't *see* the magnetism, but its effect is still working. You don't even *feel* the magnetism. Unless," she added, "it becomes so powerful that it affects the iron in your blood. Then you feel strange and queer because you don't understand what's happening."

"So your people can tap into this basic earth energy?"

Gale shrugged. "You come up with a better explanation, Indy, and I'm your girl."

"Why do people consider what the witches do as supernatural?"

"You can answer that yourself!"

"Yeah. Like curving or bending light so you see in front of you what's to the side."

"You're the one who told me about refraction, remember? Looking at the fish underwater while you're above the surface, only the fish isn't where you see it? We're simply using what nature offers us."

"Sure. Easy. After a thousand years of study."

"No one said it came quickly or was easy."

"So your magic is actually a way of using earth energies the rest of the world—the untrained world—can't see or understand."

"Oh, no, you don't, *Professor* Jones! You're not going to paste a convenient identification label of *your* making on what we do!"

"Then what would you call it?"

"It's *magic*. But that's just a label, Indy. We use natural energies as well as supernatural forces. Look, natural is what the world recognizes. What's familiar. Anything that's *not* familiar usually scares the daylights out of people and they stick the label of sorcery on it. Can you imagine going back in time a few hundred years with a Victrola and placing a piece of cactus needle onto a wax record, and the whole thing spins, and out of it comes music and voices? How would you explain *that* to the local natives? It's magic! Sorcery! They don't understand springs to wind up the magic box. Or electricity, which they can't see and can't even imagine. To them, you're a great wizard who's captured people and music and made them prisoners in that flat disk."

"I'm getting the feeling"—he grinned—"that this carrot-topped lady of the woods is teaching the professor."

"Oh, Indy, it's just that it's so frustrating sometimes! Our secret is that we use natural energies other people can't see and we mix them with what people *do* see. Sure we have magic, but I can't levitate, and I'm not a telepath. But I can see and hear things you can't. Just as ancient symbols are as plain to you as the printed English language is to me."

"You give me too much credit. That's training, experience, knowledge—"

"You've just described magic!"

"Interesting viewpoint," he murmured.

"Oh, don't be so stuffy," she chastised him. "Look at all the forces you understand, and that people use, invisible to the naked eye."

"Name a hundred."

"Easier than you think, smarty-pants. Infrared. Ultravio-

let radiation from the sun. Cosmic rays. Radio waves. Magnetism. Sounds that dogs can hear but we can't. Gravity,
inertia, acceleration—good enough for starters?"

"There's more to you than I ever imagined," he said
with honest praise.

"Let me add just one more thing."

"Oh, please. Have at it. It's nice being the student for a
change."

She laughed, a delightful trill. "How many senses do
people have, as taught in our schools to children?"

"The basic five."

"Right. Why don't we teach the tykes about a sense of
balance?"

"Your point, and well made."

"And a sense of time, timing, rhythm, past, future, the
kinesthetic senses, truth, honor—"

"I get your point. Based on what you're saying, we block
the minds from full reality while they're still young."

She smiled. He swore he could almost see canary feathers along the edges of that cat grin. "So how come *you*
escaped, Indy? What set you free to see into the past and
find wonders where most people see only dust and decay?"

He shrugged again. "Maverick, I guess."

"No guess about it. You *are* a maverick. *So are we.*
That's our magic. Sight, foresight, *insight*, acceptance."

"What about the little people?" he asked suddenly.

"I've never seen them."

Her reply caught him by surprise. "But . . . you talk
about them, what they do, you said you can *hear* them
laughing—"

"I can hear the wind, but I can't see it," was her disarm-
ing response.

"You accept them, then. Even if you don't *know* they're here, in the forest, doing all the things they do."

"What does your shadow do?"

"What?"

"You throw a shadow from the sun, from moonlight, from firelight, electric lights, even a flash of lightning. Well, is your shadow real? Can you capture it? Make it do things you want it to do?"

"Of course not."

"Then it's of no use to you, is it?"

"Not the way you're talking about it."

"The little people, the faeries, elves, what we even call the gelflings, many other names, you know what they're like to me, Indy?"

"No, but I'd like to."

"The airplane we flew today."

"Yes?"

"It flies because it's missing something. You need to learn such things if you're going to fly *well*. There's a lowering of air pressure atop the wing. Maybe a half inch or less. But there's full pressure beneath that wing. The difference between normal pressure below, and a lack of full pressure above, well, Indy, that's the secret of flight. Something you can't see, that's less of what it should be, that's missing, and wonder of wonders—we fly!"

"When it comes to cavorting in the sky, I'll yield. Strictly student time for me."

"I've never seen the little people, Indy. But I've seen shadows flitting through the bushes, glows of sunlight, phantom lights in the dark. That's good enough for me. When you become fully sensitive and open to what our vision can't see, *something* happens. It's like all of nature joins with you."

Her sudden laugh was again like music. "That's our magic. It's the sorcery of flight. We have less of what we have when the airplane rests quietly on the earth, so we soar high above it. Isn't it marvelous?"

"*You* certainly are."

"And *you*, Professor," she said with mock severity, "at times suffer from loss of memory and failure of recall."

He blinked his eyes at her unexpected remarks. "Madame," he answered in the same tone, "you have me at a disadvantage."

"I fail to understand, *Professor*, how you can see what isn't visible in your own world and use it to your advantage—and yet you find what *we* do as wizardry."

She took a deep breath after her rush of words. "So what does that make you? A sorcerer who sees what isn't apparent to people around you?"

He shook his head. "No. Just someone trained in knowing what to look for."

"*And* assemble all the pieces into a coherent picture," she said firmly.

"I yield," he said, throwing both arms into the air. "I'll accept the little people and the curving light, even if I can't see them."

"That, Professor, is the first step to true learning."

"Who's the teacher here? You or me?" he asked her.

"What's that old saying, Indy? And a little child shall lead them?"

He made a rude sound. "You hardly fit that picture. I—"

Gale turned suddenly, interrupting him, pointing. "Oh, look! Indy, do you see them?" He followed where she pointed. Lights gleaming in the woods, apparently some distance away. Twinkling lights moving behind trees and foliage.

"Are they—"

She had anticipated his question. "No. Those lights are from the everyday world. It's the police, returning. They've been driving in circles, following the roads they can see." Gale smiled. "I imagine they're very frustrated by now."

He shook her arm. "Let's get down there. *This* I want to hear myself."

5

"This place is ruddy well haunted!" The lead driver of the police convoy stood stiffly, his face beet red from frustration. His thick handlebar mustache bristled as his cheek muscles twitched. "We've been driving these roads for nigh onto two blinkin' hours, and every time we makes a turn, we're right back where we were before!" He pointed an accusing finger at Caitlin. She had changed her leather garment, and her face was scrubbed clean of dirt and blood. She could have stepped forward from someplace in time, a hunter from some ancient warrior clan.

"Haunted?" she asked, her voice on the edge of coolness. Her sword hung from a thick belt by her side, and the constable's eyes kept roving between the weapon and Caitlin's face. "And I don't understand why you needs be carrying that oversized pigsticker, either, miss!"

The tone of her voice went from controlled to icy. "The sword is none of your affair. You are on private land. We live and hunt here. Now back to your problem. Why have you returned?"

"I told you!" the constable shouted. "This place, this bleedin' forest, it's haunted! There's no way out!"

"Do not shout at me," Caitlin said quietly. "You abuse our hospitality."

The constable turned redder, making an obvious effort to regain control of himself and avoid further outbursts. "You have my apology for that," he said, grinding every word through clenched teeth.

"Accepted," Caitlin said.

Indy leaned closer to Gale. "She's playing him like a harp string," he whispered.

"Shh. It gets better."

"I would like very much, and I am asking, for your assistance," said the officer. "To find our way out of here. We have been driving through fog that settles about us from nowhere, and when the fog blows off, the road changes on us and we have no idea where we are. Except for now, and I don't know how we got *here* again."

Caitlin seemed to ignore everything he said. "You wish to leave, then. You recall, Constable, I said that whatever you did would be of no avail."

He took a step back, then nodded, his eyes lidded. "I recall, miss. This is all very strange."

"Perhaps. You need do only what we asked of you before, and you are free to leave here without problem."

"And what would that be?"

"Leave the bodies of our people here," Caitlin said in a voice devoid of emotion.

"I cannot do that, miss. I am required to—"

"We are wasting time. If you cannot do what we ask, then drive off. I assure you that you will return again."

"You mean," the man asked warily, "that unless we

leave these bodies here, we can't get out of this accursed forest?"

"Judge for yourself."

"This is quite irregular." He was fuming.

Caitlin did not respond.

Another driver came up to the officer. "Constable Harrison, may I say something?"

"Speak, man!"

"The woman tells you honestly, Harrison. Unless we do as she bids, we shall be driving these roads until we are old and gray."

"That is crazy!" Harrison shouted.

"Crazy or not, that's the way it is."

"He speaks well and true," Caitlin said.

"And if we keep driving like this," the driver added, "we'll be out of petrol soon, and I don't see any pumps about here to fill our tanks."

Constable Harrison's mustache bristled again. "Scotland Yard's going to be in on this," he said sternly.

"I have no interest in Scotland Yard." Caitlin dismissed the matter.

"Well, they're going to—"

"Harrison!" The second driver was nearly frantic. "Do as the woman says!"

Behind Harrison came the sound of angry men. The constable turned to look at the other drivers and helpers by the ambulances and lorries. Men shook their fists at him.

"Get a move on, Constable!" a beefy man shouted. "So help me, we'll do as the woman says and leave you here to rot!"

Harrison turned back to Caitlin. As he met her deep penetrating gaze he felt he was staring into the angry eyes of a wolf. Shuddering, he turned back again to his men. "All right! You heard what she wants! Bring out the bodies of her people, *and be gentle about it*."

That last gaze into Caitlin's eyes seemed to have demoralized the man. "Where can we put the, uh . . . "

Caitlin pointed to a grassy knoll nearby. "There."

Indy nudged Gale. "That woman can say more with fewer words than anyone I've ever met," he said quietly.

"When she looks at someone like she did that nit of a constable," Gale observed, "that's all she needs."

Twenty minutes later the thirty bodies, wrapped in silk and linen, lay in a neat row on the grass. Constable Harrison turned to Caitlin. He removed his helmet, holding it before him in a submissive stance.

Before he could speak, Caitlin pointed to the lead police car. "You may leave now."

"There'll be no problem, miss? Driving away from the forest, I mean? So we can return to our families?"

Caitlin remained aloof. "Go, now."

He started for his car, and the remaining drivers and assistants scrambled for their vehicles. Two minutes later all that could be seen of the impromptu convoy were taillights dwindling in the distance.

People began to leave from their homes; those who'd been left with ashes, and would be forced to live in the caverns of the Glen, tending the injured, also began to assemble by the knoll where the bodies lay. Indy could feel an ache in *his* body. By now he knew he was "receiving" the pain and sorrow of these people. The more he felt a part of them, the more sensitive he became to their feelings.

This was no place for him tonight.

"Gail, it's time for me to leave," he told the woman by

his side. "I know I've been made welcome here, but tonight isn't the time for me to stay."

"I'm going with you."

Indy showed his surprise. "Tonight? *Now?* I thought you'd stay . . . well, you know," he finished lamely, looking at the bodies.

"Caitlin wishes me to be with you tonight. I agree with her. There's so much to go over, Indy. Besides, I . . ." She let her sentence hang.

"What were you going to tell me?"

"The sense, the *presence*, of danger, is still with us." Again she hesitated. "With *you*, Indy. It's almost a dark mist about you."

He couldn't avoid the smile at the corner of his mouth. "And you're going to protect me?"

She almost flared in anger. "A lot more than you'd ever imagine," she said heatedly. "I can sense things you can't. And as good as you are, you don't have eyes in the back of your head., Indy, you're close and dear to me, but there are times when even you can use some help."

"Your choice," Indy said.

He stood alone as Gale went to Caitlin. The two women hugged fiercely, then stepped back, each looking into the eyes of the other. Indy observed them closely. They hadn't spoken a word. Gale returned to him. "I need to get some things from the hall. I'll meet you by the car. Caitlin bids you good night and hopes to see you again soon. *Very* soon."

He stopped himself from asking questions. Time enough for that later. He went to his car and waited. After several minutes Gale returned, a large leather knapsack slung over one shoulder. She averted her eyes. Indy saw tears on her cheek, and somehow knew to keep silent.

◦   ◦   ◦

The drive through the New Forest went smoothly. The only mists they encountered were the result of changing temperature and humidity. Gleaming lights appeared along the winding roadway, but they were reflections shining from the eyes of deer, rabbits, foxes, and other animals. Gale remained quiet during the drive; Indy did not intrude on her silence. Something was driving her deeper into depression.

Indy's unexpected problem was that *he* was receiving almost a physical effect from Gale. Ever since he'd been exposed to the magic of the New Forest and the inhabitants of the Glen, he was experiencing a startling sensitivity to the moods and feelings of people close to him. Finally he found it almost impossible to remain silent, but before he could speak, they drove up an incline, and as if a switch had been thrown, the trees fell away and he was turning onto the main highway to London.

Clear of New Forest, Gale began her own ascent from the depths of dark introspection. Indy glanced at her. "It might help if you talked about it."

"I'm better now. That was a very bad period . . . I was, well, receiving is what I mean."

"Gale, are you telling me you were receiving a message by mind? Telepathic?"

"No." She shook her head. "*Empathic.* Very strong. No words, no messages, but a *knowing.*"

"Empathic," he repeated. "I don't want to push, but—"

Her words hit him with physical force.

"Athena . . . Caitlin's mother. . . . She is going to die tonight."

Indy felt ice race through his body, and his muscles

jerked suddenly. "How . . . how can you know that?" He spoke slowly, choosing his questions with great care.

"It's all through the Glen, Indy," Gale told him with incredible calm. "It's like a sound wave that goes out. Athena has been the Old Mother for so many, many years. Everyone is, well, tuned into her."

"But you said she was *going* to die! Not that she's dead."

"Yes. Her wounds were much worse than anyone realized. When I was with her, I saw how pale she'd become. Not just from where they had cut her deliberately. But inside. She's been bleeding internally. I took some advanced first aid, enough to know that her stomach was perforated. There's no hope any—"

Indy slammed on the brakes and the Bentley skidded wildly with screeching tires and the smell of burned rubber. "The devil, there's no hope!" he shouted, anger exploding from him. "We can still get her to a hospital. We can be back there and get her to an emergency room. A blood transfusion! Surgery. Why is everyone giving up like this!"

"It isn't a matter of giving up, Indy." Again that impossible calm from Gale. "*It's her decision.* Or, the decision's been made for her. She can see ahead."

"You're telling me she has precognition? She can see into the future? See her own death?"

"Yes."

"But—"

"Indy, your own tribal medicine men, the American Indians, they've done the same thing for hundreds of years."

"I know all about seeing the blackness ahead," he said heatedly. "I've seen it in India, in Tibet, in Haiti . . . *but it can be altered.*"

Gale sighed, staring straight ahead. "I know this is difficult, and I'm trying, really, to help you understand. This is Athena's decision. Whatever she sees ahead of herself, her future, is not a better choice than d—than going, tonight."

"I just don't get it," he said, hands gripping the steering wheel, eyes vacantly following the headlights stabbing the night.

"She is not in pain. She is not frightened. And Athena is ninety-two years old. You would argue with her?"

"She's ninety-two? I didn't think she was sixty!"

A wan smile crossed Gale's face. "Please drive on, Indy. The farther I am from the Glen, the less I will feel, now that her decision is made."

He shifted gears and floored the accelerator, rushing into the night. He came to a decision. There wasn't any need to baby-sit or gently hold Gale's hands. She was stronger than he'd ever believed. It was already well past time for some hard questions and hard answers.

"Gale, I get the feeling I'm in deep with what happened today. You think I didn't see those cops writing down my license-plate number? And solid descriptions of the both of us? There's forty people dead, more than that wounded, and this isn't going away by itself. There'll be an investigation, and we're *both* going to be smack dab in the middle of it."

"I guess we will."

"Don't guess. It's as serious as a heartbeat. Besides that slaughterhouse today, there's the map. There's anywhere from millions to hundreds of millions of dollars, or pounds sterling, whatever currency you want to use, involved in this."

"More."

He shot her a sharp glance. "Like what?"

"Caitlin's mother. When Athena is gone, Caitlin is blood-sworn to avenge her death."

"She's got to know *who* before she can avenge anyone or anything."

"Caitlin will find out. And she'll go after him. She won't stop until he's dead. Those are the Old Ways."

"Never mind the Old Ways right now. Let's stick to the main point."

"All right."

"Before I tell you what I've learned tonight—"

Gale turned in her seat, staring at Indy. "You have a lead?"

"Later, blast it!" He gritted his teeth to remain patient. The Old Ways and the little people were starting to grate on his nerves. Indy dealt in facts, and he'd been on a merry-go-round of illusion all day. "Will you please just answer my questions?"

She slumped down. "Ask."

"I talked to maybe a dozen people tonight," he said. "When we were outside and also in the caverns. Asked them if they'd heard anyone among the attackers speaking or calling out to one another, and if they could recognize the language. One thing is definite. They were *not* English, they weren't American or Canadian. Most people believed they recognized Russian. Of course that could have been Polish or Hungarian. With all the shooting and screaming, and the fear level, it's easy to mistake one language for another. But it's definitely eastern Europe. They also heard French, and one person swears he heard orders being shouted in German."

Gale sat up straighter. "Does that help?"

"Does it ever," Indy emphasized. "It shows a pattern and it's darned clever. This group used different languages so to confuse everyone. I also spoke to several policemen who were picking up the bodies of those nine slain attackers. There wasn't any identification in their clothing. No tags, names; nothing. No one wore rings, bracelets, jewelry of any kind. But one body had strange tattoos, in the shape of a barracuda."

"We'll ask the Romanies," Gale said quickly. "If anyone knows the symbolism, the Gypsies will."

"Okay, I'll leave that up to you."

"First thing tomorrow."

"All right," Indy went on, more slowly now. "Look, Gale, there's a pattern developing from all this. That map they were after. How'd they find out it was with your people? How'd they even know about it? Or where to go once they got into the Glen? All those pieces have to come together."

"As well as where they're going," Gale added.

"I sure hope you can get Caitlin to share that other map with us. I know it exists. Then we'll know where those people will be moving."

"That's where Caitlin will be moving. It's like I said before. Whoever caused the death of her mother must die by Caitlin's sword. By her hand."

"That sword she carries . . ." He let his sentence hang.

Gale studied him. "Yes?"

"If the old legends are true, and I believe them more right now than I *ever* have, that could be the sword fired and annealed by none other than Merlin."

"Do you think it's Excalibur?"

"By now," Indy mused, "I'm ready to accept that St. Brendan's Glen is the original Avalon. Oh, I know, Avalon is regarded by most historians as part of Glastonbury, and it was considered an island because at times it was surrounded by water. But it's not and never was the wonder-ful, enchanted isle. The water surrounding Avalon at Glas-tonbury was more bog than lake. English historians have a great romantic streak in them and they'll attack you hyster-ically if you challenge their versions of the story of King Arthur and Merlin and those ill-tempered knights history regards as such dedicated gentlemen. Brigands on horse-back and violators of lovely, helpless young women is more like it."

"Oh, don't you have a rotten opinion of our cherished traditions!"

"Not at all!" Indy boomed. "There's nothing wrong with reality. Such as the great knights and warriors of England going off to the Crusades and getting battered left and right by the locals. They wore their colors and fealty as if they were armor. And the armor they *did* wear nearly killed them in the heat of the Holy Lands as much as the locals did in their loose robes and with their fast horses."

He laughed. "All right, carrot top, Excalibur is the cere-monial sword. Could be it was stuck in some big chunk of rock and the boy Arthur yanked it out because the saints were guiding him, or some other lovely fairy tale like that. But what Caitlin carries is *not* Excalibur. And through the years and the absolute hordes of definitive histories of the Knights of the Round Table, and the sorcerers and drag-ons and fair maidens, Excalibur and what Caitlin has be-came the same sword. It was Excalibur in the beginning and the name changed. But that's too convenient. It's a patsy job for some beak-nosed librarian who couldn't come up with a better line.

"Uh-uh. Caliburn is the fighting sword, the only true sword, and I know its legend. During its making, Merlin stood by the sword maker, he helped the forge burn brighter, he muttered incantations and the mumbo jumbo at which he was so good. But somewhere along the line he had some new metals, what would become alloys, and he mixed them in with the iron of the sword, and when it became steel, it was more than a sword. The blade of fire, the unconquerable, and a magic weapon—because into that blade Merlin poured *all* his magic and his power."

Indy took a long breath. "Probably why the old geezer finally died the way he did. Weak, shunned—"

"Go on about Caliburn," Gale said.

"You already know what there is to know. That's how Caitlin killed four of those men attacking her parents. With the blade of fire."

"It's not Caliburn you want to know about, is it?"

He shot a hard look at Gale. "Give the lady a cigar. She's coming out of her cocoon."

"Let's stop playing games. Go on to hard questions, Indy."

"Good. Thank you. Why is Caitlin still alive?"

"I was afraid you might ask that."

"I'm asking."

"But you already *know*. If you know about Caliburn . . ."

"I don't *know*. But I admit I *believe*."

"Please. Keep talking."

"The scabbard. Legend has it, and almost all Arthurian legends, stories, and ballads state that the scabbard has the magic power, instilled by Merlin, to heal any wound it touches."

Gale seemed somehow aloof during this exchange. "What you say is true," she said.

"I saw enough wounds—we both did—to know that Caitlin should be dead a half dozen times over."

"Yes." That was all from Gale. It seemed she was hoping Indy would run into a dead end.

"But she is not dead, despite wounds that were obviously fatal."

"Yes."

"That scabbard she was wearing. It's not the one produced by Merlin, is it?"

He heard a sigh. "No. It's not."

"What happened to the scabbard that heals wounds almost as quickly as they're inflicted?"

"I would have thought you had that all figured out by now."

"Gale, you sound almost antagonistic."

"Oh, Indy, I'm *not*." She looked at him with a pained expression on her face. "It's just that I have a lifetime behind me of *never* talking about these things."

"Until now."

She nodded.

"Where's the scabbard, Gale? The one with the life force."

"She wears it."

"You just agreed with me that's not the scabbard I saw, and—"

"The original scabbard was covered with several layers of the finest suede. Deerskin worked for months. Caitlin knew that she might one day be hurt so badly she'd be unable to reach the scabbard and apply it to the wound. So she and her mother carefully soaked the scabbard in a solution Athena prepared. They unwrapped the layers of deerskin. It was very thin but incredibly durable. Then—"

"Let me guess."

"Please."

"They sewed it into a body garment. What Caitlin wears beneath her clothes, against her skin."

"Yes."

Indy whistled to himself, a single long-drawn-out note. "Brilliant. Absolutely brilliant. If that leather from the scabbard works as advertised—"

"What a strange way to describe something with magical powers!"

"If it's all it's cracked up to be, then Caitlin is *always* protected. She can suffer those wounds and they heal immediately."

"Almost."

"What's the catch?"

"The scabbard works its healing magic only for the person fighting with the sword. With Caliburn."

"So that's it," Indy said. "That's why you're so certain that Athena will die tonight. The one thing I couldn't figure out. Why the scabbard, or its garment, wasn't used to heal Athena. It won't work for her!"

"Yes." The single word was forced out.

They sat in silence for a while, Gale accepting the night wind as a comforting blanket, Indy wrestling with myriad possibilities and trying to anticipate what the future held for them. He knew now that he was up to his neck in this caldron of mystery, and Gale was right there with him. During that time at the Glen, he'd seen one constable standing in the shadows and taking photographs of different people. He'd spent too much time shooting pictures of himself and Gale as well as several of Caitlin.

Indy would have bet a hundred dollars to a dime he was a spy in the pay of the group that had struck at St. Brendan Glen. It figured. Go in with the authorities, get a photo record of anyone who might be there who didn't "fit"—

like Indy. By now those pictures were being studied for identification.

It was time to increase his own sensitivity to trouble around every corner he might turn.

But one thing still nagged at him. "Gale, you up to some more talking?"

She'd been on the edge of sleep. She sat up straight, taking deep breaths of the night air whistling past the speeding car. "All right, Indy."

"There's a piece missing in this puzzle."

"Only *one*? How wonderful! I felt we were wandering blindfolded through a mine field."

He laughed. "Not quite as dangerous." He paused, seeking the right words. "Look, Gale, there's a rule in science—there's no free lunch in the universe. There's *got* to be an energy source for everything that happens. For everything we do. It doesn't matter if it's humdrum stuff or wizardry or magic. The rule applies to *everything*. Sometimes we can't see or understand the nature of the energy source, but it is *always* there."

"No argument, Indy. If, that is, I'm following you."

"Magic, like anything else, has to pay a price to work."

"A price in energy, you mean."

"Absolutely," he said. "Even if we draw it from the planet itself. Like the energy that collects at Stonehenge. That's not magic. The earth is an enormous gravitational energy force. It gives off all sorts of radiation. The crust of the planet shifts and generates enormous magnetic and electrostatic forces. So the energy is there for the taking, *but only if you know how*. That's why I believe in the power of the sword Caliburn. Why I can even accept the healing powers of what was its scabbard, which Caitlin now wears against her body."

She anticipated his question. "And you want to know how energy is derived from somewhere," she said carefully, "and gets to the sword and her garment."

"That puts it as well as I could," he said admiringly.

"Am I correct in judging that even if you don't yet know, you're onto something?"

"You get a second cigar."

"Don't let me stop you. If you're right, I'll tell you immediately."

Again he glanced at her. Gale looked straight ahead so as not to meet his eyes and perhaps give herself away. Indy took a deep breath.

"I saw it. Kerrie—that's her father's name?—okay, Kerrie was carrying it." He paused. "The scepter."

Gale nodded slowly. "You're onto it."

"The jewels on the outside of the scepter are pure showmanship," Indy went on. "I've seen hundreds of scepters around the world. Haitian voodoo rods, shafts worked by the American Indians, scepters for kings and queens and pharaohs. Most of them were strictly for wowing the crowd. Razzle-dazzle stuff. But every now and then I've run into a scepter that was used to collect or focus energy, or both."

"Dating from when?"

"Long before you and I arrived on the scene, lady. One of the best-kept secrets in the archaeological world is that people were using electric batteries four thousand years ago, perhaps even longer than that."

Gale half spun in her seat, staring at Indy. *"What?"*

"You heard right. Electric batteries. The Babylonians, Syrians, ancient Persians, and others. Look, Gale, they were electroplating silver and gold onto statues and figurines, and I've seen that work. Removed from tombs that hadn't been opened in four thousand years, statues and icons that could *only* have been done with electricity. In fact, pieces of those batteries are in an Egyptian museum right now. We had some electrical engineers study the pieces and try to reconstruct such a battery. The copper, lead—whatever they used. Working only with the ancient tools and materials, they did it. Built batteries that could easily have been assembled in ancient times."

"And you're convinced this is tied in with the scepter Kerrie was carrying?"

"You'd make a lousy poker player, Gale. You'd give your hand away in the blink of an eye. You *know* it was that scepter! And you also know the scepter is, like I said, strictly for show. What's *inside* that thing is what counts."

"You amaze me."

"Why? It's simple deduction. I saw the crystals glowing. I don't buy the magic potion for sale down at the local hardware store. That thing has got to have a battery inside. The battery provides the power to energize the crystals to act as an energy-collecting device. Like what happened to me at Stonehenge. The energy is real. It's radiated by the earth. The trick is to learn how to harness it. Which, I'm now convinced, is just what Merlin did. He was more practical engineer than wizard. Unfortunately he seems to have taken most of his so-called magic formulas with him to the grave. In my book, Merlin is absolutely real, an incredible genius on a par with the greatest minds of history, and he knew better than to claim he was working with quite ordinary and everyday forces. But playing it as a wizard, in a time when people believed in dragons, Merlin got away with the sorcery game. In today's world he'd be a fantastic con man."

"How do you explain the curving of light? The mists and fog? All that?"

"I don't know just how it works. But it's the greatest use of natural energy I've ever encountered. It's brilliant."

"But not magic?"

"I didn't say that," Indy protested. "I can explain some of what goes on. The rest of it? I'm hanging by my finger-nails off a cliff."

Gale smiled. "Good."

"Why good?"

"Because there's more magic than any of your science in all this."

"I'll lay odds that the garment Caitlin wears, made from the scabbard, has a lot more than suede or leather in it. Care to challenge me on my saying it's interwoven with gold threads? Or perhaps silver? Because silver is a better electrical conductor than mercury, just as a for instance?"

Gale didn't answer. She had doubled over in pain. Indy reached out to her. "Gale . . . can I help?"

She shook her head. "Athena . . . she passes on. Take me home, Indy, please, *now*."

6

Indy listened to the soft chimes of the grandfather clock in his fifth-story flat in London. Four o'clock in the morning. He was well into his second pot of coffee as he pored over notes and historical records. Merlin and Avalon and King Arthur swirled through his head, mixed with visions of the flashing blade of Caliburn and the mystical tales of the Knights of the Round Table.

Fact and fiction seemed to be interchangeable in the Arthurian tales. But one point was certain. Despite the many versions, French as well as English, the sword of Caliburn and its scabbard were always endowed with miraculous properties.

Excalibur was clearly poetic invention on a grand scale. The tale of Arthur removing the magic sword from solid rock filled in the gaps of history, because there was little to write about Arthur as a youth. Despite his kingly parentage, his childhood remained singularly unimpressive. To make the leap from relative obscurity to leader of all the knights, what better invention than a magic sword that only the "great and true" king could remove from its enchanted stone?

More than one mighty coup had been achieved through similar "politics of magic." It was popular drama on a huge scale. With Merlin razzle-dazzling the superstitious, uneducated knights, the wealthy and highborn were ripe for mesmerizing into the belief that King Arthur was, if not godlike, at least a divinely chosen ruler. Besides, being a knight bestowed all manner of freedom upon those fortunates. In the name of the king, you could rob, steal, pillage, beat, and even enslave anyone you wanted, for pleasure. The scribes, poets, and minstrels of the time who recorded the ravaging of local populaces by the knights made certain never to record the truth—or they were certain to be on their way to a merciless beheading.

But this wizard, this Merlin, was more than a master magician. More than one of history's great public-relations men. Merlin could frighten and hypnotize, astound and terrorize, and to do that he had to back up his mutterings with deeds. All his so-called magic potions and powders could not match the reality of the sword and scabbard of Caliburn.

Everything pointed to the natural energies the people of the New Forest had learned to accumulate and then utilize with marvelous effect. Like Indy's experience atop Stonehenge, hurled by invisible energies collecting in the homemade antenna he had so foolishly attached to his body—well, the way to test suntan lotion is not to throw yourself into a bonfire.

Merlin didn't create the sword Caliburn out of bat's wings or magical powder. That was nonsense. The magic was real, but it was beyond Indy's knowledge of such powers to know how *that* worked. One clue was the energy field that had smacked him at Stonehenge. If Merlin had known how to capture that energy and infuse such power into the blade of Caliburn, well, then it began to make sense, but the secrets were still locked up in the past.

Except, he thought furiously, whatever power lay within the scepter. Whatever energy was captured and then transmitted from the scepter could be tied in with the sword. Almost like a sending source. Already scientists had learned how to transmit a powerful radio signal to a distant point and pour energy into a receiving antenna or station. The principle would be the same for Merlin or any scientist today.

Indy reverted back to his exchanges with Gale. "I'll bet my bottom dollar," he had told her, "that Merlin was able to manipulate natural earth energies so that they looked like magic. And if the scepter contained a stored energy source, like a battery, that would do the trick. After all, switch on a flashlight and you get a beam of light from a tightly packed container of lead and chemicals. Stored energy is the 'trick.' "

He was convinced he was on the right track to understanding the power of the sword, but the reasons for the healing power of the scabbard remained elusive. Was it simply a tremendous force of faith? Faith was more nebulous than magic. Indy had enough experience with voodoo in African and Haitian tribes to have seen "faith" paralyze the minds of people and cripple their bodies, to the point of being frightened to death. The hex of evil spirits.

This could work the other way, as a healing instead of a wounding. After all, *something* had kept Caitlin alive despite enough wounds to kill a dozen men. Faith or magic;

he could not yet determine. But whatever it was, Caitlin was alive and well when she should have been dead.

Indy put aside the puzzles he failed to solve. More immediate concerns closed in on him and Gale. He moved quietly to the bedroom door, opened it just enough to see that Gale was asleep. He closed the door and returned to the living-room couch.

Sleep eluded him. He knew that whatever group had savaged the Glen would go to any lengths to obtain the secret map. That meant they'd be after him and Gale. The police were no protection. Not yet, anyway. They were still baffled by that attack with high-powered weapons and the ruthless murders. By people who spoke in different languages, who carried no identification, who operated as a machinelike organization. This group was brilliantly led. It knew what it wanted and would not stop at anything to find and seize whatever it sought.

There was the added tug of the past reaching out to Indy's instincts and experiences as an archaeologist. The coins that had been mentioned. Mint-condition coins from the beginning of Christianity? What an incredible find *that* would be! And where had the gold come from? What was it for? Who had gathered it originally? How did the Vatican get mixed up in so shady an affair?

Indy fell asleep in that swirling mixture of thought and riddles with which he'd wrestled most of the night.

They came down on slim cables from the roof. Two men in black clothing, black sneakers, woolen hoods. In the best manner of the dreaded Ninja, the infamous assassins of Japan. They swung well out from the buildings as they cabled down, and then with a rush, hurtling like heavy weights at the end of long strings, they shot into the living room.

Indy barely opened his eyes before the first man landed with both knees hard against his chest. Indy's eyes seemed to pop wide as his breath gushed from his lungs. Gasping for air, jerked violently from the deep sleep he'd so long fought off, he knew only that someone was hammering on his body as if he were a punching bag.

He was fully awake in seconds. Every time he fought for balance, the two men swarmed over him. In moments he knew he was being taken down and worked over by experts. Two fists grasped his hair, jerked his head back against the edge of the couch. He tried desperately to swing his body to the side, but the second man twisted his ankle, fell with a knee into Indy's stomach, and the next moment slammed knuckles into his throat.

White-hot pain shot into his brain. His windpipe felt as if it had been pounded with a lead pipe. Even as knuckles mashed his Adam's apple, he knew what his attackers were doing. He was so desperate for air that he had no chance to cry out to Gale, or make enough noise for anyone to hear him and call the police.

Indy was no stranger to physical punishment or to techniques to escape the battering he was taking. First and foremost was to get air into his lungs. He didn't know if two or six men were working him over. He managed a lungful of air and then thrashed about wildly. His foot, striking blindly, caught the man before him in the ribs. He heard the sharp cry of pain; the blows, at least for the moment, ceased. But the man behind the couch, both hands grasping his hair, was hauling Indy up over the edge of the couch. Even through his pain he recognized what they were doing; stretching him out, forcing him to struggle for air, unable to use his hands to defend himself.

Again Indy thrashed on the couch. Free for the moment from frontal blows, his body twisted until he was on his side, and then he completed the half turn, his face mashed against the couch itself. For this moment, anyway, his eyes, nose, mouth, and throat remained protected. Then he felt himself in the air as one man pulled, the other grabbed his belt, and they heaved him behind the couch and fell on him like two madmen, raining blows against his ribs and kidneys. He recognized, again, the mark of the professional. They were beating his body painfully and expertly, but they hadn't drawn any blood.

Hope flared in him. *They're not out to kill . . . they're after information. Just as soon as they stop using me for a punching bag, they'll make their move. Be ready, Indy, be ready. . . .*

The two men hauled him up suddenly to slam him backward with a jarring crash against the nearest wall. One man held his left wrist in a painful backward bend, keeping Indy from any sudden moves. Not that he wanted to get these people *that* upset as a large automatic pistol loomed before his face. The muzzle banged hard off his upper lip, then jammed against his nostril.

I guess I look like Raggedy Andy with a mop handle up my nose. . . . The idiot picture flashed through his mind and he half choked with laughter.

To the men using him for a battering ram, he sounded as if he were choking, and they relaxed. Indy seized the opportunity. He gasped and choked again, tried to bring saliva to his lips, and deliberately went limp. Now his attackers had nearly two hundred pounds of limp dishrag in their hands. That's not easy to hold up with just a pistol in one nostril for support.

He heard one man bark commands to the other. Indy wasn't sure of the language, but it sounded middle European. He understood enough to know what was happening. The second man was being told to hold him up.

Well, things were looking up. He was pinned against a wall, a heavy gun rammed into his nose, his body on fire from a hundred blows, but with one man holding him from falling and the other occupied with the gun, there wasn't much room to keep using Indy as a target for fists and feet.

Then the leader was speaking English. His voice came out as a hiss, the other man close to Indy's face, spittle accompanying every word.

"Professor Henry Jones." Clearly the masked intruder wanted to let Indy know he knew precisely who he was. Indy had regained his breath; wisely, he relaxed as much as he could to regain tautness and strength in his body. He was also adding up pieces of data and building larger blocks of information.

They knew where he lived. They knew who he was. They came through his window because he'd double-locked, from the inside, the door to his flat. And he didn't need to be a rocket scientist to conclude that this was neither a social visit nor your everyday robbery.

He had also gleaned another fact that could in an instant become vital. The contempt in the man's voice when he said the word "professor." So Indy was being held at gunpoint by a killer who judged teachers, professors—likely everyone in the whole educational system—as weak and inferior.

Indy had to work that to his advantage. "Y-yes, sir," he stammered, his voice quavering.

The man laughed. "We have a weakling here." He sneered to his companion. "I can handle this mouse myself. Go find the woman," he ordered.

"Tell me about the Caitlin woman," the man said, his voice promising punishment if Indy failed to respond. "The witch. What is your relationship to her?"

"I—I don't know her. She's a friend of—"

"You speak of the one with the fire hair," the man snapped, referring to Gale.

"Y-yes," Indy stammered.

"Worm! We know there is another map! You will tell me where it is, or—"

A voice carried from the bedroom. "She is not here! The woman is gone!"

"Fool!" the man with Indy shouted. "The ledge outside! Check the ledge!"

The man turned. The window *was* open, drapes fluttering in the night breeze. He ran to the window, climbed on his knees to the ledge, looked to his left. Empty. He turned to his right just in time to see Gale's foot coming toward his throat in a tremendous kick. He grasped his neck with his hands, choking, blood dribbling into his fingers. It was the moment Gale needed. She moved forward like a striking cobra, tightened her left hand, closest to the building wall, in a rigid fingers-extended position, and brought her hand down as hard as she could against the back of the man's neck. His hands flew from his throat. Now he was off balance, struggling to remain on the ledge.

Leaning against the wall, Gale drove the heel of her right foot against the back of his head. With a bloodcurdling shriek he went off the ledge to certain death on the pavement five stories below.

In the living room, the hooded man holding the gun to

Indy jerked his head around at the sound of the scream. Cursing in that strange language, he slammed the pistol grip against Indy's head. Indy took the blow along the side of his head rather than frontally. He reacted as if struck with a sledgehammer, collapsing helplessly. The gunman dashed around the couch.

Immediately Indy was on his feet, running to the coat-rack across the living room, then to the bedroom. Gale stood transfixed in the high window space, the man before her with the gun held steady on her.

"You are a fool," he said scathingly. "You should have silenced Ahmed first." His finger began to tighten on the trigger.

Gale stared wide-eyed as the man's head snapped back violently. She heard the sharp *crack!* of Indy's bullwhip, the leather flashed around his neck, and Indy jerked back-ward with all his strength. The gunman flew off his feet, his pistol tumbling away. Indy dragged him back toward the living room as the man struggled madly. Gale was down from the ledge, following closely.

She watched, wide-eyed, as Indy pulled the whip free. Whoever the gunman was, he was also strong and a fighter to the end. He scrambled to his feet, fingers curled into claws, rushing at Indy.

Indy smiled; a whooshing sound heralded the snap of the bullwhip. As fast as the sound cracked through the room, a deep slash opened along the gunman's cheek. He rocked backward and the whip snapped out again. Blood lined the opposite side of the man's face. A third time; skin split along his neck.

"Indy! Don't kill him!" Gale shouted.

"Oh, I'm not," Indy said, smiling. "Just paying back a little."

Another skin slice. The man staggered. Indy moved forward slowly, deliberately. And heard pounding at the door to the flat. Blows with fists, loud shouts. "Open up in there! This is the police! Open this door, I say!"

The intruder looked up, his eyes wild. Gale stepped up behind him, jerked the hood from his head and face. It spun away in a shower of blood.

Indy smiled. "What do you know?" he said with deceptive calm. "It's our photographer from the Glen."

They heard the door beginning to splinter.

"And when they find out they've had a traitor in their midst, well . . ." Indy let it hang. If there's anything a policeman hates—no matter what country and under what name they wear the uniform—it's a dirty cop.

The man's eyes widened. His fear grew swiftly. With a howl he turned on his heel and dashed for the window, running past Gale. "Indy, stop him!" she shrieked.

The bullwhip cracked hard, a pistol shot of sound. It mixed with the breaking crash of the door as policemen poured into the flat. Just in time to see the black-clothed intruder hurl himself through the window to his death.

"Stay still!" Gale spread an evil-smelling salve along Indy's head, gashed open from the blow of the pistol butt. "You squirm like a cat in a boiling pot."

"And I smell like one," Indy grumbled. "What *is* that putrid stuff you're smearing on me?"

"Would you believe bat dung, eye of newt, crab intestine, and camel spit?"

"*No!*"

"Well, then, you'd be right. It's a mixture of herbs, roots, leaves, and lichen. It must be boiled for a specific period of time, the fire must burn only wood, the caldron must be cast iron, and the mixer must be—"

Indy held up a hand to interrupt. "Must be a witch, I'll bet."

"Right again. Have you seen yourself in the mirror? Your bruises have bruises, and—Indy, stay still!"

"Easier said than done," he snarled. "What's next? This hurts you more than it hurts me?"

She laughed. "Not quite. Those two knew what they were doing. If I don't get this what you call evil gunk where they clubbed and kicked you—"

"Don't forget the punches. I think one of them was using brass knuckles."

"Whatever." She moved her fingers across his shoulders and chest, caressing him gently as she spread her healing potion. Abruptly she withdrew her hand as if stung. *I've got to watch myself,* she thought. *This is not the time to be affectionate. . . .*

Quickly she began to speak. "You think very well on your feet, Professor Jones," she said with stilted courtesy. "Coming up with that scarab jewelry to show the police was brilliant. 'Why were those people here?' the policemen ask. Using you for a punching bag and trying to shoot me? 'Why, Constable' "—she mimicked Indy as he had addressed the police—" 'here is what they were after. See these scarabs? Worth a blinkin' fortune, they are.' "

"Like I told you," he said, "I travel prepared."

She reached to the table and held up the glittering jewelry. "It *looks* expensive. What's it really worth?"

"The one you're holding? It's cosmetic jewelry. Fake. Worth the price of a good lunch."

"All of them?" She held up four other scarabs.

"No. One of them is worth a king's ransom."

"Which one?"

"Green."

"It's gorgeous."

"Gale, I'm whipped."

She put aside the jewelry. "All right. We've got a make-shift door for the night. Smart of the superintendent to take one from the spare bedroom." She propped up several pillows. "You comfortable?"

"Except for a hundred little demons jumping up and down my body, yeah, sure."

"Sleep, Indy. Sleep?"

"What?"

She passed a hand across his eyes. A small bag in her hand released the barest trace of a rare and valuable powder.

Witch's powder.

He was instantly sound asleep.

7

Indy floated on a sea of gray foam. He felt almost weight-less, a feathery drifting. He slept deeply.

A deep bass groan sent the foam shuddering. Now he felt wet sand beneath him. He was lying on a beach, at the high-water mark of the incoming surf, waves sliding in to cover his body and then retreating to sea, leaving his skin free of the water. Another boom spasmed through his body.

Gray foam again. It brightened in waves in a matching beat to the thudding booms. *This is crazy? Where am I?*

He tried to force his eyes open. Confusion again. If he could see the gray foam, how could his eyes be closed? Slowly but steadily his subconscious mind withdrew as he fought his way up from the numbing grip of deep sleep. Instantly the foam exploded silently, without any physical effect, as he looked at a tall window of his studio, through which morning sun streamed with painful brilliance. He shut his eyes, groaned with the effort of turning his body on the couch.

He forced his eyes open again. Clarity of vision and

mind came rushing back to him. Last night . . . the fight, the beating he'd taken. Gale rubbing that strange salve on his body. He remembered wanting to sleep, the effort blocked by the pain inflicted by the two men who'd attacked him. Then—

That was it. Gale, passing her hand across his eyes like a magic wand. That's when reality ended and he fell into a never-ending well of slumber.

He saw Gale. At the door, talking to several men just outside in the hallway. He recognized one voice immediately. Indy groaned again, swung his legs to the floor. Somewhere between his ears was a nasty little troll hammering on a log.

A tall man in a trench coat with a thin, perfectly waxed mustache came across the room to stand before the couch.

Indy looked up slowly from the gleaming black shoes to the perfectly creased trousers and inevitable trench coat. Above the mustache and bright, intelligent eyes was perched an old and disreputable-looking tweed cap.

"Well, well, well," came the booming greeting. "Unexpected and a pleasure to be seeing you so soon again, Henry!"

"Bug off," Indy growled to Inspector Thomas Treadwell, ace agent for MI5, British military intelligence. He looked beyond Treadwell to Gale, gesturing to seats for two other men. Indy ignored them. The troll in his head was banging with renewed enthusiasm on the log. Each blow was a spasm of pain.

"Gale? If you still have an ounce of mercy left in you, coffee, *please*," Indy groaned.

Treadwell turned to Gale, doffing his cap. "Miss Parker, you look positively lovely—"

"Watch it," Indy said. "He wants something. Where's that coffee?"

"Coming right up. It's all made and waiting for you," she said quickly. "Black as usual?"

"Stop with the questions. Just bring me—" Gale was already gone. She returned almost at once with a huge mug of steaming black coffee. If it had been larger, Indy would have climbed into the mug. He held it with both hands, surprised to see they were shaking slightly. The first sips went down slow and scalding. Wonderful . . .

Halfway through the cup the troll began packing up his log and leaving. "I think I'm going to live," Indy mumbled.

"Muffins?" Gale asked, her manner and voice disgustingly perky and bright. "Toast? Eggs? Oatmeal? Kippers?"

"More coffee. Just bring the pot."

"I'll have tea, if you'd be so kind, Miss Parker," Treadwell said. He brought a chair from across the room and sat directly before Indy.

"You're right, Indy. He *is* too nice." She smiled at Treadwell. "Tea coming right up."

Indy glared at Treadwell. Anyone listening to the two men, who didn't know just how tight and strong was their friendship, would have judged them about as cordial as two snarling dogs.

"Now, just how did I *know* I'd be seeing your pasty face this morning?" Indy asked.

"The chief wanted you brought in at the crack of dawn," Treadwell said quietly.

"You came to my defense?"

"Of course."

"You can tell the chief where to get off," Indy growled.

"Well, now, he certainly had good reason to—"

"Hold it, *hold it*," Indy broke in. He grimaced with pain as he shifted position. "That scene at St. Brendan's. I had nothing to do with that. I didn't even get there until it was all over."

"I know. You were in an airplane directly overhead when it all happened."

"How'd you know that?"

Treadwell paused as Gale brought him tea and refilled Indy's mug. "Join us, if you would?" the inspector asked her pleasantly.

Gale nodded and sat on the couch with Indy.

"For starters," Treadwell continued, answering Indy's query, "any machine flying overhead at that moment could have been part of the killing spree."

"Could have, but wasn't. I suppose you already know I was taking a flying lesson."

"You certainly need one," came the retort. "You, ah, ran out of cookie bags, I understand?"

Indy looked to Gale. "You told him about that?"

She nodded. "People who are busy upchucking, Indy, have the perfect excuse for not being mixed up in—"

"Forgive the interruption, Gale," Treadwell broke in. "We know how close you are to the St. Brendans."

Gale looked down, nodding.

"What attracted your visitors last night, Indy?" Treadwell asked, the levity in his voice gone.

Indy's head was clearing swiftly. He studied the men seated across the room. Especially one man. Stocky, powerful, yet dressed crisply, a relaxed air about him. He had all the signs of a special operative. Indy gestured to him.

"Who's he?" he said to Treadwell.

"Roberto," Treadwell called. "Join us, please."

"Professor Jones, my pleasure," the man said. His English sounded almost a bit *too* perfect for a foreign speaker.

"Let me guess," Indy said. "Italian. Which, in this case, means the Vatican."

"Roberto Matteo Di Palma, sir," the man identified himself. "Secret police, Italia. I am from Arce, southeast of Rome."

"We've asked him to join our group," Treadwell explained. "And you haven't answered my question as to what brought those two men here last night."

"You get identification on them yet?" Indy offered the question as his first "answer."

"Only one. The police recognized him. That's what makes this a bit sticky, you know. He was a constable."

"He was also a ringer," Indy said. He leaned back on the couch. "I'll lay even odds he's been with the force for some years, he's—"

"Was. Past tense," Treadwell reminded him.

"He needed money, and some people got to him to act as their eyes and ears within the police organization. He was also a photographer. In fact, he was very busy taking pictures of Gale and me yesterday. And everybody else."

Treadwell nodded slowly. "So that's how he picked you. And finding where you live is simple enough. Your tie-in with London University, for example. But what were they after?"

"Ask Gale. She can answer better than I can."

They turned to her. "The second map," she said simply. "They wanted to know where it was. If we didn't know, they were going to kill both of us."

"And they came too close for comfort," Indy added.

"*Excoosa,*" Di Palma said, a deceptively quiet tone to his voice. "This map. It is for the gold?"

"Whoa, hoss," Indy broke in immediately. "We didn't say a word about gold. You did. I don't like being at this kind of disadvantage."

"I am willing to accept the fact that you know about the gold," Di Palma countered.

"Sure," Indy admitted. "But I heard about it only yesterday. Seems to me you've known about it a lot longer."

Di Palma looked to Treadwell. The British agent shrugged. "I told you he was quick."

"Will you permit me to ask a few more questions before I answer what you have asked?" Di Palma said to Indy.

Indy placed his empty coffee mug on the end table to his left. He studied the Italian, then shook his head slowly. "No. I don't think you understand something, Di Palma. I'm not part of this whole crazy caper. I never saw St. Brendan Glen before yesterday. I didn't know scratch about gold, or a map, or those people who came in shooting like madmen. I do know that last night I got myself used as a punching bag and a target by people I don't even know, and now I have what is obviously an international undercover team in my flat. I do not feel like joining your party."

"I am very sorry to hear that," Di Palma answered.

"That makes one of us, then," Indy told him.

"Thomas?"

Treadwell turned to Gale.

"Why are you people here?" she asked.

"Obvious, my dear. This flat is invaded, through a window by swinging cable. Professionals, obviously. They, ah, work over our good professor, try to kill you, and want a *second* map that is supposed to reveal a king's ransom in gold. Both men are now dead and we find out that one of them was likely in the pocket of the same group that committed such atrocities yesterday at St. Brendan's. Where, I have learned only this morning, they obtained a map through torturing the Old Mother of the Glen and threatening to—excuse me, Gale—slit the throats of children if they did not get it. They apparently knew a great deal about this map before they ever arrived at the Glen."

Treadwell turned to Indy. "So far so good?"

"You've got the microphone. Don't quit now," Indy murmured.

"This isn't some simple robbery or just a gang," Treadwell said with increasing severity. He held up a cigarette and glanced at Gale. "Mind?"

She shook her head. "Not at all."

Treadwell lit up. "Any group with that many people and vehicles, heavily armed, represents a major organization. Which means power, political influence, financial backing, and—well, enough of counting pennies and reasons. You get the drift, I imagine."

Indy clapped his hands slowly, a pantomime of sarcasm. "Veddy good, veddy bloody good," he said, lifting his upper lip to expose his teeth.

"There's no need for that," Treadwell said brusquely.

"Then go away and you won't have to hear any more of it," Indy offered.

"Will you back off, Indy? *Please?*" Treadwell asked.

"Sorry, old man. My head is killing me."

"Thomas?" Treadwell turned at Gale's call. "What do you want of us? I mean, why this visit in this manner?"

"Well, it's obvious. Bodies flung all about, and—"

"Kill it before we need to put on high-top boots, Tom," Indy broke in. "You didn't need all these people here for that. Especially when one of them is a spy for the Italian Secret Service—"

"A special agent, if you please," Di Palma said sternly.

"A spy," Indy went on, "for Italia, and then you've got those three hoods with you—"

"Hoods?"

"Oh, come on. Bully boys. Torpedoes. Thugs. Gangsters."

"They're part of the department, Indy," Treadwell protested. "Special operations."

"Right. And my great-aunt Millie is really Queen Victoria."

"Then why," Treadwell asked, obviously nettled, "would I bring along bully boys, as you so crudely put it?"

"One, you're improving the social level of your company," Indy gibed, "or, two, they come from a nefarious background and association, which means you're hoping they might recognize somebody your people don't know."

"Somebody like who?" Treadwell pressed.

Indy shrugged. "Come on, Tom! You're going for a make on anyone from this organization you're after."

"A make? I do not understand," Di Palma said.

"Identification," Gale said quickly.

"And why," Indy asked, pointing to one of the three men seated across the room, "did you bring along a hex man?"

Treadwell's expression was pure innocence. "Which one?"

"Remind me never to play poker with you." Indy pointed again. "Your man on the left. Jamaican or Haitian, I'll wager."

Gale stared. A shudder passed through her as she locked eyes with the tawny-complexioned man. He was tall and thin, his skull as shining as a billiard ball, and his eyes seemed sunken into dark pools. He smiled at her.

That smile said many things. Above all, it was a sign of recognition from one person who saw things "normal people" could not see to another.

"Haitian," Treadwell said finally.

"And?"

"I know this is going a bit off the deep end, but—" Treadwell paused, looked to the Haitian, who nodded either agreement or permission. Impossible for Indy to tell.

"I'll finish for you," Gale broke in. "He has farsight."

Indy's interest quickened. He looked to the tall stranger. "I'm Jones. And you. . . ?"

"Antoine LeDuc. I would be pleased with Tony."

"Farsight, right?"

LeDuc shrugged. "So it is said."

"Can you cut through all this? Tell us the people that Stoneface Treadwell is after? That we'd like also to know?"

LeDuc rose slowly, like a segmented stick unfolding to a tall pole. "Now that I am here, feeling what is in your memories, I have made the connection. It is yet hazy. Miss Parker, ma'am, would you let me rest my hand on your forehead?"

Gale looked to Indy. He kept his expression blank. This wasn't his decision. She took his silence as agreement; had he sensed even a touch of danger, he would have interfered. She nodded to LeDuc and sat in a chair as he approached. He stood behind her. His hand, with manicured nails and long sensitive fingers, slid to her forehead. She felt an astonishing coolness.

LeDuc stood quietly. Then he turned to Treadwell. "You know the man you seek."

"What?" The word chorused from Treadwell, Indy, and Di Palma in unison.

"He is the same man *we* have sought." LeDuc studied

the faces of the men staring at him. "There is confusion, but that is because this is the man with three names. For some time my own government thought we faced three different men. They were moving into the drug trade in the West Indies as well as Latin and South America. Our people in Haiti are poor, so they were easy to hire out. When they learned they were no more than slave laborers in fields that grew the plants for drugs, it was too late for many of them. They died of fever, beatings, starvation, and when they grew too weak to work, they were simply shot and thrown to the sharks."

"The names," Indy said quietly. He felt a giant spring coiling within him. Whatever had been simmering was now coming to a boil.

"What I am feeling through Miss Parker," LeDuc went on, "is different names. *But only one person.* So I will start with the name of the man who led the attack in the forest."

He closed his eyes and concentrated. Then his eyes opened and he looked directly at Treadwell. "The name is Warren Christopher."

Indy, Treadwell, and Di Palma exchanged glances. Indy shrugged. "Doesn't ring a bell."

Di Palma shook his head. "English name," he said finally.

"And the blighter's been dead for six years," Treadwell said angrily. "Tony, what the devil are you doing!"

LeDuc didn't bat an eyelash. "I do not recall," he said carefully, "that I brought up the subject of alive or dead. But that is the name."

"What say you?" Indy needled Treadwell.

"Christopher was an international arms merchant. We'd been after him for a long time. We finally trapped him in Africa, selling heavy weapons to the Germans. When our people closed in on him, the Germans"—Treadwell emphasized this word—"gave him the quick. With Christopher dead he couldn't testify about who his customers were."

Treadwell jabbed a finger at LeDuc. "The next name, please. Obviously, there is either a rare similarity of names in the arms and murder business, or—"

LeDuc didn't let him finish. With a thin smile on his face he said quietly. "Konstantin LeBlanc Cordas."

Treadwell slammed a fist into his palm. "*Now* we're getting somewhere!"

"I thought you told us Cordas—or Halvar Griffin, as he was known then—was dead," Indy told Treadwell.

"That was the information we received. The information was wrong. He not only survived, but he's been building up his organization again."

"It starts to fit," Indy said, voicing his thoughts. He looked at Gale and LeDuc; the tall man had removed his hand from her forehead.

"You gave us two names," Indy said.

"You provided the third. Halvar Griffin," LeDuc answered.

"You mean," Di Palma joined in, "these three people, Cordas, Griffin, Christopher, they're all one and the same person?"

"Looks like it," Indy said, leaning back against the couch.

Treadwell nodded.

Indy snapped his fingers as he turned to Treadwell. "We heard a name last night. The guy who walloped me with the gun butt and then threw himself out the window rather than be captured. He told Gale the name of the man she dumped."

"Dumped? I did more than *that,*" Gale protested.

"The story ends the same," Indy said to dismiss her complaint. "The point is, he called him Ahmed. Any good to you?"

Treadwell scribbled notes in a pad. "Not at the moment. We'll run it through the mill." He looked around the room. "Any other names?"

Gale gestured for attention. "Scruggs," she said.

"Where did you hear that?" Treadwell said immediately.

"*I* didn't hear it. During the slaughter at the Glen, several of our people heard someone call out that name. They told Indy about it."

"Does that one mean anything?" Indy queried.

Treadwell snapped his notebook shut. Finally he reached for a chair and sat down slowly. He was obviously unhappy with the name he'd just heard.

"It most certainly does. One of the bloodiest cutthroats in the underworld. Goes by the name of John Scruggs. He's been with Cordas from the beginning." Treadwell sighed unhappily. "A totally immoral killer. Scruggs isn't his name, but he's got it on a Maltese passport. We know he has forged passports with various names. He's actually Spanish. Valdez Morato."

"I know him," Di Palma added quickly. "He sells children for slaves." Di Palma grimaced. "Among other heinous crimes. He *enjoys* killing."

Indy rose and stretched. "Well, that's the lot. Been nice seeing you, Thomas. Give my regards to Scotland Yard." He looked about the room. "What? You're all still here? Get out there and chase the bad people!"

"A comedian you are not," Treadwell countered. "Look, Indy, and this includes Miss Parker as well, we're up against the wall. Blind spots everywhere. We've got to get to St. Brendan Glen and go over the place with a fine-tooth comb. *Anything* could prove valuable."

Indy pointed to the window. "Then go! You're not going to find clues or catch anyone by staying here and jawing with me."

"I also want to talk with Miss Caitlin about that map. We know about it now. The map her father had secreted. All I know so far is that there's some enormous amount of gold that can be found with that map, that it's been with the St. Brendan family for many years, that Cordas now has a copy or the original, and—"

"Hold it, *hold it*," Indy protested. "Come on, Tom! Gale has already told your people that to save his wife and some children, Kerrie St. Brendan turned the map over to the people who invaded the Glen. The old man didn't know who they were, and at the moment it didn't matter. A map against the lives of his wife and some children. Of course he gave it up!"

"I'm not faulting anyone, Indy," Treadwell countered.

"The map is incomplete."

Heads turned to Gale. Her words seemed to thrust themselves between the men like a physical blow. "What's that supposed to mean?" Indy asked.

"Just what I said, ducks. The map is incomplete. And deliberately so. It may or may not lead Cordas, or anyone else, to where the gold *might* be. It's not as simple as it sounds."

"You seem to know a great deal about this," Treadwell said with quickening interest. "Might I ask how you obtained this information?"

"Caitlin and I grew up together virtually as sisters. For years she's been training to take over leadership of the

Glen when her parents pass on. During her instruction, I was often with her."

"For the moment," Treadwell said slowly, "strange as it seems, it's not the gold I want to talk about. It's the *map*."

"That's different," Indy said.

Treadwell ignored the dig. "Miss Parker, how did the St. Brendan family come into possession of the map?"

Gale hesitated. "You wouldn't believe me if I told you."

"Try me. Please," Treadwell urged.

"Fifty, perhaps sixty years ago, it was brought to the Glen for safekeeping," Gale said.

"I fail to understand," Treadwell said. "Why would it be brought to the Glen when, certainly, the vaults of the Bank of London would be security enough?"

"I'm not arguing that," Gale told him. "You asked me a question, I answered it. *Why* the Glen was chosen makes perfect sense to me. I know almost nothing about the bank vaults."

"Would you tell me why the Glen was preferred?"

"I said you wouldn't believe me."

"If you would . . .?"

"Sometimes"—Gale hesitated—"well, it's not always possible to get to the Glen. And if you can't get there, you can't take anything from there."

"Cordas and his people managed quite well."

"I know. The St. Brendans weren't warned that they were coming. It's like Indy said, Thomas. A case of the horse galloping away before the barn doors are locked."

Treadwell pushed the issue of the map. "You said the map was incomplete. How do you mean that?"

"There are no names on the map. Only terrain features. The land where the gold was taken, where it is supposed

to be to this day, must first be identified before the map
has any value."

"And where might that land be?"

"I have no idea," Gale told him.

"Who would know?"

"Kerrie St. Brendan. Caitlin's father. And I believe she,
too, would know."

"Thank you, Gale," Treadwell said warmly. "Might I ask
your further assistance with these people? They might be
much more willing to cooperate with us if we're together."

Gale shrugged. "I can't answer for them."

"I understand." Treadwell's mood darkened. "I hope I
needn't remind you that if this Cordas fellow fails to identify the land area, he'll return to the Glen, and this time
whatever he and his gang of murderers do could be far
worse."

"There's no fear of that," Gale said. "They cannot return to the Glen. Not after what happened. They can
never go back there."

"Pray tell, why?"

"He won't believe you," Indy told Gale.

"Why not?" Treadwell said sharply to Indy.

Indy smiled. "Magic," he said.

"This is hardly a moment for humor, Indy."

"I'm serious."

Treadwell dropped the matter completely. "I am required to talk to the St. Brendans. I hope you will accom-
pany us."

"I'll go with you," Gale agreed. "But I can't help you
unless Caitlin so wishes. Besides, she's not afraid of Cordas
returning. She is going to find Cordas. To avenge her
mother."

"In what way?"

"Cordas must die by the sword."

Treadwell shook his head slowly. "Are we in some kind of time machine? We seem to be leaping back and forth between the present and some ancient age."

Gale smiled, but kept silent.

"All right, Gale. Will you at least go with us?" Treadwell asked again.

Gale nodded. "I will. I want Indy to go, too. But you won't be able to find the Glen. Not unless Caitlin lets you in."

"You do baffle me, Miss Parker. May I say that I grew up in that region? I know every inch of it. I will most definitely find my way to the Glen."

"Better look out for the magic," Indy said.

"You're still not funny," Treadwell said grumpily.

8

Indy stood in a steaming shower for twenty minutes, the heat easing some of the strain from pulled and battered muscles. He knew Treadwell, Di Palma, and LeDuc waited for him with growing impatience. They could bloody well wait forever as far as he was concerned. He hadn't asked for their presence, he hadn't committed any crimes except in self-defense (and Treadwell wasn't arguing the issue), and sure as grass was green, he didn't want any part of the police investigation. These people were doing their best to snare him into accompanying them to chase around the globe for master criminals, and he'd already had more than his share of that. Indy was perfectly content with battling to solve the mysteries of the ages. He found dusty relics and buried tombs and learning of the wonders and marvels of ancient cultures and civilizations sufficiently fascinating. One thing special about mummified local gods from the past: They made great conversation. They spoke only the mute language of history, not the inane jabbering of the living.

Besides, he was hungry, and Gale was a wonder in the

kitchen. He'd already tasted the meat and local vegetables, none of which he'd recognized, she'd prepared in the New Forest. She was just as good in a London flat's kitchen as she was in the forest. He dressed in fresh clothes, pulled on his friendly, reliable, battered boots and a rough suede shirt. He toyed with the idea of taking his Webley, but that was inappropriate right now. However, old habits were difficult to break, and he slung the whip through his belt thong. In the Glen the whip hadn't brought so much as a second glance. Into his right boot went a long, slim killing blade, one he used far more for work and for small game than on any two-legged prey wearing clothes.

He hesitated. One never knew what might come up given the insanity of these past two days. He was doing his best to stay out of the mess, but powerful forces kept drawing him in. First, he wouldn't leave Gale on a limb. When two people have saved each other's life, unhesitatingly risking their own, a bond forms that requires no words or explanation. He didn't need a printed message to understand the tremendous pressure on this woman who'd become so close a friend. She was emotionally battered by the loss of Athena, as well as by all those adults and children killed and wounded at the Glen. Only hours before, she'd fought for her life and now she was being grilled by Scotland Yard, an Italian secret agent, and a voodoo priest from Haiti.

Besides all that, Indy knew Gale was gnawing her own knuckles at the determination of Caitlin, her closest friend, to pursue Konstantin Cordas and take his life with that infernal wizard's sword.

The sword . . . Indy didn't know whether to worship or hate that blade of fire and the wizard's scabbard she now wore as a tunic. The more he'd thought about it, the more he liked the idea of leaving Gale to her own devices. She was sharp, swift, brilliant, capable, and even dangerous when those attributes were needed. She'd done just fine before Indy came into her life. And with Caitlin, and the age-old magic of Merlin backing them up, they were a fearsome duo.

But the sword, and all that lay behind it, exerted a pull impossible for Indy to ignore. No one had asked the question that bubbled within Indy's head. *How* had the sword of King Arthur, created through the skills, potions, and magic of the legendary Merlin, come to be in the possession of the St. Brendan clan? Where was the line of history that matched the St. Brendan Glen with Glastonbury and the Tor and Avalon, the Round Table, and the sworn fealty that *had* to exist for Caliburn to end up in Caitlin's hands? And who before her? And before her father? And *his* father?

The questions clung to his ankles like lead weights. He could not resist his own curiosity, the spellbinding search for answers that was the driving force in his life.

So he *must* go with Gale, be her strength, be there to answer for her in a world of vicious international intrigue.

But not without his breakfast!

He emerged from his bedroom to greet the impatient faces of Treadwell, Di Palma, and LeDuc, who were seated in his studio room and half rose with his appearance. Indy grinned and held up one hand. "Easy, easy, gentlemen. A car doesn't run without fuel and neither do I. I eat before I drive. Anybody care for coffee or tea?" All three shook their heads.

"We've eaten," Treadwell told him. "Go ahead, Indy. We'll wait."

Indy bowed with mock deference. "Thank you, Your Lordship."

Treadwell couldn't help it; he laughed, sat back, and lit a cigarette.

Indy and Gale ate in the breakfast nook, unhurried and deliberate. "You're pushing them," she whispered.

"Uh-huh. Great herring."

"Indy . . . ?"

He was smearing marmalade on a muffin. "Mmmmpf?"

"I know you're going for me. This isn't your affair, Indy. You can just walk away from it. I'll understand."

He almost accepted. Instead he took a huge bite of muffin, herring, and eggs and picked up his coffee mug. "Ugh-rumph. Wouldn't miss it for the world." He swallowed coffee hastily.

"You sound like a water buffalo," Gale said, wrinkling her nose.

"Uh-huh." He ignored the remark. "Do I guess that Caitlin's going to do some light bending this morning?"

Gale smiled and nodded.

"*That* is going to be worth getting up early to see," Indy said between mouthfuls.

"When do you have to return to the university?"

He stopped in midswallow. "You're right. I was supposed to report to Old Man Pencroft yesterday." He shrugged. "Five'll get you ten that Treadwell's already run interference. Don't worry about it."

"Indy, I don't like interfering in—"

But he'd already pushed back his chair. He looked at the men waiting for him. "On your feet, varlets. Let's roll."

The third time they passed the same crooked tree hanging over the narrow roadway, Indy burst out laughing. Not at the tree but at the baffled and stunned expressions of the three men with him and Gale in the powerful touring auto from Scotland Yard. On the second pass by the tree, Treadwell had slammed on the brakes, the heavy auto skidding on the pebbled dirt road. He left the car and stood by a low branch, cheek muscle twitching, and slashed a clear line along the branch. Without a word he returned to the car and slammed it into gear, the rear wheels spinning wildly and slewing the rear of the car to one side.

He rounded a wide turn and gaped. White mist rolled in from a low hill to his right, covering the roadway. He had no choice but to slow down. Finally he was inching along, muttering beneath his breath.

"This is *impossible,*" he said through tightly clenched teeth. "I have driven through here all my life! I've *never* seen fog that comes and goes. No rhyme or reason to it! Even the temperature and humidity and the dew point are at levels where there shouldn't *be* any fog, or even mists rising from the streams. But we keep running into this blasted mist, and when we do, I have no idea where we are or where we've been or—"

"I told you," Indy said, not able to avoid smirking.

"You told me *what!*"

"That this would happen."

"I know, *I know,* but why? And *how!* It doesn't make sense!"

Indy reached to his right and patted the usually unflappable Treadwell, now grinding his teeth, on his shoulder. "I know it doesn't make sense, Thomas. I also told you it was magic."

"You can't be serious?"

"Oh, I am."

"Indy, you're a man of science! Now you're telling me this is magic?"

"Uh-huh."

"That's ridiculous!"

"So is this fog, right?"

"Well, yes, of course it is, I know that, but—"

"So you're in a ridiculous fog."

They rolled slowly about a sharp turn, the front fender scraping bushes crowding the road. Treadwell hit the brakes so hard everybody was thrown forward.

"My God." Treadwell mouthed the words slowly. Directly before him was the tree limb he'd marked with his pocketknife. "Indy, I am staying as calm as I can. Now, I have kept an exact track of our route. It is not possible for us to be where we were three times before."

"All right by me," Indy said lightly.

Di Palma looked about him. "The old people in the mountains, they talk about strange mists like this. They are not natural." He shuddered. "It is said that the spirits in the high hills, above where even the mountain goats go, can make these mists behave as they desire."

Treadwell gave Di Palma a withering look. "This is not the mountain country of Italy and I do not give a fig about your goats!"

Antoine LeDuc climbed from the car. He sniffed the air, his eyes widening as he turned in a circle.

"Tony!" Indy called. "Try the amulet. The one you wear beneath your shirt."

The others looked at Indy. "It's an amulet. It's real. It works for Tony."

"What is it?" Treadwell asked.

"Fer de lance. One of the deadliest vipers known. Its venom works like a forty-four slug right between the eyes." Indy laughed. "Oh, the snake isn't alive. It's been dead many years. Tony had the skeleton woven into a single strand, using sacred threads. When he's in the presence of strange energies, it vibrates."

LeDuc held Indy's eyes. "Witchcraft," he said slowly, his voice firm and confident. "It is the power of witchcraft, Professor Jones!"

To LeDuc's astonishment, Indy nodded. "You are so right," he said in a voice of great patience. "I tried everything to warn Thomas. So did Gale. Now he can experience this thing for himself."

"Miss Parker, who's responsible for this?" Treadwell asked Gale.

"For someone to be responsible," she said softly, "something must be going on. What would that be, Thomas?"

"We're on a bleedin' merry-go-round, that's what's going on!"

"But you said it was impossible."

"Withdrawn! I confess I don't understand what's happening, but I can't deny this is the third time this blasted tree has been right in front of me."

"Indy told you. So did I. It is the magic of the forest people."

Treadwell's lips were so tight they were almost white. "Are you talking about Caitlin?"

"That could be."

"How . . ." Treadwell swept his arms about to take in the forest. "How can she do this?"

"She talks to the wind. To the trees, and the streams. They do her bidding."

"Wait, wait," Di Palma broke in hurriedly. "Professor Jones, how did you know about the snake skeleton? And what does it do?"

"I will answer," LeDuc said solemnly. "He knows because he has visited my people in their villages and homes. He knows because he has walked through the dust of history. He knows because he is open to knowledge."

"He knows," Indy added, "because he—me—could see the outline of the snake skeleton beneath Tony's shirt. And knowing something about how such things are used to detect energy about the wearer . . . well . . ." Indy shrugged. "There it is."

"Indy, let me ask this calmly, seriously, please?"

Indy nodded to Treadwell.

"How can we be arriving back at the same place when we have been driving on different roads?"

"It's not *that* easy to explain."

"Try, please."

"You familiar with topological math, Tom?"

"Somewhat, yes."

Di Palma, LeDuc, and Gale immediately became silent, hanging on every word.

"Okay. You'll have to put aside some of your most cherished rules of reality," Indy warned.

"That's been done for me already," Treadwell said with a sour expression. "Like this bloody road."

"Well, then, imagine we could twist time—"

"Time?"

"Time and space. I'm no physicist, but according to what the bigdomes are saying, time and space really are the same, or they perform the same way. It's over my head, but what they stress is that you cannot picture living beings in only three dimensions. The old height, width, and depth."

"All right."

"You've got to add a fourth dimension. It's not as complicated as it sounds. It's time. We move forward constantly, from the past into the present toward the future. That's about as commonplace as you can get."

"Agreed," Treadwell said.

"But you can't move forward in time unless you've got someplace in which to move—"

"The three dimensions," said Treadwell.

"Right. So forget the fancy words and expressions. Just think of one day after the other. We move in three physical dimensions all the time. We go left, right, ahead, backward. We go into, out of, like going into and leaving a building. And then we leave the two-dimensional world—"

"Flatland," Gale burst out.

Indy laughed. "As good a description as any. Flatland would be a place where you have only two dimensions. Everybody there lives on a flat plane. They never *go up*. Up becomes the third dimension, like in our world. But since you can't be in two places at the same moment, you must advance, say, from ten o'clock to eleven o'clock. That's the fourth dimension. Now, you *can* go backward to places you've been before, but you can't go back to *when* you were there before. Still with me?"

"Rather foggily, but yes," Treadwell said, nodding.

"Okay. Now take this road. Think of it as a long strip of paper. Or a carpet. But the paper works best because you can hold a strip of paper in your hands. Stay right with me now, because we can even demonstrate this."

"I'm with you. Keep going."

"A strip of paper has how many sides, Tom? Forget the edges, I want to know how many sides it has."

"That's easy enough. Two, of course. The top, and the bottom."

Indy was in his element. He'd run into this sort of thing

as far back as the ancient mathematicians. It gave meaning to the old expression "there's nothing new under the sun."

"All right. If you connect both ends of that strip of paper, what do you have?"

"A loop," Treadwell answered quickly.

"With how many sides?"

"Same as before. Only now you wouldn't call them top or bottom. You'd call it the inside of the loop, and the outside."

"If you drew a line with a pencil along the *inside,* all the way around, until your pencil line returned to where you started, what would you have?"

"Why, that's obvious," Treadwell answered. "You have a pencil line going completely around the inside of the circle. The strip of paper that's now a circle."

"But you wouldn't have a line on the *outside?*"

"Of course not! Not so long as you held the pencil against the paper, anyway, staying on the inside."

"So that proves the strip of paper has two sides, right?"

"Indy, what the devil are you getting at? You know it does."

"Okay, Tom. Now, let's say we have a second strip of paper, same length. Before we fasten the ends with a piece of tape or glue, whatever, we give the strip of paper a half twist, and then we fasten the ends. You following me?"

"Yes. Wait. I have a large notebook here in the car." He removed a sheet of paper, cut off a twelve-inch strip. "All right, Indy, now I give the paper a half twist, right?"

"Right. Got some tape to connect the ends?"

"No. But I have some adhesive."

"Use it."

Treadwell held up the paper strip, to which he'd given a half twist. "Now what?"

"Rest the paper on your notebook. Place a pencil on the *inside* of the strip. Start a steady line, continuing all the way around the paper, along the inside, until your pencil lines join."

They watched Treadwell doing as Indy instructed. When he finished, he held up the paper strip, staring at it with his mouth open. The pencil line ran along the entire length of the paper strip, inside and outside.

"This isn't possible," Treadwell said slowly.

"Why not?" Indy asked.

"Because I never lifted the pencil from the paper, and yet the line appears on both sides of it. . . ." His voice trailed off to a disbelieving whisper.

"Tom, it has only one side," Indy emphasized.

"That is simply not possible," Treadwell said stubbornly.

Indy shrugged. "I can't argue with you. But you're holding the proof that you *can* twist into what, for want of a better description, we'll call another dimension. Look, Tom, this isn't as farfetched as it seems. Farmers and some factories have been using this Möbius strip for years. They take a fanbelt, usually something long and flat, that operates off one motor, to turn another piece of equipment. Accept that the belt needs to be greased. If you use the standard belt, then obviously you've got to grease the inside *and* the outside."

"Naturally," Treadwell acknowledged.

"But if the farmer or the machinist gives that belt a half twist and reconnects it to the machinery, all he needs to do is hold the grease brush against the top of the belt. You can figure out what happens next."

Treadwell stared at the Möbius strip in his hands. "According to this, then, the belt would be greased on both sides."

"No!" Indy half shouted. "You still don't get it! It won't be greased on *both* sides, because it's been twisted into a different dimension and it only has *one* side."

"I'll be hanged," Treadwell said.

"Any way you like it," Indy told him. "Now do you begin to understand why you can't get off this road? It always twists back upon itself."

Treadwell turned to Gale. "This is what you've been trying to tell me?"

Gale nodded. "Yes."

"How do we get off this road that goes nowhere? I really do need to talk with Miss St. Brendan."

"Talk, or perform the duty of an inspector from Scotland Yard?"

Treadwell sighed. "Miss Parker, you have my word. I will proceed with the greatest respect and consideration. I have no desire to confront black magic—"

He never finished his sentence. Gale's eyes flashed with sudden and unmistakable anger. "Don't you *ever* use that term about the Glen." Her voice was an angry hiss. "Keep your stupid superstitions to yourself! There is nothing dark here except your own limitations."

Taken aback, Treadwell held up both hands. He hurried to apologize. "Miss P—Gale," he said quickly, "I meant no offense. Forgive me. I am over my head with . . . with all this, the road that turns in on itself, this strip of paper . . . my memory serves me poorly. I know that the same devout religion has been practiced here for—"

"Never mind," Gale said, still sullen. "Apology accepted. Now, do you want to continue?"

"*Please.*"

"Then drive on. The way is clear now."

"But—I mean, how could you—"

"Talk or drive, Thomas. Take your choice."

"I'll start the car," he said.

They soon came to a fork in the road. Treadwell slowed to a stop. "I don't remember this," he said cautiously.

"Take the road to the left," Gale told him. "The one you couldn't see before."

"Leave your weapons in the car." Gale looked at each man in turn. Without a word Indy removed the long knife from his boot and placed it on the car seat. Treadwell, reluctance slowing his movements, removed a powerful revolver from a shoulder holster and set it gently alongside the knife. They turned to Di Palma. He stared blankly at them.

"Roberto, do it," Treadwell ordered.

Di Palma sighed. A small derringer came forth from an ankle holster. Then he pulled back the right sleeve of his jacket, revealing a strap assembly with a holstered gun. Without a word he slipped the weapon from his arm. Derringer and handgun went onto the floor of the car. Di Palma and the others turned to LeDuc.

Slim blades emerged from his forearms, another from his right ankle, a fourth from a belly sheath, and a fifth from a flat sheath strapped to his back, just below his neck. He held up both hands, brought the palms together.

Indy's hand shot out to grasp his wrist, turning LeDuc's arm to show the bottom of the forearm. "That's quite a tattoo," he said quietly, releasing his grip. LeDuc nodded, still exposing the tattoo. "Have you seen this before?" he asked.

"I haven't," Indy said, his tone flat but unmistakably serious. "But when the Glen was attacked, one of the people here saw the tattoo of a barracuda on the arm of one of the attackers." He paused for his words to sink in. "Exactly like yours."

LeDuc nodded slowly. "Then you have identified, no doubt, where some of those people were recruited."

"How? Where?" Treadwell broke in quickly.

"It is not Ton Ton," LeDuc replied. "But there is a group composed of Haitians, Jamaicans, and others from the islands, a mix of people and languages. French, Spanish, English, mainly. They keep no written records of their names. Only numbers. And all wear the tattoo of the *picuda* that kills in a flash and can speed off faster than the eye can follow."

Di Palma listened intently to every word. "They are a political group?"

LeDuc laughed harshly. "Only when money is involved. They are mercenaries. Almost all of them have police records. Drug and gun running, prostitution, child slavery, smuggling illegal aliens, murder for hire. They even have their own banking system set up through the islands. Ruthless, without conscience—their loyalty is to the highest bidder." LeDuc rubbed his chin. "But I have never before heard of them so far from the Americas."

"And you wear the tattoo," Indy observed with false calm.

LeDuc nodded. "Many of our government security forces have the mark. It is all that has kept us alive sometimes. Remember, there are no names. Only numbers. As we disposed of certain elements we try to replace them with our own. That way we learn—it is the *only* way—of the organization from the inside."

"One thing bothers me," Indy said.

LeDuc waited, not saying a word.

"Two things, really. The first man was sent for a long

dive outside the window of my flat"—he gestured to
Gale—"ably assisted by the lady. The second man who
went out that window referred to the first as Ahmed."

LeDuc shrugged. "They change names like their shirts.
And the second thing, Professor?"

"I've dealt with fanatical groups throughout the world.
From Arabian assassins to Hindu zealots to snake worship-
ers and everything in between. Mercenaries may not be
afraid to die, but they don't commit suicide to avoid capture like this fellow did."

"If he had been captured, and revealed anything about
his group," LeDuc explained, his face like granite as he
spoke, "he would have sought death, frantically. To violate
the fealty of this group is to condemn oneself to a very
long and agonizing death. Long before the end comes,
such violators of their oaths plead and beg for the mercy
of death."

"Then," Treadwell interjected, "if we run across some
chap with that tattoo, it could be one of this mercenary
group, or—confound it—it could be one of *your* own people! We'd have no way to tell. Anyone with the barracuda
on their arm must be regarded as a dangerous enemy."

LeDuc shrugged. "That is the way the ocean currents
run sometimes. You dive into the water and take your
chances."

Di Palma gestured unhappily. "Then we are dealing
with men of no conscience."

Again LeDuc shrugged. "That is not for you to say. Or
have you not read of the actions of European conquerors
through the ages?"

"Hey!" Indy said abruptly. "Knock it off, you people!
We're here by invitation, upon our own request. Just ac-

cept what we're dealing with and extend our courtesies to our hosts."

Gale squeezed Indy's hand in a silent thank-you. Treadwell nodded vigorously. "Well said, Indy. We *were* overdoing it." He turned to Gale. "Would you, please?"

Gale started from the car. "Stay with me, please," she said as she began walking up the hill toward the great hall.

Caitlin St. Brendan rose in stately fashion from a huge throne at the far end of an oval table, its glistening wood so polished it reflected the firelight. Large chairs waited for the visitors about the table, but for the moment they stood in silence, struck with the beauty and power of the standing woman.

"You are welcome," Caitlin spoke, her voice ringing clear and sharp through the hall, drifting back with gentle reverberations from the high rafters. Fires burned along the outer walls beneath simmering caldrons. Well back from the table, along the walls, men and women armed with swords, crossbows, and pickaxes stood silently, their weapons at rest. Behind Caitlin, and to her right, waited a small throng of Glen folk. They would serve the visitors food and drink.

"Please," Caitlin continued with a wave of her hand, "be seated."

They took their seats, Gale closest to Caitlin, Di Palma and LeDuc on one side, Indy and Treadwell on the other. Caitlin half turned and raised an arm in signal. Immediately men, women and children approached the table with great wooden platters of roasted boar, fruits, round bread, and cheese. Wooden goblets filled with wine were set before the visitors.

Caitlin sat loosely, every eye on her. Indy noticed the

new leather tunic that covered her body, the ancient sym-
bol of a cross and circle about her neck. Long dark hair
flowed over her shoulders. She was, he saw more clearly
now, a stunning woman, her face strong and lovely. Against
the right armrest of her throne lay the sword of Caliburn.

"Eat and drink, if you will," her voice sang out. "Speak
with one another as you please. But we will not broach the
subject for which you have come here until my father joins
us. He is now in the prayer chamber and will be with us
soon."

Indy marveled at the scene and the moment. They
might have slipped back in time a thousand years. The
great hall bore signs of Viking influence, subtle but real.
Along the upper half of the walls were mounted heads of
bears, stags, boars, foxes, wolves, and other animals, which
lent an atavistic air to the scene below.

His gaze froze as he spied the next animal in line. A
horse . . . *No*. Yes. But a horse with a single long curled
horn extended from its forehead.

Unicorn. Other eyes followed his. Treadwell stared, his
mouth open until he clamped it shut with an effort. "Miss
St. Brendan?" he asked, his voice quavering.

"Yes?" She sounded like a priestess addressing a child
entering a sacred chamber.

"If you would . . ." Treadwell hesitated, then raised his
arm slowly to point at the horned animal. "That . . . is it
real?" Treadwell inquired.

"It is."

"A unicorn?"

"So it seems, sir. Why are you so surprised, Mr. Treadwell?"

He showed yet more surprise at her knowing his name.
There had been no introductions, but, well, Gale or Indy

could have told her. But they hadn't had time . . . He dismissed this lesser mystery.

"I am surprised, madam. To put it mildly," he added. "I was not aware the unicorn was a real animal."

"I cannot believe it!" Di Palma echoed.

"Gentlemen." Gale spoke up. "If there is the narwhal, with its single long tusk, why not the unicorn?"

Di Palma turned to her. "But no one has ever seen a *live* unicorn!"

"And you, sir, do you know anyone who has seen a woolly mammoth? A dinosaur? Yet you believe in those, do you not?"

"Yes, but—"

"That animal," Caitlin broke in, "is no trophy. They roamed the New Forest untold years past. The one you see has been in this building more than four centuries. Like yourself, I have never seen a living unicorn. But I assure you they are real."

She turned at the approach of her father, Kerrie. Everyone stood to greet the patriarch of the Glen. He gestured for them to sit, then eased painfully into the chair by his daughter. He accepted a goblet with perfumed wine, but declined food, content to sip slowly while his guests ate.

Treadwell's impatience was almost palpable. He finally turned to Gale; she recognized his unvoiced request to get into the reason for their visit. She in turn looked to Caitlin, who understood the silent exchange.

"Mr. Treadwell, you are here officially for Scotland Yard. These two men with you are part of your investigation?"

"Yes," he said quickly.

"What may we do for you?"

Treadwell wasted no time in reviewing the events lead-

ing to this moment. He detailed their conviction that despite the many names he used, the leader of the group
was Konstantin LeBlanc Cordas, who had a nasty and evil
reputation with most police agencies throughout the
world.

"We have begun a search, coordinating with these agencies, to hunt him down."

"And when you find him, *if* you find him and his thug
you will arrest him? Take him into custody?" Indy watched
and listened. Caitlin was maintaining a fine grip on her
temper.

"Of course. We'd, ah, also like to place him in custody,
along with his entire gang, before they find the gold that
appears to be revealed by the map they came here to—"

"Take by killing and force," Caitlin finished for him.
"You will take this beast into custody," she said now with
open scorn, "and you will follow your grotesque laws, and
you will imprison him, feed him, care for him, attend to
his medical needs, and you will not prove that he is guilty.
We never saw his face."

"But—"

"And then he will go free," Caitlin added with a sharp
finality. She studied Treadwell in the silence that followed.
"You must do what you must do," she went on. "So that
there will be no question in your mind, I will find this man
and"—she grasped the sword and held it high—"I will
obey our ancient laws, and exact retribution."

"You intend to kill him," Treadwell said.

"Justice so demands. The murder of my mother so demands."

Treadwell leaned forward. He chose his words with
great care. "If my words offend, they are spoken through

ignorance. I do not intend any such offense. But I am not wise in your ways—"

"Speak without concern," Caitlin interrupted. "Words are feathers compared to what has happened here."

"Then I accept your permission to be blunt." Treadwell paused.

Caitlin nodded. Her father looked on with seeming de-tachment, as if everything had already been decided and this exchange was so much posturing.

"You are talking of revenge," Treadwell continued. "You have said you would exact retribution with the sword. If this is what you do, then you will be committing a crime yourself. Revenge in such a manner damages both parties, and—"

"Only by *your* laws," came the cold response.

"Retribution by murder under British law is still murder," Treadwell said carefully.

"If it occurs on British soil."

"Forgive me. I don't wish to preach, Miss St. Brendan, but I cannot simply ignore—"

"Consider it redress," Kerrie St. Brendan said finally. "You are a policeman. Law and order. Which has not ailed us here in the Glen. We have buried many dead. My wife is gone forever."

Caitlin placed a hand on her father's arm. She looked directly at Treadwell. "You yourself said you do not understand our ways. So I will say this to you this one time."

Again she held up the sword, this time rising to her feet. With a wicked hiss of metal through the scabbard, she revealed the blade. It seemed both to capture the blaze of the fires and to cast forth its own glow.

"This is Caliburn. The one and only true sword of Merlin. Ask no questions of me. Not now, not ever. But I tell you this so you may understand. It is forbidden to use this blade for vengeance. Forbidden, and lethal to its wielder. It may be used to right a wrong, to defend, to exact redress, just as I will use it in that manner. But it may never"—she said the words sharply, returning Caliburn to its scabbard—"be used to kill for the sake of killing. By *your* laws, it will be self-defense. I will be attacked. I will defend myself. I will follow our ancient laws and your modern laws." Her hand stroked the sword hilt. "In this metal," she said softly, "lives the spirit of Merlin. I follow and obey his spirit."

She regained her seat. Treadwell was flabbergasted. He turned to Gale; she was impassive. He looked to Di Palma and LeDuc. They looked as perplexed as was he. Finally Treadwell caught Indy's attention.

"*You* understand," the inspector said slowly.

Indy nodded.

"And you never told me," Treadwell continued.

"It wasn't up to me to tell you anything," Indy said quickly.

"We have run out of time." They turned to Caitlin. She finished off a goblet of wine. "The hour draws late. Ask what else you need to know and then it is time for you to depart. Once the mists close in the forest, the Glen cannot again be penetrated until I have fulfilled my sworn duty."

"The gold," Treadwell went on immediately. "The gold that is referenced in the map. How long have your people had this map?"

Caitlin's answers could be as infuriating as they were brief. "Since before I was born," she told him. "It was given to my father by his father and then passed on to me. I know nothing else about the map—who created it, who brought it to us. It was given to us for safekeeping, it seems. But that became a foolish idea when the madman who attacked us learned of its whereabouts."

"I've seen the copy," Treadwell said. "What about the gold? Can you tell me how much there is? *Where* it is? And—"

Caitlin raised her hand to stem the flow of words. "We do not care about the gold. My interest is in the map because Cordas must follow it to pursue what he covets so desperately. A fool's errand, but he will leave a trail for me to follow."

Treadwell knew when to quit. He could sense the impatience in Caitlin for his group to leave. He turned to Gale. "You are going with her?"

Gale shrugged, a deliberate avoidance.

"Indy, what about you?" Treadwell persisted.

Caitlin spoke before Indy could answer. "That one will make his own decision when it is time."

Treadwell was puzzled. "I don't understand," he told Caitlin.

"Jones is *different*," she replied. "He is not like you or the others. He knows the wisdom of the Old Ways. He has seen the Dance of the Giants. He enters the ancient monoliths and tombs and feels the kinship across all the centuries. He respects the past and he can read and comprehend what leaves the rest of you baffled. And most of all, this woman"—Caitlin pointed to Gale—"who is my sacred sister, *trusts* him. As I do now. He honors us, we honor him. He fights for what he believes."

Caitlin looked up, as if she could see the sky through the roof of the great hall. "It is time for you to leave. Gale will lead you through the time mists. I thank you for your concern. Do not try to return. You will not be able to come back here until the time is right. We will determine that time."

Treadwell rose. "I understand. I thank you, your father, your people, for your courtesy." He hesitated, rubbing his chin in an old habit. "And the roads . . . I understand. The roads that are like a snake that holds its tail in its mouth so that one always travels in the circle that goes nowhere."

Caitlin nodded approvingly. "You learn quickly. I am impressed."

Treadwell bowed to her.

Then they were gone. Behind them light curved, mists flowed downslope, and St. Brendan's Glen sealed off from the outside world.

9

Old Man Pencroft—Sir William Pencroft, chairman of the Department of Archaeology at London University—glared with unconcealed antagonism at Thomas Treadwell. Twice Pencroft had started to voice his anger at the inspector from Scotland Yard; both times his frail lungs had failed him. He coughed almost uncontrollably, the nurse who attended his every need holding a white linen handkerchief to his lips, her other hand pressed against his chest to ease the pain. With a sudden strength born of self-anger, Pencroft shoved the handkerchief beneath the blanket across his lap.

Not soon enough to hide the spots of red. Pencroft leaned back, drawing in as much air as he could, waiting for his breathing to slow down before he spoke. He gestured with one hand, and his nurse immediately turned the wheelchair about. With his back to the group, Pencroft brought up the handkerchief to dab away the flecks of blood around his lips. Quickly he accepted a pill and water from his attendant; the effect was surprisingly rapid, as if

the man whose skin now resembled yellow parchment had
sucked in pure oxygen.

Again the wheelchair turned. Pencroft raised a shaking
hand to point a gnarled finger at Treadwell. "Thomas,
you've become a stupendous nuisance to this institution,"
he said in a sandpapery voice. "And do *not* apologize or
tell me you're sorry. If that were true, you wouldn't be
here, disrupting my schedule, sending waves of rumor
through our classrooms."

"But I *do* regret the intrusion," Treadwell pleaded. He
was deeply fond of Pencroft. The sentiment had long been
returned, but when it came to university matters, Pencroft
was irascible. "If this were not of the greatest import—"

"Everything you come to me with is always of the greatest import," Pencroft responded with sarcasm. "I have always wondered how Scotland Yard reached the conclusion
that governmental snooping is of a higher value than edu-
cation and research."

"This matter exceeds the daily needs of both the Yard
and these"—Treadwell rolled his eyes—"hallowed halls
choking in ivy."

"Ah, a bit cantankerous this day, are we?" Pencroft
smiled. Few things in life pleased the man students called
the Ancient Mariner of Archaeology more than dueling
with friends capable of holding their own against him.

From the opposite side of the conference room table,
Indy and the others watched with open amusement. Indy
had long accepted the verbal barbs Pencroft leveled at him
nonstop. A "crude sophisticate with pure genius for ancient languages and cuneiform, unfortunately adulterated
with a swinelike lack of breeding or manners" was his favorite. Despite such insults, the two men had unqualified

respect for one another. Indy judged that it was now time to step in.

"Listen to him carefully, Sir William." Indy eased into their exchange. "If you look carefully, you'll notice that Thomas has changed his facial appearance."

Pencroft squinted at Treadwell. "He looks as common and dreary as I remember him. No, not as well. Age does him ill." He turned to Indy. "What in heaven's name is this change you're muttering about?"

"He looks more Greek than before," Indy said.

"Your remark is less curious than vapid," Pencroft snapped. "Stop your silly games and—"

"Sir?" Pencroft wasn't accustomed to interruptions when he was dispensing insults. Treadwell had caught him by surprise with that single word. Pencroft seized the moment. "Yes, yes? Do you need permission to go to the loo?" He cackled with laughter at his levity.

Treadwell sighed. No, he knew where the men's room was and he didn't need to leave the room. But the near-mummified scientist before him was in prime form. That was good. He'd need full understanding and cooperation from Pencroft before this meeting ended.

"I have something of extreme importance to discuss with you," Treadwell offered.

Pencroft turned to Indy. "I see what you mean, Professor Jones. Our friend from Scotland Yard does have a Grecian tinge to his appearance."

"What the devil are you two mumbling about!" Treadwell said with sudden impatience.

Pencroft smiled. "Impertinent, isn't he?"

"Well, you know the old saw, Sir William," Indy added, keeping a straight face. "Beware of Greeks bearing gifts."

Treadwell could have hugged Indy. He had brought this

moment off beautifully, easing their way to discussing what Pencroft would regard as interference with his university routine. The expression on Pencroft's face— interest that something of value to the university might come from, of all places, that bastion of official nosiness, Scotland Yard—was everything Treadwell had hoped for. He lost not a moment in seizing the opportunity Indy had provided.

"The gift may come wrapped in a mystery, Sir William," he said quickly to Pencroft.

"That *is* a talent of yours, Thomas," Pencroft replied, but with a warmer tone to his voice.

"Gold."

Bushy white eyebrows raised a notch. "I presume you refer to the metal?"

"Yes." Treadwell had to let Pencroft carry this in his own way. What mattered now was that he was interested. He'd never let the matter slip away without knowing more.

"In what form, may I ask?" Pencroft said easily.

"Quantity unknown, but believed to be considerable." Treadwell was again in his element as a Yard inspector. "Originally in bars. Original value, um, specifics questionable, but about sixty to eighty years past, in excess of eighty million pounds."

A low whistle escaped Indy. "You're sure, Tom? That's four hundred million dollars. Say, that was just the value sixty or seventy years ago. Better than a half billion today."

"That is only the bullion," Treadwell continued in his matter-of-fact manner. He opened his briefcase, placed a folder before him, tapped it gently. "There is also coinage. Pure gold according to a number of sources, all of questionable veracity. But definitely coins from ancient Rome. That would increase the value to where the money figures become meaningless and the historical value comes under the heading of irreplaceable and priceless."

"That is quite a speech," Pencroft said quietly. "It has all the flavor of historical fiction."

"It is *not*," came Treadwell's reply. "Indeed, a map has been unearthed that reveals certain geographic details reputed to lead to where the gold may be found, and recovered."

Pencroft snorted with disdain. "I don't believe a word of it. And this map of yours. A copy, you say? Leather and parchment, indeed! Feathers and bat droppings with a pinch of dragon's scale next, I imagine. A map without any names on it. Blindman's buff sounds more like it. Pin the tail on the donkey you can't see. You, of all people, Thomas, can come up with a better story than that!"

Gale was half out of her seat, her face flushing with anger at Pencroft's unexpected assault not only on Treadwell, but on the map, its existence, what it meant. Which, to Gale, was a slur on the St. Brendan family as well. Before she could speak, Indy grasped her arm. She turned to him. He motioned with his eyes for her to sit down and not to speak. For that extra moment she studied his face. So he *did* have something up his sleeve! That, or—she almost laughed aloud—Sir William Pencroft was putting on a show that belied his age and rumored senility.

Roberto Di Palma leaned forward, elbows resting on the table. His cheek muscle had twitched the entire time Pencroft was cutting down Treadwell. "May I speak?" he said with extreme civility to Pencroft.

"It seems you already have," Pencroft said icily.

This didn't faze the Italian agent. "I am here as a representative of His Holiness. I speak for the Vatican."

"As did Castilano before you," Pencroft observed. "And

from what I have been informed, he no longer speaks. Unless he can do so from the grave."

"He speaks, but not from the grave," Di Palma said smoothly, "and he does so with difficulty, for the gentleman is still undergoing skin transplants and other surgery."

Treadwell spun about in his seat. "Filipo . . . *alive?*"

"Yes."

"But . . . every report we received was that he was blown to bits when—"

Di Palma held up a hand. "He is as alive as Cordas. But he will be in hospital for at least another year."

"Just a moment." They turned to Pencroft, staring intently at Di Palma. "You mentioned that name. Cordas. How did he get into all this? He's supposed to be dead." Pencroft leaned back, cupping his hands beneath his chin. He answered his own question. "But if Filipo Castilano survived, then . . ." He shrugged. "How is Cordas involved in this?"

"Let me," Treadwell broke in. He described the attack on St. Brendan's Glen, the wild killing, the seizing of the map. And how Caitlin St. Brendan was sworn to hunt down the killer of her mother.

Strange emotions played across Pencroft's face. He looked to Gale. "Caitlin . . . her father is Kerrie. Then you must be—of course. The sacred sisterhood. You and Caitlin."

Gale sat straight in her chair. "Sir William, you amaze me with what you know."

"Don't give me more credit than I deserve. Kerrie St. Brendan and I were in the Royal Marines together. Six years, in fact. After I was wounded, the best doctors in England said I would never walk again. Bullet in the spine; that sort of nonsense. And I could not walk. Kerrie took me to the Glen in the New Forest. Two years I spent there while they filled me with all manner of herbs and forced me to do strange exercises. Then, when I could stand, but barely stagger about, they gave me this great sword."

His eyes seemed vacant as he rushed with his memories back to years before. Then it was Indy's turn to put together pieces of the puzzle he'd had dumped in his lap. "Sir William," he said quickly. "Would you allow me?"

"Allow you to *what*?" came the caustic response.

Indy smiled. "To tell you, and everyone here, what happened to you. How you regained your ability to walk."

"Professor Jones, you are either crazy or a mind reader. Perhaps both, but I'm more inclined to go with insanity. How could you possibly—" He shook his head.

Indy looked about the room. Every pair of eyes was glued to him. "You said you could barely walk. That means you were able to stand."

"Obvious," Pencroft snapped.

"You exercised with the sword. Against wood, straw dummies, other people in swordplay. Slowly at first."

Pencroft sat with his mouth open. He started to speak, then waited.

"The scabbard for the sword. You wore the scabbard." Indy was intense, keeping his remarks brief. "The scabbard . . . you are right-handed. The scabbard hung from a belt on your left. You regained full use of your left leg."

Pencroft stared in amazement at Indy. "Go on, go on," he whispered.

"They increased the practice. They told you to strengthen all your muscles. To use your left arm more. So you shifted the scabbard to your right side in order to draw the sword with your left hand. And when you did that, changed the scabbard from one side to the other, you regained full use of your right leg."

Indy took a deep breath. "That day you walked as well as you ever did in your life. In fact, you could run again."

Silence hung in the room.

Finally Pencroft spoke again. His mood made it clear Indy would not again discuss the sword and the miraculous recovery of Sir William Pencroft. But the old man had ceased to dismiss the reports of a gold hoard and a map that could lead someone to its long-lost hiding place. Pencroft, without further exchange between Indy and himself, now understood that the secret of Caliburn and its scabbard, which as a university professor he could never mention without fear of being branded a lunatic, was known both to Indy *and* Gale Parker. He wanted no other eye to read that page from his past.

It was high time to move on to the reason that had brought these people here. Pencroft again studied the strangers. He was familiar with Roberto Di Palma. Simple enough. A secret agent in high circles of the Italian government *and* a member of the notorious Six Hundred of the Vatican, a select group of men and women who functioned as the church's special agents, emissaries, and if need be, mercenaries. No one admitted to the existence of the Six Hundred, but then, the world was awash with secret societies and fanatical bands. One more or less made little difference.

Looking at the Haitian was like rubbing an open wound, but for the life of him Pencroft couldn't understand—

There it was. He caught sight of a portion of the snake-skeleton necklace. Long before age and bone weariness had restricted him to the halls of the university, Pencroft had been an earlier edition of Professor Jones, plumbing the depths of the hidden and secret societies of the world. Not only had he witnessed secret tribal rites and ceremonies, but wherever possible he had joined in with the indigenous groups.

That's how he had seen the fer de lance necklace. In Haiti, decades past. A witch doctor had placed one about his neck. Before the night ended, walking along a jungle trail, he felt the vibration begin along his neck muscles and tendons. Abruptly the skeleton necklace tightened painfully, a physical shock that jerked him backward. Just in time to see a snake striking where his foot would have touched the path before him.

So if this LeDuc fellow was part of Treadwell's private entourage, then he would prove invaluable in warning of certain dangers. And if the search for gold led them into dangerous territory, LeDuc could well be their ticket to survival.

Strange, Pencroft judged, a smile coming unbidden to his creased and wrinkled features. *I have played the game myself. I am the one who knows more about the gold than all of them put together.*

The old man motioned to his attendant. "Level Four," he told her, loud enough for the others to hear. "*Sub*level Four." He looked around to the group. "Follow me," he announced, and his nurse began the long descent down four ramps to Sublevel Four.

Many years before, a different age and a different time, when that strange land of America was shooting, burning, cutting, and killing its own flesh and blood, hundreds of millions of pounds of gold and jewels had been secreted where they were now headed.

◊   ◊   ◊

They watched in silence as Pencroft leaned forward from his wheelchair to work the combination lock on a huge safe. They heard the tumblers fall and the sharp click of the steel rods sliding away to release the safe door. But it was too heavy for Pencroft to move from his wheelchair.

He turned to Indy. "Professor Jones, if you would, please? The steel box on the middle shelf. On that table behind me." He wheeled around to face the others. "Kindly take seats at the table. Martha," he asked of his nurse, "lock the door to this room."

At the table, they watched Pencroft remove yellowed documents from the steel box. He arranged them neatly before him, rested one hand on the papers, and took the time to look at each person in turn.

"Gentlemen, Miss Parker, I must request that what you are about to learn not be discussed with anyone outside this room. Mr. Di Palma, Mr. LeDuc, although I am poorly acquainted with your backgrounds, the fact that Mr. Treadwell speaks for you is acceptable to me."

Both men nodded their agreement.

Pencroft took a long breath. "Then I shall get right to the crux of the matter. The stories you have heard about the missing gold are true." His hand patted the papers gently. "This is the documentation, the complete records of the gold bars, and"—he looked directly at Di Palma—"the coins in which the Vatican has so intense an interest. For your further edification, that gold, bars and coins, was stored in this very chamber."

Except for Pencroft's explanations, the only sound heard in the sealed room was the breathing of his audience, hanging on to every word.

"The gold bars were the property of two major groups, one of them being the Museum Council of Great Britain, which shared it with our government. Obviously, the Bank of England was involved as an adviser and as our representative with the international banking system. All that is of little consequence at this moment, but it is my feeling that you should have this information to round out the background and to establish where the gold and coins were located when they were, ah, stolen is the most appropriate term."

"Stolen?" Di Palma echoed.

"In the broadest sense," Pencroft replied.

"I'm not sure I understand," Treadwell said.

"To be specific, then, the gold was pirated. A popular term would be shanghaied, although I find that a bit fanciful."

"Was if from here?" Treadwell continued. "I mean, from this room, or from a museum display?"

Pencroft shook his head slowly. He began to cough; they waited as his nurse administered a syrup to clear his throat. He dabbed lightly at his lips. "Forgive me. Age takes its toll. I must be as brief as possible.

"By the year 1863, some sixty-seven years ago, England was suffering severely because of the war being fought in the United States." He smiled at Indy. "You will forgive my use of the term 'civil war,' so often referred to as the War Between the States."

"Or," Indy commented, "Yankee aggression."

"The point is that with the Union establishing a powerful blockade of Southern ports, as well as the stress and the losses of various battles, the Confederacy was unable to ship its cotton across the Atlantic to the textile mills of this country. England went through a devastating economic loss. Mills were shutting down for lack of raw materials. Recession loomed heavily upon all of us.

"At that time, representatives of President Jefferson Davis managed to elude the Union blockade to reach our shores. They met secretly with our government and struck a deal of the greatest value both to England and to the American Confederacy. England agreed to finance the war. It is that simple. We would provide the Confederacy not only with badly needed supplies and armaments, but also with enough money for Davis and his people to buy from other governments what they needed to win against the North.

"You understand, of course, Confederate currency was hardly acceptable on the world market. The only tender that would guarantee the Confederacy what they needed was gold. In return, once the South had bulwarked its military structure—evened the odds, as it is said—Great Britain would send a fleet of warships and transports to the southern ports of the United States to begin a massive transfer of the cotton we needed so badly. The arrangements called for exclusive rights of this country to continue to receive cotton from America once the Confederacy had prevailed. The United States would be split into two nations, and we, in turn, would clearly dominate the world textile market.

"So the gold, the bullion and the coins"—Pencroft looked directly at Di Palma—"were moved secretly from this museum to a port on our west coast, in an area generally inaccessible to the public and certainly guarded most heavily. Indeed, the government made certain it was closed off. All roads were sealed, teams of armed guards with dogs covered the hills, and small fast warships patrolled off the coast."

"Sir." Indy made the attempt to break into Pencroft's

narration. He knew all too well the danger of the elderly man taxing his weakened lungs. Pencroft turned to him.

"Was there any indication that the Union, Mr. Lincoln's agents, suspected what was going on?" Indy asked.

Pencroft smiled. "If nothing else, the Yankees were thorough, and ingenious, in their spy systems. They knew *something* was afoot, of course—"

"Wait! I remember something now," Treadwell said suddenly. "It's in the reports of the Admiralty. A ship, flying the Dutch flag, suffered a fire when it was off that port that was so heavily guarded. They sent up distress signals. Rockets and all that."

Di Palma laughed, harshly and without humor. "And the British, no doubt, leaped to the rescue. We also are aware of some of these events."

"What was so unusual about a Dutch ship in trouble?" Gale asked.

"Ah, madam!" Di Palma rolled his eyes. "The flag was Dutch, all right. But when the rescuers, all so eager to save lives and perhaps to claim a prize as salvage, reached the ship, why, you may guess what they discovered! A Dutch flag, to be certain. But "—he gestured theatrically—"I am sure they discovered the crew was American, and the smoke issued forth from a huge caldron burning oily rags to make great smoke but endanger no one." He sighed and leaned back in his seat. "We have done the same many times to the French and the Spaniards. It is an old game."

"But in this case," Treadwell added, "our people gave themselves away. An isolated port on our Atlantic coastline, and from this port there emerges a force of such a size that, well"—he shrugged—"it certainly, as the Americans are so fond of saying, blew our cover."

Pencroft chuckled as he looked back to Indy. "Question answered?"

Indy nodded. "So before the gold ever left England—"

"In a warship surrounded by warships," Pencroft finished for him, "surrounded by smaller, swift vessels, all of which had the added protection of another ring of ships in a great circular pattern about the main force."

"Because by then," Indy mused aloud, "the Union navy could have struck directly against the British force."

Pencroft demurred. "We do not believe that would have happened."

"Why not?" Gale asked.

"An attack against so formidable a force," Pencroft said slowly, "would require just as powerful a force on the part of the North. It would be an act of open warfare. Too many government leaders in London desired such an eventuality. Defeat the North by an alliance with the Confederacy, assure a continued supply of materials for the textile industry, *and* help the Confederacy occupy the North and seize industry and raw materials."

He coughed again, pausing once more to dab at red flecks on his lips. "History has its own sense of humor. We lost the colonies to the rebels under Washington, and now we were trying to seduce the North into a battle in which we were allied with the Rebels of the South."

"But what happened to the gold!" Di Palma exclaimed.

"That, my dear fellow," Pencroft replied, "is a question to which no answer has been provided since 1863."

"You mean . . . the bullion, the coins, just *disappeared*?"

"Not quite as simple as that, I daresay." Pencroft shrugged. "But the answer is we do not know." He turned to Gale Parker. "Have you ever seen the map that seems to be at the heart of all this—I mean, before these past few days?" he asked.

Gale shook her head. "No. Nor do I know how this Cordas learned about the map, or where it had been concealed all these years."

Indy gestured to the papers on the table. "Sir William, is that an accounting of all the gold?"

Pencroft pushed the documents to the center of the table. "Examine them, if you will."

Treadwell remained in his seat. "The papers are mere records of the past. What matters *now* is Cordas. If he deciphers the map, then we know he will move swiftly to recover the gold."

"And he'll need plenty of manpower to move whatever he finds. We're talking *tons* of gold," Indy noted.

"Except for the coins," Di Palma offered. "They are beyond any price."

"So the issue is Cordas," Indy said aloud. "Nothing else matters. All this is confirmation that the gold exists, that it left England, that it was headed for America, and then—" He threw up his hands. *"Poof! Gone!"*

"And so is Cordas," Treadwell added.

"And Caitlin," Gale said quietly.

Every head in the room turned to her. "What?" That was all Treadwell could say for the moment.

"You refer to Kerrie St. Brendan's child?" Pencroft asked.

"Not child. A woman. A *warrior,"* Gale said sternly.

"Of course," Pencroft said, his voice just above a whisper. "The oath of the Glen. Just retribution for a life of their clan." His expression showed his pain and concern. "I fear for her life," he told Gale.

"Fear for the life of Cordas," she replied.

"That," Treadwell interjected, "is a very tall order."

"You don't know Caitlin," Gale retorted.

"Then *I've* got to find her," Indy said, his words catching the group by surprise.

"And why you?" Pencroft demanded. "This isn't your affair. You're here to teach!"

"I don't *know* why, sir," Indy said, as surprised with himself as were the others. *All but Gale, I'll bet,* he told himself. "Somehow I don't seem to have much say in all this. It's as if I'm drawn to her. Look, Sir William, if there's even the slightest chance that she'll find Cordas and I'm there—"

"It could be our only chance to recover the coins!" Di Palma said, his excitement growing.

"Wouldn't do the Bank of England any harm to recover that bullion," Treadwell said, directing his remark to Pencroft. "Make a hero out of this university for making it possible."

"Make us bloody fools if Indy gets killed chasing a murdering gang, you mean!" Pencroft said angrily.

Indy sighed. "Then I'll resign my position, Sir William. That way the university will be absolved of any blame."

"*And* any credit," Treadwell added quickly.

"The Vatican would be most grateful," Di Palma offered.

Pencroft folded his hands in his lap. "Indy?" He rarely used that name with Professor Henry Jones. "You are quite serious about all this?"

"Yes, sir. Maybe I'm a fool—"

"No question of that," Pencroft said icily.

"We're wasting time," Indy said to Gale. "We need to go with Caitlin because—"

"She is already gone," Gale said.

Silence hung heavily in the room. Indy drummed his fingers on the table. "Where?"

"After Cordas."

"That I've figured out myself," he said. "But when?"

"Indy, all I can tell you is that she is following Cordas. And none of us will recognize her. She is a master of disguise. You already know what forces she controls."

Treadwell was on his feet. "You're wasting time." He turned to Pencroft. "Sir, my apologies. And my gratitude, and that of Scotland Yard, for your splendid assistance tonight."

"You're a liar, Thomas. I didn't tell you a thing you didn't already know."

Treadwell turned to Indy and Gale. "I suggest you come with me." Then, to Di Palma: "I would appreciate you and LeDuc returning to your hotel so I can contact you later."

Both men nodded. Treadwell left with Indy and Gale.

When they were gone, Di Palma turned to Pencroft. "Do you know where they are going?"

The old man laughed, a dry cackle that became a knowing smile. "Of course."

"Where would that be, sir?"

Pencroft slapped his knee. "*You're* the secret agent here, my friend. *You* find out."

10

Indy held out his hand to Gale. No words passed between them. They had learned to read the moods and needs of the other through facial expressions and body language.

Gale nodded. For a moment she hesitated as she took a long second look at the cavernous room in which she, Indy, Treadwell, and an unnamed group of men and women were gathered. Who the faces-without-names were was obvious to Gale: highly skilled professionals in the upper echelons of MI5, that bastion of British military intelligence. The room seemed to muffle all sounds. Something this huge should have echoed at the slightest report or word. But the walls and roof and ceiling swallowed sounds like living things, eating greedily at whatever pulses came their way.

Nothing spoken in this cryptographic section of MI5 could be heard outside these walls. Gale was taken aback when she noticed the windows along those walls. It took a sharp eye to recognize that the windows were false, woodwork and metal and glass through which nothing could be seen. And Gale's eye was that of the hunter.

Now Indy held forth his hand. There was but one thing he would ask of her in *this* room, so words were unnecessary. She reached within her leather jacket, unsealed an inside pocket, and withdrew the folded leather parchment she had carried now for several days.

Indy spread out the parchment on the table beneath bright lights. Treadwell motioned to his staff. "Gather 'round, gentlemen," he told them.

"I know this is obvious to you"—Indy spoke to the group—"but just for the record, you'll notice there are no names or coordinates on this map."

"Makes a ruddy good mystery," one man remarked.

"It does that. Your job is simple. Treadwell says you're the best. All you need to do is match the features here— the coastline, rivers, whatever."

"That's all?" The question came with disbelief. "You could do a jigsaw puzzle easier in the dark, sir."

Indy stood straight. "Not as difficult as it looks."

A chorus of "Oh?" met his statement. "No names, no towns, nothing but those lines."

"Look, I'm no cartographer," Indy said quickly, "but I do have some experience with maps and charts. You learn that quickly in archaeological digs." He leaned forward, tracing outlines along the map. "But there are clues. This is obviously a coastline, here." He tapped the parchment. "The map doesn't give us a fix for north of south, so it's a guesstimate at best. But the odds are that whoever made this thing followed the common rule of placing north at the top."

"Well, sir"—one man stepped in—"if that's so, then we have us a west coastline."

"Wherever that might be," another man murmured.

"Okay, we've got a coastline, and it runs along a western shore. What else?"

"What else can you tell us, sir?"

Indy looked up and grinned. "If I told you the United States, would that help?"

Treadwell resisted this conclusion. "You don't *know* that, Indy, and—"

"No, hold it, Tom," Indy broke in. "Here are the best cartographers in all England, right?"

Someone laughed. "Cheers."

"Could this be anywhere in the British Isles?"

The men leaned forward, spoke among themselves. A short man with a bristly beard stood up to look at Indy. "No way, governor. Not Scotland or Ireland or anywhere in the U.K., for that matter."

Indy looked about him. "Any arguments?" They shook their heads. "Okay, let's say, for the moment, at least, that it's the United States, and the date is somewhere between 1863 and 1870."

Someone whistled, long and low. "Mr. Treadwell, sir, is this Yank deliberately trying to stick the prod to us?"

Treadwell laughed. "Gentlemen, he's dead serious. But I know what you mean." Then to Indy: "Coastlines change over a period of fifty to sixty years. Rivers change course, too."

Indy nodded. "But not that much." He looked to the cartographers again. "How about the *southern* United States? That help?"

"Blimey, does it ever," he was told immediately.

"Well, you've got a time period, a better crack at the location, and—" Indy paused to scratch chin stubble, then went on. "The area along the coastline, um, anywhere from thirty to sixty miles, I'd say, needs some deep water.

Not for a port, but to anchor a seagoing vessel, or vessels, and enough room for longboats to work to the shore."

"You wouldn't happen to have the name of such a vessel or two, now, would you?" The query was a serious stab at humor.

Indy laughed. "Not today." Abruptly he grew serious and turned to Treadwell. "You know, Tom, he's right. There should be a full registry in the Admiralty and we can—"

"I'm way ahead of you, my friend. We'll get on those records immediately. It will take some digging, but"—he shrugged—"we are on the right track." Treadwell turned to the group. "Get cracking, gentlemen. Whatever turns up, leave word at my office, day or night."

They drove to Treadwell's favorite pub in London, the gathering place for people who wanted great food, great beer, and assured privacy: Hogsbreath Inn, announced by a large swinging sign illustrating a particularly ugly boar. Besides its large barroom, the inn also had private rooms well concealed by a long hallway and several doors. Willy Consers, who'd owned the pub for longer than Treadwell could remember, welcomed the patronage of Scotland Yard. They assured him a hand in the courts when some of his customers consumed excessive amounts of ale or bitters and fell back on their favorite pastime of bashing each other about, bringing the bobbies on a now familiar route to the pub.

Consers greeted Treadwell without a word, caught the inspector raising his eyes, and led him and his two companions down the hallway, through a private doorway, and up a narrow flight of winding stairs to a secure second-floor dining room. "I'll have Molly with you right off," he told them, and left.

"Molly's his wife," Treadwell explained as he eased into a comfortable padded chair. "Discreet, and quite hard of hearing."

They waited until they were served pitchers of ale and helpings of shepherd's pie. Treadwell locked the door from the inside. "We'll take our time with dinner and catch up on all the small details," he announced. "I'm as hungry as a bear," he added as he fell to his meal with relish, as did Indy and Gale. Then Treadwell pushed back his seat and displayed a pipe. "Mind?" he asked Gale.

She shook her head. "Not at all. Go ahead, please."

It was a comfortable shift to the business at hand. Behind a cloud of smoke, Treadwell looked to Gale. "I need, first off, to confirm that Caitlin St. Brendan has truly gone off," he said.

"She has that," Gale confirmed.

"Where?"

"I don't know. Not yet," Gale replied. "But when Caitlin is ready, she'll let me know."

"This may seem indelicate, and I intend no slight with this question, but will she, ah, use her special talents to reach—"

Gale broke in with a laugh. "No magic to it, Thomas. And no long-range mental telepathy, either. We're not quite *that* talented. But the covens, which are worldwide, do need to communicate with one another. It stands us well to know what is going on in different countries. Among other things, the Glen has powerful shortwave radio transmitters and receivers. When it's necessary to exchange sensitive information, the people on the radios use one of the ancient languages. To anyone listening in, it sounds like gibberish."

"Clever, clever," Treadwell complimented her. "What might be some of the other means?"

"Carrier pigeons in certain areas."

"Marvelous."

"Couriers. Even cablegrams with our own codes. There are all sorts of magic out there in the world, Thomas. We try to make the best use of the most modern equipment available."

"So I see," Treadwell answered. "You haven't mentioned the telephone, I note."

Gale laughed. "I save that for Indy. He doesn't like pigeons beating at his windows in the middle of the night."

Treadwell turned to Indy. "You, and Gale, of course, are planning to follow Caitlin. I assumed you were, but I must hear it from you directly."

Indy nodded. "For all the reasons you've heard, Tom."

"We can stay in touch with one another just as we did during that wild affair with the disks and that giant zeppelin. Using the transatlantic cable of course, but also high-powered shortwave radio that will go directly into my office."

"Which one? MI5 or the Yard?"

"People know me as an inspector from the Yard, of course. But everything goes through MI5. If it's sensitive, it stays there waiting for me. Otherwise it's brought immediately to the Yard, where I also maintain an office."

"I'll have to lean heavily on you, Tom. Contacts, government pressure if necessary. And money. We don't know what we'll run into or how much we might need."

"You'll have a very substantial letter of credit from the Bank of England, for starters," Treadwell told him. "And coded numbers for wiring funds wherever you need. Indy, I can best support you if I know what's happening from day to day."

Indy shrugged. "I'll do my best." He sat up straight, leaning on the table. "Question, Thomas."

"At your service."

"After all the things that have happened, and what you've seen and experienced, tell me, do you now accept the reality of magic?"

A humorless laugh escaped the inspector. He tamped his pipe, relit it, and blew out a cloud of smoke. "I have recently been in a place," he said slowly, "where people manipulate time, or what we call time, as if it were a substance they could shape in any form they desired. That's a shock to the system of an orderly man."

"And if nothing else"—Indy laughed—"you are most orderly."

"In my business, that's a necessity," Treadwell countered. "However, I also must balance incredulity against the reality of what I experienced. I don't really understand time. I don't know if anyone does. But I *do* know you can work with certain forces, use them for your own purposes, even if you don't understand them."

"Like gravity?" Gale offered.

"Precisely. We know what it does, we can measure its force and effect, and excuse me if I sound ponderous, but the reality," Treadwell said, his expression serious, "is that no one *knows* what gravity *is*."

"Point well taken," Indy added. "The astrophysics people at Princeton start their discussions on gravity pleasantly enough and usually end up screaming at one another."

"Well, back to the Glen. I told you I spent most of my

younger years on the Salisbury Plain. I often hunted in the New Forest, I made close friends among the Romanies, places like Stonehenge were playgrounds. Youthful exuberance and all that. Then I watched that most unusual young woman, Caitlin . . . well, you were there with me. Roads that twisted in upon themselves. Strange forces she describes as absolutely natural earth energies which can be manipulated like steam or electricity."

Again he paused to relight his pipe, which he'd been waving about like a baton as he spoke. "Now we come to that sword she was wearing. I am a fanatic about our legends of King Arthur and Sir Galahad, Morgan the Fay and Merlin, and the whole lot of people clanking about in armor and muttering all sorts of incantations. Wizardry and all that. And I swear that sword she carries is straight out of myth and legend—"

"And folklore and history," Gale said quickly.

"Well," Treadwell harrumphed, "I'm no longer in a position to argue the point. I feel left out of things I should have known since I was a mere stripling. The point is I consider Excalibur a convenient fairy tale, likely created to confuse the issue of the *real* sword, Caliburn. The fighting sword. Those fellows were always naming things to gain spiritual value. They named their swords, their shields and horses, even their helmets. It gave them strength and confidence. So who am I to say that Caliburn was a commonplace or ordinary sword rather than one endowed with magic powers? In short, my friends, my world of reality, in which I have rested securely, has been shaken quite severely. I don't know *what* to believe anymore."

"Believe in Caitlin," Gale said sternly.

Treadwell studied her as if he could find hard truth behind her words and expression. "She truly is going after Cordas, then."

"Absolutely. And she will provoke him until he tries to kill her," Gale added.

"Which won't be too difficult," Indy offered. "Cordas won't hesitate to cut her down like a dog. One more killing won't mean a thing to him."

Gale's lips tightened. "He might find that more difficult than he anticipates."

Indy nodded in silent confirmation.

Which irritated Thomas Treadwell. He hated when the people he wanted to protect deliberately kept him in the dark.

Indy went through his flat to give it a meaningful defensive posture. He rigged a framework with steel rods by each high window, extending at an angle against the glass. Anyone trying to swing in by rope would be impaled as he came through the glass.

Only one door led from the flat to an outside corridor. Indy rigged an electrical line from a wall outlet so that when the power was on, just moving the door inward would ring an alarm bell he'd hung on the inside.

On the floor by the couch went his Webley revolver. He had only to drop his arm to have the gun in hand and aimed at the door. Then he rechecked Gale's—his— bedroom, closed the door, and sprawled on the couch.

Sleep eluded him. His mind whirled with the idea that Caitlin's sword and tunic possessed earth energies gathered from the planet itself. But how it all happened was a curious nut he had only partially cracked. He didn't know the transfer medium from the earth to the sword and tunic. But there *was* a key in what Gale had said to him; he reviewed her words.

She had hesitated at first, then caught him by surprise. "I still don't understand, myself," she said carefully, "just how the scepter works. I mean, it's ancient. Yet it uses a battery. I've seen it. But"—she frowned with confusion— "that scepter was being used hundreds of years before batteries were even invented! Today, Caitlin's father could make anything work with electricity. Among other things, Kerrie's an electrical engineer."

"What was the battery like?" he questioned her.

"Sort of like a rectangular box. I think he once mentioned it was a dry-cell battery."

He nodded. "That means it would be an acid-type battery, Gale. They're clumsy and heavy, but they work. Where did Kerrie install it?"

"He mounted the scepter in a staff. I always thought it *had* to be an electrical system."

"I'd bet a dollar to a doughnut," Indy said firmly, "that staff had two layers. The inside is wood, around which Kerrie wound thin wire to the battery and the crystals. That's how he set up his antenna."

Gale studied Indy. "Where'd you learn so much about radios and batteries and all this electrical stuff?"

"I needed radios in the field. No telephones out there." He laughed. "And you have to know how to repair that kind of equipment if you want any reliability." Indy shrugged. "But I learned more than I ever imagined I would. I also discovered that the ancients had electricity before the modern world ever dreamed of it. That's how I'm connecting Caitlin's scepter with what could have happened centuries ago. Don't you see? If people before and during the time of Merlin had batteries, then that makes the wizardry of Merlin fit right into the known laws of energy."

"If I heard this from anybody but you . . ." She left the sentence unfinished.

"Hey, I didn't learn all this on my own. I owe a lot to a guy, Jack Silverstein. Jack was an inventor as well as a research scientist. If you mention the history of electrical power today, as we use it, and ask how it all got started, people come up with names like Edison or Tesla. It's only been thirty years since Edison produced a worthwhile light bulb."

"Just how far back did you find electricity? You, or this friend of yours?"

"More than two thousand years ago. In fact, we confirmed the presence of batteries in 226 B.C. the Parthinians, along the edge of the Caspian Sea, were using electricity on a daily basis."

"You're talking about a time before the birth of Christ!"

"Centuries before," he confirmed. "Ever hear of Wilhelm Kroner?"

Gale shook her head.

"Kroner was going through Parthinian ruins and stumbled across what looked like parts and pieces of a dry-cell battery. He got some engineers to put all the pieces together, they built a new battery exactly like the ancient pieces, and it generated electrical current. They used their electricity for plating statues and jewelry with gold."

"This is amazing," she said in wonder.

"I saved the best for last. Another four hundred years earlier. We found proof of electricity in ancient Greek writings. Thales of Miletus, about 600 B.C., described an electrical apparatus. We figured that was the absolute limit, back in time, I mean, but the ancients fooled us

again. Turns out Egyptian priests built some really powerful electrical generators for their temples. That's how they
controlled their followers. The common man really believed the priests had direct connections with the gods."

"How long ago?"

"Three thousand years. I checked the ruins myself. I
could hardly believe what we found. Multiconductor electrical cables for their altars, operated by hand-cranked
generators. They had their stoolies—"

"Who?"

"Underlings. They hid behind walls and cranked away
like crazy to generate the electrical current. The cables ran
to the altars where a priest held an insulated rod—what
the adoring masses believed was a wand of magical power.
If the priests wanted to frighten the mob, they'd point rods
at the crowd and a bunch of people would get zapped. If
they wanted to do someone in, they'd all aim at this one
person to combine their current. There'd be a dazzling
flash, an explosion, the stink of ozone, and some poor
farmer would be a smoking corpse."

Gale nodded slowly. "It makes a strange connection to
Merlin," she said, looking up to Indy.

"How so?"

"Well, the stories tell of the different ways Merlin would
dispatch his enemies. At times he'd point his finger at the
miscreant, chant something nobody could understand, and
a blast of fire—electricity, I understand now—would strike
the man. Merlin had a discharge rod concealed in his
sleeve. If he was hooked up to the kind of generator you
said the Egyptian priests had, it all makes sense."

"And," Indy added, "it always seemed that he was hurling thunderbolts out of thin air. Actually he was using the
scepter."

"I don't understand how that would work."

"Energy is all around us. We get powerful radio waves from the sun all the time. It's just that we can't feel or detect them unless we build an antenna that's in a beat with those waves. It snatches the electricity out of the air, so to speak, and concentrates it. Merlin had a staff with precious stones. Kerrie has a staff with jewels *and* crystals. You need a crystal to get maximum power. But whatever you use, you need above all an antenna to capture the energy, and then boost it so it will blast right out of the scepter. It's like a lightning rod in reverse. But you can't always count on seizing energy out of thin air. So what you do is to *store* that energy. And you do that with a battery."

"And what Kerrie has would work the way you described it?"

"Sure. He uses a battery that has only one volt. It's a lead-zinc combination, a carbon rod and gunk in between. Techically, it's what you call an electrolyte that uses acid to carry the current."

Indy snapped his fingers. "Of course! Inside that scepter is Kerrie's storage system. A capacitor. A device for collecting energy until you have enough to kick out a huge discharge. You build up power until you get a blast like lightning."

Gale shook her head slowly. "It all sounds so complicated. I mean, Egyptians and Parthinians and Merlin—"

"And now Kerrie and Caitlin," Indy finished for her.

"There's that last question neither one of us has answered, Indy." He waited for her to continue. "The tunic," she went on. "*That* is a magic neither of us understands."

"I know I don't," he admitted. "All I know is that it works, and nothing I know in science, past or present, lets me in on the secret." He shrugged. "I'm not into magic."

He suddenly became serious. "But I'll tell you this.

Tunic or no tunic, a heavy rifle slug into the heart or the brain will kill Caitlin. Instantly. She is *not* invulnerable. If she believes she is, that can get her killed faster than anything else, because then she'll take some really stupid chances."

Gale nodded slowly, fearful for Caitlin's future. "I know," she said at last.

11

What in the name of . . . !

Indy groped his way out of deep sleep. Instinctively his right hand dropped to the floor alongside the couch to grip the heavy Webley revolver. It took several moments to realize that the pounding noise booming through the flat came from the entrance door. He swung off the couch, approached the door from the side, Webley at the ready. It could be anything. The building on fire, someone with an emergency, but—Treadwell? His voice came through the door. "Open up, you nit! Open up, I say! It's Thomas!"

Indy heard the bedroom door open behind him, glanced about to see Gale in pajamas. The woman had a powerful crossbow, cocked and ready to fire, in her hands. He motioned for her to stay back and spoke through the door.

"Thomas!"

"Open up, blast it!"

"How many with you?"

"Just Roberto."

Indy opened the door and stepped back. Treadwell and Di Palma came in, stopped short at the sight of the Webley

Indy was sliding into his waistband. He closed and bolted the door.

"Sociable as always, I see," Treadwell told him.

"Its four-thirty in the morning, Thomas."

"Oh, good. Without your help I'd never know the time. I know, I know, Indy. We haven't been to sleep yet."

Gale headed for the kitchen to put on coffee and boil water for tea. When she returned to the living room, the three men were sitting at a round table. "Gale, I want you in on this," Treadwell said. She nodded, sat, and sipped slowly at her mug of tea.

Treadwell rubbed his eyes. "We believe we know where Cordas is going," he announced. "I didn't want to tell by telephone. Too risky."

Indy offered no criticism. Treadwell obviously wouldn't be here at this ungodly hour without good reason.

"We confirmed," Treadwell continued slowly, "that Cordas and a small group, appear to be en route to Hamburg, Germany. We've been running checks on every ferry, private vessel, and aircraft crossing the Channel. Cordas and his group chartered a French airliner. So we didn't have records on any of our own aircraft, but customs was notified, of course, and that was how we saw the little red flag go up."

"How many?" Indy asked.

"Eight in Cordas's group. They passed through customs without problem, with a flight planned to Orly. Lots of traffic in and out of there in the morning, so they could get lost easily enough in the shuffle."

"Customs tell you what kind of passports?" Indy asked.

"Oh, to be sure. French. I'm quite certain," Treadwell added, "they can get passports from anywhere they want."

"Did anyone pick up any information on Caitlin?" Gale broke in.

Treadwell shook his head. "Not a word."

Indy studied his friend. "You've got more than this."

Treadwell nodded, took a moment to finish his tea. "They're using codes. Letters and numbers. Our telephone monitors working all outgoing traffic managed to get this message: seven, two, one ZL. We're working on it, of course. It might be as simple as reversing letters and numbers or it might also be a preset code. Verification of communications and everything going according to plan, that sort of thing."

Di Palma drummed his fingers on the table. "What is puzzling, so far, is the choice of Germany. The map Miss Parker gave us doesn't match any coastline of Germany. It's certainly not Hamburg."

"Hamburg makes sense to me," Indy said.

"Explain, if you would," Di Palma asked.

"Port of embarkation," Indy said idly.

"We've had that in mind also, of course," Treadwell told him. "The problem is that there are exits everywhere. Will they take a steamship to Hamburg? Go by train? Fly from Orly by a circuitous route—well, we simply don't know."

"Three men booked a flight from London to Rome," Di Palma added. "Also using this code of seven, two, one ZL. Thomas is convinced it's a blind, a decoy. I see no reason to disagree with him."

"From my experience with Mr. Cordas," Indy noted, "you'll probably find a dozen people traveling all over Europe using that code just to give us fits."

"Well, if experience is any guide," Treadwell said sourly, "he may well be teasing us. Or Miss St. Brendan, especially. Cordas always makes sure he is extremely knowledgeable about any area into which he gets involved. If he knows the history of the people of the Glen, and I'm certain he does, then he knows that this young woman will pursue him, no matter what the odds."

"And he may be leaving just enough of a trail for her to follow," Indy said unhappily. He glanced at Gale. "Never ignore that possibility. Cordas is a man who enjoys a good opponent."

"He'll bloody well get more than he's bargaining for," Gale said heatedly.

"I would much rather *we* got to him first," Treadwell said, his voice leaving no doubt about his feelings about a young woman going single-handed against a murderous band. And if you don't mind my saying so—"

Indy abruptly sat bolt upright. He gripped Treadwell's arm. "That code . . . let me have that again." He wrote down the sequence: seven, two, one ZL. He kept repeating it, then wrote it backward. He tossed down his pencil and rose to walk about the room.

"I don't know why it took me so long to figure out something so obvious," he said angrily. "Cordas is clearly toying with us. All the translations of symbols and languages, codes and cuneiforms, and I couldn't see it until now. I feel like an idiot."

"Whatever are you talking about?" Treadwell asked.

"That code! It's a come-on," Indy said angrily. "Cordas made it so simple we didn't see what was under our noses."

Di Palma shook his head. "I am as confused as Thomas, I admit."

Indy stopped his angry pacing, returned to lean on the table with both hands balled into fists. "Cordas and his group aren't going east," he stressed. "They're going west."

"Need I remind you Hamburg is very much to the east of here?" Treadwell retorted.

"Sure it is, and it's a blind alley," Indy said immediately. "That gold shipment, during the Civil War, was headed for the southeastern United States, right?"

Treadwell nodded. "Yes."

"And every indication is that the convoy *did* arrive in that area?" Indy persisted.

"In that general area, yes. But you already know," Treadwell added, "that our information on the destination is at best spotty. Besides, Indy, if Cordas plans to cross the Atlantic, to go where we believe the convoy landed, he has to travel in a westerly direction."

"Sometimes," Indy said, smiling, "the fastest way between two points is the longest way around."

"You're talking in riddles at this time of night?" Treadwell said, clearly irked at Indy's roundabout explanations.

"No riddle," Indy retorted. "Look, that code. What do you get when you reverse the order?"

"Well, that's easy enough. LZ one, two, seven."

"That tells me they're headed for Friedrichshafen," Indy said.

"But Hamburg's the main port of embarkation. . . ." Treadwell's voice trailed off. He had a stupefied look on his face.

Indy laughed. "So you see it, too, now."

"Good Lord, yes."

"These games," Di Palma complained to Gale. "Do they do this all the time?"

Gale nodded. "They do. But there's always a reason for it."

"Don't you get it yet?" Indy asked Gale.

"No."

"The code isn't a code at all," Indy said quickly. "It's a designation. LZ one, two, seven. That's the designation for the Graf Zeppelin—"

"You mean—"

"Of course! A commercial airship flies a lot faster across the ocean than a steamship sails." He went to his telephone. "Everybody, bear with me, okay?" He was on the phone for less than five minutes. He hung up and returned to the table.

"That was a round-the-clock travel service in Friedrichshafen. It's confirmed. You see, LZ is the designation for the Zeppelin Transport Company, and one twenty-seven is the official company designation for the ship *we* know as Graf Zeppelin. It's crossed the ocean many times, and right now it's preparing to leave on a special flight. It's going to fly to America along a route that takes it over the North Pole. Some geographic societies want to shoot photographs and moving pictures of the flight. They're combining the expedition with a chartered flight. Remember I said Cordas was leaving a trail for us to follow?"

"Yes, yes?" Di Palma was hanging on every word.

"Well," Indy said, enjoying his revelation, "Cordas is on the passenger manifest *under his own name.*"

"Cheeky," Treadwell said quietly.

Indy sat back. "The Graf leaves in two days, Thomas. That means you've got to have confirmed reservations on that zeppelin for Gale and me in the next few hours. Use the clout of the British government to make sure we're on that thing when it lifts off."

Indy smiled. "Unless you want Cordas to get to the States a week or two before us."

"I'll do my best."

"Not good enough. We must be on that ship. Oh, and arrange seats on a commerical flight for us to Friedrichshafen."

"When?"

"Noon today. Stop sitting there, Thomas. Go!"

12

The force of the rain lashing the deck of the cross-channel cargo ferry stung Indy's face. He turned to one side, pulling his battered hat over his face, and was rewarded by a sudden spray of icy salt water thrown up by the steamer's bow as it plunged almost beneath the surface. He stared at the dim glow of yellow light from the cabin; Gale stood facing the wind and rain, reveling in the ferocity of the storm.

"Are you enjoying yourself?" Indy shouted above the howl of wind, the pounding of water, and the steamer's engines. Every few moments the entire ship shuddered, as if it was coming apart at the seams.

Gale turned, also shouting. "It's wonderful!" she exclaimed, as delighted as a child seeing open water for the first time.

"You're nuts!" Indy retorted. His stomach growled; he felt as if cotton had been stuffed inside his head. He gripped a stanchion for support as the steamer rolled sickeningly to one side. Looking up at the cabin, he caught a glimpse of Treadwell behind a window, seated comfortably, legs locked around his chair for support, enjoying his pipe.

Indy worked his way carefully along the narrow passage-way, salt water sloshing about his feet. He pushed in the door, reeling for balance as it swung away. Treadwell and the ferry crew watched with amusement as Indy slammed the door and collapsed in a seat, water streaming from his clothes.

"Remind me," he said with a snarl, "if I ever get out of this crazy trip alive, to kill you with my bare hands."

Treadwell saluted him with a wave of his pipe. "This your first touch of the sailor's life? A sailing ship is a true wonder, Professor."

"*This* isn't a sailing ship," Indy growled, hanging on to the seat arms as the ferry wallowed like a water buffalo sinking in quicksand. "It's a junk heap. Should have been scrapped years ago, or sunk before it got out of harbor."

" 'Ere now!" Bjorn McManus said loudy. "It's me charmer you're talking about, mate!"

"You're calling this roach palace a charmer?" Indy sneered. He wasn't in the mood for pleasantries. The planned flight from England to Paris went up in smoke when they were ready to depart his flat. No one had bothered to check the weather and they stepped outside just as a storm moved across their part of the city. Rushing back inside, Treadwell called the big commercial field at the edge of London. "We're down," came the explanation. "Sorry, guv. Front's come in with nary warning. We've checked across the water. Same in France."

That meant crossing a very turbulent English Channel. Even the commercial ferries were canceling their sched-uled trips. It took the clout of Scotland Yard to roust Bjorn

McManus from a warm bed and gather his crew to take Indy and Gale to Cherbourg.

As they departed the dock in London beneath low, swift-moving clouds and steady rain, Treadwell had explained the weather situation. "There won't be any flying on the mainland, either, I'm afraid. I've talked to our top numbers in France, and they'll have a car waiting for you. Off the ferry, then a straight drive to Paris. Train reservations are already made from there to Germany. You should reach the airfield at Friedrichshafen a few hours before the Graf is scheduled to depart."

They weren't out of the river passage from London before Indy was already regretting his decision to go along with Treadwell's new plans. Everyone else aboard the *Brisbane*, as the rotten channel ferry was called, was intolerably cheerful. "Of course they're cheerful," Treadwell explained when Indy wondered how a crew sailing into crazy winds and buckets of rain could maintain such high spirits. "They're being paid triple wages, and that includes the return trip."

"I'd rather fly," Indy groused.

"In this weather?" Treadwell exclaimed.

"Sure. Then I'd be sick for maybe an hour instead of the whole triple-cursed night!"

Treadwell laughed. "You'll do just fine, lad."

"Bug off," Indy snarled.

Contrary to his expectations, Indy survived long enough to reach Cherbourg. To his amazement he managed to retain his last meal. They bid good-bye to Treadwell and climbed into an old cab driven by a leathery old Frenchman who reeked of garlic and brandy and drove with complete abandon along the rain-slicked roads.

But at least Indy now had the chance to catch up on the

details of their upcoming flight. He turned on the overhead light of the cab, producing a long stream of shouted insults from the driver.

"If the light bothers you, just shut your eyes," Indy told the grumbling old man.

"I'll take care of this," Gale whispered to Indy. She reached into her bag, produced a flask, unscrewed the top, and handed it to the driver. Without a word he drank deeply, muttered, *"Merci,"* then took another long swallow.

"Are you trying to kill us all?" Indy demanded of Gale.

"I've been with these people many times before. He's drinking cognac. He has so much already inside him this won't make a bit of difference."

"If we hit a tree and die, I'll come back to haunt you," Indy promised her.

"Great," she returned. "Now look, let's go over the papers before we get to the train station. Wouldn't do for either of us to be using our own names from that point on."

Indy nodded. "All right. Let's do it. Passports first." Gale produced them from a leather bag. "They're *both* English," Indy noted.

"Right. Notice it's the address of your flat. Treadwell said it was likely that this will be checked."

"The names won't be the same," Indy remarked.

"They are now," Gale assured him. "It was very clever of Thomas to use my last name for you. All they needed to do was change your last name, and my address to yours in London, to make everything match."

"Henry Parker," Indy said aloud. "Sounds strange."

"I like it," Gale said.

"Jones is more distinguished," Indy teased.

"In a common sort of way," she riposted. "Shall we get on with it?" He nodded and she produced phony driver's licenses. "And here's the club membership for both of us at the Hogsbreath Inn. Also, your employee identification card for London Municipal Services."

"And what do I do there?"

"Zookeeper. You clean out cages." She stifled an outburst of laughter.

"Great," he said sarcastically. "And you?"

"Game warden."

"That fits," he acknowledged. "What else?"

"Oh, different clubs," she said, riffling papers and dividing them up. "Everything fits, Indy. Thomas is very thorough."

"Did he remember your pilot's license?"

She held up addtional papers. "England, France, *and* the United States."

"Thorough, all right. What about your school background?"

"Middlesex. I did go there. No need to change anything."

"And mine?"

"You, Mr. Parker, went to a university in, of all places, San Diego, California. That takes care of your accent, the terrible way you dress. After studying animal husbandry, you worked in the cattle country in Texas. You even," she said, studying him, "look like you were a cowboy. At least it explains that whip of yours. You went to work in 1926 at the London Zoo. In fact, your records will show you traveled for the zoo to bring rare animals back to London."

Indy leaned back. "He seems to have covered all the bases. Tell me, how long have we been married? So to speak."

"Seven years."

"You were how old when we got married? According to these records?"

"Seventeen. Something like that."

The driver glanced back at them. "Cradle robber." He sneered at Indy.

Indy exchanged glances with Gale. "Seems like we lost a drunken Frenchman and gained an Englishman," he said calmly, reaching beneath and behind his leather jacket.

The driver felt sudden hard pressure in the back of his neck. "Pull over. Slowly, very carefully," Indy told him. "Anything sudden and it's lights out, my friend."

"No need for that, mate," the driver said in perfect English. "Besides, I know what you've got up against me. Schmeiser, point-two-five caliber, six rounds, notched ammo, copper jacket, and scolopendra dust beneath the copper. Interesting how I knows all this, right?"

"Your advantage," Indy said. "Either you're psychic or—"

"You've already guessed it, haven't you, Professor Jones?"

"Go on," Indy said coldly.

"Not that hard to tell. You don't mind if I keep driving, do you? Clock's ticking, and all that. I know what you've got in your hand, and that holster in the back of your belt, and that a nice gentleman by the name of Sir Thomas gave you that piece as a backup. Any doubts that we're working for the same office, sir?"

Indy leaned back, the Schmeiser went into its concealed holster. "No," Indy said. "No doubts. What's your name?"

"On the license of this cab it's Jacques Voltaire. Back home, as we say, I'm known as John Pennington."

"Why all the cat-and-mouse games, John?"

"Well, sir, best way to tell just how well you and the missus was coming along was to listen to you two having at it freely. Drunken Frenchie at the wheel, now, he wouldn't care. When I'd heard enough, it was time to warn you. Before we get to the train station in Paris."

"Warn him of what?" Gale asked.

"To leave that automatic with me."

"And why would I do that?"

"You can't carry it, sir, without special government papers from the Frenchies. And you don't want those because it draws too much attention to you. If you're caught with the piece, it's a bit of a rumpus, sir. Besides, you can't take anything explosive aboard the Graf Zeppelin. No guns, no lighters, no matches. Nothing at all like that, sir. They'll even give you static-free slippers when you get aboard. Both of you. If they find a weapon like that Schmeiser on you or in your luggage—and it's going to be searched, I can assure you of that, sir—you'll both be hauled off the zep and right into jail you goes. I know about your Webley, Prof—sorry, I mean, Mr. Parker, sir. You'll have the proper equipment when you land in the United States, sir. Mr. Treadwell, he's taken care of all that. Permission from the secret service, or whatever is their organization over there."

Indy released the holster and Schmeiser and handed it over the front seat to Pennington. "That was all neatly done, John Pennington."

"Thank you, sir. By the by, I'll be staying with you to see you're well set on the train in Paris."

Gale spoke up suddenly. "Mr. Pennington, mind if I ask a question?"

"Not at all, miss."

"Do you have any word on someone named Cordas?"

"Yes'm. He's at the Zeppelin Company hotel already. He'll be boarding same time you will, like all the others."

"You seem up to everything, Mr. Pennington. Perhaps you can tell me, if we know so much about Cordas, why we didn't stop him before now or have the authorities in Germany take him into custody."

"No use apprehending the bloke, ma'am, without proof to hold him more than a day or two. His lawyers would have him out in the twitch of a cat's tail."

Indy nodded. "Makes sense."

"Any word," Gale asked their driver, "about someone named Caitlin St. Brendan?"

"I knows who you means, ma'am. Invisible, she is. Like she just dropped off the end of the earth."

"Thank you, Mr. Pennington."

"You're welcome, Miss—Missus Parker."

"I'm not used to Mrs." Gale laughed.

"John, are the Germans always that paranoid about guns aboard their gasbag?" Indy asked.

"Professor, do *you* want any guns aboard a ship that's ten stories high and more than two city blocks long, and filled with hydrogen gas and *blau* fuel?"

"*Blau?*" Indy echoed.

"Yes, sir. Hydrogen gas in seventeen gas cells and *blau* fuel—that's just like propane, sir—to run the Graf's five engines. You'll pardon my saying so, sir, but you two will be riding aboard the biggest bomb ever to take to the skies."

"Terrific," Indy said.

13

Indy emerged from the Zeppelin Company office with a uniformed crewman by his side. "We're in luck," he told Gale. "We've got a few hours before the passengers will be boarding, and the captain has given us permission to take a tour of the Graf."

"Wonderful," she said, eyes bright with anticipation.

"This is Fritz Kasner," Indy introduced the crewman. The German nodded stiffly.

"Come with me, please?" He led them to a service building away from the passenger terminal. Inside, he gestured to a bench. "You will kindly remove anything that is flammable, sir and lady. No matches, lighters, anything like that."

"We have none." Indy spoke for himself and Gale.

"Thank you. Now, these, if you will?" He held out two pairs of soft sneakerlike footwear. "These are special shoes. They do not create static electricity when you move in the Graf. With hydrogen gas as our lifting power, we must take every safety precaution."

They changed their footgear and moments later followed Kasner up a metal ladder to a catwalk, with cables on each side for balance, that led into the underbelly of the zeppelin. They stopped, feeling overwhelmed by the enormous shape stretching far away and above them. Huge rings circled the great ship; girders and cross bracing were everywhere.

"It's like being inside a cathedral," Gale said in awe.

Kasner was obviously pleased with her remark. "Thank you. Our crews feels the same way. To us, the Graf is not merely an airship. She is alive, she breathes, like a great whale of the skies." He pointed above them. "You see those cells? There are seventeen of them to contain the hydrogen, and the *blau* fuel we carry for the five engines that propel us through the sky."

"Mr. Kasner." Gale spoke, her eyes still taking in the huge shape. "How much does all this structure weigh?"

"Would you believe, madam, only thirty-three tons?" Kasner was eager to expound on the vessel of which he was so obviously proud. "The metal is a super-light duralumin alloy. Aluminum and copper and other metals. It is only a fraction of the weight of steel but equally strong."

A breeze flowing over and about the Graf became visible as the rounded flanks of the airship seemed to "breathe." Indy pointed to the undulating sides and upper reaches of the zeppelin. "It moves in a strange manner," he noted. "How thin can the duralumin skin be?"

"Ah, Herr Parker, it is not duralumin. It is cotton. Of course, the Graf is nearly eight hundred feet long and it is covered with cotton. But such superb cotton! Heavy duty, of course, covered again and again with layers of dope and special paint. It is waterproof. It will stand up under fierce winds. We have proved this, of course, by flying through storms."

"From outside," Indy said, "it is silver and it *looks* like metal."

"*Ja, ja,*" Kasner agreed. "But it is silver paint so that it reflects the rays of the sun. You understand the mechanism of heat, sir? Too much sun and the hydrogen expands and we fly higher than the *Kapitän* wishes. So the silver is our balance with the sun."

"I am impressed," Indy told him. "The way it reflects light, well—"

"You are a very good observer, sir," Kasner broke in. "I was one of the men who helped sandpaper the outer surface."

Indy seemed taken aback; he was making every move he could to please their guide. That could open doors later. "You sandpapered the *entire* ship?"

"That is so. No bubbles, no bumps, so our Graf, she slides easily through the skies. Like silk."

Indy turned to look at the heart of the zeppelin. "Are those great bags also cotton?"

Kasner laughed. "That would not be wise, sir," he said quickly. "All these cells—some people call them bags— are made from the intestines of oxen, and are connected to the structure of the Graf. Notice the bracing, Herr Parker, how the full cells push up against it. That is how the Graf lifts, from this internal force."

"You said they're intestines of oxen?" Indy repeated, as if the whole idea was impossible.

"Yes, sir. There are seventeen bags, as you can see, and each bag is lined with the intestinal membranes of fifty thousand oxen—"

Indy stared at the cells. "That means eight hundred and fifty thousand of those animals have gone into these cells?"

"*Ja!* It is a wonderful accomplishment."

"Must have been one grand barbecue," Indy murmured.

"I do not understand, sir."

"Barbecue. Big party with all that meat. Oktoberfest."

"Oh, of course!" Kasner laughed. "Yes, a very *big* party!"

Gale wanted to shift the course of their exchange. "How many engines, Herr Kasner?"

"They are Maybachs, madam. Five with pusher propellers. They are a marvelous design. Each engine in its own gondola, and our crew can service or repair them even in flight."

Kasner stopped as he heard the clear ringing of bells. "I am sorry, sir, madam. That is the call for the passengers to prepare for boarding. We must return to the ground, and I will take you to where the others gather."

They joined the passengers ascending to the gondola that would be home and hearth for the next several days. Indy was less than enthusiastic about floating over a trackless ocean in a huge machine made of the guts of nearly a million oxen, especially when the lifting power for the Graf Zeppelin was explosive gas and its engines ran on equally volatile fuel.

But there was no other way. Cordas would be aboard. No one knew for certain where Caitlin St. Brendan was, but Indy would bet his last dollar she'd be within shouting distance of Cordas, no matter where *he* might go. And the hard reality of the matter was that this was the fastest way across the ocean. Even if they were going to take the insane route of crossing polar regions, where mechanical problems or structural failure could dump them into freezing water or onto remote arctic wastelands.

His distaste eased somewhat as he moved through the long passenger gondola, nearly a hundred feet long and twenty feet from side to side. It banished all comparison with noisy, clattering, smelly, vibrating, uncomfortable airliners. Indy was, despite himself, impressed with the luxurious dining and sitting rooms. There was even a band and a dance floor!

A steward led them to their compartment. "Cabin six, sir, madam," he announced with a formal bow. "Your bags are waiting for you."

Cabin six was a bit austere compared with spacious hotel rooms, yet it was comfortable and utilitarian. Two "bed bunks," each with side rails in case they flew through turbulent weather. Nonskid flooring and a closet. The Graf had ten cabins in all, and at the end of the row of compartments were washrooms and toilets.

"Indy, look here," Gale said. She held up a map of the western hemisphere. "They've marked off our route. This is wonderful!"

They studied the dashed line marking their course. Gale didn't hide her excitement. "Indy, see here? We'll be crossing Denmark, then up to the coast of Finland. I've never seen these places! Look—we'll cross over part of Sweden and Norway—"

"Right to Jan Mayen Island," he noted.

"That'll be for a navigation fix," she remarked. "Look how the path curves a bit to the southwest across the Denmark Strait. We'll be cutting between Iceland and Greenland."

"Think we'll fly over the icecap?" he asked.

"Greenland?" She shook her head. "Oh, no! The icecap is ten thousand feet high. Much too high for the Graf. It will be marvelous to look *up* at an ice shelf, won't it!"

"Uh-huh."

"You don't seem too enthusiastic."

He tapped the chart. "This is Canada," he told her. "When this gasbag is over terra firma again, *then* I'll be enthusiastic. When I can look down and see moose and bears and wolves, I'll be happy. *You* enjoy the whales and the icebergs, okay?"

"You're what you Americans call a party pooper, Indy. You'll love it once we're flying. I promise."

14

It all came off as advertised. Passengers gazing through the observation windows watched hundreds of ground crewmen handling mooring and tow lines, gripping the rails along the hundred-foot gondola both to keep the airship on the ground and move it fully from its hangar.

"It's a three-ring circus," Indy commented to Gale. "But I've got to give those people credit. They're doing everything in lockstep fashion, precise, timed, neat."

"Did you expect anything else from the Teutonic mind?" Gale responded.

"Nope," he admitted. "Even down-to that brass band they've got oom-pah-pahing away out there."

She leaned forward to see better. "We're clear of the hangar," she told Indy. "Now's the time for the bells and whistles."

He raised an eyebrow to peer at her. "Bells and whistles?"

"Listen. You'll hear it as soon as—"

A clanging bell interrupted her and she laughed. "They are *always* reliable, our German friends. They operate this zeppelin just as they do a ship at sea. Bells and whistles instead of electricity, for one. Everybody hears it, knows what it means. And the less electricity they use beneath a hydrogen bag, the better. When they need to talk from the control room to the crew in the hull, they prefer radio to telephone lines."

"Makes sense," he agreed. He looked about him. "That means everything is fully shielded, also."

"Right. Listen? You can hear the engines starting up," she said quickly.

They felt vibrations as the Maybachs started turning their big pusher propellers. Once the engines were running, the vibrations eased and became more of a pleasant humming sound than an annoyance.

The handling crew turned the great bulk of the Graf so that the ship's nose was pointed into the wind. The engines increased in power and the Graf started moving forward slowly. Then, again smoothly and in beautiful coordination, the ground crew released their holds, the engines sped up, and the Graf was free.

"They'll keep enough speed up to move ahead slowly." Gale offered a running commentary to Indy. "Watch the ground. If you don't, you'd never know we were lifting."

He was caught by surprise, much more so than he expected. There was no sensation of rising above the ground. Instead, he seemed to be standing still before the observation window, watching the earth falling away slowly beneath him.

"This is incredible." He shook his head in wonder. "I'm in a ship that's as long as several city blocks through its midsection—and it's streamlined; slim, really—it's ten stories high, and I'm *levitating*."

He remained at the window, none of his wonder diminishing as the throb of the engines sent a tremble through the floor. Buildings became smaller and smaller. Then, two thousand feet up, the Graf finished its climb and headed for Denmark.

Finally Gale tugged at his sleeve. "Indy, you still with us?"

He turned to her, a feeling of immense satisfaction in his face. "For a while, just for a while, mind you, I was able to forget everything except what's happening around me."

"I know what you mean," she said quietly, and he had to remind himself that this woman was a pilot of great skill and experience.

Gale sighed. "Time to come back to the people world," she said slowly, reluctant to leave the vistas before them.

"Time for dinner?"

"That it is, and"—she slipped her arm through his— "dinner aboard the Graf is always formal. Besides, our steward said the Wiener schnitzel is fabulous."

"You're clutching at me like a drowning rat," he observed.

"Of course." She smiled, moving closer. "Don't forget, *Mister* Parker, everyone thinks we're just the most darling couple."

They sat by an observation window in the dining room looking out at the sky and the ocean. Indy was still taken aback by the sight of Gale in her dress. She was beautiful, her red hair agleam as if it had captured sunglow. She watched him quietly, then turned back to toy with her salad. The muted sounds of the other passengers at dinner and the engines' drone seemed to isolate them in their private conversation.

"Any idea yet on Caitlin's whereabouts?" she asked quietly.

Indy shook his head. "I was about to ask you the same question. You and she; the sisterhood. Feeling her presence even when you can't see her. Does that work even here?"

"It does." Her eyes fluttered, then opened fully. "She's with us on this ship. I just don't know where," she added with a touch of frustration.

"As you said, she's a master of disguise," Indy commented. "Then there's Cordas. He's here, too. I haven't seen him yet, but he's on the passenger manifest. What I really want to know is how many bully boys he has with him."

Gale showed surprise. "You don't seem concerned about him."

"I'm not. Not yet, anyway. We can't go anywhere, neither can he, and nobody has guns, including the crew." Indy shrugged. "Stalemate."

"From where I sit, Indy, I don't believe he'd even bother with us." Gale looked about her and gestured. "Neutral territory."

"For us," he murmured. "But Caitlin *will* go after him. So we play the waiting game."

"I know," Gale admitted. "And I hate it. I just want to get this business over with."

Indy didn't seem to be listening. He stared past her to the opposite side of the dining room. He smiled at Gale. "Don't turn your head," he said quietly. "The man sitting directly behind you, across the room. Red hair and a beard. Looks like a Viking."

"You know him?"

"It's Cordas. He smiles at me like he's almost baiting me."

"What!"

"Don't turn around! You'll see him soon enough."

Gale felt her muscles becoming rigid. "Indy." She spoke slowly, forcing words through her teeth, almost hissing at him. "We can't just *sit* here while he's—"

"Think," he ordered her. "What would you do? Confront him? You have proof that he was involved with that horror at the Glen?"

"No, but—"

"Then what would you do here? Accuse him to Captain Eckener? As the master of this vessel, he can throw anybody behind bars. But if he asked you for proof of anything you said, and you couldn't give it, you'd look like a fool."

"Indy, do *you* believe Cordas was involved? At the Glen?"

"Absolutely. Everything points to it. But we'll have to wait until we can get proof, and then try to force his hand. Gale, isn't that what Caitlin told Treadwell? Didn't she say she would not attack without being provoked?"

Gale nodded moodily. "Yes."

"Well, then we just sit and wait it out." He gestured to her meal. "Finish your dinner."

"I'm not hungry," she said, sulking.

"Well, I am," he said, keeping his tone light as he returned to his own dinner. "Tomorrow morning we're going to be expending a lot of energy. You'd be wise to eat."

"Oh? Where are we going?"

"I've been talking to the navigation officer, Karl Jaeger. I want another look inside this barge while we're airborne. Jaeger has already cleared us with Eckener for another tour through the main structure. Apparently Treadwell

carries a lot of weight with the Zeppelin Company." He
gestured with his fork. "And you never know just how important it is to know the local territory."

She showed renewed favor. "*That* sounds like the man
I know."

Morning came with breathtaking beauty, a golden dawn
rushing from the distant horizon. The Graf sailed barely a
thousand feet above the ocean. The water glowed pink and
then bright gold on small shining icebergs.

Indy stood by Gale's side, looking through the windows
of the control car at the surprisingly swift changes of light.
Even here, in the control car, the engines seemed to syn-
chronize with the new day. Their roar had become a rumbling surf of the skies.

Kurt Jaeger leaned forward, his hands resting against
the bracing bars of the broad observation windows. He
turned to Indy and Gale. "It *is* beautiful," he said, speaking their thoughts aloud. "Now, if you are ready for me to
show off our wonderful machine. . . ?"

"Please, lead on," Gale said warmly.

"This control room," Jaeger explained, "is the opera-
tional heart and soul of the Graf. These wheels and
chains"—he pointed to the controls—"enable us to maneuver through the air. In a great machine like this, unlike
a winged craft, every movement must be planned well
ahead of time. Events happen slowly, and the crew *never*
forgets that we fly by the positive buoyancy of our lifting
gas."

He gestured to a hatchway and they followed him into
the chart room, where the crew maintained navigational
checkpoints and weather reports. "Our best navigation,"
Jaeger explained, "is, of course, on a clear night. Because

we control our speed so exactly, and we move slowly, using the stars and planets for celestial navigation is most accurate."

They continued into the radio room, the communications heart of the Graf. On every side bulkheads supported huge radio sets. "Shortwave radio gives the greatest range, especially at night," Jaeger explained. "We communicate mostly by Morse code."

"And the body of the ship," Indy asked, "is your antenna for low-frequency radio?"

"That is so, Herr Parker. Of course, when we pass ships on the surface, we can maintain voice contact. In fact, we have talked with many stations along our route, both ships and the islands over which we flew."

"From here," Indy asked, studying the radios, "could you contact somewhere as distant as Japan?"

Gale tried to hide her surprise at Indy's strange question. But she knew him well enough to realize that if he asked something that odd, there had to be reason for it.

Jaeger looked doubtful. "It depends upon many factors. You are talking about the other side of the world. Conditions would have to be perfect, and at best, such contact would be intermittent."

"Well, let's say you wanted to contact Japan from where we are right now. How would you do it?" Indy pressed.

"The best way would be to send a message to the closest island station, or a ship, and request a relay for us. It could take minutes, perhaps hours. Do you have such a need, Herr Parker? I would be pleased to do what I can for you."

Indy held up a hand. "No, thank you. My curiosity was piqued by one of the passengers. That Japanese man, the one in the ceremonial attire. He might have such a need."

"Yes, of course. That is Toshio Kanamake. I understand he is a high priest. But I know nothing else about him."

A crewman approached. Jaeger excused himself, promising to return shortly. Indy and Gale moved closer to a window, where the engine sounds were louder and they wouldn't be overheard. "Why the questions about the Japanese?" she asked.

"He's a fake. It's a disguise," Indy replied. He leaned to one side as if inspecting a radio. "It's Caitlin," he whispered.

"*What?*"

"Hold it down, carrot top. I've spent time in Japan. Nobody moves so smoothly in all that heavy ceremonial garb. It's her, all right. The hair, skin color, mustache. . . . She's done a great job. I finally figured it out last night."

"But why that outlandish robe!"

"It's perfect. She's wearing the sword beneath all that garb." Indy turned with the approach of Jaeger.

"Herr Parker? Frau Parker? I am ready to continue."

This was their second visit to the capacious hull of the Graf. But now it was an entirely different world. The huge zeppelin was alive as she cruised majestically through the skies, accompanied by the distant throbbing of engines, the always shifting call of the winds, and the gentle rocking motions of the gondola. For the first time, with the light streaming in through the cotton covering, the Graf was a gleaming forest of technology. They could have been within a cathedral, as they had felt before, but just as easily they could have been in an enormous cavern under the earth's surface.

They followed Jaeger along the duralumin catwalks, climbed ladders that soared to the very top of the zeppelin, where hatches opened to the outside of the hull. There, a man on the heaving upper flanks might ride a silvery vessel nearly eight hundred feet long and supported by magic.

Here was the true community of the Graf, the bunk-houses for the crew, storage for cargo, food and water, washrooms and workrooms for the men who ran the machine. A deep humming noise increased as Jaeger led them to the generator room, and finally they stood within a mass of rumbling, whirring machinery. "In here, of course, everything is heavily insulated, static free. We are isolated from the rest of the world." Jaeger smiled. "We call this place the devil's workshop. Whatever happens to the Graf originates from here."

"The heartbeat," Indy said to the German officer.

"Wunderbar!" Jaeger exclaimed. "I could not have said it better."

They continued their journey through spokes and ladders and gangways fanning out in all directions from the central keel. Men a hundred feet above them called out to one another, a singsong of human voices mixing with thrumming power.

Jaeger gestured for them to begin their return to the passenger quarters. "It is time for breakfast"—he smiled—"and our chef will be annoyed with me if I cause you to miss one of his wonderful meals. He prides himself on his skills. Besides, as you enjoy his food you will have a bird's-eye view of the first large icebergs coming into sight."

"And whales?" Gale asked.

Jaeger laughed, the perfect host. "Yes, Frau Parker, I promise you the whales also."

15

To be floating beneath a giant time bomb filled with hydrogen over a bitter-cold sea gnawed at Gale's patience. She stared moodily through an observation window.

"How much longer are you going to sit around like a piece of furniture," she finally exploded, "while that murderer struts about, tipping his hat to us and smiling? He *smiles* at us!"

"And no harm done," Indy said calmly. "It doesn't hurt us—or Caitlin, for that matter."

Gale lapsed again into a brooding silence. Indy held the reins on his own growing impatience. He knew how Gale felt. But timing was everything. This wasn't simply a case of exacting their own punishment against Cordas. Indy knew all too well that revenge for its own sake rarely equaled justice. They couldn't take the law into their own hands. They would be no better than criminals. The more he chewed over the situation, the more he understood Gale's despair and anger.

Gale and Indy were now on the right side of the Graf, facing north. They had passed Denmark, the Baltic Sea,

Finland, and Norway, had crossed Jan Mayen Island, and finally were into their long curving course over the Denmark Strait. Iceland would now be to their left and Greenland to their right as they headed directly for Cape Farewell on the southern tip of Greenland.

Icebergs had appeared, floating islands of gleaming white. Chin cupped in her hands, Gale pushed aside her troubled thoughts as she opened her senses to the wonders below. The sun sat low on the horizon, a pale and distant star. They cruised above an utterly flat sea, without a ripple, except for those caused by great whales spouting thin plumes of white spray that were tossed away by the surface winds.

In the late afternoon Jaeger joined them. He pointed to the north. "Those wispy clouds up there. See them?"

Long streamers and curlicues sailed miles above their own altitude. Gale didn't need explanations from Jaeger. "Mare's tails," she said. "The beginnings of a front. How far from us?"

"Fifty miles, perhaps sixty," he answered, unsmiling. "I do not need to hide from you what is coming, Miss Parker. It is a strong front and it is bearing down on us with great speed."

"We're going to be in it?" Indy asked.

Both Jaeger and Gale nodded. "I am afraid so, sir. Among other things, the thermometer is dropping as fast as the barometer. Sometime during the night"—he shrugged—"we will know more. Unfortunately there are very few stations to the north that can send us information." He stood. "But tonight? A marvelous meal. I invite you to enjoy."

In their cabin Gale offered her own advice to Indy. "Forget the fancy dressing. It's going to get much colder."

"I've noticed," he said.

"And these cabins are *not* heated," she added.

"I know. My goose bumps are sending messages to each other."

"You hungry, Indy?"

He grinned. "Always."

"Let's do it," she said. "Oh, by the way. We'll be seated with an American navy captain. A scientist. He's along to gain some experience on flying in the northern regions."

Indy removed his favorite leather jacket from the closet. "Follow your own advice. Get dressed. Bundle up. I'll wait for you in the lounge."

Dinner was everything that Jaeger had promised, and more. The sense of floating without apparent effort across a great ocean while seated in a lounge with rich draperies and luxurious fittings, sailing along at nearly eighty miles an hour, returned again and again. But now there was an unwelcome visitor. The forward edges of the downrushing front from the northernmost regions stabbed at the Graf Zeppelin, trembling and prodding with fingers of wind. They could feel the airship rising and falling as downdrafts made them feel lighter in their seats. Minutes later, as the Graf sailed beyond a current of downflowing air, the ship returned to its former level.

As if to remedy what the coming hours could bring, the crew went all out to please the passengers. Dinner began with a choice of wines, fresh fruit and sherbet, shrimp and lobster tidbits, pâté de fois gras, sizzling lamp chops, a variety of vegetables and potatoes, smoked salmon, and four brands of caviar. Gleaming Bavarian chinaware graced every table, and no wineglass went empty. The dessert trays offered lush pastries from a dozen different nations.

And the Graf trembled, a bit more, it seemed, with each course.

Indy studied the crew. The quick smiles of the stewards looked forced. An air of tenseness grew stronger. It was, he was pleased to note, not a feeling of fear or apprehension, but a determination to secure the airship against the approaching violence.

Their good weather, that wonderful air ocean that had given them so graceful a passage up to now, departed almost with reluctance. By now the Graf was revealing the pressures that were being applied to its huge shape. Strange slapping sounds could be heard. Captain Richard Pruett, USN, raised his eyes as if seeing off into the distance. "That's the Graf, breathing," he said with an air of comfortable calm immensely pleasing to Indy.

"Of course," Gale said, placing Pruett's words into her own knowledge of the forces of flight. "The outer envelope. If it didn't have elasticity—breathing—it could tear the material. But this way . . ." She left the rest of her sentence unvoiced.

Indy leaned forward. "I'm not as sanguine as Mrs. Parker about something this size, and yet so delicate, standing up well in a real storm. You increase my confidence," he told Pruett.

The navy captain laughed. "Let me put it this way. It could get a bit bouncy before this is over, but this is the best, and the strongest, airship ever built. Fortunately, a dirigible of this design doesn't have to remain in the heart of a storm and fight it out with the elements. Captain Eckener is the most experienced airship officer in the world. We'll move along *with* the winds if he decides that's the best way to minimize air loads on this vessel."

Indy held up his wineglass for a silent toast to the captain and "Mrs. Parker."

After dinner, the Graf trembled in ever-stronger gusts, making complaining sounds as the structure twisted and yielded. They watched a sun diminished in brightness by an ever-darkening haze along the western and northern horizon. The familiar deep red of sunset failed to make its appearance; instead, lowering with extraordinary slowness, the sun changed to a salmon-pink color. The hue, never before seen by most of the passengers, unnerved them more than the wind gusts and thickening clouds.

Passengers left their tables, returning from their cabins with heavy fur coats, hats, boots, and gloves. They became more and more subdued, watching crewmen packing away everything that could be secured. Captain Pruett turned from watching crewmen lashing down loose tables and chairs. "Just like being aboard a ship at sea," he commented. "Battening down the hatches against the oncoming storm."

"That's the first time you've used that word," Indy noted. "Storm, I mean."

"Sorry, it wasn't deliberate. I've been watching the sky for some time. Spoke to that fellow Jaeger earlier. We agree on what's causing this bit of fuss in the atmosphere. Major low-pressure area across northern Canada. Behind it, in the arctic regions, high pressure. You know the old saw. Nature abhors a vacuum. Likewise, a high-pressure area always displaces one of low pressure. So the arctic is pushing downward, and the low that's starting to dump on us is heavy with moisture. Being hammered this way from the north, the air is unstable and begins to pile up in strange masses, and that's the turbulence we're feeling."

As if in response to his words, a heavy gust pounded the

zeppelin. The Graf rolled and twisted, and Captain Pruett grinned. "Just like an old sailing ship creaking and groaning in heavy weather. I sort of like the sound."

"How interesting," Indy said with a straight face. He did *not* like the sound at all. A long time ago, as a youth driving a cranky old Ford on a rutted country road, he'd heard sounds oddly similar to those he was hearing now. The difference was that the Ford was in its final gasps of life. A burst of creaks and groans heralded falling fenders, an erupting radiator, breaking fanbelts, a cracking engine block, and finally a transmission dropping with a great dusty thud. Anything that moved and creaked and groaned at the same time, Indy found less than relaxing.

Within the hour light rain enveloped the zeppelin. They were long done with dinner and had braced themselves in their seats, struggling to keep the contents of coffee cups from splashing about their tables. The icy rain made a hissing sound against the observation windows, and a deeper hoarse echo proceeded from the body of the Graf. "This," Captain Pruett said quietly, leaning closer to Gale and Indy, "I do not like. The temperature is at its worst. That rain we're hearing—it freezes onto the outer surfaces of this ship *after* it strikes. And I'm sure you know what that means."

He sat back, wrapped in his own unfinished warning. Gale understood. Indy didn't yet know, but he was figuring it out rapidly. Icy rain that froze as it reached a surface. Ice forming on the outer cottony skin of the Graf Zeppelin. *Ice equals weight, weight reduces positive buoyancy, and the ocean is already too close for comfort.* . . . As if in response to his conclusion, they all heard the powerful Maybach engines throttling up, the propellers whirling faster to offset the growing weight of ice.

"Things are getting interesting." Captain Pruett grinned as he rose to his feet. "I must see to my cabin. Dinner was most enjoyable, Mr. and Mrs. Parker."

"Toodle-oo," Gale said merrily.

"Aren't we the social set," Indy said with a frown. "You trying to hide your real concerns about this storm?"

She gripped his forearm. "You had bloody well believe it," she whispered.

Indy laughed. "That makes two of us. Do you feel like a coward?"

"*Yes!*" She moved closer to Indy for comfort. "Now, if I were flying a *real* machine, something with wings on it, I'd feel much better, and—"

She stopped short with the approach of Kurt Jaeger, who bowed quickly and then handed a sealed envelope to Indy. "This is for you, Mr. Parker. It just came over the wireless. We were fortunate to receive it now. Communications are going down."

Indy held the envelope. He'd open it in private. "Thank you, Mr. Jaeger."

Again Jaeger bowed. "Hang on tightly, my friends. You will now excuse me, please? Duty calls."

"Of course," Gale said pleasantly.

Jaeger smiled. "I shall see you again when the sun shines," he said, and left.

"Sure hope so," Indy murmured to Gale.

The Graf was now shaking like a wet dog.

16

Indy locked the cabin door behind them. Gale eased onto her bunk, watching him as he opened the wireless message. He studied it for a moment. "The sender is Sherwood," he said.

She showed her surprise. "Sherwood?"

"The forest. Obviously it's from Treadwell. It's difficult to read aloud. Sounds crazy, I mean. You read it."

She waited with impatience, studying the deepening furrows along his forehead. Several times he smiled, frowned, then went poker-faced. Finally he handed the paper to her.

HORSE NOW BEHIND CART. STOP. CONFIRM PYRAMID
CONFIGURATION JOHNNY ROUTES NINETEEN. STOP.
CLOTH YELLOW KINGSLEY SOUTH PRAY ST. JOHN DE-
LIVERANCE DEAD MAN. STOP. OLD GRAY MARE IS
DEAD. STOP. FOLLOW GHOSTS SEMINOLE PURSUIT
TRAIN SIXTEEN EARS MANY. STOP. END.

She held out the paper as if looking at it from a distance might bring clarity to the tangled words. "Indy, I think I could understand Sanskrit easier than this jumble."

He laughed. "Okay, here goes. The first line reads, 'Horse now behind cart. Stop.'"

"Which means?"

"It's telling us that certain events are out of order, we're on a blind trail, and we've got to get back on track."

He stopped as a cabin loudspeaker sputtered to life. "All passengers. All passengers. Captain Eckener requests your presence in the lounge immediately. Please report to the lounge immediately. Thank you."

Indy folded the paper and slipped it into his jacket. "This will have to wait. Let's go."

The loudspeaker message was being repeated in different languages as they left their cabin. Many of the passengers were clearly frightened at the hard blows of wind that rocked the Graf Zeppelin. At times the nose pitched up sharply and the crew fought to bring the great airship back to an even keel. Maintaining balance was difficult for all, and some of the passengers, already suffering the first pangs of airsickness, needed help. People clung to the vertical structural beams of the lounge or sat in chairs secured to the decking, their hands gripping the chair arms for dear life.

Captain Eckener walked slowly to the lounge from the control room. His uniform was perfect, his bearing calm and confident. To their surprise he stood, legs apart, balancing into the rocking and pitching moments of the zeppelin, disdaining any support. A lifetime of sailing ocean storms at sea and flying in balloons and zeppelins had given him an extraordinary sense of balance.

"Ladies, gentlemen, thank you. I will not keep you long.

You are entitled to know just what we face. First, we are in no danger. That is most important for you to understand. The Graf Zeppelin was designed and built to withstand any storm we could foresee. I believe you know that although our metal structure is light in weight, it is as strong as the best steel ever made. Our crew is experienced. But it is likely that when we encounter severe updrafts and downdrafts, this zeppelin will seem to pitch up or down at alarming angles. The steepness of a climb or descent, however, is not at all dangerous. Please consider all I have said. Until further notice, I advise everyone to remain in their cabins, where you will be able better to brace yourselves against any unexpected turbulence. We hope to escape the worst of the storm in just a few hours. Thank you for your attention."

Moments later only three stewards remained, helping passengers back to their cabins. Indy and Gale preceded the group, anxious to return to the coded message from Treadwell.

"We started with the dancing of the runaway horse," Gale said, "right?"

"Almost," Indy corrected. "The precise wording was 'Horse now behind cart.' "

"Sorry. That means we've been barking down the wrong road."

Indy had to laugh. "I believe you mean we've been barking up the wrong tree."

She made a face at him. "Colloquial or colonial expressions leave much to be desired, Professor." She pointed to the paper. "Go on, *please*."

"Okay. The next line reads, 'Confirm pyramid configuration Johnny routes nineteen.' "

"That makes even less sense." Gale frowned, then fell back at a sudden sharp gust. They felt the Graf's nose swinging around in a high rolling circle. Gale rolled her eyes. "Give me *wings*," she murmured. "Sorry, Indy. Please go on."

"Well, Treadwell has confirmed a triangular route over which he believes the gold was shipped. The pyramid is three-sided. Now, 'Johnny routes.' That confirms a route used by the Confederate military forces in the American Civil War. The soldiers of the South were best known as Johnny Rebs."

"What about the word 'nineteen'?"

"Treadwell's counting on us to be able to work that one out. He's basing the number on our working out what went first."

"Indy, you're losing me," she complained.

"Just hang in there, carrot top. Look, the number we all know fits is for the year 1864."

"How do you get that?"

"Add it up. It comes out to nineteen, and we already know the time period of the war. The gold was shipped to the southern states at just about that time."

She shook her head. "Oh. I see. But not," she added hastily, "until you explained it. Now explain that 'cloth yellow' to me."

"That jumps right out at you, Gale. 'Cloth yellow' refers to both cotton *and* gold. The cotton to be shipped to England—which we know the Crown was prepared to escort with warships—and the gold as payment to the Confederacy. Now . . ." He opened a map of northern Florida and spread it out on the lower bunk. " 'Kingsley.' It's a plantation near Franklintown and Little Talbot's Island. We go south from Kingsley and we end up smack in the St. John's

River. Treadwell used the word 'pray' simply to emphasize the 'Saint' in the name of the river."

"All right, so now I'm in this river with you. What good does that do?"

"The key is the next phrase, 'deliverance dead man.' Look here." Indy's finger traced a line east and southeast of Port Jacksonville. "The gold was obviously brought in here. A deep-water port would have been necessary for those ships. From Jacksonville it was to be delivered to Steinhatchee. There, Confederate ships would load it and take it to New Orleans, which at that time was still well out of reach of the Union forces."

"But . . . Steinhatchee isn't even in the message! How could you—"

"You're right," he broke in. "It's not in the message, so clearly we were expected to return to the map. Look at it, Gale. Steinhatchee is on the gulf coast of Florida. It sits right on Dead Man's Bay. That's the key. 'Dead man' tells me the people handling this project were killed, probably in a battle.' "

"And now we get to the horse," she quipped. "That reference in the message. Isn't that from a song?"

"Almost. The song is about the old gray mare, she ain't what she used to be. The message reads, 'The old gray mare is dead.' That's a direct reference to a land convoy. Most transport at that time was by rail or horse-pulled wagons. 'Gray mare' is obviously a reference to a horse or many horses, and 'dead' means that for the most part the people were killed in some kind of battle."

Indy was interrupted by a long trembling wave passing through the Graf Zeppelin. Everything blurred before their eyes as the dirigible shuddered from one end to another, the resonance rushing back and forth from nose to stern. They heard a scream from a nearby cabin.

Gale shrugged. "While we're still airborne, would you like to finish deciphering this code? My curiosity knows no—*oops!*" Another blow nearly toppled her to the deck. She laughed as Indy grabbed her arm to keep her upright.

"You know what battle was what?" she prompted.

"Well, at that time of the war, the Seminole Indians, who had good reason to hate both the Confederate *and* Union forces, were killing off the palefaces—"

"Who?"

"The whites."

"Oh."

"They considered them invaders of their territory, and killed or stole their horses. So the Rebs turned to mules. And a mule train was made up of heavy wagons, each pulled by eight mules. That's pretty good on Treadwell's part."

"Does that mean that the 'sixteen ears' he refers to is a wagon pulled by eight mules? Eight mules, sixteen ears?"

"Right. Now put together the whole sentence. 'Follow ghosts Seminole pursuit train sixteen ears many.' "

"Who are—who *were*—the ghosts?"

"The Seminoles. Indian trackers could move like wraiths through he densest undergrowth. They'd follow the mule trains for miles, unseen and unheard, until they were ready to attack. So Treadwell is telling us to follow the same paths the mule trains and the Indians took."

She studied the map, rocking back and forth with the motions of the zeppelin. "I'm impressed. I really am, Indy. Until now we didn't know where we were going, and now we've got a map, rivers, trails, and historical markers to follow. You're incredible, Professor."

He looked directly at her. "You're pretty great yourself. If you weren't with me, the way this ship is shaking and being slammed around, I'd be scared half to death."

"And you're not because I'm here?"

"You bet. Right now I'm taking my cues from you."

"Great. So long as you're doing that, let's ride out this storm in the lounge. I hate being cooped up in this little cabin while everything is rattling and shaking around me and I can't see very much of what's going on. In the lounge we've got those windows to look through. Besides, if everything falls apart and we go down, I'd like to see it happening so we can do something to protect ourselves."

They spent the next hour hanging on for dear life, pushing themselves into the chairs, bracing their legs against structural posts. The Graf rose and fell in great soaring swoops, following the dictates of the wind that swirled and pounded the giant structure.

"They're doing everything right!" Gale called to Indy.

"You mean the elevator ride?"

"Absolutely. Eckener is working to keep the attitude of the ship level. If he was fighting to hold altitude he'd be overheating the engines and putting some serious stress on the structure. It may feel like a roller coaster, but they're keeping the loads on this ship as low as possible. I'm really impressed with the way they're taking us through this mess."

"What about the ice?" Indy had been staring at torrents of sleet blowing against the observation windows. The temperature in the lounge remained cold, and ice had formed along the window frames. He could only imagine how bad it was on top of the zeppelin.

"It could be a lot worse," Gale told him. "You know what they're trying to do?"

"Sure! Get us out of this storm alive!"

"That, too. But they're chasing levels of warm air. That will melt the ice faster than you realize. And sometimes a difference of just a few hundred feet in altitude can take us out of a freezing level."

Another pressure wave rolled over the Graf. This time the effects were far more frightening. Invisible waves of turbulence, like a pounding surf on a shore, thundered against the Graf, sending spasms through the great ship. Then would come intervals of respite when the rain stopped and, amazingly, the moon shone through. Then it was again swallowed up by the storm. The Graf Zeppelin was a huge living whale of the skies, tossed to and fro, the crew in the control room working constantly to meet and then offset blows of turbulence and to keep the ship level.

Lightning tore through the clouds and rain. Indy stared at the green-and-blue bolts flashing about them. Lightning and hydrogen gas; what a combination! Gale read his expression correctly.

"The lightning's not a problem, Indy."

"Why not?" he demanded.

"The structure is designed to pass the electrical charges right through us without damage. The electricity will flow through the ship from one side to the other and—"

"Look at those blue flames along the windows! That's not something to worry about?"

She followed his gaze. Indy was right to be concerned, but only because of the dancing blue flames and flickering small bolts playing along the window frames. "Static electricity," she explained. "Every now and then the clouds around us are highly charged, and they pass off the charge to us. This ship gathers the static, and finally it builds up to the point where we see it. Indy, I've seen that a hundred times in airplanes! When it builds up high enough, we'll discharge the electrical field away from the zeppelin structure."

"Away from us?" He stared, fascinated, at the miniature electrical storm dancing and sparkling only feet away from him.

"*Away* from us," she emphasized. "In fact, sometimes the discharge is a lightning bolt itself. We've had that in airplanes. An electrical charge builds up and we fly between two clouds, the charges are opposite, and *wham!* We'd discharge the—"

BANG!

Indy froze in his seat. A flicker of pure electricity, then a blue-white ribbon of fire flashed. The blast of thunder followed immediately, booming and echoing about them and then through the body of the zeppelin.

"You didn't have to do *that*," he told her. "A mere explanation would have sufficed."

Gale laughed with delight. "You have a wonderful sense of gallows humor, Indy."

"Thanks." He grimaced as his hearing slowly returned to normal. He turned his head, staring. Gale followed his gaze. They stared at the "Japanese man" in ceremonial attire moving through the lounge, turning neither left nor right, walking purposefully for the hatchway that led to the interior of the airship structure.

Gale grasped Indy's arm. "Indy . . . it's *her*."

"I know," he said quickly, climbing to his feet, grasping the table for support as the zeppelin began another wide swing. "Stay here. I'll see where she's going."

Gale watched Indy exit, the hatchway door closing behind him. She sat nervously until she could wait no longer and went after him. As she reached the hatchway the door opened and he came through.

"She went up a gangway, then started up along a ladder. I've got a funny feeling. Caitlin was moving as though she knew where she was going and was heading toward some*one*."

"And we both know who that someone is," Gale said. "Indy, we've got to go after her. She might need us."

Gale started for the hatchway and Indy grabbed her arm. "The cabin first."

"You're right. Let's go. Indy, please hurry."

In their cabin they opened their luggage. Gale snapped together the interlocking pieces of a small but powerful hunting crossbow with spring-fired arrowhead darts. She slipped a flexible metallic baton into her belt. Indy knew the weapon. With a flick of her wrist it would extend into a steel rod that bent as it was swung, striking its intended target with tremendous force. Indy slipped his whip to his belt, opened the door, and they hurried out.

Moments later they were closing the hatch door behind them. For a moment they stared up at the cathedrallike vessel. The Graf Zeppelin seemed to be writhing in pain, the outer shell pulsating. Thunder boomed and echoed like the continuous crash of giant kettledrums. High above and to the sides floodlights cast eerie lights and shadows.

They moved toward the midsection, climbing steadily, at times gripping stanchions and rails. Several times they froze in position, assailed by great hissing sounds as sheets of loosening ice slid down the sides of the ship to the storm-whipped ocean. Indy could hardly believe the deep groaning booms as duralumin girders and rings bent and flexed. High above them static electricity danced and flickered in ghostly blue light. Indy could taste the sharp ozone in the air. He had never felt so helpless.

"Indy! Hurry! This way!" He saw Gale gripping a girder with one hand, pointing with the other. Lightning flashed, sending a brief but intense glow through the fabric shell.

In that sudden flare of light he glimpsed a tableau that turned his blood as cold as the ice crashing down the sides of the huge airborne cavern.

Three men stood on a catwalk. Lightning reflected from the long gleaming blades they held in their hands.

Facing them, alone, Caitlin St. Brendan had shaken off the heavy, Japanese ceremonial robe and large hat and dark wig.

She was braced, legs wide to counter the shuddering movements of the Graf. A deep red gleam of light came from the great sword Caliburn, withdrawn from its scabbard. On that narrow catwalk her three adversaries would have to face her one at a time. Caitlin had selected the best of all possible places to face Konstantin Cordas.

Indy and Gale climbed faster. The first man before Caitlin lunged, his steel blade stabbing.

Indy watched in disbelief.

Caitlin made no move to defend herself as the man's blade slashed her arm, sending blood spraying from the wound.

17

Indy sucked in air; the sight of steel ripping through Caitlin's arm was almost a physical shock to his own system. Lightning flashed, turning the air about Caitlin into a crimson spray as the glare reflected from the blood that spattered outward.

In almost the same moment, even as his feet propelled him higher toward the catwalk, he understood. Caitlin had explained it days before. No matter how terrible the actions against her or her family, she could not strike the first blow in a confrontation. Caliburn's great powers, the legacy of the fabled Merlin, would come into play only if Caitlin was defending herself.

But now the ancient rules had been observed. Indy hauled himself up by the ladder cables. Caitlin faced three adversaries, each of them a formidable opponent, skilled in the art of killing. He heard Gale racing after him, desperate to reach Caitlin.

But it was not quick enough to prevent another slashing move against her. Indy saw an arm upraised from one of the three men, a glint of reflected light, and a throwing knife.

Indy had seen great swordplay in his time; he had become skilled in fencing. But never had he seen the moves now made by this warrior woman from the deep forests of southern England. Caitlin's moves were subtle; at this distance and in the deep gloom, speared intermittently by lightning flashes and booming thunder, she seemed hardly to be twisting and turning as Indy knew she must to survive the assault against her.

The knife hurtled at Caitlin . . .

Her timing was perfect. She did not flinch left or right; instead, she leaned *toward* the knife flying at her. Caliburn came up and forward in a blade-twisting motion to strike with a sharp ringing cry of metal as it struck the knife and hurled it aside, where it clattered and banged through the zeppelin structure.

One of the three men started a climb up along a steel cable angling from the catwalk to a position well above Caitlin, where he could strike at her out of the reach of Caliburn. As the man struggled along the cable the other two lashed out at Caitlin in an attempt to divide her attention.

To remain where she now stood would be an open invitation to disaster. The last thing the two men expected was for the woman to rush forward directly at them and their weapons.

"Indy—" Gale gasped, but they were still too far away to help. Still climbing, almost to the catwalk, they watched Caitlin rush forward, stop, crouch, and spin with Caliburn singing its deadly song through the air. The sword came up in a slicing thrust from right to left, cutting through the rib cage of her nearest attacker. Slashed nearly in two, he sagged to his knees, his eyes bulging, and then collapsed.

The third man, the one remaining opponent directly before her, struck as quickly, his sword stabbing swiftly. Caitlin's gasp of pain came with a sharp sword point thrusting into her rib cage. By now Indy and Gale were close to her.

"Help her!" Gale shouted. Before Indy could stop her, Gale dashed past Caitlin and dropped low just beyond the slashed and now still body of her first victim. The swordsman, face obscured by a cloth wrapped just beneath his eyes, laughed and brought his sword to the ready. Quickly Gale brought up the small crossbow from beneath her leather jerkin. Just as she placed the barbed bolt into position for firing, a fierce blast of wind rattled the Graf Zeppelin, swerving the airship's nose wildly to one side. Gale instinctively reached one arm out for support. Her small but deadly bolt fell away from her, bounced on the metal catwalk, and dropped away forever into the recesses of the zeppelin.

Gale could not go forward, left or right, and to go back meant getting up and crossing over the body behind her. No time! Steel flashed as her attacker brought his sword down. She knew she must die.

A pistol shot cracked loudly just behind her. A *pistol*? Impossible! No one had a gun aboard this—

She stared, eyes wide, as a long dark shape whistled over her head. Indy! His whip! She just had time to glance upward as the thick leather smacked against the sword blade, tearing it free from her attacker's grip and hurling it far to the side of the catwalk. The whip snapped again, louder this time. Before her the man now without a weapon stared in disbelief as the leather cut through his face as if it were butter. His scream echoed and mixed with thundering blows of the storm still raging against the Graf.

As he fell back, collapsing in pain and shock to the catwalk, Gale remembered the man who had climbed the cable leading well above them. She knelt, this time fitting a bolt snugly within her crossbow. In a single smooth motion, balanced on one knee, she turned with the crossbow raised and cocked to fire. Above her the man, holding to the cable with one hand, held a throwing knife in the other. Gale squeezed the crossbow trigger. The small bolt shot in an upward blur.

The man's eyes bulged as the bolt pierced his throat. He tried to scream but emitted only a strangled, gurgling cry. The throwing knife whirled away to one side, the man clutched his throat, and fell from the cable. Gale watched his body plunging, arms and legs waving about madly, as he dropped against another catwalk, bounced against a girder, spun about like a rag doll, and plunged through the belly fabric of the zeppelin, lost in a blur as he began the long fall to the merciless ocean below.

Indy watched the man he had struck with his whip stagger back, trying to stanch the blood flow from his face with one hand, the other holding the guide cable as he struggled to escape the maddening pain. Indy let him go. He was no danger now. Indy came back quickly to where Gale knelt alongside the bloodied, wounded Caitlin.

"Indy . . ." Gale's voice faltered. "She's hurt, badly."

Indy saw with a glance just how severe the wounds were. And he understood now how Caitlin had survived shots fired directly into her body when the Glen was attacked. Under her outer garments, the covering from the scabbard of Caliburn was already working whatever sorcery Merlin had wrought in the leather. Open wounds were closing before his eyes, blood had dried. Yet she had been struck so severely it would take time for her strength to flow back into her body.

"Caitlin," Indy said to her, studying the glaze in her eyes. That upset him, for it spelled shock that could still overwhelm her. She took several deep shuddering breaths and grasped his arm for support. "I hear you well."

Gale was wrapping the crumpled Japanese robe about Caitlin to keep her warm and cover the terrible wounds and caked blood on her body. "Can you make it to our cabin?" Indy asked.

Caitlin nodded.

"Indy!" exclaimed Gale. "We just can't *send* her there! She needs our help to—"

Indy pointed. Two large men moved menacingly from the stern of the zepplin along the catwalk leading directly to them. He didn't need to say that Caitlin must leave the scene with or without help. She pulled herself to her feet. "I feel stronger," she said, despite what he knew was tearing pain.

"You're in no condition to fight. You need time. Leave *now*," Indy pressed. "Go slowly but carefully. Go to our cabin. *Now*, Caitlin; go."

Strong fingers squeezed his arm. He was surprised by her strength. Most men would have been unconscious from the punishment she'd taken. "Thank you," she said quietly, then started down the ladder, holding carefully to the guide cables as Graf Zeppelin rocked and swayed.

"Indy, three more," Gale warned. She was right. First the two men that he'd seen. Now three others behind them. He knew they couldn't all have come aboard the Graf before departure. Not from Cordas's group, anyway. So Cordas must have members of the crew who would fight for him. That made the situation doubly dangerous; they were experienced in moving around and through the structural maze of the dirigible.

The last thing Indy wanted was a struggle in the territory of his opponents. "You see any weapons?" he asked Gale.

She shook her head. "Indy, I don't understand . . . I mean, the others had swords and throwing knives."

"They were the pros. These are crewmen," Indy said quickly. "It looks like hand-to-hand. You have more of those bolts?"

"Another dozen."

"Load up, lady. The game is about to begin," he said a lot more casually than he felt. Gale had that small but deadly crossbow, he had a whip. It wasn't easy now to figure what these three men coming at them would use. Hand-held knives. As crewmen of the Graf, they could never explain to their superior officers why they were carrying anything with a long blade. Anything that could shoot was out of the question. So they'd come in close, grapple, and go for direct thrusts with knives. Indy looked about him. He wanted to be higher than these menacing figures. A ladder was *almost* in reach and—

There *was* something else. All these three knew about him and Gale was almost certainly restricted to what the passenger manifest read. A zookeeper and a game warden. Easy targets, then. That would be their judgment, and the last thing they'd expect would be innovation and daring.

Well, Jones, he told himself with an inner humorless grin, *guess it's time to be daring. . . .*

He had to get higher. Immediately he lashed out with his whip, curled the end tightly about a ladder rung, and launched himself across the yawning space between the catwalk and the ladder. His left hand grasping a rung, he planted his left foot solidly beneath him just as one attacker lunged toward him, knife in hand. At that moment the man was off balance and Indy snatched the advantage. It was a stupid move on his attacker's part. A hard driving kick to the man's face was all it took. Caught between catwalk and ladder, he was stunned by the blow, his arms flailing for balance. The knife flew from his hand, the man's eyes widened, and his mouth hung agape as he felt only thin air beneath his feet. He fell downward with a long scream, bouncing off girders and through the belly fabric to vanish from sight.

Indy clung tightly to the whip for balance and security. "Gale! Up here!" he shouted. "Come up the ladder *over* me!"

She didn't need a second call. She scrambled up the ladder, reached Indy. He grasped her jacket to help haul her upward. One foot shoving hard against his belt, she pulled on his shoulders, grasped a ladder rung above him—scraping her boot across his face in the process—and climbed quickly to a higher position.

The two remaining men shook their fists helplessly. They spoke quickly to one another, then ran to another ladder farther back in the swaying, rocking zeppelin.

"They're going to climb to the top of this thing," Indy told Gale.

"But why—"

"I don't think it's for sight-seeing," he interrupted. "They can get on top of the hull and work their way forward to the hatchway directly over us. If they do that, we'll be at the bottom of the well and they'll have us right where they want us. Move! Go *up*!"

She nodded, turned, and began another rapid climb up

their ladder, Indy right behind her. She stopped to undo the hatch while he grasped her ankle to give her greater support. As the hatch opened, a blast of icy wind rushed over them.

"I don't like this," she complained to Indy. "We're supposed to walk on top of the ship?"

"*Go!*" he repeated.

"Indy, it's blowing like mad out there . . . and the surface is icy. We—"

He shoved upward on her ankle, explaining as she went through the hatch. "Toward the stern!" he shouted above the wind. "There's a glass cupola there. Jaeger told me about it. He uses it for celestial navigation and it's got grab rails." He reached into his jacket. "Here!" he called out, handing her a rope with snap hooks on each end. "Lock one end to your belt and snap the other one on the guide cable!"

"Got it!" she shouted back.

They they were both atop the zeppelin. The world was mad and beautiful and violent all at the same time. For a long moment they clung to a guide cable running the length of the outer hull. As the nose of the huge airship dipped they felt themselves lifting off their feet. They clung tightly to the rail, their bodies swaying with the motion of the ship, still being hammered by the wind. Beneath their feet the hull was slick with melting ice. Patches of open sky were now showing, through which they saw a brilliant moon and stars. Navigation and work lights along the top of the hull gave them dim but effective illumination. They glanced downward, beyond the ice-glistening hull. Far below, white shadows seemed to be drifting from another dimension, icebergs reflecting moonlight in ghostly form. Specks of white, barely visible, revealed the wind-whipped ocean surface.

"Move!" Indy ordered. "Save the sight-seeing for later!"

Clinging tightly to the cable with her right hand, left hand outward for balance, Gale shuffled and slid toward the stern, working her way to the glass cupola and its beckoning handrails. Indy stayed close behind her, ready to help if she slipped or started to fall. He heard voices behind him. Another crewman had come up swiftly along a ladder and was on the hull, moving toward them, a curved blade visible in one hand, the other gripping the guide cable.

His hand went up and back, and in a single swift motion the knife flashed toward Indy. He tried to twist his body away from the oncoming blade. One foot skidded out beneath him. Instinctively he fought to retain his balance, to keep from losing the security of the rope holding him to the cupola rail.

Fire seared along his ribs beneath his left arm. A cry of pain escaped Indy, but his reaction was as immediate as the sound of pain. The blade had pierced his jacket and shirt and scraped along the skin. His right arm went up and to the side, and the powerful whip cracked with the report of a pistol firing. The lash whipped about the feet of Indy's attacker; Indy yanked back with all his strength.

The man's feet flew sideways from the icy hull; for a moment he kept his handhold on the cable guide, then his own weight and the sudden movement pulled his hand free. With a thin wailing scream, he tumbled down the side of the zeppelin and vanished toward the ocean.

The two men approaching from the opposite side had stopped to see the outcome of the attack by their associate.

Indy prepared himself for their rush, watching for throwing knives or swords.

No blades appeared. The unexpected happened. The second man held to the guide cable by his left hand, then withdrew a revolver from a shoulder holster. Indy stared in dismay. Of course! No passenger could board with a firearm, but a member of the crew? Absolutely.

The man smiled, brought up the weapon slowly and carefully, balancing against the wind and the heaving motions of the zeppelin. Indy felt he was staring all the way down the barrel of the gun. He tried to push Gale behind him. "Get out of there," he snapped. "Quickly! You can make it back to the ladder to—"

"Don't move."

Her words seemed to come from a stranger. "Balance me," she directed Indy. He had no idea of what she was about, but with death staring at them both over the sight on that gun, he didn't bother to reason it out. He grasped her waist, doing his best to keep her still. Moonlight broke as clouds scudded past, and in the silvery light Indy watched Gale staring at the two men. She was pressing her hands against her temples, concentrating fiercely. A low moan, a sound he could barely hear, escaped her.

He turned back to the man about to fire. *He wasn't there.*

An icy mist enveloped the two men, glittering and swirling in a cloud moving with the zeppelin, as though there was no wind, no other movement anywhere. Above the crescendo of engines, the groaning of the ship, the wind everywhere else, Indy heard an eerie tinkling sound, as if thousands of pieces of crystal shimmered in a chandelier. *The sound of things within the glittering mist turning to ice . . .*

He'd heard that sound before on an expedition north of Finland in bitter winter. Cold fell upon them within an arctic blast. Cold so intense and swift that ice crystals formed in the air and rained down like glass snowflakes.

Yet . . . he felt none of the cold! Through brief breaks in the mist he saw the faces of the two men contorted in fear and pain as their skin froze; their limbs seemed encased in huge blocks of ice. But this was impossible!

He turned back to Gale. Her body trembled with some unknown effort; the knuckles of her hands ground into her temples. So great was her concentration she would have fallen were he not holding her upright.

He heard a strangled cry of terror, choked off before it could be completed. One of the two men emerged from the icy mist, his body frozen and stiff, to begin the long slide to death down the side of the zeppelin. Indy looked quickly at Gale, then back to the second man, the one with the gun. What had been black was now ice-covered. The gun fell from his hand, bounced off the catwalk, fell from sight. Moments later, frozen as stiffly as if he had been in a bath of super-cold liquid nitrogen, their attacker began that long drop from which there could be no return.

Gale's legs, trembling, gave way. Indy held her as close as he could in the wind and swaying of the zeppelin.

"J-just hold me . . . cold . . . so cold," she said, huddling against him, shivering.

They were alone on top of a floating world, racing away from the storm front, the moon shining cold and amazingly clear.

Indy held Gale to ease her trembling. Finally he understood what had happened. Gale Parker, soul sister to Caitlin St. Brendan, raised amid sorcery and the power of the witches' clan that had endured more than a thousand years.

"You never told me," he said to Gale, "that you could do something like this."

She looked up, still shivering. She managed a weak, tired smile.

"You never asked me."

18

Gale tended to Caitlin's wounds with the efficiency and knowledge of an experienced nurse. Indy stood and watched, helping whenever Gale requested assistance. Anyone who had spent the time, as Indy had, in distant lands, burrowing deep underground, hacking through jungles, suffering cuts, bruises, bites, stings, slashes, scrapes, torn muscles, and broken bones, could survive without the presence of a doctor. To say nothing, Indy reminded himself, of all the men with him who'd been shot, stabbed, struck with shrapnel, or gassed.

Caitlin suffered, but with gritted teeth and in silence. Indy helped remove her outer garments, then stepped back in the cabin, sitting on the opposite bunk, as Gale carefully, almost reverently, removed the golden leathery tunic. Then, as gently as she could, but with hand pressure she knew must hurt Caitlin terribly, she pressed parts of the tunic against the worst wounds.

Of all the wonders Indy had seen in his travels throughout the world, none matched this. The worst bleeding had already stopped from the pressure of wearing the garment woven from the scabbard of Caliburn. Now the slash wounds closed and began to seal before Indy's eyes. Gale washed away the caked blood, revealing purple and dark bruises about each wound, all the clearer now for him to witness the sorcery of Merlin.

"How was the scabbard turned into her tunic?" Indy asked finally. He'd been told before; he wanted to hear it again.

"Kerrie, her father, knew the ancient secrets," Gale replied. "They placed the scabbard in a caldron containing oil and other liquids to loosen the fastenings from the metal beneath. This way the leather, with its gold threads, unraveled slowly, without tearing. Then her mother, with several of the elders assisting, worked the strips on an ancient loom. That's about the only way I can describe it; everything had to be done by touch and feel. Then they stitched the strips together with more gold thread. That formed the tunic perfectly to Caitlin's size and shape, and the additional gold threads gave it great strength."

Indy nodded. "I know she's in shock. Can she hear, can she understand us now?"

Caitlin's voice came whispered but strong. "Yes."

"I need to say some things to you, Caitlin. I'm asking you not to argue with me," Indy told her. "This isn't a matter of right or wrong, but of experience."

"I will listen."

"No matter what happens in the next day, or the next few days," Indy began, "you've got to stay out of it."

Caitlin struggled to raise herself up on one elbow. Her look at Indy was dark and brooding. Through pain-filled eyes she managed to speak. "That is not for you to decide," she said in a tone that would not brook argument.

Indy didn't take the hint, strong as it was. "It *is* for me to decide," he snapped. "Listen well to me, Caitlin." He was amazed with himself for slipping into her tone. "The authority to decide isn't a matter of who's in charge about anything," he said sternly. "Both Gale and I have placed our lives on the line for you. Several times we've been a hairsbreadth away from being killed." He gestured to forestall comment. "No one is asking you for gratitude. Gale, as she's told me and I've seen, is your soul sister. You two have been bonded through your lives."

He took a deep breath as he looked down on Caitlin, doing her best to conceal the pain still coursing through her body. "But *I'm* not part of the family tree, so to speak. I'm here more because I believe in you, and Gale, than for any other reason. I don't give a hang about gold. Ancient coins, yes. Historical artifacts, yes. But even those are hardly worth skidding around the top of this blasted oversized hydrogen bag in an ice storm over the ocean! Especially when people are doing their best to slice us into strips. Okay, that's behind us. For the moment, anyway. But if someone comes after us now, you, lady, are not strong enough yet to defend yourself, and you sure as thunder can't protect *us.* It's the other way around right now. In short, when you're hurt, we look after you. When we're cut down and hurt, you look after us."

He paused, knowing he was getting in over his head. "Caitlin, the long and short of it is that you can still die. *You can be killed.*" He reached down to lift the edge of the tunic Gale was still pressing against Caitlin's wounds.

"Not even this great magic can save you if you take a bullet through the heart, or the brain. Magic, like everything else, has its limitations. Confound it, Caitlin, we're in this together. I'm on *your* side. But avoiding reality won't do a thing for any of us."

Caitlin motioned for Gale to help her sit up. She gritted her teeth, holding back any sounds to indicate the severe pain she still suffered. She closed her eyes and took long, deep breaths to clear her mind. When she opened her eyes again, they were clear and sharp.

"If everything you say is true," she said at last to Indy, "then what Merlin hath wrought shall be put to its greatest test. If I fall, if I succumb, another will take up my sword and my banner." She looked to Gale. No words were needed to tell Indy that Gale would step forward to assume Caitlin's role were that necessary.

"The death of my mother," Caitlin continued, softly now, "must be put to right. No matter how many others have been defeated, no matter how many have gone to the permanent terrible darkness beyond, Cordas must die. And not until that moment will my mother's spirit find peace, and the long rest awaiting her."

Indy stared at her for a long time. He made his decision. This was not the moment for arguing. Caitlin must sleep. Her wounds were far more serious than she realized. Even with all the sorcery of past ages, her body required time to heal.

Caitlin also recognized this. Indy's words, and what she read in his eyes, ended all resistance. "Gale, you know what I need," she said suddenly.

Gale nodded, rose to her feet. "I'll be right back," she told Indy. She left the cabin. Less than five minutes later she returned, holding within her jacket a large vial containing a liquid unknown to Indy. Gale held the vial for her friend. Caitlin drank slowly but emptied half of it. She nodded to Gale, leaned back, and her eyes closed.

Indy watched her breathing, deep and steady. "Is she asleep?" he asked Gale.

"More than sleep. Yes, she sleeps, but she is also in a

trance. The liquid will permit her body to heal faster. Don't be concerned with our voices. She cannot hear us and," Gale said somberly, "we still have much to talk about."

Slowed by the storm, more than a hundred and seventy miles off course, the Graf Zeppelin made a painful return to its former steady flight. The tears in the cotton fabric of the hull raised no alarm. The Graf had been in worse shape from wind damage before, when one entire rudder was torn open, the duralumin twisted, the cotton cover flapping like a rag. Yet even that damage had been repaired by the crew.

Indy was far more concerned about the loss of men from the zeppelin. No one among the crew, especially its officers, seemed to have noticed anything unusual. Which was patent nonsense. Whoever kept the records of the crew and worked those men knew all too well that men had been lost overboard. There were still several men with terrible wounds aboard the airship, but Indy knew this could be explained away by the storm, throwing men against metal, causing them to fall and smash into equipment. And whoever knew what was going on was managing very well to keep the injured out of sight—not only from the passengers, but from Captain Eckener.

A visit from Kurt Jaeger, the ship's navigator, settled most of Indy's questions. "I do not know if you are aware that during the storm last night," he began, "we suffered both illness and injury to several of our passengers."

Jaeger hadn't come to their cabin for chitchat or a run-down on who threw up or twisted an ankle. "I must ask your confidence on another matter," he said, his words uttered slowly and carefully. "We have kept this information from the passengers, as you will understand in a moment."

Indy and Gale glanced at one another, a silent agreement to go along with whatever this man was bringing them. Jaeger was stepping far beyond the bounds of his job.

"During the night we sustained rather serious damage to some of the structural elements of the Graf," Jaeger went on. "It was a most tragic event. Several of our crew fell from their work positions within the hull. Some were caught by catwalks and beams, but several men also fell completely through the lower outer covering of the zeppelin. They were lost, of course, swallowed up by the ocean."

Jaeger went silent, but Indy was immediately aware of the import of his message, and grateful for his careful phrasing of it. Indy wondered who the devil he was working for; most certainly it was not only the Zeppelin Company. For Jaeger, without specifically saying so, had just told Indy and Gale that officially, there had been no fighting within the zeppelin the previous night, that no one had battled anyone else, that everyone involved would remain nameless. And most important of all, the matter would not only be dropped from the airship's records, but what had taken place would never be noted in the logs.

"Herr Jaeger," Gale began suddenly, "do you know—"

Indy moved swiftly, clamping a hand across Gale's mouth. She resisted by reflex, but then went silent and unmoving as she felt a steady, deliberate pressure from Indy's hand. Slowly he removed his hand. Gale offered him a slight nod; she would go along with whatever it was he wanted.

"Herr Jaeger, thank you for your consideration. It is . . ." Indy paused, searching for the proper words. "It is gratifying to know that the situation, and the records, are indeed in such capable hands."

Jaeger offered a brief smile, aware that Indy had caught

all his meaning. He bowed slightly. "Thank you, Mr. Parker. It is my fervent hope that the remainder of this flight
will go smoothly for you. In perhaps thirty-six hours we
will be at Lakehurst. I have sent a wireless ahead. You will
be greeted upon landing and your transport will be waiting
for you. I bid you pleasant voyage." He turned, closing the
door quietly behind him as he departed.

Gale stared at the closed door. She shook her head slowly
before turning back to Indy. "Pinch me, I think," she whispered. "Do I get the idea that our peerless navigator does
more than steer this gasbag about the skies?"

Indy leaned back against the cabin bulkhead. "How
might Merlin say it?" he murmured. He smiled at Gale.
"Methinks the gentlemen doth tarry on both sides of the
brook."

Gale grimaced. "Indy, that's terrible. Talk American.
Merlin would flip-flop in his grave if he could hear you."

"With all due respect, I believe he can," Indy said softly.
"However, the point you're chasing . . . Either Herr Jaeger
is on our side, and we won't say any more than that, or
he's working for both sides. I wager he's no stranger to a
certain gentleman by the name of Thomas. And that *is*
enough." He tapped the bulkhead. "Ears grow in the
strangest places. We'll play it safe and drop it."

"The, ah, visitor mentioned thirty-six hours to go. By
then, Caitlin should be fully recovered."

Indy blinked. "That's incredible. Are you sure?"

"I've seen it before."

"What happened?"

"She has an affinity for animals. Almost as if they're in
communication with one another," Gale said, her voice
showing excitement at the memory. "One day she was in

the deep woods, her hunting bow on her body, plenty of arrows in the quiver. A bear rushed her from thick undercover. That alone is unusual. Normally there's a warning of some kind. Bears are like that."

"Was this one wounded?"

"That was what we thought at first, but—" Gale shook her head. "Infected tooth. The animal must have been crazy with pain. It rushed her and caught her unawares. Before she could defend herself, she was slashed open by its claws. It tried to sink its teeth in her throat, but by then she had her hunting knife, the one she always carries, in one hand. The bear mauled her and got a good grip on her shoulder instead of her neck. She knew the knife couldn't kill the bear before it killed her. Caitlin never loses control. She brought up the knife and slashed the animal across its eyes. It dropped her immediately, pawing wildly at its eyes."

"Which let Caitlin get away," Indy offered.

"No. She wouldn't leave the animal like that. Bad as she was bleeding, and hurt, she went after the bear. Not with the knife, but she managed to get an arrow strung, and her aim was true. Right into the heart. At that close range the arrow had great penetrating power. What also saved her was the roaring of the bear as it tried to kill her. The sound carried, men came running. They found the bear dead and Caitlin, unconscious and near death herself, atop the animal. Wisely, they stopped the bleeding, kept her comfortable, and a man ran back to the Glen to get her father and the tunic made from the scabbard. It was touch and go, Indy. For a while we thought we'd lost her. Three days later Caitlin was up and about. And that bear tore her up a lot worse than what she's taken here."

Indy shook his head. "I'm ready to believe just about anything where she's concerned." He turned to go through some papers. "Anyway, the time won't be wasted. We do not leave Caitlin alone, not for a moment. I'll have meals brought to the cabin. When we leave here, it will be with the other passengers."

"Do we dress her again in that Japanese outfit?"

"Yes. Let the other people see the same person leaving the ship that they saw board."

Gale nodded. "Mind some questions?"

"Ask away."

"From everything you said before, Indy, you know, going over the maps, and that coded telegram, well, I'm still confused about how certain you are about where the gold is."

"You're not alone, Gale." He laid out a map for her to study. "We're playing a game of blindman's buff. A jigsaw puzzle with broken and missing pieces. The best we can count on is that the gold was transported between Jacksonville and Steinhatchee. From that point on it is simply"—Indy shrugged with resignation—"lost."

"But what about the railroad? The tracks should let us follow the path that the gold followed." She looked at his face. No agreement there, she saw.

"Nice try, Gale. If we were working with should-be's you'd be right. Unfortunately, the railroad line, here"—he tapped the paper—"and here, and the points in between, is gone. After the war the South needed metals desperately. So these rail tracks, like many others, were torn up and sent to the ironworks for reprocessing into tools and other items. This is semitropical country. It didn't take long, what with heavy rains, horses, and heavy undergrowth, to destroy any sign of the old railbeds."

"And I suppose the roads used by the mule trains didn't fare any better," Gale said.

Indy nodded. "Dead ends in all directions. *But*," he emphasized, "now we get down to guesstimates and experience in searching out other ancient sites, heavily traveled a lot earlier than this area. There are other clues and we'll be falling all over them."

"Fascinating," she said, not quite believing Indy. She had visions of thick undergrowth, snakes, alligators, and other creatures in an abandoned countryside.

"My opinion," Indy went on slowly, "is that the gold was lost, abandoned, or concealed somewhere between the Gulf and the Atlantic coastlines. Either on or near the site of one of the last great battles fought in that area. That means they've left clues almost everywhere."

"And you talk about me and Caitlin using magic?" She leaned back and sighed. "You run around in riddles that would make even Merlin envious."

Indy patted her hand. "It's all in knowing where to look and what to look for."

"What isn't?"

"Blast it, Gale, you're not thinking. Or more to the point, you're thinking in contemporary terms. Where we are going is like traveling down a time tunnel."

He seemed so perturbed she paid him her full interest. "Try to imagine the war fought here. It was more than seventy years ago. No tanks, no modern artillery, no communications lines, no airplanes, no bombs from the sky. Just rough, dirty, wearying slogging, a savagery of wounds and a killing ground that turned the earth to blood. Now concentrate on the weaponry and the debris it leaves behind. *That's* how we'll find the greatest battles. By what they've left behind."

"Indy, I'm trying, but I don't understand what—"

"Cannonballs, for one. Archaic, heavy, monstrous pieces

of artillery. Machines of war so massive and heavy they had to be abandoned. The horses and mules, for the most part, gone. Killed, eaten, or run away. But the wagons, well, the wood is likely all gone by now. Insects, sun, rain, that sort of thing. But we'll look for the iron that was placed around the wooden wheels."

"Iron wheels?"

"Right. Iron was secured around the heavy wooden wheels, and the iron was then shrunk to produce an extremely strong wheel. Most of that will be rusted, but with so many wagons abandoned in the field, well, there should be signs."

"Indy, from what you're saying, hasn't this occurred to other people?" Gale queried. "I mean, why wouldn't they have found just the things you're describing?"

"Oh, they have. But they've all been looking in the wrong places. I think, I just *think*," he said with a thin and enigmatic smile, "I know where we've got to do our search."

Gale mulled over his words. "What about Cordas? Does he have the same information?"

Indy shrugged. "I don't know. But I hope so. Besides, he'll be looking over his shoulder everywhere he goes, knowing that Caitlin will be dogging his every step. And Cordas has an Achilles heel."

"Which is?"

"Try and think like him. If he were pursuing a group of heavily armed men, professional killers, would he do it alone? No way!" Indy laughed. "He's got to figure that Caitlin will have accomplices. Plenty of them and all spoiling for a showdown."

"And what she has," Gale said moodily, "is you and me."

"Which might be enough," Indy concluded.

19

The Graf Zeppelin cruised slowly beyond the eastern borders of New York City, over Nassau County on Long Island. Captain Eckener had planned his arrival with great skill, swinging the great dirigible southward over Long Island Sound. He had urged his passengers to move to the right side of the main lounge, where they had an extraordinary view of the great skyscrapers of New York. The morning broke with splendid clarity, a sky washed clean by an evening rain shower and light wind. The sun rose behind the left flank of the Graf to flood the world with crystalline golden light.

Of a sudden, Manhattan came ablaze with the glory of that sun splashing and reflecting brilliantly from thousands of windows. What had been a city of steel and concrete became a magic wonderland of golden light. Even the drab concrete flanks of the towering structures glowed. Then the Graf was droning along the south-shore beaches of Long Island, turning slowly to cross the huge bay area and head for its final destination of Lakehurst in New Jersey.

Lower Manhattan now passed to the right flank of the dirigible. The Hudson River stretched far out of sight to the north, and below the Graf, the port area of New York went wild with welcoming horns, whistles, all heard clearly at the Graf's height of barely a thousand feet. Fireboats in the bay sent up huge plumes of sparkling water; ocean liners boomed with their deep bass foghorns. Newsreel airplanes and curious sightseers in their private planes buzzed about the Graf like noisy but friendly little hornets, pilots and passengers waving at the faces visible in the lounge windows and control car of the German airship.

The Graf settled gently toward the long flat grounds of the naval air station. Bringing the huge mass down proved a delicate balancing affair of engines revving up and idling, water ballast being dumped when descent became too rapid. Mooring and grab lines tumbled like pencil-thin snakes from the airship; far below, men rushed to grasp the lines and pull them taut, their combined weight providing the ship with a solid balancing keel and continued slow loss of buoyancy. A heavy truck waited in position as hundreds of men walked forward, lines over their shoulders like Russian peasants hauling barges on the Volga River. Slowly and deliberately the Graf moved toward the mooring mast, then her nose was eased with precision into the locking cage. The Graf Zeppelin was down, the journey completed. A brass band played with enthusiasm, thousands of awed spectators cheered, and motorists blared their horns. It seemed like a holiday to mark the arrival of the amazing queen of the skies.

When the Graf finally emptied, there was no Japanese passenger to be seen. Instead, newsreel cameramen recorded Mr. and Mrs. Henry Parker leading a very old bearded gentleman, quite ill and supported by the Parkers, to a waiting limousine.

In the limo, a fretful and agitated Caitlin glared at Indy. "Get this bloody sheep mat off my face!"

Indy grinned. "Right away, Grandpa."

Indy leaned back in the thickly padded seat of the limousine, still chuckling at Caitlin's irritation with the scratchy false beard, thick eyebrows, and detestably long wig. She cared even less for the large dark glasses she wore, to say nothing of the thick padding about her body and the oversized trousers she'd donned only after a mixture of cajoling and growing impatience from both Indy and Gale.

"They'll be looking for a Japanese!" Indy said heatedly. "The last thing we want is for you to walk out in all your Oriental splendor, and—"

"You told us this Jaeger fellow was helping us," Caitlin protested angrily.

"Sure," Indy told her, "but I also cautioned Gale that Jaeger could be playing both sides of the fence."

"He said brook, actually," Gale quipped.

"Tell me what you mean," Caitlin insisted.

"He's being paid to do his job as a navigator for a German zeppelin. So that makes him a skilled, valuable, and likely very patriotic German," Indy answered. "But we also know that he's in league with Treadwell. But why? Is he really working faithfully for jolly old England? We don't know, which means we have no way of knowing if he'll sell out to the highest bidder. Most likely he's being paid by Treadwell's people, with the added fillip that if he rats on us—"

Caitlin raised an eyebrow. "Rats?"

"If he squeals. If he lets the Cordas people know who

you really are. If he does the job for Treadwell but is also being paid by Cordas. They're not that certain it was you in that donnybrook aboard the Graf. There are still plenty of questions. So *I'm* not taking any chances, and that's why an old sick man, um, rather portly, too, came off the Graf with us."

"Could Cordas's people be following us?" Gale asked.

"I doubt it," Indy said. "First of all, three identical limos, all with the same license number as the one we're in, left Lakehurst at the same time. No way for anyone following to know who's in what. Second, why would he bother? We don't *know* what Cordas is thinking, so that's why we're going with this mystery-man routine."

"I do not know where we are going," Caitlin said finally, "but remaining here, somewhere in New York, is not what I want to be doing."

"I'm aware of that," Indy told her quickly. "It won't be for long. We're on our way to some very well-concealed quarters in the heart of Manhattan. We'll be there only a day or two."

"You seem willing to forget Cordas and what he might be doing," Caitlin said icily. "Or where he is going. I could lose track of him. I see no sense in staying here."

"We won't be losing track of him," Indy assured her. "Treadwell has been working with the American authorities from the beginning. There's full cooperation both ways. Our people—the Americans—have been sticking like glue to Cordas's tail ever since he climbed down the steps of that gasbag we rode here from Germany. And they'll stay with him."

Indy shifted in his seat. "Anytime we want to know where Cordas is, we can find out. The point is, Caitlin, you won't accomplish anything by trying to track him. First, that could take days. He could lay in a bunch of false leads that would have you going in circles. And if he does catch on to your shadowing him—"

"Do you mean my trailing him?" Caitlin broke in.

"Sorry. Brutish colonial phrases and all that," Indy told her. "Yes, if he knows you're just a few steps behind him, it's a simple trick to lay in some nasty traps for you. You're in territory you don't know."

"He's right, Caitlin," Gale added. "You've never been in the United States before, have you?"

Caitlin shook her head.

"Then you'd stick out like a sore thumb," Indy went on. "Not because you're British, but because you sound unmistakably British. You'd be on your way to where the clock acts like it stopped a hundred years ago, and you'd be like red flares on a dark night. Which only makes you extremely vulnerable."

Caitlin had never been one for long conversation. "We'll be here no more than two days?"

"Yes."

"Then we're going after Cordas?"

"Yes."

"How long is the train trip from here to this place in Florida where Cordas is going?"

"At least two days. It's a rotten ride. I don't recommend it."

"Then how—"

"We make like a bird when it's time to go, Caitlin. And that way we catch up to Cordas a lot faster than he'd ever dream possible."

For the next thirty-six hours the threesome of Indy, Gale, and Caitlin "vanished." They drove to one of Indy's favor-

ite haunts in New York; he was both a professional associate and close friend of the curator and staff of the American Museum of Natural History, on the west side of
Central Park in mid-Manhattan. The museum kept a
sweeping underground chamber of private apartments and
conference rooms for its guests from throughout the
world. Privacy was assured in these secure chambers. Indy
fired off a cable with the code name of Shiloh to Thomas
Treadwell to "get things rolling."

Within an hour Indy was notified by the curator's office
that several men were being brought down to their underground apartment. If they were "sent through" that
quickly, it meant they were part of the combined operation
of the American and British governments.

Indy almost laughed aloud when two men, carrying
briefcases and large leather bags, entered their apartment.
He had always wondered why undercover or secret-
service agents could be spotted a half mile down any road.
Dark gray suits, gleaming shoes, impeccable shirts and
ties, and as clean-cut as a safety-razor. He pushed aside
the unimportant judgment; what these people brought and
what they had to say was what counted.

"Fred Carruthers, sir," said the first agent, extending his
hand. "This is my partner, Ron Judson." The second man
shook hands with Indy, who introduced the two women.
Caitlin leaned back on the couch like a great cat, her eyes
following every move. Indy had to force back a laugh. Caitlin was making the two federal agents uncomfortable with
her air of total self-confidence, which seemed to tell other
people how really insignificant they were.

Indy pushed aside these thoughts to concentrate on the
serious matters at hand. He nodded to Gale and a notepad

was in her hands immediately. She flipped open the cover and spoke two words. "Identification papers?"

Carruthers recognized impatience when it stared him in the face, and to his credit, he put aside whatever speeches he might have been instructed to present. He opened his briefcase and withdrew a sheaf of documents.

"You, sir," he said to Indy, "are once again Professor Henry Jones. Whoever was Henry Parker no longer exists with customs or immigration. Madam, you are once again *Miss* Gale Parker."

"The marriage was amusing while it lasted," she teased Indy.

Carruthers looked to Caitlin. "And you, madam, are no longer Japanese. That was an excellent performance on your part, Miss St. Brendan. I have here your British passport and whatever American documents you will need while you are in this country." He looked from one to the other. "And for the record, you all work for the American Museum of Natural History, and you are doing research for a new exhibit."

"Well done," Indy told Carruthers.

"Weapons?" Gale asked.

Judson opened one of the leather bags. Carruthers turned to the weapons Judson was placing on a table. He turned again and handed Indy a burnished, heavy revolver. "One of your specific choices, I believe. A Webley, and of four-fifty-five caliber. One hundred rounds of ammunition go with the piece, more if you desire."

Indy hefted the Webley. It was like handling an old friend. He examined the weapon closely. "This," he said, looking up at the two men, "is the finest Webley I have ever had in my hands."

"It is yours to keep," Carruthers told him. "Along with

this particular document." He handed Indy a federal permit to carry the Webley. "There is a separate permit for Miss Parker and Miss St. Brendan."

"Don't stop now," Indy urged. "You're doing great."

"Thank you, sir." Another handgun appeared. "Since you had to leave this before boarding that German airship . . ." Carruthers said smoothly as he handed Indy a blue-barreled Schmeiser .32-caliber, flat automatic.

Judson held up two rifles with telescopic sights. "Excellent hunting rifles," he said.

Indy studied the rifles from halfway across the room. "British make, point-three-oh-three, six-power sights, I'd say from here. Magazines?"

"Excellent call, sir," Judson said. "A three-oh-three it is. You have your choice of eight rounds as standard in a magazine, as well as a special magazine that will hold twenty."

Next came a repeater pump shotgun for close-in work. Judson then displayed a half-dozen round metal balls. "Grenades," he explained.

"Indy!" This sharp exclamation came from Gale. "What in the world are we going to do with hand grenades? We're not going off to war!"

"Oh, but we are," Indy said quietly. "Besides, those aren't for killing."

Both women leaned forward, curiosity showing in every look and movement.

Judson picked up Indy's remark. "That's right, ma'am. These are flash grenades. They'll make a healthy racket, but there's no shrapnel or killing metal. The grenade jacket is very thin and it vaporizes when the charge detonates."

"Intended to temporarily blind people who are after us

and have the upper hand," Indy said, as if he handled these explosive charges every day in the week. "I carried several of these in Africa. One day, when I was in the Congo doing my best not to upset the local wildlife, a leopard took an immediate dislike to my presence. He charged, and I tossed one of these little beauties at him. Covered my eyes, but the big cat didn't know about that. When the grenade went off, it blinded the animal. He got his sight back about twenty minutes later, but by that time I was gone. Besides, he was eager to go in the opposite direction."

"Do you have what we requested?" Caitlin asked.

"We certainly do, ma'am," Judson replied, opening the second leather case. "The finest, strongest hunting bows made in this country. You'll notice the arrowheads are what you asked for. Three-pronged, notched like a shark's tooth."

Caitlin and Gale were on their feet at once, testing the bows, pulling them back for the heft and feel. "Ma'am, if you don't mind my saying so," Judson said to Caitlin, "I am greatly surprised at what you're doing." Caitlin held his gaze, waiting. "I'm pretty good with the bow myself. But you brought that thing into position faster than I've ever seen anyone before."

"She's also an Annie Oakley with it," Indy offered.

"A who?" Caitlin asked.

"A famous American marksman," Indy answered.

"Thank you for the compliment," Caitlin replied.

Indy turned to the two agents. "Was there something said about a vehicle?"

Carruthers nodded. "Yes, sir," he said brightly. "It will be waiting for you on the northwest shoreline of Port Jacksonville. It's an army field truck, civilian license plates. The registration and other papers are all properly made out and waiting in the truck for you. It has a four-wheel drive that should get you through anything except swamp. It will take that pine-barren country real well."

Gale glanced again at her notebook. "Radio?"

"In the truck, ma'am. The frequency is preset to link up with our field outposts. Oh, yes, there are also emergency food rations and drinking water, extra fuel cans, first-aid kit. Just about anything we figured you might need."

"There is one more thing, please." They turned to Caitlin. "I am in need of several batteries, if you would be so kind."

Judson had a notepad in his hand. "What kind, miss?"

"I require a stand-up one-volt battery," Caitlin said. "It is an acid-type battery."

"No problem, miss. How many?" Carruthers asked.

"Four, please. But let me be more specific."

"Of course."

"The batteries, for my purposes, must be no greater than three inches in diameter and nine inches tall."

"Excuse me, ma'am," Judson broke in, "but I'm pretty sure I know precisely what you want. Would those batteries have two screw terminals at the top?"

"Why, yes."

"The screw terminal at dead center is the positive, and the second one, at the edge, is a negative. I sure know them, ma'am. The outside casing is a lead-zinc combination, and the carbon rod is the center post, just about three quarters of an inch in diameter. And between the two, there's a mixture of what we call gunk. That's what becomes the acid-based electrolyte."

Everyone in the room was staring at Judson. Finally Carruthers found his voice. "How in thunder do you know all that, and how can you be so sure that this is what Miss St. Brendan needs."

"But he is right!" Caitlin exclaimed. "I am as surprised as anyone. Tell me, sir, how did you know all this?"

"Well, shucks, ma'am, there's no real mystery to it," Judson explained. "You see, my son flies radio-controlled model airplanes. Small gasoline engines. Powerful little things. And this battery you want is just what *we* use to start those engines, see?"

Caitlin nodded. "Quite remarkable," she said. "They are available?"

"They'll be in your hands tonight."

Indy could hardly wait to see just how Caitlin would use those batteries.

20

Caitlin held up the scepter Indy had seen only once before, at the Glen deep in the thick woods of the New Forest. The scepter that according to legend, Merlin himself had used to control powerful energies in the earth and the atmosphere. Ancient science and an affinity with nature explained for Indy many of the feats of wizardry ascribed to the ancient magician.

"As I have said before," Caitlin told him, "this scepter has been passed down through many generations of my family." She released a catch at the bottom to open a space within the scepter, and twisted free the top with a dull red ruby in its center. Indy and Gale watched Caitlin insert the battery, then twist a thick wire of pure gold to the screw terminals. She closed the top and then the bottom.

"When I press this crystal, here"—she pointed to the side of the scepter— "the battery closes its circuit and maintains an electrical energy field. Indy, would you please lower the lights in this room?"

He did as she asked and returned to the couch alongside Gale. A deep gloom filled the room; Caitlin was a shadowy figure perhaps ten feet away from them. In the dim light they could barely make out the scepter in her hand.

"Watch closely, listen carefully," Caitlin instructed. Indy had the strangest feeling that she was drifting away from him, floating almost phantomlike through some distant tunnel. Her voice took on an ethereal quality, coming to him with the soft ringing tones of an echo.

"This is the wand of the great Merlin," she called out. "It has the power to draw energy from the earth, from the air about us, from the waters in the streams and rivers and lakes. It reaches into the clouds to reap pure energy as a farmer clears his fields. The scepter; a goddess of energy."

Indy saw her move the instrument in a wide circle, then stop its movement, holding it out before her. "You wish to see, to feel its effect," she said to Indy, a mixed statement and question to which there could be only one answer.

"Yes," he said quietly.

"Your mind will leave you," came a dire warning.

"It has more than once," he said dryly. A bit out of line for the solemn moment, but a retort he couldn't hold back.

He felt Gale squeezing his hand. A touch of reassurance, he knew. But why? What was so terrible about energy gathering?

"We begin," Caitlin said. She held the scepter aloft, her finger pressed against the yellow crystal, and power flowed through it. More crystals began to glow as energy streamed up, like liquid mercury, to the top of the scepter. A low humming sound seemed to come from everywhere. Indy felt the room temperature dropping. There was a slight glow from the red ruby at the top, becoming brighter with every moment.

Indy felt as if he were being elevated out of his body. He was physically seated on the couch, Gale by his side, squeezing his hand, yet he was ascending. Mind? Body? *What?* He couldn't tell, but he had no desire to fight for control of himself. *Go with it.* . . . The voice was his own, an inner voice releasing him from his natural survival reactions.

Pressure built against his ears. No sound, but a cooling pressure as smooth as a summer breeze. It flowed through his ears, through his skin, through muscle and sinew and bone *into his mind.* The crystals blazed before his eyes, highlighting the goddesslike figure of Caitlin. Her voice floated toward him like ripples shimmering on a silver pond. "Tell me," she said softly, "what you fear the most."

Indy tried to speak, but no sound issued from his lips. He found himself falling backward through a mist that was condensing all about him. Then he *was* falling, down through a well with glowing walls, falling forever. Yet it was so strange . . . no air rushed past his body, no sudden gasp shook him.

"Think of what you fear. . . ." *The voice . . . Caitlin? Who was Caitlin? And where—*

He heard his own voice, thin and from a distance, as if he were calling across some unfathomable void. He struggled to recognize words, but they danced just beyond his grasp. Old memories rushed up, swept over and through him and sailed beyond. Moments of past dangers, fears, struggles.

They vanished and abruptly he no longer fell. He was walking, the surface beneath his feet an endless stretch of blazing coals that should have instantly set his shoes ablaze, but he felt no heat from the flames. There! Before him, out of shimmering fire mists . . . a huge form taking shape, swirling, in and out of focus. He stopped, concentrating on the form.

It towered over him. He seemed to be rushing toward the creature, his feet unmoving, but his body was impelled forward until he stood beneath an enormous dragon, a great scaly creature with huge fangs and firebreath, massive tail lashing angrily, glowing eyes staring down at him.

A whip was in his hand, magically. The biggest whip he had ever held, impossibly huge and long. It sang like a screech of torment, and he snapped it with all the strength at his command. It cracked like a peal of thunder, booming and echoing.

Leather slashed into scales, ripped through a dragon foot, tore it apart from the leg. The creature raised its head and roared, its other front leg extending gleaming claws, plunging toward him.

Again the whip struck. Indy brought the leather across the snout of the enraged beast. Blood spurted from a long slash across the mouth of the dragon, splashing over him. Huge teeth bore down on him, and he ducked, slipping on dragon blood. Again the whip cracked, again scales tore away, blood spurted, but the dragon head was closer, and flames roared downward. He threw up his arm to protect his face, feeling scorching heat, the whip forgotten. The great fangs clashed again and again, snapping at him, and—

A woman's voice cried out to him. *"The sword! Take the sword!"* He could hardly breathe, but *there!* In the air hovered a sword, light blazing along its cutting edges. He flung away the whip, pushed into the fiery breath to grasp the sword hilt. Shouting with his anger, he rushed forward and rammed the blazing steel into the throat of the beast. A scream of pure agony burst about him, flames everywhere, needles stabbing his entire body—

He stood in the center of the room, soaked in perspiration, gasping for breath. No mist, no fog, no thunder or needles . . . *no dragon*.

Caitlin talked to him softly, soothing. "You're out of it now, Professor Jones. Breathe deeply, stand your ground. You're back with us."

He looked down on his own body. No scorched clothing, no dragon blood.

What . . . ?

"Do you understand now?" Caitlin's voice was clearer now; lights came on in the room. It seemed she knew his thoughts, knew the confusion leaving him slowly, saw the clarity returning to his eyes.

"Do you understand now, Professor? It is the scepter. It works with *my* mind. It gathers energy to me, which I can then radiate outward. It is a mind wave from me that matches that of your own mind. So I created the images you encountered. Our minds were as one."

"It was . . . it was incredible. It was *real*," Indy said quietly, his breathing again normal.

"It can be used many ways," Caitlin added. "And it can be a terrible weapon because it brings up your own forbidden, forgotten memories."

"But you said you created the images."

"Yes. But if they were not already in your own mind, you would never have seen them." Caitlin gestured with a wide sweep of her hand. "All of us have memories, terrible dreams, so awful we remove them from conscious memory. But they are always there, always waiting to get out."

"So I was fighting myself," he said, barely above a whisper.

"Yes."

"But . . . what about the sword?"

"You learned to fence with a sword, did you not?" He

nodded. "And you have seen Caliburn, and experienced its great power, and all those were your memories also."

"Then . . . this must be how many of the ancient priests and shamans controlled so many people," he said aloud, but as much to himself as to Caitlin and Gale. "What we have discussed before. Merlin . . . he had electrical power, as did the ancients six thousand years ago. The Assyrians and the Babylonians . . ."

"And it will help me to destroy Cordas," Caitlin said. "When do we leave, Jones?"

"Dawn tomorrow."

21

"Five o'clock! Everybody up and at 'em!"

Indy pounded on the door to the apartment shared by Gale and Caitlin. He grinned as he heard the thump of a pillow thrown against the door.

"Ten minutes. Coffee's hot. Eggs, bacon, toast, ham, potatoes. Get with it, ladies!"

He could just hear Caitlin. "Bloody barbarians, these colonials. Coffee, indeed! What's wrong with piping hot tea?"

Gale's laugh followed. "Tea will be waiting. And I'll wager Indy's all packed and ready to go."

They gathered in the small dining room. The museum staff had a "frontier breakfast" waiting for them, including biscuits, gravy, and a half-dozen varieties of jam. Carruthers and Judson arrived moments after they were seated to join them for the early-morning meal.

"We'll travel from here in two taxis," Carruthers explained. "No limousines at this point. I can't see any reason for attracting any unnecessary attention."

Indy nodded in agreement. "Where to?"

"Floyd Bennett Field. It's a navy airfield on the edge of Long Island Sound. South shore. We've got a Sikorsky S-38 amphibian waiting and ready to go. In fact, we'll fly down to Florida with you, make sure all your arrangements are satisfactory, and then you're on your own. Our, um, our office would prefer to have the Sikorsky land in the river, and we can then taxi to an army depot out of sight of everyone else. Everything you requested will be waiting for you there. And if anyone *is* watching our approach and landing, and then the people deplaning, why, the airplane will leave the river with the same number of people who went ashore."

"Neat," Indy said.

"That," Gale said as she stepped from the taxicab at the airfield, "is undoubtedly the ugliest flying machine I have ever seen."

Indy and Caitlin stood by her side, studying the ungainly winged creature on the flight apron. "It looks like some kind of prehistoric reptile," Indy added. "One that mutated in the egg and was then kicked out of the nest by its mother."

That the S-38 was. It barely resembled an airplane, and had it not possessed a seventy-two-foot wingspan, as well as a lower sesquiplane, half-wing and half-hull support, it would have been difficult to identify as such. Its long forward hull resembled the beak of some huge, awkward pelican, while its blunt and stubby fuselage seemed to have been chopped off at its aft end. The upper wing loomed above the boatlike hull on enormous struts, and from the wing, its two four-hundred-horsepower Wasp engines were suspended in seemingly precarious fashion. As if to emphasize the Erector-set-like design, the tail assembly and the upper wing were connected by two long booms, partly supported by a long strut attached to the stubbed rear fuselage.

The S-38 bore the markings of Pan American Airways. Indy turned to Carruthers. "I thought this was a navy job."

"It is. But Pan American has been running commercial test flights from here down through Florida and Central and South America. It's a common sight right now and won't attract undue attention. But your pilots *are* navy."

As if on cue, two young men in civilian clothes approached from the hangar, introducing themselves as Jim Barrett and Rex Silber. Gale tugged Barrett's arm. "I hope this thing flies better than it looks," she said, doubt clear in her voice.

Barrett laughed. "You're in for a great surprise, Miss Parker. This old girl is the best handling and flying job of its kind. Nothing ever built can match its ruggedness or reliability. I know it looks like it has more drag than an overstuffed balloon, but we'll be flying nonstop to Florida at a steady cruising speed of a hundred miles an hour. We can get her up to a hundred and thirty for shorter ranges. She'll get into the air like a homesick bird on migration. Catch this, ma'am. We can climb out with a full load at a thousand feet per minute."

Gale *was* impressed. "Really?" Then she cast a baleful eye at the ungainly-looking flying boat. "But if ever you lose an engine, with all that drag . . ." She shook her head to emphasize her doubts. "I suppose," she added slowly, "that's the advantage of the flying boat. You can always land her on the water."

Jim Barrett drew himself up to his full six feet three inches. "Miss Parker, I will have you know that on test flights we have shut down one engine in the air and on just one engine remaining, we have flown nonstop from this airfield to Jacksonville."

Gale slipped her arm around Barrett's. "Then I'd love to try her out myself."

She took him completely by surprise. "You, miss? A girl?"

"Try *woman*," Gale said sharply.

"Sorry." He cast a pleading eye at his grinning partner. "All right. When we're on our way, you certainly can have a go at it."

They started for the Sikorsky, Gale still held the navy pilot's arm. Sweetness wafted from her like a mist. "I'm interested in something," she said as coyly as she could manage.

"And what would that be, Miss Parker?"

"How much flying time do you have, Mr. Barrett?"

"Why, I'm not sure of the exact figure, but it's something on the order of about fifteen hundred hours." The pride was evident in his voice.

"Impressive," she told him.

"You seem to know a few things about the flying game, Miss Parker. Have you had some time at the controls?"

"Oh, yes. Dear me, I certainly have," she said, dripping honey.

"There! That's great." He patted her hand. "Would you mind telling me how much time?"

She squeezed his arm and looked up with a childish innocence. "You said you had fifteen hundred hours? What's three times fifteen hundred, Mr. Barrett?"

"Why, that's forty-five hundred hours."

"How wonderful! You've guessed how much time I have logged. I'm looking forward to our trip."

Before Barrett could close his mouth, Gale had rejoined Indy and Caitlin.

The navy pilots took off smoothly, swung out to sea, and climbed steadily to three thousand feet. Scattered puffy clouds a thousand feet below them offered an exceptionally smooth ride. Barrett came back from the cockpit to check the cabin and gave them the added good news of a fifteen-knot tail wind that would reduce their time to Port Jacksonville.

"Let's put these few hours to good use," Indy told Gale and Caitlin. He spread maps and charts across a worktable unfolded from the side bulkhead. "The better you memorize details of these charts, the better our chances of doing everything we're on our way to do, especially if we get separated."

His finger moved along a chart and stopped at a small town marked *Olustee Station*. "Note this place," he said. His finger moved to a nearby location. "And this one as well. It's called Ocean Pond. From everything I've gathered so far, this is the main area we'll be working."

"Olustee," Caitlin said aloud. "What a strange name. Does it have special meaning?"

"Sure does," Indy told her. "It's an old Indian name for an outpost that became a small frontier town in northern Florida. Biggest place close by is White Springs. In the American Civil War, some terrible battles were fought in this area. Gettysburg or Antietem, hardly anyone knows the name of Olustee. But there were some ghastly casualties on both sides." He tapped the chart again. "Besides, this area is the last *reported* position of the wagon train carrying the gold."

"Then that should be our best chance to find the gold. Maybe even before Cordas," Gale said with conviction.

"What makes you so sure?" Indy pressed. Seated behind him, leaning forward to hear every word, were Judson and Carruthers.

"If the gold *is* still in this area," Gale explained, "the ancient coins will draw us to its location. If what we have been told of these coins is true, and they really date back to the Roman Empire, and most especially if Jesus did handle them, then they will have a powerful psychic aura." She gestured to Caitlin. "And she is like a divining rod. Her body and mind perform as one. She can find water, metal, anything, beneath the ground. It does not have to be visible."

Indy nodded slowly. "Well, I've seen divining rods used all over the world. I don't question that in any way."

"There is also the scepter," Gale added. "No one knows its strange and wonderful powers better than you."

"Don't remind me," Indy said, a cold shiver suddenly running through him. "But the scepter. The way I understand it is that it's also a divining rod on its own radio frequency. Like the way it worked with—on—me."

"That is how," Caitlin broke in, "the mists were formed back at the Glen. How the roads twisted in time. How we may even cut ourselves off from the rest of the world by going into another time."

Indy nodded slowly. "No argument on that from me."

Caitlin laid her hand on Indy's arm. "This is important, Indy. What can you tell me about the battles that were fought in that area?"

"Confession time," Indy replied. "I've been a Civil War buff for a long time, but I did some heavy reading the night before we left. After that session with the, ah, dragon, I couldn't sleep. So I went into the archives."

They waited for him to continue.

Indy looked through a cabin window for several moments as he arranged his memories. "The major battle was known as the Battle of Ocean Pond. Others call it the Battle of Olustee Station. Depends on who was writing the history. But it's all the same fight. Lots of rapid troop movements. Infantry, cavalry, artillery. Both sides winning, then losing. Both sides advancing, then retreating before the final actions."

"When?" Caitlin asked.

"Early February 1864."

"What started the battle?" Gale asked.

"Early in February," Indy replied, "the Confederacy received intelligence reports of Union forces closing in on the city of Gainesville. The worry factor in the Rebel camps went right through the top of the tents. The Rebel commanders figured accurately that if they didn't stop them, the Yankees would smash right through Gainesville, advance along the low hills to the north, soon be in position to burn the town of Lake City to the ground, then fan out with their cavalry and wreck the Columbia Bridge"— he tapped the chart—"that spanned the Suwannee River.

"The only way to break up the enemy advance, besides moving defensive infantry and artillery into position, was to strike with Confederate cavalry. Unfortunately, there was little enough of cavalry forces. They'd have to use smarts and courage to make up for an overwhelming Union advantage in mounted troops.

"Well, as soon as they'd gathered their forces, the Union set off under the command of Brigadier General Truman Seymour. They started their movement with thirty ships carrying men, guns, and horses out of Hilton Head." His finger again tapped the charts. "They moved fast, and with skill, but before they knew what was coming down on them, the Yankees swept in from St. John's River. They stormed into Jacksonville with such surprise and strength they took the entire city without firing a single shot."

Indy leaned back. "While the Union forces were having a high old time rolling through Southern territory, not suffering a single casualty, the Rebs worked day and night at Olustee Station to put together one battalion of cavalry, which they hoped to use to bring the Union cavalry after them. If that ploy worked the Union forces would chase the Rebs straight into an ambush of Confederate artillery and infantry breastworks and be cut to pieces. That's what they hoped, anyway.

"One of the most important elements was how to operate in that countryside. It's almost all low-lying pine barren, swamps, streams, and hundreds of small lakes. If the Union forces were to advance deep into the Confederate defenses, they'd have to stay intact. The only way for them to do that was to keep along the rail lines and the dirt roads used for wagon transport."

"Did the cavalry of the South also have to remain along these railways and the roads?" Caitlin asked.

Indy shook his head. "Nope. The pine-barren country hasn't much going for it, but it's wide open for the most part. Easy enough for some smart cavalrymen to skirt the lakes and swamps and use the open country for full speed.

"The way things turned out, the Rebs had Clinch's Regiment, Georgia Cavalry, and also a regiment of the Florida Cavalry led by a Colonel Carraway Smith.

"They were, as I mentioned, terribly outnumbered. Coming after them would be the Union's Tenth Massachusetts Mounted Infantry, and the Stevens Battalion of Cavalry. All well equipped, well fed, heavily armed, and spoiling for a fight."

Indy pushed aside the charts. "The official records, however, make absolutely no mention of the gold that had already been landed by British men-of-war. They came to the Florida coast at night, the crews unloaded everything before daylight, and the British then sailed to the Caribbean in order to avoid Union warships.

"The point is, while the Confederates were doing everything possible to hold off the Union, they were also driving day and night to move the gold as far west as possible. The Union knew nothing of the gold shipment, and the Confederacy wanted to keep it that way. So their ranks were thinned out even more because they had to use every available horse and wagon, as well as mounted troops and a force on foot, to carry the gold."

"Indy, please," Gale interrupted. "What happened? How did it turn out?"

"It was back and forth for quite a while. The Rebel commanders sent out their cavalry on full-force cut-and-run strikes against the flanks of the Union army. Their plan was to slice deep into those ranks, and kill as many men as possible, but also kill off as many horses as they could and wreck Union artillery teams. That way, doing their best to fight off the concerted cavalry attack of the Rebs, the Union forces would be wide open to devastating fire from massed Rebel infantry and artillery."

"Did it work?" Gale persisted.

"Unfortunately, no," Indy replied, surprising his listeners.

"What happened?" Caitlin asked.

"Turned out the Rebel cavalry didn't know that country

as well as they thought," Indy said. "They charged, all right, but they got bogged down in swamps, they broke ranks trying to get through, and they never managed to make the assault in full strength."

"So they lost, then," Gale judged.

Indy shook his head. "One thing about combat is that quite often a poor move turns out brilliantly. You see, the Union generals had figured out what the Rebels might do. They were all ready for the cavalry strike along their flanks. Had the Confederate cavalry attacked as planned, they would have been cut to pieces. Instead, their problems with the swamps broke them up into many small forces. This let them operate with greater speed in fast cut-and-run attacks. They'd sweep in from the pine barrens, let loose with everything they had, and then disappear into the woods. They hit the Union army so many times and so fast that they demoralized the Blues. In this way, they managed to carry out their original plan."

"You mean to lead the Union into a trap?" Gale queried.

"Bingo. The Rebs were raising such havoc, and inflicting so many casualties, that the Union commanders ordered their cavalry to cut them down at any cost. It cost them, all right. The moment the Rebs saw the powerful line of Union cavalry coming after them, they ran back to their own lines. The Union cavalry went after them hellbent for leather—right into the artillery and fortifications the Rebels had set up in the first place. They cut the Union cavalry to pieces. The Rebs regrouped their cavalry and led wild charges into the heart of the Union forces. The battle went on for several days, and when it was over, the North was in full retreat. For a while no one knew who was winning, but as it turned out, the Union took terrible

casualties in their infantry, and without their own cavalry
to protect them, the Yankees had to abandon most of their
artillery, which the Rebels seized and used against them.
When the battle was in full swing, and the Union was retreating, the Rebs had three times as much artillery, powder, and ammunition as they had when the battle started.
So the South took the field, chewed up the Yankees, and
ended up with a terrific victory."

"But the gold!" Gale exclaimed. "What happened to the
gold?"

"Nobody knows," Indy said.

"That's it?" Gale said with disbelief. "The gold just *disappeared*?"

"Nothing ever really just disappears," Indy countered.
"The best way to explain what happened to the gold is that
whoever was involved in the mule trains carrying the gold
was killed in battle, by Union cavalry who had no idea what
they were carrying. And they never had the chance to stop
and check things out, because as fast as they hit those
wagon trains, they were set upon by Rebel cavalry. It was
a running battle. No definite lines or anything like that.
The main fighting kept moving back to the north as the
Union was retreating, the Rebs hammering them with everything they had. The fighting, where the wagon trains
were, was simply left behind. From what I was also able
to determine, shortly after that battle, the weather turned
terrible. Heavy rains and thunderstorms for several days.
It made the ground virtually impassable. And since the
enemy was on the run and the Confederacy was more interested in killing Yankees than in sending vital combat
forces to see what was left of wagon trains, the whole thing
was ignored—and then forgotten."

◦   ◦   ◦

"What you have just said," Caitlin responded to Indy's recitation of the past battles, "may be of great value to me."

Indy studied the woman; she seemed strangely confident. "How so?" he inquired.

"The ground across which we shall travel," Caitlin said slowly and deliberately, "clearly still harbors the metal debris of the struggles. Debris, and the skeletons of the forgotten dead. They are more than broken bones. They suffered, they died terribly, and the psyche from these men was intense. That is energy. It is never lost. It will be possible to detect what happened in the past. That may help guide us to what we seek. I am certain Cordas is no amateur and he certainly is no fool. He may have already learned just what you have described to us. So now we know what path he must take. It is a journey we will share."

Carruthers moved closer and spoke to Indy. "May I ask a question?" Indy nodded. "Do I understand from what Miss St. Brendan has just said that the spirits of the dead will help her find what you're looking for?"

"Correct," Indy answered, smiling.

"I don't understand." Carruthers was honestly perplexed by everything he'd heard, most especially by Caitlin's words.

"Let me put it another way," Indy told him. He started to speak, stopped, and turned to Caitlin. "I shouldn't speak for you."

Caitlin surprised him. Her eyes seemed to glow with delight. "I am fascinated by what you might say, Indy. Please." She gestured for him to continue. "Your opinion, how you judge all this, can mean much in what is yet to come."

Indy nodded and turned to Carruthers. "Keep one point

always in mind," he began. "We're going to be traveling through an area that's just about drenched in the metal and other debris of the battles. Musket balls, the muskets themselves, all kinds of artillery, the metal structure of wagons, shoes for horses and mules, metal canteens, uniform insignia . . . But there's more than physical debris. Picture those battles. Hundreds of men shattered by bullets and bayonets, screaming in agony, dying slowly.

"Something like that leaves a psychic effect. I don't care if scientists can't quantify it. It is there. It affects people, affects animals. Some people are extraordinarily sensitive to the psychic aura that remains after a battle. Ever have a hunch? You can't tell what it is, you don't *know* what it is, but you feel something that's disturbing, that grabs your attention and won't let go."

Carruthers found himself torn between his own dogma of "seeing is believing" and what he was hearing from Indy. "This effect, what you call psychic," he asked carefully, "is it only a sense, or a feeling, or can it be something physical?"

Indy laughed. "I'll tell you right now, it not only can be physical, it can knock you head over heels. At Stonehenge, for example, I stood at a specific spot where the energies are supposed to come together. I used a two-foot antenna that was supposed to collect the energies."

"What happened?"

"It was like being hit with a bolt of lightning," Indy said soberly. "A blinding flash and then I was hurled from the car. Like being swatted by a huge invisible hand. I didn't try it again. The point is, there's a link between the past and the present. It's there at Stonehenge. It's powerful at Avalon, where King Arthur is believed to have held court."

"Mr. Carruthers," Gale broke in. "The Olustee battlefield is like a psychic magnetic storm. And Caitlin is attuned to that kind of energy. She could move through empty ground, open fields, with her eyes closed, and *feel* what happened in the past."

"The whole thing is incredible," Carruthers answered finally.

Indy reached into a pocket of his jacket. "Well, there's more than one way to look back through time." His words drew their immediate attention. "I can also see through the ground. I use the Jones Unique and Wonderful Underground Detector." He held up a circular metal object and flipped open the top to reveal an extremely sensitive magnetic compass, the needle floating in watch-lubricating oil. "This thing will pick up just about any metallic object as deep as ten feet below the ground surface. It may not be magic, but it works."

A bell rang in the passenger compartment. Judson went forward to talk with the pilots then returned. "We start down in ten minutes. The pilots would like everybody to take their seats and secure their seat belts."

Barrett and Silber brought the Sikorsky down on feathery wings. They checked the wind direction across the river and settled the flying boat down. As the Sikorsky settled, the hull threw back a foamy cascade on each side of the cabin, leaving no doubt that they were now in a boat rather than an airplane.

Several minutes later the pilots eased the S-38 alongside a mooring dock; an army team secured tie lines.

One hour later Indy, Gale, and Caitlin were driving southward toward the ghostly battlefields.

22

Loaded down with weapons, maps and charts, cans of water and provisions for several weeks, Indy and his two companions drove into increasingly wild and remote country. Small towns and communities became more distant until they had gone for miles without seeing another human being. The pine country seemed abandoned by nature itself with stunted brush and sparse tree growth. Only hordes of biting insects kept them aware that they were still in an alive and angry world.

"This is like traveling back in time." Gale lowered powerful binoculars and turned to Indy. "I've been in desolate areas before, but *this* place, well, it's like no one ever *lived* here."

"They did," Indy offered in answer. "Seminole Indians, Spanish explorers, and even the first settlers moving down from the Georgia hills. Of course they were pretty well spread out. The kind of people who settled here, farmers and lumbermen for the most part, liked the empty spaces. Their idea of being crowded was to have some neighbors less than a couple miles away from where they lived."

"There are others here," Caitlin remarked.

"Tell me," Indy prompted.

"The birds. Look about you. I recognize many, of course, especially the crows and ravens. And in the distance, at times, vultures," Caitlin said.

"And that's to say nothing of snakes, armadillos, raccoons, possum, field mice, woodchucks, foxes, lizards, well, it's an amazing list. What's missing are the people," Indy added.

"There were many here before," noted Caitlin, surveying the countryside. "You only need to look in order to see. It has been how many years?"

"About sixty-six years since the last great battles," Indy answered.

"Those trees, over there." Caitlin pointed. "All this time and many trunks are still splintered. The way they are broken tells how they were struck. The poison of so much lead and gunpowder leaves its mark. That hillside, to our right? Torn away by terrible explosions. And more recently, many fires."

"The last one is common enough," Indy said quickly. "They get a long stretch without rain and everything dries up. It's like a tinderbox. Heavy weather rolls in, lightning hits all around, and before you know it, half the countryside is burning. If the wind is strong, the fires go on for mile after mile."

"But there is something else," Caitlin said, her eyes narrowing. "It is what I *feel*. Many have died here. I felt much the same hushed cry of voices when I visited the Holy Lands where the Crusades were fought. Here, all about us. It is as if the dead were still calling for a final reckoning."

"Maybe they are," Indy said, not wanting to voice his

own feelings on the matter. He pushed the issue to something more positive. "That list of animals I gave you before?" he offered. "Remember, that's just the small stuff. This country is also well populated with larger creatures."

"We talked about that before," Gale came into the exchange. "You mentioned bears—"

"Mainly black bears. Not as big as the northern animals, but they're fast and can be dangerous," Indy cautioned.

"You said there were wild boar here?" Caitlin asked.

Indy nodded. "Wild boar. And the panthers. Also called cougars. Some are all black, others brown. There are wildcats. Tough as nails and they'll tackle just about anything."

"And"—Gale shuddered—"alligators."

"They stay pretty close to the wetlands," Indy explained.

"There are very few people," Caitlin mused.

"More than you'd expect," Indy told her. "Indians, for the most part. Like the gators, they're mainly in the wetlands and the swamps."

"We will be alert," Caitlin said.

"Indy, you've been doing this for years," Gale said. "Looking for ancient things. Forget the scientist part of yourself for the moment. What do you *feel* happened to the gold?"

Indy didn't answer immediately. He'd thought about it often enough, but understanding historical events was tricky. You had to try to think as did the people in the bygone times, and that sounded a lot easier than it really was. More often than not, the researcher had to follow the same trail a dozen or even a hundred times to separate fact from supposition.

Indy had to figure in the Confederate victory at Ocean Pond and Olustee Station. Even victorious, the Confederates were aware of how precarious was their position, especially if the Union knew they had a hoard of bullion in their hands. If that were discovered, Lincoln's army would overrun them like an avalanche.

"The Rebs would do everything they could to make the gold invisible," he said. "And their best bet would be to bury it."

"Sounds sensible," Gale agreed.

"But it has its pitfalls," Indy cautioned. "If you bury something, you need to dig deep and make certain the exact burial spot can be found in the future. The Rebs didn't have the luxury of time. Their need was either to deliver the gold to New Orleans or to get it out of sight. But they had another option. And that was to leave it so clearly in sight, blending in with everything around it, that you could walk through the area where it was hidden, stare right at it, and never see it."

Gale smiled. "That's something that Caitlin can do. But I don't know if the Confederacy employed witches."

"We'll see what we can see," Indy said noncommittally. The truck slammed over some deep ruts, bouncing them around, then came to a stop. Indy pointed ahead. "It's the end of the road. We can't go any farther in this thing. Too many tree stumps, marshy ground. Our best bet is to se-cure this truck and leave it here if we need it to get back to Port Jacksonville."

Caitlin was already gathering her material, checking her backpack. She waited for Indy and Gale to do the same.

"Hold it," Indy ordered the two women when they were ready. He reached back into the truck and withdrew three pairs of thick leather leggings. "Put these on," he said, demonstrating by securing them to his legs from his ankles to his knees. "A rattler or copperhead or water moccasin can hit you before you can see it coming. Their fangs won't go through this leather."

Leggings on, backpacks secure, they were ready to begin their arduous walk. Once again Indy paused as an idea came to him. He dug through the tool supply kit, removed a roll of heavy wire, and stuffed it into his pack.

"What's that for?" Gale asked.

"Just an idea," Indy said mysteriously.

The eight miles became ever more difficult as underbrush and tree growth thickened. The long open barren pines had changed through the years. "Whatever they saw back in 1864 sure isn't the same," Indy growled. "All this, according to the maps, was just open land. Nothing like these trees. And the ground—"

"I know," Gale said, trying not to limp from pulled muscles in her left foot. "I expected rough ground, but those traps—"

"Gopher holes," Indy corrected.

"You mean these are natural?"

"Furry little critters. Gophers. They dig tunnels like mad all around us. *And* gopher turtles," Indy added.

Both women stared at him. "Gopher *turtles?*" they chorused.

"Right."

"Caitlin, you hear what he's saying?" Gale said jovially. "He expects us to believe there's turtles everywhere, burrowing underground like moles!"

"Gopher turtles," Indy repeated. "See those raised humps along the ground? Gopher turtles made those. The smaller raised areas are moles and woodchucks."

Caitlin shrugged and walked on. She had little use for idle conversation. Her senses seemed especially sharp as she traveled into the old battlegrounds. Wildlife became ever more noticeable. None of them wanted to say that wild animals and birds had feasted on the thousands of bodies left strewn along the battlefields, since not enough men were left to bury them.

To break the gloomy mood that descended on them, Gale asked questions about what lay ahead. "Three miles or so to go," Indy told her, stopping short as several deer streaked through the trees. He showed Gale their route on his map. "We'll cross an old trail, two streams, and then we'll find an old railbed. The rails are long gone, but we can't miss where they ran through this country. About a mile along the railbed we'll come to the town of Macclenny, an important rail depot in the old days. Not much there now, but the state of Florida has forest rangers working there. One of them has been contacted by Carruthers and Judson and been told to give us whatever help we need."

They forded the streams and crossed the trails, found the roadbed; soaked in perspiration and covered with welts from insect bites, they trudged the final mile to reach Macclenny. Just outside the town, while bearded men in overalls and slouch hats watched their approach and dogs barked, they discovered a huge rattlesnake barring their way. Caitlin and Gale started to walk off the railbed into nearby thick brush to bypass the snake.

"Don't move," they heard Indy's harsh order. Both women froze. Moments later Caitlin had her bow strung and ready; Gale was in a crouch, machete ready to swing. Moving in slow motion, Indy brought his whip to hand. They all heard a strange rattling sound. Neither Caitlin nor Gale had ever before heard the warning chatter of the pit viper, the American rattlesnake.

Indy's whip flashed in a blur, swung down with the cracking sound of a pistol shot. In a frenzied, turbulent motion, the severed head of the poisonous snake flew off in one direction, the body twisting wildly in the other. Gale looked at Indy. "It's safe now," he said easily, wiping snake blood from the whip.

Gale moved forward, using the machete to lift the deadly creature from the railbed. Draped over the machete blade, held at arm's length, both the tail and the severed neck touched the ground.

"How bad is it truly?" Caitlin asked.

"You start dying within ten seconds," Indy said with deceptive calm. "The venom hits the nervous system immediately. It's like a tremendous electric shock or being hit by a bullet." He smiled without humor. "But you know that feeling very well, as I recall."

"Is there an antidote?"

Indy shook his head at Caitlin. "Not out here. Get nailed by something of that size and it's lights out in just a few minutes. Normally they strike between the foot and the knee. *That's* why you're wearing those leggings."

Gale tossed aside the snake body. "You should have brought it with us," Indy told her.

"What on earth for!"

"Those men watching us. They'd appreciate it."

"A souvenir?"

"Not likely. They'd skin it and cook it. Tastes like chicken."

Gale shuddered. "Then *you* eat it."

"I have," Indy said. He picked up the snake.

"You're not going to eat it now, are you?" Gale asked with disbelief.

"Nope. But it's always best to bring a gift into a strange town."

They continued along the roadbed the remaining short distance. On the porch of a ramshackle saloon and restaurant, boards weathered and warped, several old men watched them with mixed curiosity and suspicion. Indy stopped by the porch.

"Howdy," he called out.

All eyes were on the snake, then the women, back to Indy, and then once again to the snake. "Enjoy," Indy sang out and tossed the snake to the porch.

One man picked it up, hefted the body for its weight, and nodded with satisfaction. "Obliged," he said.

A hundred yards down the dusty main road, they climbed onto the porch of an old hotel, pushed through the doors into what passed for a mixture of lobby, lounge, and bar. A man in a neat green uniform emerged from the eating room.

"I'm Dave Barton," he said, extending his hand to Indy and nodding to the women. "State ranger for hereabouts. You must be Jones. Been expecting you. Let's go into the restaurant. Got some iced tea waiting for you. Beer if you'd like it."

They sat about a round table, served by a limping black man. "This here is Jethro," Barton explained. "Runs this place. He also knows this country better than anyone else. Far better than me, in fact."

Indy shook hands with the elderly man. "You got any questions, you ask Jethro. And whatever he tells you, you listen," Barton added.

"Thank you." Indy spoke both to Barton and Jethro. "The horses available for us?"

"In the stable. They'll be saddled and waiting for you in

the morning," Jethro said. "I imagine the ladies would like
to freshen up before dinner. Cooked it myself. You ladies
like venison?" Gale and Caitlin nodded. "I'll show you to
your room. Hope you don't mind sharing it with each
other. We don't get much company here." He studied
Caitlin. "That's a mighty fine bow you have there, miss.
You real good with it?"

"Jethro," Indy said quickly, "she can put it through a
man's heart at two hundred yards. Dead center."

Jethro smiled. "I'll make sure her venison is done *just*
right."

Early the next morning Jethro treated them to a heaping
breakfast of eggs, ham, bacon strips, pancakes, grits, biscuits and gravy, and assorted honey and jams. And coffee
strong enough to awaken a dead man. He handed Caitlin
a cloth-wrapped package. "Ham and bacon for your trip.
Tastes even better the day after cooking. Remember what
I said. Wild pigs are pretty mean this time of year. They
can come out of the brush without warning. Be right onto
you before you knows it."

"Thank you," Caitlin said, accepting the package.

On the horses, ready to leave, Indy turned to Jethro and
Barton. "One more question." Both men looked up at him.
"I should have thought of this last night. Has anybody else
come through here lately?"

"Sure have," Jethro said, catching them by surprise.
"Never stopped. Six, maybe eight men, on horseback and
a team of mules hauling a right large-size wagon. Never
said nothing to us, we never spoke to them. Ain't polite to
ask questions of them kind of people unless they speak
first."

"What kind of people would that be?" Indy asked.

"Armed," Jethro said. "Armed to the teeth. Everyone we saw wearing a gun *and* carrying a rifle. Somehow, though, I don't think they were here for hunting."

Not unless you include humans as targets, Indy thought. *But at least we know where Cordas is.*

He slipped a round into the chamber of his rifle.

23

For the next several days, sleeping in tents at night with small fires burning to ward off sudden invasion by bear or wild pig, they searched and crisscrossed the sprawling landscape of the Olustee battlegrounds. The horses acted nervous as they carried their riders over fields once soaked heavily in blood and littered with the bones of dead soldiers.

Caitlin withdrew from even casual conversation. Indy needed no explanation from her or Gale. Whatever her psychic connection to this terrible and grisly past, it struck her with both emotional and physical pain.

"She could be an Indian tracker the way she finds things," Indy told Gale. "It's almost as if she could see what happened and she knows how to thread her way through the worst of the past."

"And you're not doing well at all, are you?" Gale asked, referring to the sensitive compass that Indy had brought with him.

Indy shook his head. "This blasted thing is crazy enough to discourage anyone," he said in frustration. "It works *too* well! Everywhere we go, metal is scattered everywhere. Especially iron. The needle of this compass just spins in all directions, picking up stronger targets as we move along. And every one we've examined has been an iron ball or a cannon." He pointed ahead. "We're getting closer to the main battlefield. The heaviest fighting was over that way. Just southeast of that lake." Caitlin pulled up beside him, listening carefully. "If the gold-shipment wagons were caught up in that fight, there's no way the people moving that gold in those mule trains could have gotten out of the way."

He stood in his stirrups for a better view of the area. "Give me your feelings," Caitlin asked.

"My guess," Indy said slowly, "is that they buried the bullion and the coins. But not deep. They didn't have the time or the manpower to do that." He offered a crooked smile that reflected his dislike of guessing. "It's like looking for the proverbial needle in the haystack. Only the haystack covers several square miles, and the needle"—he gestured with his compass—"has gone bananas on me. Our best bet is to try to locate where the final battle lines were drawn. That will narrow the search, let us concentrate more on what's around us."

"What about Cordas?" Gale asked.

"If anyone knows about that, it's Caitlin."

"He is nearby," Caitlin said stiffly.

"How close is nearby?" Indy pressed.

"Dangerously," came the short response.

"Which means," Indy said cautiously, "they may have doubled back on us. If they haven't had any luck in finding the gold, which I feel sure they haven't, then they're following us to see how we do." Again he looked about him.

"If we don't see them and Caitlin feels they're close to us, they may have us in their sights."

Indy couldn't have used a worse selection of words.

He whirled suddenly in the saddle with a cry of pain. Gale and Caitlin, startled, saw a crimson welt appear just beneath his ear. Half-conscious, he slid awkwardly from the saddle.

Not until then did the crack of a distant rifle reach them. Before Caitlin could move, Gale threw herself from her horse against her, taking her to the ground. "Look after him," she snapped. In the same moment she pulled her rifle from its saddle scabbard, a shell in the chamber, crouching and looking toward the area from where the shot had come.

She stayed low, moving to Indy and Caitlin. Indy was now fully conscious. "The bullet creased his upper cheek," Caitlin said, pressing a bandanna against the bleeding. "Another inch and he would be dead."

She moved aside for Gale to reach Indy. "Whoo, man," Indy said softly. "It burns. Did I hear a rifle shot?"

"You did," Gale told him. "Lie still. I've got to stop the bleeding." Indy brought his revolver from his holster into his right hand. "All right," he said, aware that he was still bleeding heavily.

"Sniper," Gale told him.

Indy started to nod, but winced in pain. "Better get our rifles," he told Gale. "They may be moving in closer."

Caitlin brought their rifles to them. "Stay with him. Tie the horses," she said brusquely. "Whoever is out there may want all of us dead. I've got to find the sniper first."

Before Gale or Indy could protest, she had disappeared in the tall underbrush. Almost at the same time a mist ghosted into being about them. Before it cut off their vision, they saw it flowing steadily across the pine barren.

"We'll be safe now," Gale said. "At least I'll have a chance to get you sewn together."

He looked at her in disbelief. "You're going to do *what*?"

"Sew you up. We could bandage you but then you'd lose some hearing from the bandages, and besides, you'd look like an Egyptian mummy." She rummaged in her backpack and Indy stared at a long curved medical needle. "I suggest, Professor Jones, you make yourself comfortable and grit your teeth."

"How long has she been gone?" Pale, the side of his face afire, but regaining his composure and strength, Indy was already eager to get on with their search. *Two can play this game,* was his first thought. *Remember the old rule, Jones. Never fight the other man's fight. Draw him into your own.*

Gale's voice interrupted his thoughts. "Indy, we can use this mist to our advantage. We know where the shot came from, so we can backtrack and come in from their side without their knowing it."

Indy shook his head, wincing at the sudden pain. Drawing in a deep shuddering breath, he spoke slowly and carefully.

"Gale, this isn't the New Forest. This is the Florida barrens, and those people out there have guns. Don't forget it for a second."

"But we can fight them!"

Again, Indy shook his head, and groaned at the pain. He gasped for air before he could speak. "Listen to me, Gale! For all we know, we're ringed in. They fire from one spot, then wait for us to show ourselves again after they're in closer. We've got no protection here. They may be able to see our horses through or above the mist, but so long as we stay low, they can't be sure if we've slipped away. And we've *got* to keep them guessing. Right now we're in a really lousy situation."

"That's strange hearing that from you," Gale responded, honestly surprised at Indy's cautiousness. "We're experienced trackers and hunters, we could make mincemeat out of these people!"

"You think wrong," he said, more harshly than he intended. "You're thinking like you're on a hunt in your home territory. Out here, Gale, you're the neophyte. Look around you. Feel the grass and the undergrowth here. It's like tinder. Now check the wind. You know what that means?"

Comprehension dawned slowly. "Fire," she said softly, almost breathing the word.

"That's right. This whole area would go up like a tinder-box. A fire could drive us into their sights. We couldn't go upwind, obviously, so we'd have to work our way downwind with the fire following us. Oh, we could survive, because of that lake over there. We could even save the horses by taking them into the water with us. But we'd be forced along a path they could easily follow. Like right in their sights."

Gale averted his eyes. "I didn't realize. . . ."

"Don't blame yourself," he said quickly. "It's just that you're in new territory. When I was in the New Forest with you, I saw what Caitlin could do. Then *she* had the upper hand. You did the same thing on top of the zeppelin. But right now, we wait for Caitlin. She took the initiative away from us by running off the way she did." Indy scanned the swirling mists that would appear to Cordas and his group as a normal fog. "But before she went, she covered us beautifully."

"What now?"

"We wait for Caitlin. If it's a game of hunter and hunted, she's got the upper hand. I have no doubt she could be right on top of Cordas and his bunch and they'd never see her."

He studied Gale for several moments. "You created the fog before. In the Graf, or rather, on top of it. Could you do the same here if we needed it for cover?"

"Yes. It drains me of energy for a while, but yes."

"Then we could do it again. I mean, we'd have to leave the horses, because this mist pretty well hugs the ground. But we could move as if we were invisible."

"We *would* be invisible," she emphasized. "It's more than just a mist. Especially if Caitlin does it. Remember the roads that disappeared in the New Forest? The way you explained the Möbius strip? How things turned back on themselves, and were twisted in time?"

"I still have a headache when I think of it."

"When Caitlin does it, she shifts us into a different time. Literally. Those men could walk right through us and never know we were there." Gale sighed. "But I guess that's just postponing the inevitable. I know we can't stay in this mist forever."

She grasped Indy's arm. "Besides, I know Caitlin is going to bait Cordas. She won't forgo the old rules. I know it. She *must*."

Before Indy could answer, the mists swirled and parted; Caitlin stepped out of the fog. She had a grim smile on her face. "The fool has played into my hands." Instinctively her hand gripped the hilt of her sword. "There are eight of them, including Cordas. All armed."

"And three of us," Indy reminded her.

"It matters little," Caitlin said with confidence. "He has attacked us. Everything changes now. The old laws are in effect."

"Not quite," Indy told her. "*I* was attacked. Not you."

Caitlin ignored him as she caught sight of the stitches Gale had sewn into his head. "That will take forever to heal," she said critically. "And it can open easily. We cannot chance any of us not being fit for what is yet to come. Gale, a mirror. Indy, please sit."

Gale held the mirror so Indy could see his stitches. Caitlin moved closer to him, leaned forward, and lifted the waistband of her tunic. She pressed it fully against his wound, where the stiching had left his skin a nasty purple. He felt a strange itching sensation. His skin seemed to crawl beneath the tunic. Several minutes later Gale removed the tunic and stepped back.

"Look closely," she said to Indy.

He took the mirror from Gale, holding it until he could see the wound clearly. The dark purplish bruising was gone! The pieces of skin sewn together by Gale like the stitching on a football had blended. As he watched, several stitches came loose. He brushed at them and they fell away from his face.

"I've seen you do it before," he said, overwhelmed by the miracle. "But this is . . . it's just . . . incredible."

Gale studied the healed wound. "Any pain?" she asked.

"No. It feels like a slight electrical shock. Mild, fuzzy, almost." He looked from Gale to Caitlin. "In fact, I feel terrific!"

Caitlin stood tall, arrow notched in her bow, the sword

hilt within immediate grasp. "It is time, Jones. The old laws call. I must go after Cordas now."

"No!" Indy shouted.

Caitlin stared at him, confused. This man was her ally. They had saved each other's life. Why, then, did he seem to protect her enemy?

"Speak quickly," she told Indy. "I care little for your words of caution."

"Blast it, listen to me! You know I'm behind you all the way," Indy said, rising to his feet. "But it's like I told Gale. You're out of your element here. They've got the advantage. Fighting them head-on is not the way to go. Look, Caitlin, this just isn't bow-and-arrow time in the New Forest!"

He walked back and forth, putting all his conviction into his words. "I want Cordas just as badly as you do. Did you ever think about that? Maybe not for the same reasons, but I've lost good friends to that madman. You're making a mistake. All your attention is focused on the hunt for this one man. He has seven professional killers with him. You might even get through to kill Cordas, *but you won't come out of it alive.* And a hundred dead Cordases aren't worth one of you."

He took a deep breath, hoping against hope he was getting through to this vengeance-mad woman. "Anytime we step out of this time twist of yours, we're sitting ducks for snipers with scopes and long-range rifles. I know these weapons. Enfield three-oh-threes. They can take out a target with dead-on accuracy at more than a mile, *and we're the targets.* I saw plenty of them in the war."

He stopped, spun about quickly, stabbing his finger at Caitlin. "This isn't the time of Merlin's magic—"

"It is more powerful than you understand," Caitlin said, her face a stone mask.

"It can't stop a high-velocity rifle bullet!" Indy half shouted at her. "Remember, one shot into your heart or your brain and you're dead! And Merlin and Caliburn and all the witches that ever lived can't help you then!"

"I am wasting time," Caitlin said angrily, starting off.

"Wait! One question, Caitlin."

She stopped. "The *last* question, Henry Jones."

"Did all the magic of the New Forest, of the covens, or Merlin prevent the death of King Arthur? Magic swords or not, he died. And if Arthur could fall, so can you."

Indy took a long, deep breath. "And if Cordas takes you out before you get to him, your mother's death will *never* be avenged. Everything you've done so far will be a waste."

Caitlin hesitated, struggling with the words that conflicted so strongly with what she considered a holy mission. But much of what this man said had worth to it. And he was right; Cordas alive . . . and her dead would be unacceptable. She must hear more.

"I have come to know you, Jones," she said carefully. "I know you are a brave and worthy man. You do not speak without reason. Tell me, then, what you have in your thoughts."

Indy felt relief surge through him. "There *is* another way. I think I can manage some time twisting of my own."

Both women stared at him, incredulous. What he said didn't make sense. Indy was no warlock! He could not control the ancient secrets. Caitlin shook her head in disappointment. As she started to rise Gale restrained her with a gentle touch on her arm. "Listen, Caitlin."

Indy faced Caitlin directly. "Can you keep Cordas and

his men busy? Chasing shadows or whatever. Anything to keep them where they are, in this open pine barren, until ten o'clock tomorrow morning. That's when I will need all your powers, Caitlin. When I want this mist to cover *all* these fields, low to the ground."

"Yes." Caitlin showed her question in her expression as much as her words. "But why do you want this?"

"Please. I'll explain it all later. Right now I need you to trust me, to do as I ask. If I fail, well"—Indy shrugged—"Cordas will still be here. He won't leave without turning this whole country upside down for the gold."

"I accept your reasoning, even if I do not understand."

"Great. Now," Indy said with sudden intensity. "It's getting dark. When night falls, see if you can get that bunch to make some noise, to let us know where they are. Can you do this?"

"Yes. That is your wish and I will do it. I will wait for the dark." She turned and disappeared into fog.

"I just hope she'll do what I asked," Indy said to Gale.

"She will. When it is dark."

"It's almost midnight." Indy looked up from the radium-phosphorescent numbers on the watch face. "I haven't heard a sound yet and—"

Abruptly he clutched his head in both hands as sudden pain stabbed at his skull. Gale rushed to his side. "It will pass soon," she said, placing her hands over his.

His face showed his pain. "W-what is it?" he said hoarsely.

"It's not the wound. That's healed," she assured him. "The pain is from Caitlin. Not directed at you. She is calling the animals."

"I don't understand—"

"You will. *Listen.*"

Across the pine barren, rushing through the low-lying mist, came the thudding sound of racing hooves, mixed with grunts and shrill squeals. Abruptly, the squealing noises became angrier and louder. Moments later Indy heard men shouting in surprise and fright and then yelling in pain. Shots boomed across the flatlands and hummocks, mixed in with howls of pain. Then, silence.

Indy stared across the darkness, a thin moon reflecting along the upper layer of mist. A glow in the distance became brighter, sending wisps and streamers of orange and red along the curling fog.

"That's their camp," he murmured. "Cordas and his men. I don't understand that kind of fire. If we were after them, all they're doing is making perfect targets of themselves."

"Except two, who are now dead." Indy and Gale turned to see Caitlin appearing wraithlike through the mists. Her bow was still slung over her shoulder. In her hand she held the glowing scepter.

She joined them by the fire, sitting cross-legged on the ground. She smiled at Indy. "I have done as you asked. Now you know where they are. There were eight. Now there are six, and they will not leave the safety of their fire in the dark."

"Two of them are dead?" Indy echoed, wanting to be certain he had heard her correctly.

Caitlin nodded.

"Did you—"

She cut him short. "No, Henry Jones. Before you even complete your question. I did not kill anyone."

He glanced in the direction of the roaring fire, sparks drifting high into the air. "What happened?"

She gestured with the scepter, the crystals gleaming pinpoints of light. "With this, I called the wild pigs. The tusked ones. They came in a herd, stampeding directly into the camp. They are vicious animals."

"I know," Indy remarked.

"Before these men knew what had appeared, the tusks ripped several of them. One man died from being gored."

"You said two were killed," Gale broke in.

Caitlin nodded. "Yes. The men reacted with panic. They were shooting wildly. They killed one of their own." She smiled. "There is great satisfaction in that. It is fitting."

"They get any of the animals?" Indy asked.

"Yes. At least three. They are, as you say, professionals. They have not had fresh meat for days. So tonight they will roast the meat of the boar. By their fire and smoke we shall know they remain in their camp."

"Caitlin," Gale asked her friend, "you are certain they will stay there?"

Caitlin laughed. Indy wasn't sure, but this seemed to be the first time he had ever heard that sound from this woman. "Would you wander about in the dark, the ground concealed by mist, knowing there are the tusked ones nearby, ready to charge? Remember, the animals are invisible to them."

"Beautiful," Indy said slowly. He looked with admiration at Caitlin. "Just beautiful," he said. "Tomorrow morning, it's my turn."

24

That night, by flashlight and a pale moon and reflected glow from their campfire, Indy pored over the battle campaign maps of Olustee Station. Caitlin slept. Gale had napped, but now she felt irresistibly drawn to Indy's studies and the marks he was making on the maps.

"What do you have in mind?" she persisted. "I mean, you just left us hanging."

He patted her shoulder. "Not yet, carrot top. Still got some details to work out. If I'm going to be successful, I can't afford not to have every last item drop into place."

"All right." She sighed. "Can I at least look over your shoulder?"

He made room for her by his side. "Good. Now you can hold the flashlight."

She took it from him, but pointed the light away from the maps. "Question, oh wise one."

"Very nice. Very nice indeed. Ask away."

"We're sitting here by this fire. Which makes us as much an open and visible target as Cordas and his group. Why are you so relaxed about our safety?"

"Caitlin took care of that, remember? Wild pigs, strange shadows, and all that."

She took patience as her cue. "Indy, that doesn't mean that one or more of those people won't *try* to attack us. You said yourself they're professionals. To me that means they'll take chances."

"You're right. But they'd also have to come in very close to us," he said, smiling.

"What's so funny?"

"They couldn't get a shot at us unless they got close, like I said. The fog and all that. Gale, walk out into the field. That way"—he pointed—"not toward their fire."

"What on earth for?"

"Just do it, Gale."

"Sometimes, Indy, you are the most exasperating man I have ever—"

"Walk!"

She rose, started moving westward. Perhaps twenty yards off into the mists, something snapped against her ankle. She froze as metal clanked noisily.

Indy's voice came through the darkness. "Okay, carrot top, you can come back now."

She emerged from fog and sat by him. "What was that all about?"

"Trip wire," he said casually. "While you were asleep Caitlin and I set out stakes and then ran a thin wire in a large square around our camp. Pieces of metal hanging from the wire. Shake it even a little and you get all sorts of metal pieces banging against each other. You clanked pretty good out there."

Caitlin stood by them. Her approach had made as much sound as a wraith. "The wire," she said to Indy. "Visitors?"

The sword Caliburn was unsheathed, reflecting firelight like a beacon.

Indy shook his head. "Nope. Gale was testing our alarm system. Since you're up, how about going over what I've set up for the morning?"

"I'll get coffee," Gale offered. When she returned with three enameled mugs, they went back to Indy's maps.

"All right," he began, his tone serious. "You both know the essential details of the battles. What I need to do now, with your help, is to bring forth some powerful energy from the past." He didn't wait for a response, but went back to the maps.

"Look, right here. South of us. We know there's an old wagon trail here. What's left of that road is clearly visible. More important, along that old trail there are some large open spaces. Now, if these maps are accurate, then during the Olustee campaign, the Rebels were camped along the perimeter of the woods down that way." His finger drew a line along the map. "So the Union cavalry had to have made their mass attack from the north."

Gale glanced again at the map. "Right past where *we* are now."

"Carrot top, you are exactly right," Indy complimented her. "What I need from you and Caitlin is your help. And whatever ideas you have to get Cordas and his thugs to that area south of us. And it *must* be close to, but before, ten o'clock in the morning."

"But why?"

"A little trick out of the past," he said mysteriously. "It will all become very clear tomorrow morning." He watched them nod in agreement, if not in understanding.

"In that area, over there"—he pointed again—"there's plenty of brush for them to conceal themselves, but only if they're lying down or crouched low. There aren't any trees for cover. If they stand up, they'll be visible to us. And we're just as much a danger to them with our rifles as they are to us. The stalemate won't last too long, but I just need it to last long enough."

"You make no sense, Jones," Caitlin said, scowling.

"Caitlin, I trusted you completely in your own backyard in the New Forest," Indy said, his tone and manner brusque. "Now I'm asking you to do the same."

"I do not like your mysteries, but I will help all I can," she answered stiffly.

"All right. I'll go over the critical move again. We've got to get those people into that area I've pointed out and keep them there for a while. Let's get to work."

They made dummies from brush and their bedrolls. From even a short distance away, in dim flickering firelight and the night, the bedrolls looked like three people sound asleep around the fire. They loaded thick wood that would burn the night through and still be smoking in the morning to "give away" their position. "Even if the mist lifts in the morning, or the wind blows it aside, through a sniper's scope or binoculars it will look like we're still in camp." Indy grinned. "Stupidly dozing away the morning." The grin faded.

"Now, Cordas has no way of knowing if we've been joined by anybody else. I want to keep him guessing. If he believes our three may be five or six, he'll tighten up his security and stay right where he is. We can't get to him without exposing ourselves to any rifle of decent range."

"All right. That much makes sense," Gale noted. "But what do you want us to do now?"

"We leave this camp setup," he told them. "As we move toward that lake I showed you, we'll zigzag our way through the field. We stay low, every now and then firing a few shots in their direction. With the sound reaching them from different places, they'll start to worry about our number here."

Indy checked his rifle and the Webley. "They won't try to reach us in the dark. Too dangerous. But come morning," he stressed, "their patience should run out. With us lobbing shots at them through the night, they'll also have to worry about our having found the gold. That should scrape their nerves a bit more."

He turned to Caitlin. "There's usually heavy mist hereabouts in the morning. All those lakes, the marsh and swamps. Cordas already knows this, so a heavy fog won't seem anything but natural to him. Usually it burns off about eight or nine in the morning—"

"But you wish me to continue the low mist," Caitlin broke in. "Very low to the ground."

"Precisely. So that's the whole package," Indy said. "We want Cordas and his bunch to be in the area I've noted at ten o'clock sharp. And *we* have to be along the shores of this lake. In fact, just as I said before, we'll have to be standing in the water."

"Indy, you amaze me," Gale said quickly.

"Tell me," Indy answered.

"You warned us about alligators," Gale said, shivering at the thought. "How they can attack without warning and—"

"Don't forget the water moccasins," Indy broke in.

"Then why are we going into the water?" Gale said with open confusion and anger.

"Because Caitlin can keep them away from us," Indy said gently. "Just as she maneuvered those wild pigs. If that scepter works as well in water as it does on land, we're safe."

"I will do it. The scepter has the power," Caitlin confirmed. "But your words are a puzzle, Jones. You said we must be out of the way. But you have not said out of the way of what."

"You'll see in the morning."

Gale let out a sigh of frustration. "I hope you've got some very good aces up those sleeves of yours!"

Indy laughed, holding out his arms. "Big sleeves. Lots of aces."

The night passed slowly. They moved furtively through the tall grass and the mists rising from marshy ground. The company they found—or that found them—was unwelcome and aggravating. Mosquitoes and gnats swarmed about them, drawn by perspiration, body heat, and scent. They did their best to ignore the bites and stings. At irregular intervals they fired rifle shots in the direction of Cordas's encampment. His men returned the fire, but aimed at the campfire glowing in the mists.

"It's working," Indy said in a half whisper. "They don't know where to shoot, but I'll bet a dollar to a wooden nickel they're convinced we've been joined by friends. We'll keep them pinned down just as they are."

"Don't forget the wild pigs," Gale reminded him. "They're still circling around their camp. Only the fire keeps them away."

Caitlin tapped Indy's shoulder. "I can send the animals into the camp, fire or not. Is this what you wish?"

"No!" he hissed. "They could break up and spread out, and that's the last thing I want."

Morning came cool and damp, the fields glistening with dew, dripping from trees and bushes. From the streams and marsh and the nearby lake, heavy mist curled and floated in a light morning breeze. It lay over the ground like a thick blanket.

Indy watched the rising sun with growing exasperation. "It's burning off the ground fog too fast!" he said angrily. "By nine o'clock most of it will be gone. Both of you, start some intermittent fire with your rifles. Aim to the left of where that ground opens up into the low brush. I'll keep up some shooting to the right. I want Cordas and his men to feel they're safer if they stay low and work their way into that open area." He snapped off three fast rounds, the bullets smacking into tree trunks.

He rolled to one side and looked up to Caitlin. "How long will it take you to create the mist?"

"It can be done as quickly as you ask."

"Great." He nodded with satisfaction. "Just keep your talents ready to go when I say so. Now listen carefully. At five minutes to ten, we all go into the lake. Stay alert for those gators and snakes. And just in case those nasties aren't tuned into your frequency, Caitlin, both of you keep your weapons handy. Especially that sword. Whatever happens, no shooting unless it's a matter of life or death."

"Indy, none of this is making sense," Gale complained.

"It will. No time for a conference now."

The sun beat down, and the fog lifted until the ground was clear and low scud floated twenty feet above them.

Indy's watch showed eight minutes before ten o'clock. He led the two women, Caitlin with the great sword Caliburn, Gale with her crossbow. Their guns were slung over shoulders or in holsters as Indy had asked.

Five minutes to ten. They stood at the edge of the lake. No question; the alligators were present. Indy turned to Caitlin.

"I need everything you've got, *now*!" he told her. "Bring

the mist to the fields"—he pointed toward the Cordas camp—"out there. Cover these fields. We'll handle the gators right now."

Caitlin turned to face the long open pine barren. She held the scepter high, the crystals gleaming. Indy felt that strange pressure squeezing his ears, thrusting into his brain. He winced with the pain.

"Indy!" A low gasp from Gale as a huge prehistoric form glided toward them. Gale brought up the crossbow. A powerful bolt slammed into the eye of the gator. The huge creature bellowed and thrashed madly, spraying the water with blood. Other gators moved in swiftly to feast on their wounded brother. Again the crossbow sang, again a bolt struck, this time into the soft underbelly of another animal.

"We can't hold them off like this!" Indy spat amid the roaring and thrashing sounds. He drew the Webley, desperate *not* to fire the shots that would reveal their presence. He turned to Caitlin. She was barely visible in the thick white mist heaving across the barren. It rose everywhere to several feet above the ground. No higher, but so dense that only the higher foliage and trees were visible.

Caitlin turned, saw the alligators still rushing in. She pointed the scepter at the water. The pain in Indy's head increased, throbbing, stabbing at him. But the alligators had stopped their assault. They were turning, leaving!

He forced out his words. "Into the water! Quickly!"

Gale slipped on the muddy bottom. Indy grasped her arm, helped her regain her balance.

"This is insane!" she yelled at him.

"Quiet!" Caitlin's voice, urgency commanding their attention. "Can you hear it?"

They stood in silence. Then both Indy and Gale heard it. A sound of distant thunder, a shaking of the ground, sending birds and insects fluttering wildly into the air. The thunder grew into a roar, rushing toward them, the earth itself seemed tortured, the rumble and thunder like the hollow booming of thousands of drums. Even the water about them began to dance, tiny spouts of white lifting above the surface as shock waves raced across the ground and along the lake.

"Thunder . . ." Gale stared at Indy. "What is it? I can't believe this . . . the sky. It's clear."

She started for the shore. Indy grabbed her, held her back. "Stay here," he gritted.

The whole world seemed to be pounding. An enormous, invisible, thundering surf rushed closer and closer.

Indy had to shout to be heard. "Ten o'clock!" he called out in triumph. "The past is now the present!" Unmistakable jubilation in his voice.

"Bugles!" Caitlin shouted.

Gale's eyes were wide. "I hear them! Bugles! But . . . Indy, what's happening?"

Indy ignored her. "Caitlin! Cordas and his men! They've got to be covered with the mist!"

Caitlin remained impassive. "They are invisible to whatever magic you have brought here."

Indy laughed, a roar of mirth. "Magic? It's not magic! I promised you a time twist, remember? I would bring the past into the present. Don't you know yet what you're hearing?" He didn't wait for a reply.

"Look!" he cried, pointing. "Here they come! Right out of time! The Union cavalry attacking! More than four hundred horses, running right at Cordas and his men! Listen! Hear that?"

Sharp, cracking sounds sounded above the thunder. "Musket fire! A thousand men on foot, behind the cavalry, firing!"

Indy threw both arms into the air in a gesture of triumph. Before the stunned eyes of the two women, the Yankee cavalry charged into view, four hundred horses and their riders, the men holding sabers high in the air, shouting war cries, whooping and yelling.

Straight to that open space between the copses of trees where Cordas and his killer band lay, invisible to the riders tearing through the swirling mist.

Gale's face registered shocked disbelief. She clutched Caitlin's arm. Neither woman could utter a word as the cavalry crashed along, like a huge engine of destruction, four hundred horses, messengers of death, smashing through Cordas's camp, grinding and pounding them underfoot.

Caitlin found her voice. She grasped Indy's shoulder, turned him to look directly into his eyes.

"Truly, you are a wizard," she gasped.

25

The thunder of sixteen hundred hooves pounded away
from them. In the trail of the cavalry charge, fog swirled
and dust and grassy debris spilled high into the air. The
ground still shook, then heaved and rolled beneath their
feet in the muddy lake, as if they stood on the edge of an
earthquake.

"Cordas . . ." Gale clutched Indy's arm and shoulder for
support. Birds still whirled and darted about in fear and
confusion over the pine barren. And beyond the feathered
creatures they knew men had been trampled, heavy animals and sharp hooves crashing into their bodies, cracking
bones like brittle twigs.

"Look!" Caitlin cried, pointing. Indy's time twist was
still exploding past them as more than a thousand blue-
uniformed troops, cheering and shouting at the top of
their voices, ran steadily after the cavalry charge. Muskets
popped and exploded as the men fired on the run. The
charge had torn the ground mist to swirling wisps. They
could see the men in their headlong charge, continuing
their firing, running faster as they went directly for the

Confederate breastworks still out of sight to Indy and the two women.

"I . . . I can't believe this!" Gale shouted above the exploding din of running feet, muskets firing, and the cries and shouts of the attacking Union soldiers. "Indy, this is impossible! How could you bring back from the past an entire army?"

"Out of the water," Indy called. "Quickly. We needn't remain here any longer. And that kind of noise will only confuse and madden the gators and the snakes. Let's move."

They struggled through the muck to the shore, still gaping. Caitlin touched Indy's shoulder gently. "I am . . . I am overcome by what you have done. If ever I doubted you, I beg your forgiveness. This would astound the mightiest magicians of all history. It is incredible. . . . "

The cavalry was gone, its thunder distant and muted, the rumble and musket fire and shouting from the soldiers heard clearly across the pine barren.

"If anybody in the Cordas camp is still alive, it will be another miracle," Gale noted. Indy lifted his binoculars to his eyes, studying their enemy's camp.

"I see one—no, two people moving. Barely moving, let me add. All that's left of their camp is wreckage."

"Cordas?" Gale asked the question.

"Can't tell from here. But let's not waste any time." He pointed to Gale. "Have your rifle ready, one in the chamber and the safety off," he directed. "You walk to my left, at least ten feet away. Caitlin, would you please do the same to my right? I want us spread out, and I want to get over there right away."

They started across the pine barren, three rifles loaded,

ready to fire instantly. Mist began to form again about them. "Caitlin, can you get rid of that stuff now?"

"After what I have seen," she replied, "I would think a wave of your arm would do the trick."

"But I can't," Indy told her, keeping his eyes directly ahead of them. He watched one man stand, then fall, obviously hurt.

Moments later, as if a switch were pulled by Caitlin, the mist evaporated in a rush of cool air.

"Indy, would you tell me how you worked your magic?" Caitlin asked.

He didn't answer immediately. He was still taken by surprise that Caitlin was calling him Indy. Before, it had been Jones or even a stilted-sounding Henry Jones. Now she'd dropped all barriers. That small shift signified the enormous shift in her relationship with him. He was now "family." And as sure as the sun rose and fell every day, he hated to tell her there wasn't any magic in that incredible performance they'd all just witnessed.

Unless, of course, you considered intensive research, studying, knowledge, and persistence on the same level with magic. Maybe they were. They took longer, but they were always reliable.

They were too close to Cordas's camp for long explanations. "Caitlin, I'll tell you all of it, but not now. We've got other business at hand."

As if to emphasize Gale's words, deep groaning rolls of thunder boomed from someplace faraway. Gale's head snapped around. "I know that sound. That's artillery fire."

Both women stared again at Indy. He ignored the looks and almost snarled at them. "Watch what you're doing! Don't look at *me* . . . keep those rifles up. Move in!"

Indy dropped to a crouch, started running in a zigzag

like a football player. Beneath his feet the ground was chewed to fresh dirt from pounding hooves. Hardly a blade of grass or brush could be seen.

He came up fast on the camp.

What had been a camp . . .

All but two of the men lay dead, bodies crushed and broken by the cavalrymen, who, because of the mist, had never even seen Cordas and his men. One man lay on the ground, legs broken, moaning, but alive.

Cordas was the other man. Seated with his back propped against an old tree stump, face bloodied, one arm hanging broken.

In the other he held a rifle, bringing it up slowly to aim at Indy. Too slowly to do him much good. His eyes were glazed in shock and pain; he was holding the rifle from instinct and rage. Indy held his rifle pointed at him. Then, suddenly, Indy's rifle fell, his whip lashed out, snapped around Cordas's rifle, and jerked it away.

Cordas didn't make a sound. His one good arm was raised as though it were still holding a weapon. His mind was as battered and broken as his body.

Yet the strength of the man showed in the anger that shone in his eyes. Indy understood. He'd known men like Cordas. He would rather die in a fight than be a helpless prisoner. If Indy had fired his rifle, Cordas would have escaped his just punishment. Once dead, he would no longer be accountable for his crimes.

Indy's swift movement with his whip had placed the man in a cage with bars stronger than any steel. Helpless, he stared with mixed anger and hatred not only at Indy, but at Caitlin St. Brendan.

To Cordas, Caitlin had become his worst fear. An avenging angel. His only hope was that her own anger might be so great she would kill him.

Gale had already walked through the smashed remains of the encampment. She shook her head at the carnage about her. "They never had a chance," she finally said aloud. "That one over there." She pointed to the only man alive besides Cordas. "He'll live, but he has both legs broken and he's in shock."

"We'll need him," Indy said.

Gale gaped at him in disbelief. "For what?" she shouted. "He's one of those people trying to kill us! Blood mercenaries is all he—"

"Whoa," Indy said sharply. "This isn't a matter of killing. Treadwell, and the American authorities, need to know who else was involved in what's happened. Terrible crimes have been committed. They'll only find out what the real story is if they have someone they can question. He's no use to them if he's dead."

"You really want him to live?" Gale said, her disbelief undiminished.

"You've got it," Indy said. "You kill him here and now, helpless like he is, and you commit murder. We get him back to England and into an English court, and when he's through singing like a canary to save his own hide, they'll hang him high and long for his crimes. No one gets away with committing mass atrocities in your country."

Gale swallowed; finally she nodded slowly. "I hate every word you've just spoken." She shook her head at not being able to finish off the last of the killers. "But you're right."

"Think of it another way," Indy added. "The people at the Glen will see, and they will know, that justice will be done. You don't want to rob them of that."

Gale leaned on her rifle, yielding to Indy's words. "That, too, is true," she said at last.

Indy turned to Caitlin. She stood tall and strong before Cordas, still propped up against the tree stump. Her rifle lay on the ground and in her right hand she held Caliburn. The sword gleamed in the morning sun, casting off glistening beads of light.

One thrust and Cordas would be dead. Caitlin wanted revenge for what had happened in the Glen. One thrust and her family would be avenged, the honor of the Glen would be upheld. Yet she hesitated.

She turned to Indy.

"Before I kill him," she said, her face as frozen as stone, "I must know of your magic. I would not be here with this garbage before me without your help. I cannot complete my oath without my understanding how you did your magic. And I have wondered, deeply, if you are not of the line of Merlin himself."

"This," Gale murmured, "I want to hear."

"No magic," Indy said, watching Caitlin and still keeping Cordas in sight. Broken legs notwithstanding, that man was dangerous. Suddenly Indy realized how stupid he was being and quickly broke off what he had started to say.

"Caitlin, hold the sword at his throat. *Do not kill him yet*. But if he makes a sudden move, act quickly." He studied Cordas's eyes. The man could understand every word he was saying, and that made him doubly dangerous. "If he moves his arm, either one," Indy said, harshness in his voice, "cut it off with the sword."

Gale was shocked by his words, but remained still. Caitlin moved forward, the razor point of Caliburn just touching Cordas's neck. Quickly Indy went to Cordas and began a search of his pockets and clothing. On his side with the good arm he found and removed a revolver. He tossed it aside and continued the search. When he stood, he held two hand grenades he'd removed from under Cordas's leg. He put them gently on the ground near Gale.

Cordas looked at him with pure hatred in his eyes. "The party's over," Indy said to the man. He motioned Caitlin back. She didn't move; Caliburn remained poised for a final thrust.

"Tell me what you were prepared to say," she told Indy.

"I said there was no magic," he said, as calmly as he could. One thrust of Caliburn, one short movement of Caitlin's arm, and Cordas would be skewered like a helpless animal. Indy wanted desperately to avoid his death. This was the ringleader, the mastermind, of a ring of international criminals. Bring Cordas back to England and Thomas Treadwell could break the back of that organization.

Dead, he would simply leave an open space for another leader to fill.

"If there were magic," Indy said to Caitlin and Gale, "then I would know where the gold was hidden. I do *not* know."

"And it is not in this camp," Gale broke in. "I've searched everywhere."

For the first time Cordas spoke. Not easily, for the effort brought a trickle of blood from the corner of his mouth. "You'll never find it," he forced out through cracked lips. "If we could not find it, no one can. You're amateurs. Clumsy and stupid and—"

The point of Caliburn nudged closer. A spot of blood appeared. Enough for Cordas to choose silence.

Caitlin glanced at Indy. "Please. Continue."

"I hate to disillusion you," Indy began again, "but there is no magic to what I did. I don't know how to do magic. What I do have is information and, above all, an ability to bring different things together at the same moment in time."

"Is that not magic?"

"*No*," Indy said emphatically. "It is using knowledge and timing. Properly used, history, as well as knowing what is going to happen, produces desired results."

"You said what is *going* to happen," Caitlin answered cautiously. "Is that not magic?"

"No. It is *scheduling*."

"You confuse me."

"That's not my intention, Caitlin. Look," Indy said with all the sincerity he could put into his voice, "today is the sixty-sixth anniversary of the Battle of Olustee Station. As I studied the historical documents, confirming everything I could with the records kept here in Florida, I realized I had stumbled onto something. When we stayed at that hotel in Macclenny, I had a long talk with that forest ranger, Dave Barton. That's when I began gathering all the pieces that I might bring together at the right time. Which was ten o'clock this morning."

"Indy, get to the point!" Gale scolded.

"The point is," Indy said, ignoring her impatience, "that each year the people from this entire countryside, and even from a few hundred miles away, gather to commemorate the Battle of Olustee Station. It's a reenactment of the *original battle*. Thousands of enthusiasts, buffs, historians, they all come together. They've re-created the original regiments and battalions, the uniforms, muskets, and artillery. It is an exact duplicate of the forces that were involved in the fighting at Olustee and at Ocean Pond. And that includes all the horses, weapons.

"Everything except live ammunition."

He paused to look across the pine barrens, seeing in his mind's eye the powerful charge of Union cavalry that had swept through where he now stood.

"They *did* fire their weapons, but they were using blank ammunition. The cavalry charges, the infantry, reenact *exactly* what happened back in the war between the North and the South. That's why marking the maps was so vital. That's how I knew that at ten o'clock this morning the Blues would come charging through this area with those four hundred horses, going headlong against the Confederate positions.

"It's a wild and terrible battle, but *no one gets hurt*. Unless, of course"—Indy chuckled—"he falls off his horse. And when the battle is over, everybody gets together and they have a marvelous feast of barbecue and catfish and their favorite foods, and they get drunk and they fight the war all over again, but this time with beer and white lightning and bourbon instead of guns and swords.

"So what I did was to learn the exact times and the route. That's why we had to maneuver Cordas and his cutthroats into this very position, because I knew the cavalry would come thundering right through here.

"They never expected anyone to be in their way. All the local people know just where they're coming from and—"

"The mist," Caitlin said softly. "You had me bring on the mist so that the men on their horses could not see Cordas and his band."

"Right. If they *had* seen them, they would have gone around them. And if Cordas and his bunch knew what was coming, they would have gotten out of the way. But the cavalry couldn't see this group, here, and *they* couldn't see the cavalry, and what they heard sounded like thunder approaching. The rest you know. But you see, Caitlin, *we* were out of the way. And just as important, and I'm sure it's more important to you than anything else, you haven't violated your ancient rules.

"You didn't do this to these people. The ones who murdered so many of your clan. They did it to themselves."

"I am astonished," Caitlin said. "But now the time has come for Cordas to leave this world." She poised to thrust the sword deeper into his neck.

"Caitlin . . . *don't!*" Gale's voice burst from her in a frightened scream. *"Don't kill him!"*

The terrible sword remained still. Slowly, almost with disbelief, Caitlin turned to the woman who had been, all through her life, her soul sister.

In a voice as cold as the steel she held in her hand, she asked quietly, "And why not?"

Gale pointed to Cordas. "Your enemy is unarmed, Caitlin. He lies helpless before you. Caliburn was never meant for slaughter. Its power is meant for use in battle. If you kill this mad dog, this human wretch, no matter how terribly he has wronged you, all of your family, you will kill out of hatred and vengeance. *You will break the pact with our past.*"

For a long time Caitlin did not answer. Nor did she move as she struggled within her own mind. Kill this murdering wretch and avenge the death of her mother . . . and at the same time break the code of honor and tradition. What Gale said was right. Caliburn was meant for battle, not execution of a helpless prey.

Slowly the sword lowered. "What are you doing!" Cordas spat at her. A coughing spell racked his body; blood appeared on his lips. "Go ahead, she-devil!" He fought to get out the words. "Do it! Finish me off!"

Caitlin brought up the sword again. Slowly she drew the

tip of Caliburn down the side of Cordas's face. Just enough
to create a long red welt. She leaned forward, moving the
sword aside.

"No. I will not kill you now." Her smile was icy cold. "I
will bring you back to the king's law. And I will see you
hang by the neck. As it was so long ago, it shall be again.
You will swing at the end of a rope."

For the first time in long minutes, Indy breathed easy.

"How are we going to take them back with us? At least as
far as Macclenny?" Gale studied Cordas and the second
man. "That one has two broken legs, and Cordas can't ride
a horse."

"And I'm not leaving you here to ride for help," Indy
said. "We've been together through all this and we'll stay
together. I can get them back with us. They'll have a
bumpy ride, but that's better than being dragged behind
us by rope."

"Your plan, Indy?" Caitlin asked.

"You stay here with them," Indy told her. "And try not
to kill them, please?"

He'd never seen a colder smile. "Only if they try to run."

"Fat chance," Indy said, going along with her grisly
humor. "Gale, come with me. We'll get the horses."

Indy and Gale rode the two horses, the third behind
Indy's animal. They left Caitlin's horse with her. Indy
pointed to a nearby copse of trees. "Over there," he told
Gale. "Let's go."

In the trees, he selected long saplings. The survival ax
from his pack soon had them cut and stripped of branches.
He tossed Gale a long coil of rope. "Tie them together so
we can take them back to Caitlin."

Caitlin watched as Indy tied two of the thickest saplings

with crossbars of thick branches. "We'll build a travois," he told the women.

"What is that?" Caitlin asked.

"It's how the old Plains Indians of America traveled. Two long poles, tied with smaller poles crossways. It's like a sled. We attach one end to the horse and the saddle. Then we lay these two on the back of the travois, and off we go. Oh, yes, tie them down tight. Like I said, it's going to be a bumpy ride. Especially the way they're all busted up. When we get to Mcclenny, we'll have a doctor set splints. Dave Barton can notify the authorities to come get them and transport them to the coast. We'll get word to Carruthers and Judson, they'll let Treadwell know we've got these two, and the rest is detail."

He walked to the far side of the wrecked encampment to confirm how many bodies were sprawled on the ground. "Gale, give me a hand here. We haven't the time or the desire to bury these people, but we can cover them with branches until Barton can send a wagon back here. I'm sure they'll want to try to identify the remains."

They pushed their way through tall grass, heading toward nearby low trees. Suddenly Indy tripped and tumbled headlong through the growth. He let out a howl of pain as he landed with his back against a concealed rock. Gale ran to his side, helping him up.

"What happened?"

"Blasted rock. In the grass. Didn't see it and"—he grimaced—"when I came down, I landed smack on my back against another rock."

Gale glanced down. Her voice seemed strained. "Indy?"

He groaned with the pain in his back, struggled to stand erect. "Good grief . . . of all the ways to—"

"Indy, listen to me."

The strange tone of her voice alerted him to her call. He shoved a fist into his back, forcing himself upright.

"W-what? What's so important?"

"You didn't fall on a rock," she said.

"What then?"

"A cannon. The barrel of a cannon, Indy." She made a sweeping motion with her arm. "This whole area, Indy. There are these strange barrels all around us."

"What's so strange about them? Both armies left their artillery all over the countryside."

"Will you come here and look for yourself!"

He stumbled to reach her. She pushed aside the grass, revealing an old cannon barrel. "Okay, it's a cannon. So what?"

"Don't you see it? What's so strange about these cannons?"

Indy went from one to another. The Rebels had obviously been forced to dump a whole contingent of artillery here.

Then he understood what had Gale so worked up. "You're right," he said. "Something's wrong here. There are cannon barrels all over the place. But . . . no mounts. And no firing mechanisms."

He moved through the grass, stopped, and looked up at Gale. "Have you seen any metal rims from old wagon wheels?"

"None."

"Neither have I." Indy withdrew his hunting knife. He tapped the hilt against a barrel. "It doesn't sound right, does it?" he said to Gale.

"No. It doesn't ring. The sound is too dull. Indy?"

"Go ahead."

"Try to cut the barrel," she said.

He understood what she hesitated to put into words. Gale held up one hand, fingers crossed. Indy felt the same way. This could be that stroke of fortune combined with perseverance. He shifted the heavy knife, hilt in hand, placed the sharp blade at midcenter of the cannon barrel, bore down with all his strength, and slashed against the barrel.

The blade cut through the curved surface of the barrel and left a gash behind it.

He stared at Gale; she held his gaze, her eyes wide. They both looked down again at the cannon barrel. He pushed the blade into the groove opened by his first thrust, put all his weight behind his hand, and slashed again.

The blade cut through old gray paint.

Beneath the cut, beneath the gray paint, the cannon barrel gleamed with a clean color.

Gold.

"Indy . . . I can hardly believe this." Gale spoke in a whispered, stunned voice.

He looked back at her. "This knife will *not* cut through a cannon barrel." The words sounded stupid to him, but it was all he could say at the moment.

"I know," she said.

"So do I," he repeated.

"It's . . . well, who would ever expect . . ." Her voice trailed off.

Indy went to another cannon barrel, slashed several times at the curving shape. Gold gleamed at them, reflecting brightly in the noon sun.

"We've found it!" he exclaimed.

"This whole area . . ." Gale turned, holding out her arms to include the tumbled cannon barrels half-buried in ground and grass.

"It's the gold, all right," he said.

"The missing treasure," she murmured. "It's been right here all the time!"

Indy cut through the top of another cannon barrel. Gold glittered before them.

"They melted down the bullion," he said quietly. "They couldn't transport it through the battle area. Maybe they didn't have enough mule trains to carry it through. Fighting, the weather, disease; anything could have stopped them. So they melted the gold into the shape of cannon barrels and dumped it just like so many other pieces of artillery were dumped and abandoned."

"And hoped to come back here when the South won—"

"Or the North. They'd retrieve the gold and help rebuild what was shattered by the war."

Caitlin watched them from a distance, wondering at the excitement that carried their voices across the field.

Indy went to a sapling, slashed the trunk, and hacked off the branches until he had a long pole. He went to another cannon barrel. "Pray there are no snakes," he said to Gale.

He pushed the pole into the open mouth of the cannon. Halfway down, it stuck. He prodded whatever had blocked the pole. "There's something in there. Could be a dead animal."

"Or . . ." She left her words unfinished.

"Yes," he said, sharing her thoughts.

He leaned down, inserting his arm deep into the cannon. "It feels like leather, or oilskin," he told Gale. "It's too heavy for me to pull out like this. Grab my arm and help me."

Together they dragged out a heavy oilskin packet, a large sheet rolled over several times and bound with wire. Indy laid it on the ground, cut the wire with his knife. They unrolled the packet until its contents shone brilliantly in the sunlight.

The ancient coins of Rome flashed in their eyes.

26

Caitlin St. Brendan walked through the administrative halls of London University with all the muscle-tensed wariness of a feral cat in dangerous territory. She felt as out of place as the stiff-collared professors she passed would feel in her own beloved forest. Robed men with bewhiskered faces stared at her leather garments as much as she looked upon them—they might as well be visitors from another planet.

Not that Indy, walking by her side, was much help. Again, as she had done so many times since their return to England, she couldn't avoid furtive glances at Professor Henry Jones, authority in archaeology, ancient languages, and medieval literature. Clad in a three-piece gray tweed suit and polished shoes, wire-rim glasses on his face, and his hair as neat as a barber's advertisement, he was far from the daring and dangerous man she had finally come to know so well.

Caitlin felt an instant dislike for and discomfort in her surroundings. The New Forest and the Glen seemed a million miles from this stuffy, massive, corridor-laced building with its strange sounds, strange smells, and even stranger people. Yet Indy had convinced her that she was needed in a conference set up in the office of Sir William Pencroft. Indy had called him the "biggest wheel of all" in the university system of London.

"He's old, feeble, unpleasant, argumentative, insulting, and he gnashes his teeth a lot," Indy had described the chairman of the Department of Archaeology of London University.

"Then why do you trouble yourself to be in his presence?" Caitlin asked, honestly confused.

"There's a couple of good reasons," Indy went on breezily. "First, he runs this entire university. Second, without his assistance, and his cooperation with government authorities, we would never have been able to go after Cordas and his men the way we did. That venture cost lots of money."

"This terrible old man paid for it?"

"Not directly. But he convinced the board of directors, and Whitehall, to foot the bill, arrange for special diplomatic freedoms, such as our carrying weapons, and provide us with the full cooperation of the American Secret Service and a half-dozen other agencies in Florida."

"Then we are in his debt," Caitlin said solemnly.

"Unfortunately, yes."

"Why is it unfortunate?"

"Because he has a memory like an elephant. He never forgets the favors he bestows. He considers them debts he collects in the form of favors *he* wants from *me*."

"It is only fair, Indy."

"Caitlin, *please*. Don't defend the old buzzard. He doesn't need any help."

They rounded a corner, sending startled students scurring out of their way. "Tell me again why you need me here, Indy."

"I don't *need* you, Caitlin. I confess I *want* you with me and—"

"Your words please me," she said quietly.

"Every time you talk like that I feel I'm falling down a long well back in time," Indy told her. "Caitlin, you're here because your government needs you. You were witness to Cordas committing murder. Not only of your mother, but many of your people. You will have to swear to that, describe what happened, when Cordas and the other man—whose name is Scruggs—are put on trial. Your eyewitness accounts will send them to the gallows."

"I wish to be there when that takes place," she said grimly.

"We'll talk to Treadwell about that. I'm sure he'll make the proper arrangements."

"Thank you, Indy."

There it was again. That stiff, formal manner of speaking, as if Caitlin still lived in a world of knights and castles and magicians. *Well, maybe she does,* Indy thought suddenly. *Maybe that's what I've been missing all this time. Caitlin isn't acting. She really lives it! To her we're the outlanders and her world is the real one.*

They made a final turn and faced a set of large double doors. Entrance to the private office of Sir William Pencroft. The hallowed inner sanctum of the university.

Armed British soldiers barred their entry. They snapped to attention. "Sir, madam! Your names, please!"

"Professor Henry Jones and Miss Caitlin St. Brendan," Indy announced.

"Sir! One moment, please!"

One soldier pressed a buzzer, turned, and snapped back

to attention. Moments later the doors opened. Indy and Caitlin looked upon the frail figure of Sir William Pencroft.

"Ah! The colonial black sheep has returned to the fold. "I suppose"—Pencroft spoke in a mixed wheeze and growl—"I should defer to the amenities and tell you how glad I am to see you. But I never did lie very well."

"Sir William, I—"

"Oh, shut up, Jones. And get out of the way!" The old man brandished a cane at Indy. "Move, *move*!" he shouted. He stared at Caitlin. His eyes narrowed, widened, and narrowed again. "So you are the maiden from the Glen. I have heard much of you, Caitlin St. Brendan. You are a most beautiful young woman."

"And you are as grouchy as I have heard," Caitlin said, a smile tugging the corner of her mouth, "but there is fire in your heart."

"How long is this mutual admiration society to continue in session?" Indy said with feigned weariness. He could not have been more delighted.

"Before we venture back into my chambers and the dregs of our modern society, Caty, I feel I should—"

"You called me Caty." The words came forth in a tone of wonder; it was as if a secret had been suddenly exposed.

"Yes, I did, my dear," Pencroft said, folding his hands on his lap. His eyes seemed to be laughing.

"But . . ." Caitlin looked to Indy. "That was what the people of the Glen called me when I was a . . . a—"

"It's not so difficult to say. When you were a little girl," Pencroft said gently.

"But how . . . how could you know!"

"Ah, I am betrayed by a slip of the tongue, I fear," Pencroft answered with full pleasure in the moment. "Because your grandfather and I were the closest of friends, Caty. Or Caitlin, as you now seem to prefer." He leaned forward. "Give me your hand, child." He held her fingers in both his frail hands. "Long ago, so long ago it seems lost in the mists of time, Caty, I held you on my lap. And carried you on my shoulders."

Caitlin's eyes widened. "They called you the oracle," she said in a half whisper.

"*You?*" Indy stared at Pencroft. "The man who could read the secrets of the ages with only a glance? *You*. The one they compared to a crystal ball!"

"Shut your mouth, you sassy pup!" Then, more quietly: "It stays among us three, you understand?" Pencroft said in a hushed tone.

"If that is your wish—" Indy began.

Pencroft's lapse into gentleness vanished in a flash. "Leave this bungling fool, Caitlin. I would like you to push me back into the room." He swung the cane with a solid whack against the leg of his assistant, who quickly yielded to Caitlin.

Indy followed. *Miracles will never cease . . .*

Neither-would surprises, he discovered, for as Indy entered the room behind Caitlin, who wheeled Sir William before her, a large man in a glittering uniform detached himself from a group to rush at him. His first reaction was to assume a defensive posture, then he recognized the hulking form of Matteo Di Palma. He never expected the Italian agent to wrap his arms about him, hug him fiercely, then holding him tightly by the arms, kiss him once on each cheek in true Italian fashion.

"You have done it!" he cried. He turned to point to another room adjacent to the large office. Indy saw armed guards at the door. "The coins. Ah, truly a wonder, a miracle! Others may not see it in this way, but I"—his fist pounded his chest—"*I know!* The coins, Indy, my friend, have been examined by a dozen of our greatest scientists, metallurgists, and historians. They are authentic. Their loss for so many years has been a grave disappointment to the Vatican, which is now overjoyed."

Indy blinked and separated himself from the unfettered enthusiasm of Di Palma. "What's with the uniform?" he asked quickly to change the subject. "You look like a doorman from the Waldorf-Astoria."

"Ah, for several weeks I am again Admiral Matteo Di Palma, of the venerable and ancient Di Palma family, which helped bring Italy into the world. It was thought best by Rome if my appearance this time"—he leaned forward for a conspiratorical whisper to Indy—"was not, as we say, as an undercover or secret agent. This time I lead the group that will return the coins to their original place in the palace in Rome. A group that is most heavily armed. Indeed, the English are sending with us one of their special raider units for added security. But"—he waved a hand in the air—"all that is nothing compared to what you, and this wonderful lady with you, have accomplished. Someday, Indy, you must tell me what really happened aboard that piggish German balloon on which you made such a perilous crossing of the ocean!"

Indy patted Di Palma on the shoulder, unable to keep from laughing with the excited Italian. "I promise. But right now you will excuse me."

"Of course! Thomas awaits you and the lady in the next room."

o o o

Thomas Treadwell shook Indy's hand with a firm, almost intense grip. He turned and with a small bow offered his greetings to Caitlin.

"I won't burden you with a speech," Treadwell told them both. "But I bring you the deep gratitude of our government and the Italian government. You already know that Sir William's testiness with you, Indy, is simply his way of expressing his own gratitude for once again raising the name and reputation of London University to great heights."

"I thought you weren't going to make a speech," Indy observed.

"Right. Cordas and Scruggs are the first order of business. There will be a speedy trial; that I assure you. Your presence as witnesses is vital. Caitlin for what happened at the Glen, and afterward. You, Indy, for the attempted killings on the zeppelin flight and also what happened in Florida. I also assure you the trial will be brief."

"I wish to be there when he hangs," Caitlin said. "That is essential."

"I understand." Treadwell nodded. "It is already arranged, and you will be present as an official witness for the Crown rather than for, ah, personal reasons."

"What about other governments who want him?" Indy asked. "Does anyone else get a crack at him in trials?"

"Germany wants him. So does the United States. *And* Austria, Italy, and other countries." Thomas smiled coldly. "We will let them haggle with one another as to who gets the *remains*. Neither Cordas nor Scruggs will ever leave England alive."

Treadwell poured tea for himself and Caitlin. "I'll take coffee," Indy said. Steaming pots stood on a table by a high window.

"You already know from that greeting of Di Palma that the coins are being returned to Rome," Treadwell told them. "The gold, to our immense pleasure and gratitude, is being sent by the American government to the Bank of England. It is remarkably generous on the part of the United States. There *are* positions they could take to retain the bullion. But they have worked it out cleverly on the grounds that the gold was payment for raw goods, mainly cotton, that delivery of those goods was never effected, and therefore the payment should be returned."

"Neatly done," Indy said.

"And a most generous donation is being prepared for London University," Treadwell added.

"Well, that might even bring a smile to the face of our curmudgeon in the next room," Indy observed. "Anytime the University receives a donation, Sir William manages a hint of a toothy smile."

Suddenly Indy sat up straighter. "Wait a minute. Something's wrong here. Where's Gale?"

Treadwell hesitated, and immediately both Indy and Caitlin knew something was wrong.

"Out with it, Tom," Indy said impatiently. "It's not like Gale to just take off somewhere."

"Gale Parker is in South America."

Indy stared at Treadwell. *"What?"*

"Pan American is testing new routes with their Sikorsky flying boats. It's their feeling that if they have a woman pilot, it will build great confidence among their passengers. Gale Parker is that pilot. They are being quite generous, and I needn't tell you what this kind of flying means to Gale."

"There is more to it than that," Caitlin said icily. "Gale

is my soul sister. For her to leave without a word to me, or to Indy . . . No, there is more than the flying."

"Level with us, Tom." Indy said, his face reflecting doubts and suspicion.

"There is, well, perhaps something else," Treadwell admitted.

"Tom, you're beating around the bush! Out with it, man!"

"I may not have the exact words," Treadwell cautioned.

"What is it you are afraid to say?" Caitlin said, staring hard at Treadwell.

"Gale wants you two to get to know each other better. Indy, she said she was feeling like a fifth wheel. And when Pan American made its offer, she jumped."

"So she just steps out of the picture?" Indy clenched and unclenched his fists. "The three of us were a team!" he burst out.

Treadwell looked miserable. "Indy, I'm only the messenger in this."

A long silence followed his words. Then they turned as the door of Pencroft's office opened, and the old man pushed his way into the room. "Get out," he said curtly to his aide, "and close the door behind you, *and* don't open it until I call you. Not for anyone, you understand?"

Pencroft pointed to the soldiers. "Clear them out of here, Treadwell. I want just the four of us in this room for a while."

Within moments they were alone in the room. Pencroft wheeled himself closer to them, stopping at the far end of the table. "Have you told them yet, Thomas?" he asked.

"I've told them several things." Treadwell parried the question.

"You know very well what I'm talking about!" Pencroft shouted, the effort bringing on a coughing fit.

Caitlin moved immediately to the old man, holding him erect in his wheelchair. "Speak gently," she said, her hand rubbing his back.

"And whatever you want Treadwell so badly to tell us," Indy said, still annoyed at the news about Gale, "why don't you do your own dirty work and tell us yourself?"

"Well, well, our unmannered guest from the colonies still has spirit, I see." Pencroft sneered at Indy. "All right, Jones, here it is. I have received a lengthy message that may have some slight interest to you as an amateur archaeologist and whatever else you putter about in."

"Amateur—"

Indy knew the old man. Every word he said, his mannerisms, his way of broaching this subject, spelled something big. Indy kept silent.

"I have taken the liberty of arranging for you to investigate," said Pencroft.

Indy shifted position until he was sitting upright, staring hard at him.

"Wait a minute!" he said. "You haven't even *asked* me if I'm interested in this crazy caper of yours!"

Pencroft smiled. He had set out the bait. Indy would bite.

"Is there really any doubt?" he asked.

AFTERWORD

In the story of *Indiana Jones and the White Witch* we have stopped at the edge of the historically recorded, stood and contemplated what lay beyond, and then made that "great leap" into wonder, magic, and wizardry.

Before venturing beyond "harsh and established reality," in the words of historians who want everything carved in stone, let us first visit the locales where such wonders are commonplace and as ancient as the oldest recorded events and names. A central locale in our story has been, of course, the New Forest in the southwestern regions of England. It is important that the reader be aware that every single town, village, forest, and plain described in this book is real.

The writer some years back was one of the pilots flying the Atlantic Ocean in an "ancient" Consolidated Catalina amphibian, a great lovely flying boat that was in wide use with the United States Navy and several commercial airlines well before the Second World War. In our resurrected Catalina, flying over the Azores in midocean to Portugal, Spain, and finally to a smooth water landing in

Plymouth Harbor, we began a "second adventure" by personally visiting the very places you have encountered in these pages. Leaving Plymouth, we became guests of the Fleet Air Arm main airbase and its nearby town of Yeovil. Then, sometimes by air, at other times in "motorcars," and quite often on foot, we traveled through the Salisbury Plain and moved with no small sense of awe through the New Forest.

This was a return visit for me; I had been there after flying a Boeing Flying Fortress to England in 1961. One of my closest friends for many years was Dame Sybil Leek, the renowned "white witch" of Wicca and its adherents who lived not only in the deeps of the New Forest, but also in different towns and villages of this fascinating southwestern extension of the United Kingdom. From what Sybil told me, I located St. Brendan's Glen.

The trees, the particular foliage, the twisting roads and strange mists, the practice of magic, it is all there. The New Forest, and that magic place of St. Brendan's Glen, the Midlands and the Plains, the purple-hued hills and mountains, the Gypsies—they are all very real, most remarkable, and provide a keen and rich look into a past filled with wonder and mysteries.

Which led me directly to the great and wondrous tales of King Arthur and his beloved Guinevere. The legends tell of a violent, fierce battle at Camlin, in Cornwall. Here King Arthur was wounded, and his men carried him from the field of combat to a monastery, either in or close to Glastonbury, to be cared for.

Glastonbury and the local terrain is considerably different from what it was a millennium ago. The land has changed. Glastonbury lies along the foothills of famed highlands, such places as Tor, Chalice, Edmund's, and

Weary-all. The Bristol Channel was a main thoroughfare for barges and boats and commerce. There was much more water over the land than at present, and all these towns were on the hills that actually constituted the center of an island. There were, in fact, many such islands in the sprawling water-divided land: Wedmore, Beckery, Athelney, and Meare.

What we know today as Glastonbury was in ancient times Ynyswitrin, a tongue twister of a name that means Glassy Island. Ynyswitrin was settled, and farmed, and astonished its people with bountiful crops. Its reputation for productivity led to tales that its soil was so rich that apple trees, instead of taking years to mature and produce fruit, grew to maturity within days. Glassy Island assumed a richness that people believed could only come from the power of wizards and sorcerers. The names of Ynyswitrin and Glassy Island faded in time, and the rich farmland became known as the Isle of Avalon, the latter name deriving from *Avalia*—the apple.

Through the centuries, Avalon would become confused with legends of a faraway magical island of the same name. Arthur and his bride were transported by sorcerer's magic to this mysterious isle, to be kept in some form of suspended animation until the need for Arthur's prowess in battle would rouse him from his deep sleep and he would again march against England's enemies.

The Isle of Avalon, on the coast of England, faded to give way to the name by which it is known today— Glastonbury. In the year 1705 it was incorporated as a municipal borough of England.

It soon became a world-renowned center of learning, where libraries and teaching flourished. It was also the first place in the British Isles where the name of Jesus Christ was heralded.

History and legend mixed here as well, for the ancient scribes recorded that Joseph of Arimathea arrived at Avalon as far back as 60 A.D. to spread the word of the new religion. At that time the old name stood strong, and Arimathea settled for a time in the Isle of Ynyswitrin.

Here is the direct connection between Arthur, the Knights of the Round Table, and their devotion to the new religion. It is believed without question by the descendants of the early settlers that Joseph brought with him to England the Cup of the Last Supper. He and his closest friends are reputed to have buried the cup in what is now known as Chalice Hill.

Many years after the legends say Arthur died with his queen, their coffin was removed from its original burial site and buried again in a church at Avalon. Some eighty years later the burial site was visited by Edward I and his queen. Disturbed that so great a figure should be left in the church burial grounds without proper recognition, Edward had the remains interred directly before the high altar of the monastery. This new resting place was then completed with an inscription that may still be seen today:

Site of King Arthur's tomb; in the year 1191 the bodies of King Arthur and his Queen were said to have been found on the south side of the Lady Chapel. On 19th April, 1278, the remains were removed in the presence of King Edward and his Queen to a black marble tomb on this site. This tomb survived until the dissolution of the Abbey in 1539.

Which brings us to the question of whether the swords Excalibur and Caliburn were in fact the weapons of wizardry wielded so famously by Arthur in his battles.

Consider that the ancients loved a world of magic, mystery, sorcery, and wizardry, and that the vast majority of the people of ancient times could neither read nor write, and lived in a world of wonder they could never truly understand.

To these people, history was carried by songs, poems, and storytelling around glowing fireplaces. The reality of Arthur as king was absolute and unquestionable. Along with this reverence for the king went the stories of his sword, which gave him a splendid advantage over his adversaries in combat.

The most popular tale of the fighting sword of King Arthur, from which thousands of versions have sprung, is of course the Sword in the Stone, which suddenly appears before a village that is host to many fighting men at a time when a new king is to be chosen. As the men gather in wonder about this huge lump of rock, staring at the sword with its blade locked within the stone, Merlin appears, and says that whoever is able to withdraw this magical blade from the rock is the *true* King of England. After a parade of muscled knights and other husky fellows fail, amid huffing and puffing and gnashing of teeth, the boy Arthur shows up, grasps the hilt of the sword Excalibur, and pulls it effortlessly from the stone. The boy demonstrates his rightful succession to the throne by sliding Excalibur in and out of the stone with giddy ease.

The volumes on the history of Arthur, Excalibur, Camelot, and the Knights of the Round Table disagree on how Excalibur came to be. According to one tale that solves this thorny problem, Merlin, in his mountain hideaway, mutters incantations and, with potions, powders, and secret ingredients, brings into existence Excalibur, the Sword of Flame, the Invincible.

In contrast to this tale is the equally well-known story of the Lady of the Lake, who represents the unsullied spirit of goodness. Arthur is somehow urged to go to the lake, where the arm of the Lady of the Lake thrusts upward in a dazzling light, holding the sword for him to grasp and accept as his own.

For some time it was believed that there were *two* swords. Excalibur was the ceremonial blade inserted in the stone (in other versions, in an anvil laid atop a great stone) and served its purpose by "selecting" Arthur as the new and rightful King of Britain. Caliburn, however, was the sword of combat. Over the centuries, Excalibur was either lost or, as most tellings go, was finally hurled back into the lake whence it had emerged, and was snatched in midair by the upraised arm and hand of the Lady of the Lake, then drawn down into the waters, never again to be seen.

That, of course, left Caliburn to be passed on from one generation to another. Caliburn, the fighting sword, thus survived and eventually was placed in the care of the clan or clans who lived in the New Forest. In our specific instance, the clan of St. Brendan's Glen.

The deeper the research, the harder one scrabbles down through the torrent of words and stories, the clearer it becomes that the sheer variety of versions of this story obscured the single most enduring fact about Excalibur and Caliburn.

Which is that they are but one sword, and known by two names.

Stonehenge at Wiltshire is famed the world over, and the subject of more stories, investigations, studies, and changing conclusions than perhaps any other man-made structure on this planet. The collection in a circle of mammoth stones, topping a gently rising hill, is but the centerpiece of colossal stone structures radiating outward in absolutely straight lines for miles. The incredible feat of manually tugging and heaving these monster pieces—*as long as five hundred years ago*—boggles the imagination. There are arguments yet raging as to whether Stonehenge was religious in origin, or employed for astronomical readings, or perhaps served a mixture of purposes.

Our interest here, as referenced in this book in one of Indy's misadventures, is personal. I have been there and seen people react strangely to whatever energy collects at and/or emanates from Stonehenge. It has a powerful effect upon certain visitors, who seem to be possessed of a body field of energy attuned to that of Stonehenge. Some people have become faint from the energy field; others have been struck as though with a blast of electricity. This is not a fanciful tale, but a reality this writer has witnessed and felt. The nature and characteristics of Stonehenge as portrayed in this book are *not* fiction.

Which brings us to a journey that smacks more of fiction than reality: the journey of the Graf Zeppelin from Friedrichshafen to New York City. Every word, every detail, every description of the Graf Zeppelin is accurate. On one voyage, battered by a severe storm, the Graf was so badly pummeled that the winds smashed part of the tail structure and the crew discovered to their dismay (and the horror of the passengers) that the great port fin had been torn, as if shoved into a giant shredding machine. Behind the great airship there now streamed and fluttered huge sections of fabric. If the damage was not repaired, there was every chance the fabric would get tangled in the external control surfaces, jamming the rudders and elevators and ripping control of the Graf from its crew.

Captain Hugo Eckener sounded the call for volunteers from the crew to go outside the vessel, still hammered and pounded by severe turbulence, cut away the torn fabric, and make swift repairs to the tail. Four men volunteered, among them Knut Eckener, the captain's son. They crawled outside along exposed structural girders and repaired the damage!

Consider that the Graf Zeppelin kept flying until it was retired in 1937, and that it was the first airship ever to exceed one million miles of flight. During its commercial life of nine years, it often flew from Europe to North and South America, cruised around the world, crossed the Atlantic 144 times, and carried more than thirteen thousand passengers in perfect safety.

How did it end its time with us? Under the direct orders of Hermann Göring, head of the German air force, in 1940, engineers emptied the gas cells and dismantled the Graf—and used its duralumin girders to erect a radar tower pointed at England to detect oncoming British fighters and bombers.

Now we come to the little-known details of the attempted alliance between the American Confederacy and England in which the British were to exchange gold and convoy protection in return for immediate shipments of raw cotton. The story told in this book is just the way the "deal" was attempted between the two governments. The exact figures offered in gold have not been revealed, only that an enormous amount of money was involved, and England also promised to meet the needs of the Confederacy in weapons, ammunition, and those materials of which the South was in short supply.

The flight from New York to Port Jacksonville in the U.S. Navy Sikorsky S-38 required no invention of detail. It did fly as a navy patrol bomber, enjoyed tremendous success with Pan American, and was used, in fact, by several other airlines as well as industrial and exploration firms. The routes and the countryside covered by Indy, Gale, and Caitlin, across the pine barrens of North Florida, are exactly as they existed in 1864.

Finally, we come to the sweeping movements of cavalry, artillery, and infantry of both combatants in the Battles of Olustee Station and Ocean Pond. Here again, every description is accurate.

I am indebted to Stephen Knight of Lake City, Florida, one of the prime players in the incredibly realistic reenactment scenarios. I have been there and felt the earth shaking and been hammered by the thunder of hundreds of horses, the smashing blast of heavy artillery, the firing of muskets, and the war cries of the Blue and the Gray. I consider it an honor to be invited back again, this time to participate in full uniform as one of the "combatants."

And last of all, your own touch of magic. Go back in these pages to the drive through the New Forest and the manner in which a strip of paper can be twisted so that it has only one side.

Half twist your paper strip, connect the ends with tape, and you will be holding a Möbius strip.

And no matter what you do, it will have only one side.

Which we all know is impossible.

In *this* dimension, anyway.

ABOUT THE AUTHOR

The author of nearly 200 published books, several dozen technical and flight manuals and several thousand magazine and newspaper articles and series, MARTIN CAIDIN is one of the outstanding aeronautics and aviation authorities in the world. He has several times won the Aviation/Space Writers Association top awards as the outstanding author in the field of aviation and has also been honored as a "master storyteller" by aviation and science organizations throughout the world. He is the only civilian to have lived and flown with the USAF Thunderbirds jet aerobatic team (and won high honors for his book on that experience). He is also a member of the Ten-Ton Club of England for his supersonic flying in the earlier days of "Mach-busting," and is as well known for his stunt flying and airshow performances as he is for his writing. He has flown dozens of types of military and civilian planes throughout the U.S. as a movie stunt pilot and airshow performer. Caidin is the former Consultant to the Commander of the Air Force Missile Test Center and was involved in rocket, missile and spacecraft development from its earliest days. Of his more than 40 novels, *Cyborg* became his best known work when it was developed into the "Six Million Dollar Man" and "Bionic Woman" television series. Caidin lives with his wife, Dee Dee M. Caidin, in Cocoa Beach, Florida.

INDIANA
JONES

Bold adventurer, swashbuckling explorer, Indy unravels the mysteries of the past at a time when dreams could still come true. Now, in an all-new series officially licensed from Lucasfilm, we will learn what shaped Indiana Jones into the hero he is today!

❏ **INDIANA JONES AND THE PERIL AT DELPHI**
> by Rob MacGregor   28931-4 $4.99/$5.99 in Canada

❏ **INDIANA JONES AND THE DANCE OF THE GIANTS**
> by Rob MacGregor   29035-5 $4.99/$5.99 in Canada

❏ **INDIANA JONES AND THE SEVEN VEILS**
> by Rob MacGregor   29334-6 $4.99/$5.99 in Canada

❏ **INDIANA JONES AND THE GENESIS DELUGE**
> by Rob MacGregor   29502-0 $4.99/$5.99 in Canada

❏ **INDIANA JONES AND THE UNICORN'S LEGACY**
> by Rob MacGregor   29666-3 $4.99/$5.99 in Canada

❏ **INDIANA JONES AND THE INTERIOR WORLD**
> by Rob MacGregor   29966-2 $4.99/$5.99 in Canada

❏ **INDIANA JONES AND THE SKY PIRATES**
> by Martin Caidin   56192-8 $4.99/$5.99 in Canada

❏ **INDIANA JONES AND THE WHITE WITCH**
> by Martin Caidin   56194-4 $4.99/$5.99 in Canada

Available at your local bookstore or use this page to order.

Send to: Bantam Books, Dept.   FL 7
> **2451 S. Wolf Road**
> **Des Plaines, IL 60018**

Please send me the items I have checked above. I am enclosing
$_____ (please add $2.50 to cover postage and handling). Send check or money order, no cash or C.O.D.'s, please.

Mr./Ms._____

Address_____

City/State_____ Zip_____

Please allow four to six weeks for delivery.
Prices and availability subject to change without notice.   FL 7 3/94